For Alexandra and Irène
with love

ACKNOWLEDGEMENTS

Star of Heaven is a work of fiction and I must stress that none of the characters to be found here is based on anyone, living or dead. It is true, however, that the character of Sharif Khan would never have evolved without the background research suggested by Imran Khan, former cricket captain of Pakistan, and for this I wish to express my most sincere thanks.

As with my first novel, *Samson and Delilah*, I have again found that experts in the field are most generous with their time and knowledge. For their help and support I should like to thank the brilliant jeweller and designer David Courts (M.Des.RCA) of Courts and Hackett; Harry Garnett and Michael Grantham of the Central Selling Organization; and Susan Farmer of the Diamond Information Centre.

I am grateful to all my many friends (past and present) at my publishers Pan Macmillan. Invidious though it is to select individuals in such a team effort, I would nevertheless like to express special thanks to my editor, Jane Wood, who is a tower of strength. I am also very grateful to Hazel Orme for her meticulous copy-editing, and to Peta Nightingale, Jane's ever cheerful assistant. I should also like to thank Debbie McInnes (publicity director, Pan Macmillan, Australia) for looking after me so well in Oz. They tell me she has now recovered. Many thanks also to Robert Craig, Pam Wood and Sabrina Knipe (Pan Macmillan, South Africa) for making my promotional tour there so enjoyable.

Star of Heaven has involved a fair amount of travel. I am deeply grateful to Francis de Souza (Special Services Executive, British Airways), who always ensures that I arrive back home in better shape than when I left.

To write a novel is a long and lonely process. I count myself very fortunate indeed to have Desmond Elliott as my business manager, friend, confidant, advisor, shoulder-to-cry-on and general Father Confessor. I do not know what I would do without his help and guidance. I should also like to thank his assistant, Lisa Moylett, who 'fixes' everything for me.

On a more personal note, I would like to thank my family, especially my mother, without whom I would be lost.

London, November 1993

CHAPTER ONE

Laura let the half-read letter slip from her fingers and watched as it fluttered downwards, coming to rest on the pile of books strewn across the coffee table. Black copperplate on ivory vellum, it was the work of an artist, all right – Caroline's letters always were. Laura flinched, the pain of rejection the years could never erase. Who needed a pen pal for a mother – and an erratic pen pal at that? Irritated, she picked up the letter and stuffed it into an already overflowing wastepaper basket. The same old farrago of promises and fibs – she had read it all a hundred times before. Laura bit her lip. If only she could bring herself to ignore the woman completely, but that was too hurtful even to contemplate. Despite everything, a small, almost buried voice kept insisting that a mummy, even an absentee mummy, really must care. Perhaps, thought Laura ruefully, such illusions never died.

She glanced at her watch. Ten o'clock! Better get a move on! Even after an hour's housework the flat still looked a shambles. Designs scattered all over the place, books on art, gems and precious metals – margins heavily annotated, yellow markers stuck on relevant pages – hell, she wished she could be more organized. She picked up a folder and, muttering to herself, began to collect her sketches. 'I bet Paloma Picasso doesn't operate like this.'

'Paloma Picasso, Paloma Picasso.' From his cage, a glorious blue parrot squawked happily away. Amused, Laura wagged an admonishing finger at him. No, there were no secrets in this household. The bird saw to that. Everything he heard or was told

1

was repeated without discrimination. It was for that reason that Laura had decided on his name.

'I'm going to miss you, too, Backbencher.'

'Miss you, too. Miss you, too.'

In her book, there could be no doubt about it. For company, this parrot was streets ahead of any husband.

She sauntered into the kitchen and switched on the kettle. Despite the radiator, the room was bitterly cold. From the window of her second-floor flat, she could see the frost glistening on the roofs of the large Victorian houses opposite. For a few minutes she stood there, watching the watery February sunshine illuminating the street, doing battle with the frozen rivulet emanating from a fractured overflow pipe. How she loved European winters – the crispness, the cold, the purity of the northern light. After three years in Bangkok, studying gemmology, London seemed calm, sober, restful even. To her surprise, she had even found it an inspirational place to work as her bulging portfolio testified.

Warming her hands on a mug of coffee, she returned to the sitting room to water her plants. Fragrant purple hyacinths nurtured through the winter in bright ceramic bowls, crimson-leaved poinsettias, multi-coloured geraniums: Laura had her own enlightened version of what was meant by urban jungle. Even here, in her cold and draughty flat, she had never known a casualty. It was all in her artist's fingers, according to her father. Her mother, he had once confided, had been exactly the same.

'For goodness sake,' she chided herself, 'you've really got a head like a sieve.'

She returned to the kitchen, opened the fridge and removed a piece of Gruyère cheese. She knew it was extravagant, but city birds needed all the protein and fat they could get to help them through the winter. She cut the cheese into cubes and wandered back into the sitting room.

'I'm a pretty boy,' shrieked Backbencher, whose concern for underprivileged urban bird life was more limited than his mistress's. Ignoring the parrot's demands for attention, Laura opened the french windows, which led onto her narrow, south-facing balcony, and placed the offerings on a wooden table. They were spotted by a robin which swooped down and, after nodding politely, impaled one large chunk on his tiny beak before flying off again.

The clock of the neighbouring church chimed a resonant eleven o'clock. Laura jumped at the first stroke, her thoughts miles away as she stared dreamily at the skyline. Now she really *was* pushed for time. Heavens! She had not even started to pack her suitcase. She raced into her bedroom and began rooting through her wardrobe. There was not that much to choose from. A selection of jeans and cotton shirts for the summer; the same jeans and shirts plus a few baggy jumpers to see her through the winter. The only decent item there was a cashmere trench-coat, which Maisie had insisted on buying for her. Laura rummaged around hopelessly. What on earth could she wear for her father's eightieth birthday party? It was going to be a sumptuous affair – Gaston Gautier never did things by halves – and *le tout Paris* had been invited.

She spread her miserable collection over the bed and studied it disconsolately. A stickler for tradition, her father always insisted on a degree of formality for his parties. It was one small aspect of home life that had always irritated her. To hell with it, she thought. She would just have to ask Maisie if she could borrow a dress. The only problem with that was that she was bound to make her keep it. Laura tossed a few shirts and underclothes into her battered old suitcase. Dear Maisie . . . she had always been more of a mother than a sister-in-law. It was all Laura could do to stop her from showering her with gifts. Despite her gratitude, however, she often wished that she could be left to pursue her own individualistic style.

Laura snapped shut her suitcase and carried it into the hall, pleased that it weighed almost nothing. Indifference to clothes had its advantages, after all. Fashion, couture – to Laura such fripperies seemed so ephemeral compared to the permanence of her craft. How she scrimped and saved, using whatever money she accumulated on the raw materials for her art. Despite falling prices, gold was still expensive, platinum exorbitant, and silver bad enough. She had a small but dwindling cache of precious and semi-precious stones, lovingly acquired over the years. For students of jewellery at London's Royal College of Art, there were no easy options. Running costs were high.

The buzzer went as she hunted for her passport. She picked up the Parlaphone. It was her friend, Jenny, come to fetch Backbencher. Her head swathed in a large maroon shawl, Jenny clattered up the stairs. 'Gosh, it's cold,' she said, removing the shawl to reveal a dark-eyed, elfin face. 'I hope poor old Backbencher doesn't pop his clogs on the way back to Fulham.' Her eyes scanned the room, taking in the familiar mess, and focusing at last on the object for which she was searching. She walked across to the dining table and picked up the small rectangular box she had watched her fellow student working on for months. She gazed at it in wonderment. 'It's fabulous.'

Laura's present for her father, the miniature masterpiece of jade plaque openwork, had now been set with rose-cut diamonds on platinum. The lid was scattered with tiny cabochon emeralds and the sides were inlaid with mother-of-pearl. Jenny tapped the baton diamond push-piece and instantly the box sprang open. A typical example of Laura's work, it combined artistic genius and technical precision to perfection.

Nervously, Laura studied her friend's reaction. 'Do you really mean it? Do you think Papa will think it's good?'

'Good?' Jenny shook her head in disbelief. Poor old Laura, she had always been the same, even at boarding school, so full of hang-ups, so unsure of herself. No matter what she did, however successful she became, she would always be short on confidence. Of course, the scandal of her mother could not have helped: Jenny knew how such traumas could scar people for life.

'Good? It's bloody brilliant. And what's more, your father will be the first to appreciate it. "Gaston Gautier, the king of jewellers and the jeweller of kings". For goodness sake, didn't you read that profile in last month's *Vanity Fair*?'

Laura blushed. Such publicity always embarrassed her. At college she never mentioned her connections with the celebrated House of Gautier. Desperate to be judged on her own merits, she had even applied for a place under her mother's maiden name. As far as most people at college were concerned, she was simply

4

Laura Jay, a highly trained and extremely pretty if somewhat shy postgraduate.

Laura drew her fingers through her long blonde hair, a tell-tale gesture of discomfort. 'It's just – well – you know . . . I don't want to let anyone down. The materials alone cost a fortune and Maisie insisted on buying them. I promised to pay her back but she wouldn't hear of it. She said we could call it a joint present if that made me feel any better.'

Jenny slumped down into an old bean-bag. 'I really don't know why you insist on making life so difficult.' She opened her handbag and retrieved a packet of cigarettes. 'Maisie and your father are both loaded. If I were in your shoes, I wouldn't say no to a little extra help.'

Laura offered her friend a light and continued the search for her passport. This facet of her life was strictly private, a definite no-go area. 'I wish you were coming to the party,' she said, deftly changing the subject. She shoved a few stray magazines into a rack. 'You know you'd have a riot.'

Jenny inhaled deeply. 'A whole weekend getting brasseried in Paris! Don't think I wouldn't have loved it – hell, I'm still in a daze from my last trip! But I've really got to get some work done. We've not all been as conscientious as you, I'm afraid. My portfolio looks about as thin as a budgie with bulimia.'

Laura laughed and picked up Backbencher's cage. 'You've just reminded me.' Upset at this unexpected disturbance to his habitat, the parrot squawked his disapproval. 'I hid my passport under here. I didn't think any burglar would risk upsetting a bird with a voice as loud as Backbencher's.'

Jenny stubbed out her cigarette in the Indian *papier-mâché* pill box which served as an ash tray. 'Passport under the parrot – makes about as much sense as anything else in this place.' She scrambled to her feet from the squashy depths of the bean bag. 'It's time I was off. I'm double-parked outside and if I hang around any longer, those bastard clampers are sure to nab me.' She reached for her shawl. 'Anything else need looking after while you're away?'

Laura thought for a minute and then slowly opened the top

drawer of her ancient, ink-stained desk. She rummaged around for a few seconds before pulling out a chamois leather pouch. She untied the drawstring and, without a word, poured the contents on to the desk. Jenny stared, open-mouthed, at the small pile of stones which glittered brightly against the wood. 'What on earth are they?' She picked up one of the rugged purple chunks and held it to the light. 'I've never seen anything like it. It's absolutely stunning.'

Laura looked vaguely pleased with herself. 'I came across them in Natal. It's a gem called sugilite. Hardly anyone here has seen it before.'

'These must have set you back a packet!'

'Not really.' Her eyes began to sparkle. 'Can't you just see it, though, a necklace of this surrounded by turquoise, opals and tourmaline? It'd be the talk of the degree exhibition.'

Jenny nodded enthusiastically. It was fascinating to watch the metamorphosis in her shy, retiring friend. Whenever Laura talked about her projects she became animated, less self-conscious, more genuinely sure of herself.

'Sorry, but I wouldn't want the responsibility of that little lot. We've got the builders in, sorting out the damp. Backbencher will be OK. Nobody in his right mind would want to nick him.' The parrot shrilled, offended. 'But these little beauties . . .' She stroked one of the stones appreciatively, as if it were a living creature. 'You know, you really should invest in some sort of safe or deposit box.'

'I'd only lose the key or forget the combination.' Laura began to ferret around in the drawer and finally located a large lump of Plasticene. Indeterminate grey in colour, it was wrapped in kitchen cling film. 'Looks like this'll have to do, then.'

Intrigued, Jenny watched as her friend moulded the stones into the Plasticene. She followed her into the kitchen where Laura stuck the amorphous grey parcel to the U-bend under the sink. Pleased with her handiwork, she stood up and washed her hands. 'Who goes looking for gemstones in among the Brillo pads?'

'You're a head case!' Jenny smiled and picked up the parrot's cage. 'But at least it looks like you've got the main things under control. Next move – the man!'

Laura's face coloured. She ushered the odd couple towards the door. 'I'm just keeping my fingers crossed.'

'Brillo pads!' wailed Backbencher, distressed at his imminent departure.

His mistress opened the cage door and gently patted him on the head. 'Thanks, Backbencher. I knew I could rely on you to keep a secret! Look after him, won't you, Jenny? I'll see you in class around Wednesday.'

The phone was already ringing as Laura closed the door behind them. She lurched for the receiver, tripping over a stack of travel books which went skimming across the floor. 'Hello?'

The caller turned out to be Maisie, ringing from Paris. 'Are you OK, honey? You're sounding kind of hassled.'

Laura collapsed on to the sofa and tried to catch her breath. 'Sorry, I'm fine, just trying to tie up a few loose ends. How are things over there?'

'What can I say? Even your father is excited. Mind you, party or no party, he always gets that way whenever you're coming home. Me too, I've got to tell you.'

The sound of Maisie's soft Texan drawl was warm and comforting. Even after twenty-three years in Paris [and married to Charles], she had never lost her accent. Laura had always thought it part of her charm. For her half-brother, Charles, Maisie's husband, it was simply something else to sneer at. 'Thanks, Maisie. I'm looking forward to seeing you, too. I hope you're going to like Papa's present.'

'If you made it, I just know it's got to be great.'

'I feel such a fraud,' continued Laura, skirting the compliment. 'You've done all the work for the party and I just tip up, like the prodigal daughter, at the very last minute.'

'But, honey, you're busy at college, just like you ought to be. Besides, work? What work? All I did was call the caterers. Your father put himself in charge of invitations. All his old Resistance comrades – you can imagine they took some tracking down!'

Laura paused for a moment, wondering how to frame the

question uppermost in her mind. In the end, she decided to keep things vague. 'And how are things with you?'

Instantly Maisie recognized the shorthand. Laura never mentioned her half-brother by name if she could possibly avoid it. 'Oh, fine,' she answered, rather too quickly. Laura grimaced. Maisie was so impossibly loyal. Why on earth did she stay with that bastard? 'Now square with me,' continued Maisie, resolutely chirpy. 'Do you have something stunning to wear for this party? There's no point fixing you up with eligible young actors if you can't look your prettiest.'

Laura swallowed hard, a combination of pride and principles. 'Well, the point is, I've been meaning to go down to Harvey Nichols to see what they had in stock . . .'

It was hopeless trying to fib to Maisie. 'Hold it right there,' she interrupted. 'What you're trying to say is no.'

'Sorry.'

'Look, I picked up a lovely red silk number in the avenue Montaigne the other day. Now I look at it, it seems a bit on the young side for me. I'd be happy if you'd take it.'

For once, Laura did not argue. 'I know I shouldn't, but I *do* so want to look good for Robert.'

Maisie stared out of her drawing-room window and tried to remember how it felt to be in love. Swiftly, she pulled herself together. 'I'll be waiting for you at the airport,' she said brightly, 'so I'm warning you, don't go missing that plane.'

Laura replaced the receiver. By now she was really racing. She wrapped the small jade box, first in tissue paper, then in glossy gold gift paper. Finally, she tied the neat rectangular parcel with a black bow and popped it into her handbag. She pulled on her cashmere coat and, tumbling out into the street, hailed a passing cab. It was only ninety minutes later, safely ensconced aboard the Paris-bound flight, that Laura suddenly remembered. The french windows leading on to her balcony had been left wide open.

CHAPTER TWO

Maisie roamed around her sumptuous house in the Bois de Boulogne, looking for things to do. She glanced at her watch. Two hours to kill before leaving for the airport. She wandered into her study and began to sort through the heap of documentation which had accumulated on her desk, catalogues of antique furniture . . . Her attention meandered from the glossy pages and outside into the garden. Where on earth could she put a stick more furniture? In the shrubbery, perhaps? Half-heartedly she continued to flick through the heap of brochures. Another sale of modern art – what was the point of even going to the preview? Already she had one of the finest collections in Paris. Her study alone boasted a Mondrian, a Picasso and a Klimt. Maisie sighed. Call this place a home? It looked and felt more and more like a museum. Too many things and too little warmth. She flicked on an electric fire.

Outside, the gardener pottered into view. Her eyes followed him as, slowly, he swept the few remaining leaves from the path. There were days when she envied him his simple, structured life, an existence dictated by nature and the seasons. At least he always had something to do, new developments to look forward to, a natural, inexorable cycle to follow – at least he never looked lost.

A single tear trickled down Maisie's cheek. She pulled out a handkerchief and swiftly mopped it up. No. She must not let herself get into one of those states, not today of all days, not the very day her darling Laura was arriving. She poured herself a glass of water and tried hard to think positively. There was no

9

excuse for this depression, not for someone with all her privileges and wealth. She straightened her back. It was simply a question of organization. She ought to do more with her time. Time! Despite her resolution, Maisie let out a small strangled sob. It was not as if she ever had much of that to spare. She always seemed so busy with her charity committees, exercise classes, therapy sessions, bridge evenings, dress fittings and auctions. By now, the tears were running freely down her face. Who was she trying to fool? Forty-six years old, Maisie Gautier had everything in the world apart from what she wanted most. The love of a good man and some children to call her own.

She pulled a tissue out of the box and dabbed her eyes. She had tried her darnedest to fulfil those deepest desires. When children failed to appear, she had raced around every specialist in the world, hoping for a solution, but no one had been able to find anything wrong with her. At first, Charles had been sympathetic – he so desperately wanted an heir. But, as time wore on, he had grown bored of her fad diets, health regimes and relaxation techniques. She begged him to let her try artificial insemination, but he would not hear of it. Unnatural, he called it, disgusting, even. He, too, had seen specialists and, according to him, it was simply a matter of time. After twenty-three years there were still no children and little chance now of there ever being any. Five years ago she and Charles had taken to sleeping in separate bedrooms.

It was all her fault. Mentally Maisie lacerated herself a thousand times a day for her failure to produce an heir for the Gautier name and Appleford fortune. She meandered into the drawing room and paused to look at herself in the mirror. Despite the tears, she was an attractive woman in an unconventional sort of way, *une jolie-laide* as the French were inclined to say. Tall and elegant with kind brown eyes, her mouth was perhaps too generous, her forehead too high for contemporary tastes. All the same, she still drew admiring glances wherever she went. Maisie's reflection stared back at her blankly. What was the value of other people's admiration compared to the treasure of inner joy?

It had not always been this bad, at least not at the beginning, not when she still believed that Charles had married her for herself and not for her fortune. The thought upset her. Eager for a distraction, she cast around, searching for her handbag. There it was, slung on the sofa where she had left it the previous evening. She opened it and checked her purse for change for the airport car park. A photograph, curled with age, fell from one of the partitions. Maisie bent down to pick it up. A picture of Charles and herself, it had been taken the first time they met in New York. God knows why she still kept it – nostalgia, perhaps, or self-deception, it hurt too much to say.

Restless now, she padded up the staircase to her bedroom. The sound of a car in the driveway stopped her in her tracks. She looked out from the large bay window on the landing to see Charles pulling up outside the door. At once she felt ill at ease. What on earth was he doing home at this time of the day? She hurried into the bathroom, checked her make-up and swiftly applied a coat of lipstick. Despite her husband's indifference, she still tried to please. After all, who could blame him? It was all her fault, her failure, her sterility . . .

She felt her heartbeat grow louder as she heard his footsteps in the hall. Even now, his presence had a curiously unsettling effect on her. There was, however, one difference. In the early years, it was the excitement of love that had made her pulse race faster. Nowadays, she realized glumly, it was simply tension.

'Anyone at home?' Charles's booming voice reverberated around the hall.

'I'll be with you in a minute.' Quickly she checked her hair in the mirror before joining him downstairs.

He turned as she entered the drawing room and gave her a peremptory kiss on the cheek. 'Glad I caught you in,' he said, staring at something past her eye-line. 'I'm afraid something unexpected has cropped up – you know the way it is. I've just dropped in to pick up a few papers from my study.'

'Nothing serious?' she queried anxiously. She knew the purchase of the new Hong Kong property was causing a lot of headaches.

His smile was broad and easy. 'Nothing I can't handle. But I'm afraid it means I won't be able to make the theatre this evening.'

Maisie looked downcast. 'But you promised—' She stopped herself immediately. Charles could not bear anyone remonstrating with him. It made him so bad-tempered and sometimes his moods would last for days on end. No, decided Maisie swiftly, this was not worth an argument, even if he *had* promised, even if today *was* their wedding anniversary. 'Never mind,' she said lightly. 'I'll phone Betsy. I don't think she's doing anything tonight.'

Betsy *was* and Maisie knew it. Moreover, at such late notice it would be impossible to find anyone else to accompany her. Gaston was organizing a quiet *tête-à-tête* supper for himself and Laura. She stilled her quivering lip as she weighed up the alternatives. Another evening alone at the theatre or another evening alone at home.

'Good,' continued Charles, oblivious to her disappointment. 'I'm sure Betsy will enjoy it.' He sauntered towards the door.

'Oh, Charles, and by the way . . .'

'Yes?' He turned on his heel.

'You haven't forgotten it's your father's birthday party tomorrow evening?'

His face grew suddenly thunderous. 'How the hell could I forget that day?'

She felt the blood, hot and crimson, rushing to her cheeks. 'Oh, God, how stupid of me.'

Charles just stood there glaring at her. She wished the ground would open up and swallow her there and then. How could she have been so insensitive? As if that date, of all dates, could ever be erased from Charles's memory.

'I'm so sorry. I wasn't thinking.'

His lip curled cynically. 'Another privilege of the idle rich.' He walked across the hall to his study and slammed the door behind him. Safely inside, his hard, handsome face dissolved into a smile. It was easy, almost too easy. Manipulating Maisie was like falling off a log. Guilt made people so ridiculously malleable. That was something he had learned for himself at a very early age.

It was some ten minutes later when Maisie, still quivering in the drawing room, heard her husband's Lagonda roaring off

12

down the driveway. Not a word, not even the most perfunctory of farewells – it was so typical of him. He could maintain such moods for days; sometimes even weeks on end. Sullen, awkward, taciturn, his behaviour reduced her to tears. Sooner or later, however, he would need something and then the full force of his Gallic charm could be turned on like a tap. She felt like an emotional punch-bag. It was like living with Jekyll and Hyde.

She heard the knock on the door and turned round, quite startled. Immersed in her thoughts, she had not heard a second car arriving at the house. 'Yes?'

Young and pretty, the new housekeeper was Charles's latest appointment. With a certain easy insolence, she popped her head around the door. 'Madame Lamielle is here to see you. Shall I show her in?'

Maisie jumped up, flustered, and put a cooling hand to her cheek. 'Sure. How nice. I mean, I wasn't expecting company.'

A tall, impeccably groomed lady was ushered into the room. Another expatriate American living in Paris, Betsy Lamielle was one of Maisie's closest friends. Ten years older than Maisie, she had recently lost her husband after a long and painful illness. For months she had nursed the irritable sexagenarian who, though suffering from cancer, had stubbornly refused to give up his cigarettes. Now, as the gossips of Paris were whispering, she looked quite radiant with trauma.

'You've been crying,' she said, after a brief appraisal of Maisie's red-rimmed eyes.

Embarrassed, Maisie stared fixedly into the middle distance. 'It's nothing, honestly. I'm a bit overwrought about the party tomorrow. It's all been such a strain.'

Betsy sat down next to her friend, and placed a comforting arm round her shoulders. It was a simple gesture of warmth and affection. Maisie dissolved into tears.

'Hush, now,' said Betsy, retrieving a freshly laundered handkerchief from her handbag. 'Here, take this.'

Gratefully, Maisie blew her nose.

'You can't fool me, Maisie Appleford. I'm far too long in the tooth. And I'm telling you that if your pa were still alive today, he'd have that husband of yours horse-whipped.'

'But Charles can't help it,' countered Maisie, loyally. 'He's had such a terrible childhood.'

Betsy sniffed, unconvinced. 'That don't give him the right to go making *your* life a misery. That man's just bleeding you dry!'

'I can afford it.'

Betsy bristled. 'We all know you can afford it, but that's not the point. Do you honestly think this is what your dear daddy would've wanted for you? A parasite for a husband?'

Maisie's head lolled listlessly to one side. 'If only we'd had children, maybe he wouldn't be so bored—'

'Bored?' Betsy laughed mirthlessly. 'The guy loves skiing, so you buy him a chalet in Gstaad. Then he's bored with that and thinks he'd like to sail in the America's Cup. Let me tell you, Charles was fine just berthing at Cannes. Cudmore or Connor he wasn't!'

Maisie winced at the recollection. Her husband had been the laughing stock of the entire event. He had sailed so badly that even the Italian syndicate had awarded him a rubber duck.

'And then there's his horses.' Betsy was too sensitive to mention his mistresses although everyone in Paris knew. 'His cars, his gambling, the entire bloody lifestyle you're funding.'

Maisie looked sad and crumpled, like an orange from which all the juice had been squeezed. 'I don't mind,' she lied unconvincingly. 'Like he says, until his father dies, he's still an employee.'

Harsh though it was, it had to be said and Betsy was determined to say it. 'And when his father *does* die, what then?'

Maisie shook her head. It was something she struggled desperately to ignore: the fear of Charles leaving her for a wife who could produce an heir. So long as she could bind him to her with her money, so long as she could be useful, she felt there was always hope. Her shoulders heaved as she stifled a sob. Men were so lucky. However old they were they could still father children. For her, life was anchored in a law of diminishing returns. At least, so it seeemed right now.

'I honestly don't know,' she murmured despondently, 'but, whatever happens, there's always Laura. She still needs me.'

Betsy sniffed, impatient. 'You're going to have to do better than that for excuses. Laura's no longer a child. We all know you've been like a mother to her. So much the better. She'll be there for you, believe me, whether Charles is around or not.'

'I guess so.' Maisie's voice trailed off wearily. In her head, she had this argument a hundred times a day.

Betsy patted her arm. A kindly woman, she was determined to pull her friend out of the doldrums. 'You know, I didn't call here to make you feel bad. I've just been thinking, that's all. It's time you took a vacation.'

'But I'm always away.'

Determined not to be put off her stroke, Betsy soldiered on. 'Art galleries and museums with books and guides and a headful of facts, that's not what I call a proper vacation. Take a look at this.' She pulled a letter from her handbag and handed it to Maisie. 'My friends, the MacLeans, are involved in this brand-new hotel in Cairo. It's called the Seraphim.'

Maisie glanced, unseeing, at the letter and attempted a watery smile. 'I've read about it. It's supposed to be superb.'

'Well, they have invited me for August. I thought it'd be more fun if we went along together. Come on, what do you say?'

Maisie's smile grew stronger. 'A trip up the Nile – we could visit the pyramids. And then there's this wonderful museum—'

'OK. OK. We'll get our quota of culture, if you insist. So I take it the answer's yes?'

Maisie shrugged, not unhappy to have been steam-rollered. 'Why not? I could do with meeting a few new people. And besides, there's nothing here to stop me.'

A further ten minutes of good-humoured chivvying, and Maisie looked distinctly better. Happy to have lifted her friend's ailing spirits, Betsy got up to leave. Maisie insisted on accompanying her outside to where a brand-new Porsche was waiting.

'My daughter-in-law thinks I'm a lunatic,' with some difficulty, Betsy manoeuvred herself into the low-slung seat, 'but I reckon you can't take it with you so you may as well blow it. See you tomorrow at Gaston's.' She started up the powerful engine and idled down the drive, waiting for the electric gates to swing open before accelerating loudly on to the road.

Maisie watched as the car disappeared from sight. Then she turned to walk back to the house. The merry widow and the miserable wife: despite everything, the image amused her. She quickened her pace. It had just begun to drizzle and it was time to leave for the airport.

CHAPTER THREE

'Anything you would like, M'sieur, before I leave for the market?' Madame Deschamps, known affectionately to all the family (even to Charles) as Madame D, was dressed to withstand a hurricane. Heavy black overcoat, thick lisle stockings, black woollen scarf, she looked like one of the more morose peasant women from her native Cahors.

Gaston Gautier looked up from his reading. 'No, I don't think so.'

The woman nodded and turned to leave.

'Oh, and, Madame D,' he smiled across at her benignly, 'if it's raining, promise me you'll take a taxi home. We old-timers must stick together. I can't have you going down with pneumonia.'

The heavy front door clanged shut behind her. Despite his protestations, he knew she would never take a taxi even if it were pouring. Tough, simple, self-sacrificing, Madame D was a true daughter of the soil. Of all the many gifts Gaston had given her over the years, beautiful brooches, pendants and bracelets, he had never seen her meagre selection of black wool clothes embellished by any of them. According to Laura, she kept them on her dressing table, to be loved and admired but never used, just like her holy relics.

Gaston switched on the reading light by the side of his armchair. In the summer, the apartments on this side of the avenue Foch were bathed in sunshine. But already on this dark, miserable February day, the shadows were closing in. He glanced at his watch, rectangular and solid-looking, one of his own designs. Today the minutes seemed to be ticking by slowly, as if Old Father Time himself were getting weary. Gaston wished Laura and Maisie would hurry up and come. Today, of all days, he did not want to be left alone with his memories. Tomorrow, his birthday, would mark the actual anniversary. Tomorrow, it would be fifty years precisely since the Gestapo took Marianne away. But tomorrow, too, there would be the party. Tomorrow, he would be surrounded by friends and the people he loved. Tomorrow, he could again be Renard, 'the Fox', the most cunning and audacious of all Resistance heroes, feared and hated by the Germans, adored by his fellow French. Right now, however, Gaston Gautier was feeling alone – alone and utterly terrified.

He put down his book and stood up. Handsome and distinguished, with shocks of silver-grey hair, Gaston still bore himself erect, unbowed. He moved around the room, turning on lamps as he went. Light, lots of bright light, light to block out the pain. Burnished in the glow of a yellow-red Tiffany lamp, a silver photograph frame claimed his attention. He picked it up and stared at it. A photograph of Marianne tenderly holding their son, Charles, it had been taken at the baby's christening. What a happy day that had been. Despite growing unease about Hitler and his seemingly unstoppable war machine, guests had endeavoured to enjoy themselves and to drink to the health of the new-born Gautier heir.

Gaston studied the faded image of his first wife intently. Yes, Charles had inherited her thick dark hair, her proud features and, so it seemed, her inalienable Auvergne business sense. But her smile, her kindness, her warmth, her sense of fun? Gaston replaced the photograph on the table. He knew he was being unfair. Any child would have been scarred by Charles's traumatic experience. He slumped back into his chair. How, in honesty, could he blame his son for the way he had turned out?

Blame? If anyone were to blame, then it was he, Gaston. Perhaps, he had allowed his work for the Resistance to become too exhilarating, its duplicity a buzz. One evening, Gautier, the celebrated jeweller, would be entertaining German generals to dinner, the next, the legendary Renard would be blowing up the same men as they made their way to the theatre. As the months slipped by, Gaston began to find the subterfuge exciting, the danger a positive thrill. All the same, he had played the game with caution. It took years for the German authorities, many of whom considered him a friend, to suspect him. Eventually, however, the inevitable happened. Under interrogation, someone had informed. When the Gestapo arrived at Gaston's home in the middle of the night, he had been out. After refusing to disclose her husband's whereabouts, Marianne was badly beaten before being dragged off to the infamous avenue Kleber for further questioning. Hours later, neighbours found the three-year-old Charles, abandoned and screaming hysterically. For twelve months after the event, the child had refused to speak to anyone.

Gaston closed his eyes. What was the point? A national hero, he knew his own son dismissed him as nothing but a coward. Coward, coward – like punches, the word still pained him physically. Reunited with his father after the war, these were the only words the young Charles would spit at him. Coward, coward. Citations, honours, medals – what did such baubles matter to a child who had lost his mother? Desperately, Gaston had tried to explain to his son. He told how he had wanted to give himself up in return for his wife's safe release, but that his comrades had forbidden it. There was no guarantee that the Gestapo would let her go, they had argued, and, besides, Renard knew too much. He was a brave man, but even brave men had been known to break under the Gestapo's notorious techniques. And if he cracked, the entire Resistance operation would have been placed in serious jeopardy.

Gaston had known his explanations were falling on deaf ears. From the small boy's cold, expressionless eyes, he could see that Charles blamed him for Marianne's death. Whatever he did, he knew his son would never forgive him. Deep down, he even accepted it. Why should anyone forgive him when he could never forgive himself?

Gaston felt suddenly cold. Even now, fifty years on, the nightmare returned to haunt him. The facts had emerged soon after the war. Twelve months after her arrest, Marianne had died in the concentration camp at Ravensbruck. It had been a particu-

larly brutal death. Caught stealing scraps of food from the
kitchen, the starving young woman had been pinned down to a
stove. Another prisoner was forced to stoke it until the heat
became unbearable. The guards had laughed as their victim
screamed and watched as her tortured body writhed in agony.
The smell of burning flesh permeated the kitchen and one of the
younger soldiers had vomited. Irritated, a superior officer
ordered him to finish off the by now unconscious woman. Taking
out his revolver, the young soldier had put a bullet through her
head. It transpired that her mangled and blistered body was later
fed to the dogs.

Gaston clenched his teeth. Not a word, not one single word
of this story had he ever breathed to a soul. This was a burden
of guilt he must carry alone to his grave. He looked over again at
the christening photograph. There could be no doubt about it.
Charles really *did* take after his mother. He sighed deeply.
Whatever he did for his son, whatever he gave him, he could
never make amends. Gaston stood up, walked across to the
drinks cabinet and poured himself an Armagnac. He took a sip
and savoured it. The spirit burned the back of his throat but
seemed to alleviate the pain. He took another, more generous
sip. He was drinking more, nowadays, sometimes even in the
middle of the day. It was a habit he had tried to break but, for
once, his will-power failed him. How he hated this time of year
with its darkness and its drizzle. He could not wait for the spring
to arrive. Sunshine, birds, flowers, laughter – the spring
reminded him of Caroline. The winter would always belong to
Marianne.

Caroline. If he closed his eyes he could still see her the way
she was on the day he met her, in that grubby *atelier* of hers just
off the rue Mouffetard. Dressed in faded blue jeans and a kaftan
she had been decidedly unfazed by his visit. For ten minutes
after his arrival, she had continued to feed the birds on her
balcony before finally turning her sapphire-blue-eyed attention
on him. Inured to French formality, Gaston had been amused by
the hippie nonchalance of this young English designer. He had
never met anyone, not even an artist, as dreamily impractical as
this. Yes, she had nodded vaguely, she had heard that he was

impressed by her designs and was naturally very pleased about it. But no, thank you very much, the last thing she wanted was a regular job. Who wanted to be shackled by the requirements of any major outfit (no insult intended), even if that outfit was the House of Gautier?

For a good two hours Gaston had argued with her. The more he argued, the more he realized that, far more than anyone else in the world, he wanted this precious, dazzling new talent in his workshop. Her jewellery, he had already seen, was exciting and vibrant, precisely what was needed for the rich young pop and movie stars who now frequented Gautier. Caroline, however, was as stubborn as she was beautiful. Money, she maintained airily, had never interested her, only her freedom and her art.

It was then that Gaston knew he had her. Who, he asked pointedly, was she trying to kid? What freedom could there possibly be in her current hand-to-mouth existence, scraping a living from one commission to the next? And as for her art? Second-class materials would never produce anything but second-class jewellery. At Gautier, she would have the finest of everything, fabulous gems, precious metals with which she could never otherwise afford to work.

Gaston had watched, his heart in his mouth, as Caroline stared up at him from beneath her over-grown fringe. OK, she had finally conceded, she would accept his offer so long as he would guarantee her complete artistic freedom and integrity. Gaston agreed to her terms at once. Her unfettered genius was precisely what he wanted. Even now, Gaston could remember leaving her *atelier* and stepping brightly into the warm spring sunshine. He had felt happier on that day than he had felt for many years. It was ridiculous and he knew it, but he had just fallen head over heels in love with a woman young enough to be his daughter. That woman, he had been the first to recognize, had the makings of a star.

From the beginning, theirs had been a deeply passionate affair. Within weeks, Gaston knew that he wanted to be with Caroline for the rest of his days. Since his wife's death, there had been no shortage of mistresses in his life, but such relationships had always been maintained on a strictly physical basis. With

Caroline, it was different. Like Gaston she, too, was an aesthete, a craftsman and an artist. Despite an age difference of thirty-five years, the two were soul-mates. Instinctively they felt the same about an idea, a jewel or a design. Under Gaston's loving tutelage, Caroline's genius began to blossom. Within months of her arrival at Gautier, a new range was created as an exclusive showcase for her work. J for her surname, 'Jay', and J for *Jeunesse*, Youth, Gautier's J line was an immediate and resounding success. Thrilled, Gaston watched as his adored *protégée* gained in confidence and renown. And their love-making acquired a new intensity as a grateful Caroline did everything to make her mentor a happy man.

At home in the avenue Foch, Gaston Gautier sipped his Armagnac. His happiness, he recalled, had been complete the day that Caroline discovered she was pregnant. Not that he had ever verbalized the desire, not even to her, but (deep-down) he had been longing for a child to compensate for his dour, grasping son. Caroline's reaction had astounded him. She was, she declared, still too young for the responsibility of a baby and had already made plans for an abortion in London.

Horrified, Gaston had begged her to keep the baby and to marry him. After all, he argued, he loved her desperately and wanted to care for her. He even promised that her burgeoning career would be in no way affected. He would organize someone to take care of the baby and she would be free to pursue her art as before. Stubborn as ever, Caroline resisted. She did not want to be tied down by either marriage or children. She wanted to be free (the meaningless hippie clichés soon surfaced) to do her own thing.

Never had Gaston been so insistent. It was as if his life, his every hope of happiness, depended on her acceptance. In the end, Caroline reluctantly gave in. Clasping her tightly in his arms, tears of joy and relief streaming down his face, he promised she would never regret it. He said she had made him the happiest man in Paris. That, at least, was what he thought at the time.

Gaston jumped as he heard the sound of the door-bell ringing. At last, he thought gratefully, Laura had arrived. With the push of a button, he opened the front door to the building.

Then, leaving his own apartment, he walked down the corridor and waited by the lift. The old-fashioned elevator cranked and whirred its way to the top floor. Impatient, Gaston tapped his foot on the highly polished parquet floor. It seemed to be taking an eternity. At last, the lift arrived and shuddered to a halt. He moved forward to open the gilded-metal grilles. As the dark mahogany doors swung open, he moved forward to embrace his daughter.

'Charles!' Both surprise and disappointment were audible in his voice.

'Welcoming as ever,' sneered Charles, emerging on to the landing. 'I'm sorry to intrude, Father. It seems you were expecting someone else?'

'I thought it might be Laura. She's arriving some time this afternoon.' Embarrassed, he ushered his son back into the apartment. Charles, he noticed, was putting on weight. Always beefy and heavy-muscled, he was beginning to look quite fat.

'The darling daughter.' A cold, hard smile played on Charles's lips. 'Well, I shan't be taking up too much of your time. We can't have family business intruding on the unalloyed pleasure of Laura, can we?'

There were days when Charles's sarcasm made Gaston want to strike him. But then the memories came flooding back and forced the old man to bite his lip. Once inside the drawing room, Charles opened his briefcase and pulled out a folder full of documents. 'I thought we'd better get these out of the way before you race off on another of your painting expeditions. It's the lease-back agreement for Gautier's new Hong Kong outlet.'

Gaston sat down, put on his spectacles and started reading slowly through the contract.

'You needn't bother dissecting the whole thing.' Charles's voice was tetchy. 'The lawyers and I have been through it with a fine-tooth comb. Just sign the last page here, would you?' He took out his fountain pen and indicated the relevant spot.

For a moment, Gaston demurred. 'I'm not sure I understand completely—'

'For heaven's sake, what's the matter? Do you think I'm trying to pull a fast one?'

23

'Please, I wasn't suggesting—'

'Then sign the bloody thing, would you? I haven't got all day.'

The indomitable Resistance hero heard himself babbling excuses like a child. 'But the whole idea is so new to me, I'd like some time . . .'

Charles towered over his father, implacable and grim, like the north face of the Eiger. 'I thought it was agreed. Property is my side of the business. Have I ever let you down? Have I ever done anything that wasn't entirely in Gautier's interests? Have I ever double-crossed you?'

Gaston could feel his objections being seized and flung out of the window. 'No,' he murmured.

'No,' continued Charles, pointedly. 'Not like some people we could mention.'

It was a cruelly effective blow. However obliquely, he never missed an opportunity to have a swipe at Caroline. Without further ado, Gaston picked up the pen and added his signature to the contract.

'And here too.' Charles handed his father another copy of the document. This time he signed without even looking. 'I think that's about it for now.' Charles briskly returned the documents to his briefcase. 'I'll see you tomorrow evening.'

'If you've got another minute,' Gaston moved swiftly to stop his son leaving, 'there *is* something I'd like a word about.'

Charles arched his eyebrows. 'Yes?'

'There are rumours circulating.'

'Rumours,' repeated Charles in a neutral tone of voice. 'Don't tell me Caroline has gone and done another runner.'

'Just leave her out of this!' Gaston's eyes blazed with a sudden anger. He forced himself to regain control. There was no point in exacerbating the situation by arguing over her. Obsessively jealous after so many years as Gaston's only heir, Charles had always hated his father's second wife as a threat to his future fortune. The adventuress and her bastard daughter: Gaston was well aware of how Charles referred to Caroline and Laura behind his back. He stared hard at his son. How could Charles ever understand the joy Caroline had brought into his miserable, guilt-ridden existence? True, soon after their marriage she had run off, leaving him with their small baby to look after. Nevertheless, whatever people said, Gaston could never think unkindly of his wife. Caroline had given him the most exquisitely happy years of his life and, most important of all, the precious gift of Laura.

Charles walked across to the drinks cabinet and poured his father another Armagnac. 'Now then, there's no need to get upset.' As he handed him the glass, he smiled with faintly sardonic courtesy.

Gaston watched him intently. He was in no mood for Charles's switch-on charm or for any other of his diversionary tactics. 'I was in London the other day,' he continued, more aggressively this time, 'to buy diamonds.'

Charles flicked an imperceptible speck of dust from the cuff of his suit. 'I know.'

'And you also know,' Gaston struggled to moderate the growing anger in his voice, 'that we at the House of Gautier are privileged to be sight-holders at the Central Selling Organization.'

Charles resumed the inspection of his cuff. 'Our dear, dear friends at De Beers. What would we do without them?'

Despite his resolution to keep cool, Gaston felt Charles's sarcasm bite. 'I'll tell you what we'd be doing,' he replied heatedly, 'we'd be fending off total chaos. Prices would be in free-fall if we allowed the diamond market to be swamped with illicit stones. You know as well as I do that it's in everyone's interest for the industry to be organized.'

'Rigged, wouldn't you say?' Charles's smile was thin and taunting. He loved to bait the old man.

'No, I wouldn't!' Gaston could feel his blood pressure rising. His doctor had warned him against this kind of excitement and he knew he would have to take a beta-blocker as soon as he had dealt with his son. 'Production and sales have to be controlled,' he shouted. 'You know it makes sense all round, even to consumers. Look at our own clients, for heaven's sake! No woman wants a diamond ring today that may be worth half as much tomorrow.'

Charles picked up a newspaper from the coffee table and ostentatiously started to read it.

'Are you listening to me?'

'Of course. It's a very interesting homily, I do assure you, but I've heard it all before.'

Suddenly, Gaston's temper snapped. 'Don't play games with me. I hear you've been seen in Antwerp.'

'And in Rome, New York, Hong Kong, Dubai . . . I do get around, you know.'

'Stop playing silly buggers! Everyone knows that illicit diamonds from Angola and Namibia are being channelled through Antwerp.' Gaston paused for breath. He was wheezing badly. 'My friends in London believe that you've been buying up stocks.'

'Oh, really?' Charles walked angrily towards the door. Tall and broad, at his full height he made a daunting figure. 'A regular little espionage service you've got going, haven't you? I thought you'd given up playing the avenging angel at the end of the war.'

Gaston ignored the gibe. 'For God's sake, this is important! I *must* know. Have you, or have you not been purchasing illicit stones?'

Charles turned and flashed his father his most brilliant smile. 'Who's to say what's "illicit"? An "illicit" diamond has been in the earth for four billion years, just like any other.'

It was as good as an admission. Unable to contain himself further, Gaston leapt to his feet. 'You fool. You complete and utter fool. Does the good name of Gautier mean nothing to you? A hundred and fifty years—'

'All very laudable, I'm sure.' Charles snapped shut the clasps on his briefcase and made to leave once more. 'Why don't you save it for your birthday speech?'

With a bound, Gaston placed himself between his son and the door. 'This business has got to stop!' He stared him straight in the eye.

Unflinching, Charles returned the stare. 'Defender of other people's interests. How very noble and selfless.' Charles's lip curled with unconcealed contempt. 'Too bad you weren't around to defend your own family when they needed you.' He watched as his father deflated, and secretly congratulated himself. This time it had been a close shave, but the well-worn strategy never failed. He pushed his father aside and continued on into the hall. As he opened the front door, he stopped for an instant. 'Don't bother seeing me out,' he called. 'I'm used to looking after myself.'

Gaston stood motionless for some minutes before staggering off into the bathroom. His heart thumping loudly, he reached for the dark brown bottle in the medicine cabinet. He filled a tumbler with water and sluiced down a couple of tablets. Gradually, he became aware of voices talking in the drawing room. He had no idea how long he had been sitting there, just slumped on the side of the bath. It all seemed such a blur.

'Hello? Anyone there?'

Surely, he thought, he must be dreaming. It sounded as if Caroline were calling.

'Gaston, are you home?'

Through the haze, he recognized the sound of Maisie's voice.

'Perhaps he's out.'

He struggled to stand upright. What on earth was he thinking about? The other voice belonged to Laura.

'I'm here, in the bathroom.' He tried to shout but, somehow, the words tumbled out in a whisper. Neither woman seemed to have heard him. Panicking now, he struggled to open the bathroom door. The voices continued still.

'It's a good job you keep a key. Looks like there's no one at home. Strange, though. When I spoke to Papa this morning, he said he'd wait in for us. Papa . . .' Laura broke off, horrified, as her father stumbled into the drawing room. His face white, his hands clenched, he seemed to be trembling all over.

'Oh my God!' She rushed to help him to his armchair. 'Please, Maisie, call the doctor. He's having another of his attacks.'

'No!' Gaston's voice, surprisingly clear and authoritative, stopped Maisie in her tracks.

'But, Gaston . . .'

He silenced her with a wave of the hand. 'I'll be all right. It's nothing – just palpitations. If you call that old fuss-pot of a doctor, he's bound to order me to bed. We'll end up having to cancel the party.'

'But, Papa, you don't look well.' Close to tears, Laura knelt beside her father's feet and held his hand to her cheek.

He bent down to kiss her halo of hair. 'I'm feeling much better already. My poor Laura! What a homecoming!'

'Come now,' ordered Maisie, swiftly assuming control, 'at the very least, I think you ought to spend the rest of the day in bed.'

'Stop fussing,' said Gaston, the colour already returning to his face. 'Honestly, you're worse than Madame D.'

'Do I hear my name being taken in vain?' In all the commotion, no one had heard the housekeeper returning from her errands.

'Madame D!' Laura raced across the room and flung her arms around the old woman, who beamed at her with pleasure.

'My, my!' Gaston had noticed Laura's jeans, torn and tattered at one knee. 'Is this the student look nowadays?'

'I'm afraid so. The rip's supposed to be all the rage. I acquired mine on a barbed-wire fence.'

Madame D tutted in mock disapproval. 'Always been the same. Even when you were a baby, we could never put you in a dress. Don't ask me how, but somehow you always managed to tear it. Such an angelic smile you had,' fondly, the old woman swept the fringe from Laura's forehead, 'but even your father ended up calling you the Wild One.'

Laura was relieved to hear her father's laugh. Sonorous and comforting, it brushed away all her qualms. Maisie's concerns, however, were not so easily alleviated.

'I'm sorry to play old bossy-boots,' she interrupted, 'but I really do think you should go to bed.'

'M'sieur,' exclaimed Madame D, alarmed, 'you've not had another turn?'

'I'm perfectly fine.' Gaston's voice was dry and precise. 'And I am *not* going to bed the moment my daughter arrives to see me.'

Madame D eyed him with affectionate anxiety but, sensing a family confrontation in the offing, decided to repair to the kitchen. From experience, Maisie knew there was no point in arguing further. Accepting defeat, she set about plumping up cushions and arranging them behind Gaston's back.

'Well, at least let me fetch you a blanket,' she said, as if seeking to regain lost ground. 'And if you dare move from that chair this afternoon, you know you'll have me to deal with.'

Gaston suppressed a smile as his daughter-in-law marched into the bedroom. How she blossomed, he thought, whenever Charles was out of the frame. Self-confident and decisive, she was a completely different woman.

She returned with a heavy tartan blanket which she wrapped around his knees.

'What would the pair of us do without you?' Laura shot her sister-in-law a grateful smile.

'Oh, I expect you'd manage somehow. At least you have one another . . .' The words trailed off painfully. 'You must have lots to talk about and it's high time I was off.'

From the tone of her voice, Gaston knew something was wrong. 'Is Charles still taking you to the theatre this evening?'

Maisie looked away. 'He's been so terribly busy, you know, with this business in Hong Kong. And then, with your party coming up tomorrow, I said I'd rather take a rain-check on the theatre. It's no big deal. I was never too hot on Corneille.'

'Great,' Laura piped up immediately. 'Then you can have supper with us.'

'That's sweet of you, honey. But really, I don't want to upset your plans—'

'Nonsense!' Gaston straightened in his chair. 'Laura and I have never had plans that didn't include you.'

'I'll second that.' Already Laura was on her feet. 'I'll just go and tell Madame D that tonight we'll be three for dinner.'

Maisie blushed with sheer pleasure and settled down contentedly on the sofa. 'Seems like I'm being overruled by just about everyone today.'

'And a good thing, too.' Gaston's face was peaceful and contented. He smiled across at her. 'So here we are again, the same old *ménage à trois*. What must the *beau monde* think?'

It was well past midnight when a slightly tipsy Maisie decided to head for home. Happy but exhausted, Gaston embraced the two women he loved best in life and made his way to bed. On her own, at last, Laura felt free to roam through the apartment, adjusting the position of an ornament here, a candelabrum there, recalling just how things were in the days of her childhood.

The Gautier apartment had never been a particularly busy home. For years after Caroline's departure, Gaston had been virtually a social recluse. He still kept an eye on the business, visiting the Gautier workshop every morning and continuing to deal personally with favoured clients, but his heart was no longer in it. His wife's adultery, the manner of her leaving – the pain and humiliation was difficult to bear for a man of Gaston's passionate nature. It was not as if he had not been warned, especially by his son. When Caroline finally ran off with the dashing Ralph Buckingham, Gaston's debonair young horse trainer, Charles had gloated openly to his friends. What a scandal! For months the whole of Paris was talking about it. A delighted Charles could hardly believe his luck. Overnight, his hated stepmother was out of the way and he had yet another hold over his father.

For Gaston, however, there was one compensation which outweighed all the hurt and shame. From the day she was born, Laura had been the apple of her father's doting eye. A placid baby, forever smiling, she returned his adulation with a fervent baby passion. As soon as she could crawl, she would follow him around like a puppy, cooing and laughing whenever he picked her up, trying to encircle his neck with her chubby baby arms. Caroline, of course, had always been fond of the child, but by that stage her career had really taken off. The success of the J line had made her reputation as one of the world's most brilliant and innovative young jewellers and she was heavily in demand. Increasingly self-centred in the pursuit of her art, she had no time for her gorgeous little daughter. Silently, Gaston watched his young wife's progress. Who, after all, was he to complain? It was he who had taken this impractical dreamer and forged her into an ambitious artist, hungry for success. Not one word of criticism would he tolerate about his increasingly absent wife. It was he, after all, not she who had so desperately wanted this child.

In the drawing room, the oval-faceted Mystery Clock struck one. Lapis lazuli and silver gilt with hands of diamonds on yellow gold, Laura had always loved this masterpiece of craftsmanship. As a child she had often wondered how a clock, seemingly transparent and without inner mechanisms, could possibly function. Tonight, as she studied its garland motif of emeralds and rubies, she could still remember sitting on her father's knee and listening, eyes as large as saucers, as he explained the illusion. Of course, at four years of age, she did not understand everything he told her. How the hands – which had no axis and apparently moved by magic – were linked to a crystal disc and covered by another crystal disc, cut like a diamond. To the little girl it had all seemed so beautiful and clever, just like her daddy. It was then that the desire had first taken hold in Laura's imagination. When she grew up, she promised, she too would create wondrous objects.

Laura rubbed her eyes. It had been a long day and she was tired, but her head was too full to sleep. Adulation and indifference, safety and insecurity, the memories of such conflicts returned to torment her whenever she came home. Whatever happened to a child, however she was subsequently brought up, she always had two parents. Two parents, two genetic contributions, two sets of influences. Whatever she tried to do, Laura knew she would still remain the creature of her mother as well as her father. The thought petrified her. The poor man had suffered enough. She had to be someone of whom he could be proud, a world-famous jeweller in her own right. Unlike her feckless mother, she vowed she would never let him down.

Restless now, she decided to expend some energy tidying up. Large and panelled, the drawing room was full of exquisite eighteenth-century furniture. On the parquet floor, polished until it shone like a mirror, was an antique vase, filled (courtesy of Maisie's florists) with white lilac even in February. A Greek sculpture adorned one table, a piece of underglazed blue Ming another. An Aubusson carpet, pale cream and pink, lay at the foot of the sofa. She had always loved this room. Here, the sensitivity of the artist and the passion of the collector combined to create a feeling of both luxury and simplicity. Classical and original, balanced and proportioned, it exemplified everything that Gaston Gautier the jeweller had always striven for.

Suddenly, she spotted something shining on the carpet and bent to pick it up. A gold fountain pen. Someone must have dropped it. In the lamplight, she tried to decipher the initials engraved on the clip. CDG – Charles Daniel Gautier. She almost let it fall. It was as if the distasteful object was burning the tips of her fingers. Swiftly she placed it on the mahogany coffee table, disturbed by the vehemence of her own reaction. She never discussed such feelings with her father or with Maisie – that would not have been fair. Nevertheless, despite genuine efforts to understand her half-brother, she had grown to hate him. What had started as mild antipathy in her childhood had now blossomed into contempt. She despised the way he treated Maisie and how he manipulated Gaston. Indeed, Laura often wondered how on earth she and Charles could have been sired by the same father. Most of all, however, she despised his philistine materialism: it was so alien to everything she and her father believed in. That, in Laura's view, was Charles's most serious crime. He valued things and people for what they were *worth*, never for what they *were*. She wondered how such a man could ever understand the heritage and tradition that was Gautier.

It was then that the thought struck her. Madame D, an obsessive cleaner, would never have missed that fountain pen during her morning sweeping ritual. That meant that Charles must have been in the apartment some time that afternoon. She felt sure it was his visit that had been the cause of her father's attack. Laura clenched her teeth. It was one more reason, as if another were necessary, to hate that wretch of a man. God knows how he had upset his father this time, but from experience she knew Gaston would never complain. It drove her wild, the way he excused and protected Charles, even when he was in the wrong. She heard the Mystery Clock chime two. Angry now, despite her fatigue, she began to turn out the lights. She knew she must do her best to catch some sleep. After all, tomorrow was to be a big day.

CHAPTER FOUR

For the tenth time that afternoon, Caroline Buckingham dialled the number only to hang up before it was connected. Outside, the fading Californian sunshine still reflected invitingly on the pool. She poured herself another glass of cold white wine and collapsed exhausted on to her bed. Perhaps she should have a swim, or go shopping, or invite a few people round for supper – something, anything to alleviate the boredom. Her eyes glazed over as she contemplated the possibilities before dismissing them all as too energetic. She was, as usual, far too listless to do anything. The only thing she seemed to manage, nowadays, was pointless gossip over the telephone.

Without thinking, she reached for the locket Gaston had once created for her. Fashioned in platinum and set with pearls and diamonds, it had been his gift on the birth of their daughter. Inside, he had placed a lock of Laura's fuzzy baby hair. Caroline stroked it affectionately. Nowadays, it was the only piece of jewellery she ever wore. She sniffed self-pityingly. Neither Gaston nor Laura would ever believe it, but she never took it off.

It was not quite so bad when Ralph was around. At least he forced her to get out and about. But although he had more than enough to do in the States – horses to train, stud fees to negotiate, sales and races to attend – he was overseas increasingly often. Early on in their marriage, Caroline had accompanied him everywhere, but the excitement soon waned. The horsy crowd were not her type: too hale and hearty, she always complained, with all the sensitivity of the average rhinoceros hide. Besides, by the time they reached Los Angeles her infatuation for Ralph had cooled dramatically. What a little fool she had been. Why, in the end, she had gone through with marrying him she would never know. Perhaps she felt that she had burned her bridges. What did it matter? It was all academic now. Never having asked the question, she would never know what would have been the response. But surely, she reasoned, after the way she had behaved, Gaston would never have taken her back.

Gaston. There was never a day passed that she did not try – and fail – to call him. She wrote to Laura, of course, but nowadays her letters all went unanswered. Who could blame the girl? In the eyes of the world, in her own eyes, even, she had been the most dreadful mother. Remote and unreliable, she now had no emotional rights whatsoever over the two people who filled her every waking thought. Caroline drained her drink. If only they knew how much she missed them, how ashamed and guilty she felt, how much she longed to see them both again.

She turned on the radio. She must have some noise to distract her from her thoughts. 'Stand by your man . . .,' loyal an' lovin', some big-hearted country-and-western singer was pounding out her stuff. Caroline flicked the OFF button. So bored, so lonely – if only she had managed to continue with her art. Not that there had ever been anything to stop her. Man of honour that he was, Gaston had never done or said anything to jeopardize her burgeoning career. On the contrary, he had done everything to ensure her continued freedom to create. Despite the brevity of their marriage, he had provided generously for her, too generously, perhaps. For years after their divorce, Caroline had no real need to work.

It was not long, however, before another, far more serious problem surfaced. With every day away from Gautier and Paris, Caroline's inspiration seemed to fade. At first, she tried to dismiss the phenomenon. She was, or so she thought at the time, head over heels in love with Ralph. When things calmed down, she rationalized, the creative muse would return with a vengeance. Caroline waited as the months, sterile and unproductive, turned into years. Now, it was hopeless. In two decades she had produced absolutely nothing. Her talent, once so exuberant and energetic, had atrophied.

Far too late in the day, Caroline had come to understand. Basking in the warmth of Gaston's love and approval, her genius had flourished. Removed from that warmth, the delicate flower of her creativity had shrivelled up and died. His love had been so selfless, his munificence so freely given, that she had failed to recognize her total dependence on him. With Ralph, the attraction had been uncontrollably physical, but it had never developed from there. Dear Ralph, it was not his fault. He had been, still was in fact, a bloody good lay. But spiritually, emotionally and artistically, Gaston was her soul-mate. She still needed him to function. What a stupid little fool she had been! She had gone and sacrificed everything for the briefest of hormonal aberrations.

Caroline poured herself another drink. Well, why not? Why not get roaring drunk again? Why not get so drunk that the entire unholy mess would be obliterated, at least until the morning? After all, what else was there to do in this God-forsaken place? Tonight she should have been in Paris. Yes, in Paris, in the bosom of her family, loved, protected and admired, busily organizing her husband's eightieth birthday party. As it was, here she was, alone with nothing but a telephone for company and a bottle for a friend.

CHAPTER FIVE

'Time I was going,' announced Charles, suddenly leaping out of bed. Yolande made no effort to restrain him. He had been in a foul mood all evening and, not for the first time, she would be glad to see the back of him.

'Maisie will be home.' The explanation was proffered through half-clenched teeth. He pulled on his boxer shorts.

Yolande shrugged dismissively. She never asked for explanations and it was quite unlike Charles to offer any. Like a cat, she snuggled down under the grey-blue luxury of the satin sheets and looked on idly as he dressed.

'I don't want any hassle in that department.' He buttoned up his shirt.

'No, of course not.' Yolande studied a broken fingernail. She knew better than to prompt.

Swiftly, he knotted his tie. 'I've got enough on my plate right now.'

'You certainly have.' She closed her eyes. 'In fact, I think you'd better get a move on, darling. There can't be too many "business meetings" that run till two in the morning.'

Charles caught sight of the luminous dial of her alarm clock. 'Hell! Is that the time?' He zipped up his trousers and cast around for the jacket he had left slung across the chair.

The young woman yawned loudly and rolled over. Something was bothering him and she was dying to know what it was. Over the past two years, however, she had learned precisely how to deal with her odd, awkward lover. The best way of keeping him was not to cling. And the best way of extracting anything from him (gifts, money or information) was to feign complete indifference.

The effect of her unconcern was instantaneous. 'I'm sorry.' His hurry apparently forgotten, Charles sat down on the side of the bed and started to nuzzle her cheek. Naked under the sheets, Yolande stretched languidly and yawned again. 'I know I've been a bit preoccupied this evening,' he continued, his fingers straying down her throat to tease her nipples, 'but I promise, I'll make it up to you next time.'

She smiled secretly into her pillow. 'But there's really nothing to be sorry about. Now if you don't mind,' she reached to switch off the bedside lamp, 'I've got an early start tomorrow.'

'An early start?'

'Yes. Our first flight out to Hong Kong.'

Alarmed, Charles switched the lamp back on again. 'What do you mean, "our first flight out to Hong Kong"?'

Nonchalantly, Yolande rubbed her eyes. The strategy never failed. Uncertainty – she knew it was the one feeling Charles simply could not bear. Accustomed to manipulating the people around him, a sudden loss of control unnerved him completely.

'I'd have thought it was self-explanatory.' Her voice was a curious amalgam of boredom and irritation. 'Our first flight out to Hong Kong. What's the big deal? That's what air stewardesses do, you know. They take planes. Now please, if you don't mind . . .' She reached to switch off the lamp once again.

This time he caught her hand. 'But you never said.'

'I don't recall you bothered to ask.'

'And how long will you be away this time?'

'Who knows? Two or three weeks. Nowadays, they keep changing tours while we're on them. The way things are going, I could find myself transferred on to the Hong Kong/Australia sector.'

'But when am I going to see you again?' There was panic in his voice.

Yolande suppressed her smile. Older men, if only they realized how pathetic their silly egos made them. Talk about manipulation! 'Play it mean and keep 'em keen' – her sometime flatmate had been right. 'Don't worry,' she patted his hand almost patronizingly, 'I'll let you know when I'm back.'

Charles stood up and started to undress. Yolande arched an eyebrow. 'And what do you suppose you're doing?'

'I'm coming back to bed.'

'But what about Maisie?'

'Forget Maisie. I'll deal with her tomorrow.' He slid back beside his mistress's warm soft body and took her in his arms. 'You won't be seeing that pilot while you're gone, will you?' He turned her insolently beautiful face towards him and kissed her long and hard on the mouth.

'Who knows?' she whispered, surfacing for breath but still determined to make him suffer. Charles was such a push-over, he was not difficult to tease. It was like dealing with a small, possessive child. Yolande knew he saw other women when she was away but it did not bother her. In her book, you had to be emotionally involved with someone before you could start to feel jealous. But with Charles it was different. Men in the so-called prime of their lives were often so pathetically insecure. She had often thought about it. Perhaps it was the very fear of ageing, the need to prove their diminishing virility that pushed them into affairs in the first place. In any event, whatever Charles's neurosis, the thought of her sleeping with other men seemed to drive him to distraction. Perhaps it was the dread of being compared and found wanting. She decided she would never know. Charles was such a morass of hang-ups, he was impossible to fathom.

'Please.' He kissed her neck and buried his face in her mass of unruly auburn hair. 'Please, don't see him. I . . .' He could not bring himself to say 'love'. He knew it was dangerous to bandy words he did not understand. 'I *need* you, Yolande, especially right now.'

'But you have Maisie. Good old wholesome-as-apple-pie Maisie. She's so loyal and understanding.' Yolande's laugh was cold and brittle. 'You're a lucky man, Charles. You really should count your blessings.'

Agitated, he hoisted himself up on one elbow. 'You don't

understand. I can't go into it now. But if what I have planned comes off, I won't be needing Maisie around much longer.'

Yolande lay motionless, totally intrigued. Never before had Charles spoken to her so openly. 'So you don't love her any more?'

'Love her?' he snorted. 'Do me a favour, will you? I never loved her. She was rich and I needed her money. I had the name and she had the ridiculous, social-climbing daddy. The whole thing was a deal. As far as I'm concerned, I've kept my part of the bargain. What more can the stupid bitch want from me?'

Yolande shivered. She had seen Charles in a rage before and he seemed to be winding himself up for one now. She stretched out a placating arm to encircle his increasingly generous waist. She felt him trying unsuccessfully to pull his stomach in. 'Calm down,' she said soothingly. 'Why don't you come here and I'll massage your neck for you? Then, when you're feeling nice and relaxed, we both must get some sleep.'

Charles shook his head vehemently. For once, the urge to speak, to explain, to get a few things off his chest was overwhelming. Angrily, he punched the pillow. 'I can't tell you how much I hate the whole rotten bunch of them!'

'Them?' It was the gentlest of encouragements.

'My family,' he sneered contemptuously. 'Some bloody family! That gutless coward of a father, the simpering Yank and now, oh, yes, now guess who's coming to dinner?'

Yolande said nothing. There was no need to reply. The boil, it seemed, had finally burst and the poison was spewing out freely.

'I'll tell you who. That bloody bitch of a half-sister. Why can't she just run off and lose herself like her mother?' The vein in his neck was pulsing alarmingly.

Yolande looked on, concerned. 'You mustn't get so worked up about it,' she pleaded. 'Please, darling, try and calm down.'

'Calm down? How can I calm down when some tart and her little bastard have deprived me of what's mine?'

'Deprived?'

'Yes. The House of Gautier belongs to *me* – just me! No one else. After everything that's happened, my father owes me at least that.'

'Poor Charles!' Gently she began to stroke his hair. There were times like this when she felt genuinely sorry for him. Everyone in Paris knew the story of his mother.

Tonight, however, he was not to be placated.

'My father had no right to marry that woman. He had no right to have more children!'

He paused for a moment but Yolande stayed silent. She knew the subject of children was a sore point.

'He had no right to divide the company between Laura and me.' He sank back, exhausted, into her arms.

Sorrow, pity and compassion – suddenly Yolande felt awash with emotions. For the first time in their relationship, she thought she might almost understand him. 'It's OK—' she began, but her mollifying efforts seemed to incense him even further.

'No, it's not OK!' He was shouting. 'Now it's my turn to show them who's calling the shots! Oh, yes, they all think good old Charles can break his neck building up the company. And then, when Father dies, he'll be happy to sit back and let darling Laura take half of everything.' By now the sweat was streaming down his back. 'But, of course, Laura's an artist, isn't she? She's Daddy's little pet. And you can't expect artists to go around sullying their pretty little hands. The dirty world of business, well, that's all right for the likes of me. In their eyes, I'm no better than a pocket calculator.'

'I'm sure your father values—'

'No, he doesn't. He doesn't give a toss about anything I do! But don't you worry. They think they've got it made. They think they can steal from me and plot against me but they've got a few surprises coming.'

Yolande looked at her alarm clock and sighed inwardly. By now it was hardly worth trying to sleep. Tomorrow's flight would be a struggle but, at least, she was looking after First Class. Her colleagues would help her out. As soon as the passengers settled down after breakfast she would be able to catch a snooze. Tonight, for the very first time, she felt that Charles actually needed her. 'Charles?' Her voice was soft and mellifluous, the pettiness erased.

'Yes?' Still breathing heavily after the outburst, he sounded quite exhausted.

'I want you to make love to me.'

Surprised, he leaned across and kissed her cheek. 'I'd like that.'

She continued to stroke his hair. 'And I promise you, you needn't worry about the pilot.'

He knew she was probably lying, but he felt grateful for the gesture. Gently, he cupped one firm, round breast in his hand and, bringing her breast to his mouth, kissed her hard, round, crimson nipple.

CHAPTER SIX

Gaston looked up from his breakfast of coffee and croissants as Laura appeared at the door. 'Good morning, darling.' The sun streamed in through the large picture windows, bathing the room in light. Gaston felt the warmth envelop him like a blanket. It seemed to penetrate the very marrow of his eighty-year-old bones. Today his face was composed, his eyes smiling. He felt better and more at ease with himself than he had for many months. Of itself, the glorious morning was enough to lift anyone's spirits. But somehow the sun always seemed to shine whenever Laura was at home.

'Good morning, Papa.' She kissed him lightly on the cheek and took her place opposite. 'And happy birthday!' Slightly self-conscious, she pushed the glossily wrapped gift across the table.

Gaston picked it up. 'Now let me guess.' Playfully, he shook the parcel. 'Small, hard, heavy. Is it something you made yourself?'

She blushed and unfolded her stiffly starched napkin. 'I do hope you like it.'

'I'm sure I shall.' Enjoying their childish game, he shook it again. 'Do you want me to open it now?'

'Please,' she said earnestly, 'and then I want your *honest* opinion.'

Slowly, savouring every moment, Gaston unwrapped the neat, rectangular package. At last the gift was revealed. Her heart fluttering, Laura watched as her father appraised the small jade box in silence.

'It's quite beautiful,' he murmured at last. 'London seems to have worked wonders on you.'

Relieved, she felt like flinging her arms around his neck. Her father's artistic approval was never lightly given and especially not to her. From his daughter Gaston always demanded the very best and, for as long as she could remember, she had been determined to produce it. 'I'm so pleased you like it.' With an impish grin, she pointed to the lid. 'I thought, at your age, you might need the odd emerald.'

Gaston sniffed and did his best to look offended. Emeralds, according to an old jewellers' superstition, were supposed to protect the eyes. 'I'm grateful for your concern, young lady,' he winked at her, 'but I'm still managing to keep track.'

Clattering in with fresh coffee, Madame D was cheered to see her charges in such high spirits. She placed the pot on the table. 'I hope you two will be getting out from under my feet this morning.'

Gaston caught his daughter's expression and both suppressed a smile. Mumbling and grumbling was simply Madame D's way, it did not mean a thing. Underneath that morose exterior, there really was a heart of gold. She had nursed her darling Laura through all her childhood ailments – chickenpox, measles, mumps and whooping cough – with the selfless devotion of any mother. Madame D's loyalty to the family was beyond question and everyone made concessions to her somewhat offhand nature.

Laura poured herself another cup of coffee. 'I thought you'd like me to give you a hand.' It seemed politic to offer although she knew the likely response.

'Ask *you* to tidy up?' Incredulous, Madame D folded her arms underneath her pendulous bosom. 'No thanks, the caterers will be here by lunchtime.' She sniffed. Caterers, indeed – what a ridiculous extravagance! For her niece's wedding in Cahors, she herself had prepared a six-course meal for over a hundred guests! 'And I want the place to be spick and span by then.'

'Don't worry,' interrupted Gaston, 'we'll get out of your way as soon as we've finished breakfast.' He smiled at his daughter. 'Everyone in the workshop is dying to see you. Would you like to come with me this morning?'

Her mouth full of buttery croissant, she could do nothing but nod her agreement.

'Good.' Carefully Gaston picked up the jade box. It sparkled in the sunlight. 'I want those people of mine to see how well their favourite pupil is getting on.'

Situated in rue de la Paix, the Gautier workshop was as starkly functional as its adjoining salerooms were luxurious. Laura could not wait to see her old friends, some of whom had worked for her father for over fifty years. It was here, much to her father's delight, that she had insisted on spending her holidays as a child. While her schoolmates were away, skiing and sailing, she was happy just to watch, fascinated, as priceless objects were created before her eyes. By the time she was fourteen, she already knew how to blend metals, handle leather and sculpt in ivory. With an enthusiasm which staggered everyone, even her father, she soon assimilated moulding and pressing, the traditional techniques of jewellery-making. At home, her bedroom was littered with books on mineralogy and gemstones and, if asked, she could recount the history of the world's most famous diamonds as if they were treasured loved-ones.

She quickly mastered the art of filigree, the technique of working an object in an open pattern and of soldering in gold, silver and glass. Under the strict eye of Maurice, Gautier's oldest employee, she learned the age-old technique of *champlevage*, a process involving the hollowing out of a surface so that it could be encrusted with enamel and precious stones. Of all her many teachers, Maurice was by far the young Laura's favourite. She loved the way his instructions were accompanied by free-flowing lessons on art and history.

She learned, for example, that Louis XIV had exiled the Protestants who were the supreme masters in the art of enamelling. She discovered how platinum had become fashionable at the end of the nineteenth century. A white metal, malleable and ductile, which never oxidized and resisted all acids, it was perfect for the creation of light settings of infinite suppleness. With the increasing popularity of precious stones – sapphires, rubies, and

emeralds from South America – Gautier's jewellers were determined to abolish ugly claws as far as possible. The use of
platinum, explained Maurice, ensured an almost invisible mount.

For Laura, the holidays could never be long enough. Eagerly,
she listened to the stories and legends which attached to the
precious stones she loved. The aquamarine, so she heard, was
the sailors' stone, which had once belonged to the mermaids.
The opal, regarded as unlucky in the West, was a talisman in the
East, blessed by the deities Vishnu, Brahma and Shiva. It was
one of Laura's favourite stories, the tale of three gods all in love
with the same woman. The woman, tragically, was turned into a
ghost by the Eternal One, and each god gave the spectre his own
colour: Brahma blue, Vishnu gold, and Shiva red. Eventually, the
ghost was turned into opal by the clemency of the god of gods.
Even now, whenever Laura worked with opal, she still looked
for a woman's face.

Maurice's descriptions were like poetry, which made his
lessons easy to learn. The young Laura would listen, spellbound,
as he described the colours of his beloved stones, 'those daughters of fire and water', as Colette had called them in *Gigi*. His
favourites were the reds, from the violet-red of the almandine –
the Crusaders' stone – to the purple-pink of the rhodolite. He
told her of his love for the yellow-brown citrine, which, like rock
crystal, belongs to the quartz family; for the grey-blue-green of
the falcon's eye, the blue-brown of transanite, a member of the
jade family, and the mica green of the aventurine. Laura assimilated his every word with the fervour of a disciple and Maurice
grew to love the girl as much as he despised her loutish, elder
half-brother.

Unlike Laura, Charles rarely visited the workshop. Even now,
on the few occasions when he did, it was only to talk of reducing
costs, increasing profits and improving salvaging methods. Maurice viewed the prospect of Gaston's retirement with increasing
trepidation. He complained to everyone in the workshop that
Gautier *fils* knew the price of everything and the value of nothing.
He was no better, opined Maurice archly, than a common or
garden grocer.

Laura and Gaston entered the workshop through the watch-making department, which had been established by Gaston's father at the turn of the century. Clocks had been the late François Gautier's unassailable passion and he had spent a fortune accumulating his collection of eighteenth-century timepieces. His whole life had been devoted to reimposing the notion of aesthetics in twentieth-century clock-making and for years he studied the work of his heroes, Caron and Jaeger. Gaston had inherited his father's passion but his mastery of mechanisms had been put to far less edifying use. Whenever the Resistance needed an explosion timed to absolute perfection, the impeccable Renard had always been called in to do the job.

A buzz of excitement went up as father and daughter progressed through the workshop, stopping to embrace an old friend here and to admire a particularly beautiful object there. At last, they reached the diamond department which was, as usual, a hive of activity. Unaware of their arrival, Maurice did not look up as Laura and Gaston moved towards him. Hunched over his workbench, a bright angle-poise light focused on his latest creation, he was completely oblivious to everything else around him. For a few minutes, Laura watched in silence as he continued his work on a necklace of rubies and diamonds mounted in yellow gold. He still had the most wonderful hands, she thought. Strong and sensitive, with long tapering fingers, they belied his four score years. Smiling to herself, Laura recalled how he would stroke beautiful stones as if they were living beings. Of course, as she had learned, they *were* living beings, some full of sparkle, personality and fire, others more secretive and mysterious. A stone was indeed like a person. There were no two alike of either.

As Laura looked around her, she was ten years old again. It was here, at Maurice's side, that she had learned about the various cuts of diamond: heart, brilliant, emerald, pear, oval and marquise – the shapes that modern tastes demanded. She remembered blanching the day she heard that there were over five thousand categories of diamond. With her customary zeal, however, she had soon set about learning everything she could about the celebrated 'C' quartet – cut, colour, clarity and carat weight.

The light flickered on the ancient picture of Saint Eloi, the patron saint of jewellers, which Maurice always kept beside him on his workbench.

'I've brought someone to see you,' said Gaston at last.

Maurice looked up, slightly puzzled, as if suddenly aroused from a dream. 'Laura, my dear!' Slowly, he stood up from his bench.

A tiny cloud of concern scurried across Laura's face. Like her father, he seemed to have aged dramatically over the previous few months. 'Maurice.' She embraced him warmly, kissing him on both cheeks. He was so overcome with emotion that for a while he could not speak.

'Let me look at you,' he said at last, his eyes watery. He stood back to admire her. 'My, my, I hardly recognize you. Tell me, how are they treating you in your fancy London college? Do they work you as hard as I did?'

Laura smiled and took his hand. 'Even harder, if you can believe it. They've got some very talented people there. I only hope I can make the grade.'

Gaston caught his old friend's eye and shrugged with wry amusement. 'Perhaps we ought to take an expert opinion. Maurice, what do you make of this?' He extracted the jade box from his pocket and laid it on the workbench.

For a full five minutes, Maurice studied it under the light, checking every aspect. Eventually, he turned to Laura. 'You do us credit,' he said simply.

Gaston beamed. That was the highest accolade Maurice could bestow. 'Doesn't she, though? Do you know, I've been thinking—'

'Monsieur! Monsieur! Ah, there you are.'

Gaston turned to find his diminutive secretary, Madame Goffinet, breezing towards them.

'Excuse me, Monsieur – ah, Mademoiselle, how lovely to see you again – I'm sorry to interrupt, but your dealer is on the phone from Antwerp.'

'Harry Blumstein?'

She nodded. 'He says it's very important.'

'In that case, will you please tell him to hold. I'll be there in just a minute.'

Impeccably coiffed and couturiered, Madame Goffinet wafted back to the office on a cloud of Patou's Sublime.

'I'll leave you two to talk,' said Gaston, smiling benignly at his daughter. 'Maurice, we look forward to seeing you at the party tonight.' He kissed Laura on the cheek. 'I'll see you later in the office. There are a few things we need to discuss.'

For a few seconds, mentor and pupil stood in silence, trailing Gaston with their eyes. He still walked proud and erect, a definite elegance in his bearing, but of late he seemed to have lost that spring in his step which Laura recalled so vividly. Even the legendary Renard, it appeared, could not escape the ravages of Father Time.

'It's a bad month for him,' ventured Laura, at last.

Her friend sighed. 'Not so bad when you're around, although . . .' he hesitated for a moment, '. . . although it's impossible to be with you and not be reminded of your mother.'

Laura tossed her long blonde hair defiantly. 'I can't help the way I look.'

'It wasn't intended as a criticism.'

'To me it is. I'd like to blot that woman out of our lives.'

Maurice shook his head. 'You could never blot her out.' He picked up the box and caressed it lovingly. 'Whenever I see your work, I think of Caroline. The same flair, the same unerring eye, the same daring.'

Laura stared at the floor. It was always the same. Despite her protestations, she was always desperate to learn more of the mother she had barely known. 'Was she really so very good?'

Maurice closed his eyes and let his memory wander free. 'A genius, in a class of her own. Somehow, her work just captured the mood of the time. Innovative, liberated – well, you've seen the J line for yourself.'

She nodded. Of course she had seen it, and for most of her adolescent life she had struggled to find fault with it. For years she had felt that to criticize her mother's work was another way of exorcizing the woman from her system. The notion had proved a failure. Caroline's work, to her daughter's distress, was utterly superb.

Sensing her disquiet, Maurice put his arm around her. 'You

mustn't hate her, you know. In many ways, she saved this company. The Gautier boutiques are our major money-spinner nowadays and they were all her idea.'

Laura's jaw dropped. 'But Charles always says—'

'Yes, Charles always takes the credit for everything and your father lets him get away with it. But it was your mother who intuited the way the market was going. Not everyone could afford a diamond necklace or a platinum wrist-watch. But access-ories – a gold fountain pen, a lacquered cigarette lighter, even a beautiful key-ring – she could see that these would reach a far bigger market.'

'I never realized she was so smart.' Laura felt slightly ashamed.

'Smart? Your mother would have made a brilliant business-woman if it hadn't been . . .' Maurice's voice trailed off. 'You know, in my heart, I still believe she loved you both . . .'

'Sure she did.' Cynicism was the only defence she had mastered to camouflage the hurt.

He caught her hand. 'Believe me, she just didn't know it at the time.'

Laura could feel the tears welling up in her eyes. 'I'd better be off.' She picked up the box. 'It's been good talking to you.' A renegade tear rolled down her cheek and on to the workbench below. It clung, a tiny globule of pain and rejection, to a beautiful cabochon ruby.

'I'm sorry.' Maurice felt as though he might have overstepped the mark. 'I didn't mean to upset you.'

'Oh, no.' She squeezed his fingers hard. 'You haven't upset me, really you haven't. If anything, you might have helped.'

Gaston was still busy on the telephone when Laura walked into his office.

'So you think you might be able to locate the current owner?' As he spoke, he gestured towards a seat, but Laura shook her head. After her conversation in the workshop, she felt too edgy to sit down. She prowled around the large high-ceilinged room stopping, as ever, to admire the royal warrants (the House of

Gautier boasted thirteen) displayed along the walls. Warrants from the Empress Eugénie, the kings of Spain, Portugal, Greece, Romania, Yugoslavia and England, sultans and maharajahs. It was an impressive collection.

Gaston's tone was insistent. 'Harry, I don't care what it costs. You've got to get it for me.'

Like a dog, intent on re-establishing its patch, Laura continued her saunter around the office. Despite Madame Goffinet's best endeavours, the place was never tidy. Like his daughter, Gaston hated paperwork with a passion and letters and documents lay scattered all over the place.

He had begun to sound positively tetchy. 'Of course I know. Do you honestly think I wouldn't know a thing like that? No, believe me, it doesn't bother me.'

Laura scanned the bookcase and spotted a large, anonymous-looking folder. She picked it up and started to flick through its leaves. Soon, she was engrossed in the most fascinating of history lessons: a list – still in the process of being compiled – of every major client Gautier had ever dealt with. Her fingers tingled with excitement: it was like being transported back in time. Eagerly she turned the pages and gazed, wide-eyed, at what she found. Detailed drawings of a tiara for the Princess of Metternich; a necklace created for the mistress of Prince Demidoff, a man whose zest for living was extraordinary, even by aristocratic Russian standards; a brooch for Empress Eugénie of Montijo; pieces for Napoleon III; a pearl choker for Hortense Schneider, actress, courtesan and darling of the Tsar, the Sultan of Turkey and the kings of Prussia, Greece, Belgium, Spain and Portugal throughout the 1860s.

Laura smiled. Good old Hortense, she thought. She must have given all those gentlemen a jolly good run for their money! As her father said, mistresses and courtesans had always been the backbone of the jewellery business. She turned another page to find a bracelet design for Anna Deslions, the inspiration, so it was generally believed, for Zola's infamous, grasping Nana. Elsewhere was a jewelled case, commissioned by the Russian Prince Youssoupof, the architect of Rasputin's assassination. The

Maharajah of Kapurthala, the Duchess of Windsor, a few Princes of Wales – the loves and foibles of the world's nobility lay chronicled in the folder. The New World, also, was duly represented. The Vanderbilts, Rockefellers, Carnegies and Pierpont Morgans were all in evidence. A fabulous emerald necklace commissioned by the tragic heiress Barbara Hutton; a diamond pendant for Elizabeth Taylor; pieces for Onassis and Thyssen and later, for Trump and Spelling. Laura's eyes came to rest on the final addition to the folder: a jewel-encrusted elephant commissioned by the eccentric pop star Scorpio.

She stared out into space. Wonderment and pride combined, perhaps, with a little fear; she felt every one of these emotions. Although it was still incomplete, the folder was a testament to the history and traditions of a House which had excelled since 1850. This, she realized, was her heritage; like a child, it was both a joy and an enormous responsibility. The idea filled her with trepidation. Would she ever be able to live up to her father's expectations? And, even if she could, would she manage to sustain those standards for an entire professional lifetime? The spectre of her mother sped fleetingly across her mind. Like a brilliant firework, she had dazzled and faded swiftly. Laura prayed for a kinder fate.

She looked up to find her father staring at her. 'I'm sorry,' she smiled, 'I was miles away.'

'I see you've found my latest little undertaking.' He looked quite pleased with himself.

'It's incredible. How long have you been working on it?'

'A couple of months.' Gaston shrugged. 'Slightly more, I suppose. All the information I need is around here somewhere. It's just finding the time to collate it. I call this my labour of love.' He rummaged around in his drawer and finally pulled out a sheaf of papers, loosely clipped together. 'Look what materialized last week.' He handed her the pile.

Laura frowned as she struggled to decipher the morass of letters and figures. 'I'm afraid I can't make head or tail of it. What on earth does it all mean?'

'A secret code,' Gaston chuckled, 'based on the word ARTI-

CHOKES. A equals one, R equals two and so on until S which equals zero. The letter X indicates repetition. It was my grandfather's invention. I'm told he had quite a sense of humour.'

Her eyebrows knitted, Laura still struggled to comprehend. 'But what was the point?'

Gaston took out his pen and began to mark the letters down on a pad. 'It was used to value the major pieces of jewellery. So a ring worth five thousand five hundred francs would be marked down as CXSX.' He showed Laura the results of his scribbling.

At last, the light began to dawn. 'I see. So he used it as a form of security.'

Gaston nodded and reached into the drawer again. 'And then this turned up . . .' He handed her a battered black book, its leaves dog-eared with use.

She pounced on it and began to read. 'My God,' she whispered, 'talk about low behaviour in high places!'

'Fascinating, isn't it?' His grin was almost boyish. He, too, had been riveted by the contents of the book. As jeweller to the rich and the royal, Gaston's grandfather had kept a personal file on every customer. Details of wives and husbands and, more important, mistresses and lovers had all been carefully recorded. Every *liaison dangereuse* in contemporary Paris was right there in that little black book. 'So you can see why I've decided to spend the rest of my life collecting what I can, while I can.'

Laura's blood ran cold. She snapped the book shut. Already she considered herself the child of a one-parent family. The idea of losing that one cherished parent was more than she could bear. 'Please, Papa, don't talk like that. Today's your birthday, not your funeral.'

'I know.' His voice was placatory. 'But the traditions of this place must continue when I'm gone. That's why I've started to put some order into things. There are debts that must be paid.'

Laura's face clouded over. 'What kind of debts?'

'Debts of honour.' His eyes twinkled. 'I think it's time I told you. I'm leaving my collection of clocks and jewellery to London's Victoria and Albert Museum.'

She brightened visibly. 'But, Papa, that's a wonderful idea!'

'I hoped you'd think so. It's a token of gratitude to the British people for everything they did in the war.'

A sudden shadow crossed her face. 'What does Charles have to say about that?'

'I haven't told him yet. I don't suppose he'll be too pleased.'

'You won't let him talk you out of it, will you?'

'No,' he gave her a slightly world-weary smile. 'On this one I'm sticking to my guns.'

From his face, Laura knew that he meant what he said. Whatever the objections, the Gautier Collection was to be Gaston's gift to posterity, his own immortality guaranteed.

He stroked his chin as he continued. 'The trouble is, there's something missing. The collection needs a focal point, something really spectacular. That's why I've been talking to Harry Blumstein.'

'Good old Harry!' Laughter lines creased Laura's face at the memory of the Antwerp diamond dealer. As a very special treat when she was young, her father would take her on his buying trips to Blumstein's. She could still recall the smell of strong black coffee and expensive cigars which always permeated the office. It was difficult to imagine but there, in that tiny, smoke-filled room, billions of francs-worth of diamonds changed hands every year. 'So,' she cajoled him, impatient now, 'you've asked him to find you something special?'

For a split second she felt as if her father was trying to avoid her gaze. He answered in a studiedly casual voice. 'I've told him I want the Star of Heaven.'

Laura's face turned ashen. She felt her stomach turn. 'But, Papa! How could you even consider it?'

The Star of Heaven. The very name sent shivers running down the length of her spine. Everyone in the diamond business knew of the curse attached to this most fabulous of diamonds. Stolen, so the legend ran, from the head of an Indian idol, the stone was first sold in Europe to Louis XIV of France. A top colour, flawless diamond, weighing over one hundred and fifteen carats, the Star of Heaven was soon the talk of Versailles. After some manipulation, the king presented it to his mistress,

Madame de Montespan, who then had it set as a pendant. The diamond was subsequently acquired by the ill-fated Marie-Antoinette and then stolen, along with most of the French crown jewels, soon after the Revolution. It reappeared in Spain, but the duke who owned it was killed in a duel. Then it was stolen by his brother, who took it to London to sell. The brother, so the legend ran, was shipwrecked on his way back but by that stage the diamond was safe in the hands of a wealthy London banker. He died shortly afterwards and his nephew, who inherited it, went bankrupt. The diamond was then bought by an Arab prince who was involved in a fatal riding accident together with his favourite son.

Laura pulled her woollen shawl around her. She knew the legend by heart. It had been one of Maurice's favourite tales. Misery and misfortune had followed that stone wherever it went. In the early eighties it had again disappeared and its whereabouts were now uncertain. Some thought it was in Tel Aviv, others believed Saudi Arabia. One thing was sure, however. Wherever it was and whoever was holding it, the incomparable Harry Blumstein was bound to track it down.

'Please don't buy it,' Laura stammered at last. 'That diamond is nothing but trouble.'

Gaston laughed, a trifle too heartily. 'You're even worse than Harry. Diamonds and curses – I'm surprised a modern girl like you believes in that sort of nonsense.'

Her eyes were pleading. 'I'm begging you. There are so many other fabulous stones.'

'You're just being silly. I want the Star of Heaven. In fact, I've set my heart on it.' He tilted her face towards his. 'Come on, cheer up. Forget those superstitious tales. Do you know what *really* concerns me?'

She pulled her head away and turned to stare out of the window.

Ignoring her resistance, Gaston caught her by the hand. '*You!*'

'I'm fine!' she said gruffly.

'No, you're not, you're whacked. You've been working too hard, haven't you?'

A flush suffused her slightly pinched cheeks. 'No harder than anyone else.'

'Knowing you, I find that difficult to believe.'

He watched as she stared from the window to the floor, then back to the window again. She looked just like a small child. He longed to pick her up and cuddle her as he used to do, not so long ago. 'Laura, please, give yourself a break. Why not just finish your course and come and work for me? We're always on the look-out for fresh, talented young people.' The words resonated in his memory like an old refrain. He had used the same arguments on Caroline almost twenty-five years ago.

She shook her head with unexpected vehemence. 'Charles would hate it. He'd make my life a misery.'

'To hell with Charles! I still run—'

'I'm sorry. I shouldn't have dragged him into it. He's not the main reason. It's just . . . I don't know how to explain it, but I feel I still have to prove myself.'

'But you already have. Your work—'

'I'm not talking about my work! I'm talking about *myself*. Look what happened to my . . . to Caroline. You gave her everything – instant fame and fortune—'

'Your mother's own talent was the reason for her success.'

'Sure, but the weight of Gautier behind her didn't hurt. I have to prove that I'm a success in my own right – without that sort of help. I have to prove that I have . . .' the words stuck in her throat '. . . staying power, that I'm *your* daughter, that I'm really worthy of your name. When I've proved all that, Papa, then I'll come and work for Gautier.'

He could feel the tears pricking behind his eyelids. If it were possible, he would have loved his daughter even more for that confession. He gazed at her tenderly. 'So, I must let you go to keep you?'

'I'm afraid so.'

Gaston thought for a moment, then smiled a sly, mischievous smile. 'In that case, you must do something else to accommodate an old man on his birthday.'

Relieved to be let off the hook this time, Laura was happy to enter into the spirit of his game. She raised her hand in the air, as if on oath. 'Anything. Scouts' honour.'

'I'm sending you on holiday.'

Her forehead puckered immediately. 'But I haven't the time—'

Gaston would hear none of her objections. 'A promise is a promise. Besides, I know the change will do you good. You'll come back bursting with energy and new ideas.'

She flicked her hair back, half annoyed, half pleased. Perhaps her father was right, after all. It was true, she *was* tired and she hadn't taken a real holiday in ages. She did not want to run the risk of going stale just before the degree exhibition. All the same, she could not help but feel that her hard-earned independence was once more being threatened. 'Why do I always end up feeling like *la petite fille de Papa*?'

Gaston had experienced his daughter's stubborn streak all too often before. He decided to tread cautiously. 'Just this once,' he urged. 'I may not be around to spoil you for much longer.'

'You win,' she relented ungraciously. 'You play dirty, but you win. Anything to put an end to this dying-old-man routine.'

'Thank you.' The corners of his mouth were twitching dangerously. It was fortunate she did not see.

'Actually, I've been meaning to do a bit of photography – birds, landscapes, wildlife – it generates ideas.'

'So it's a deal, then?'

Laura thought for a second. She did not want to give in without some semblance of a fight. 'Only if you let me pay you back.'

'Naturally.' Gaston's voice was matter-of-fact. 'Out of your first Gautier pay-cheque.'

'That could be some time.'

'I can wait. After all, I'm only eighty. Where were you thinking of going?'

She hesitated for a moment. 'Up to the Afghanistan and Pakistan border.'

Gaston was genuinely taken aback. 'The North-west Frontier province?'

Her eyes took on a faraway look as she stared dreamily out of the window. 'Yes, the land of the Pathans, the most inspirational place on earth.'

'Smugglers, gun-runners and impossible terrain!' Suddenly Gaston began to laugh. 'You really are a headache, you know. Will you *ever* start taking life easy?'

CHAPTER SEVEN

The sunglasses fooled no one, especially not the insatiably inquisitive Madame D. As soon as she opened the door, she knew something was wrong. The tinted lenses failed to camouflage Maisie's eyes, still bloodshot and red from crying. Underneath, the large blue-black bags bore testimony to a disturbed and sleepless night. This morning, Maisie's clothes, usually so well co-ordinated, looked as if they had been thrown on at random. A pink blouse, a brown sweater, blue slacks and a black coat. No, concluded the housekeeper, Madame Gautier was not herself today.

A retainer of the old school, however, Madame D knew better than to question or to comment. Monsieur and Mademoiselle were out, she informed Maisie, but would Madame care to take a seat in the drawing room and telephone them at the office? Graciously, Maisie declined all offers of hospitality. Gaston and Laura had so little time together, she felt, they must be allowed to enjoy it. Besides, her husband and her marriage were *her* problems, no one else's. Neither Gaston nor Laura should be burdened with her unhappiness – especially not today.

Maisie handed Madame D the red silk dress she had brought for Laura and asked her to hang it in her bedroom. 'I'm rushed off my feet this morning,' she prevaricated, sensing an unwelcome hint of pity. 'I'd better be getting along.'

The housekeeper looked at the outfit with obvious approval. 'It's beautiful,' she said and then, catching Maisie's indulgent glance, decided for once to express an opinion. Laura, after all, was their joint surrogate child. Opinions on her and her well-being were thus permitted from time to time. 'You spoil her, Madame, but she's worth it. She'll stun everyone in this.'

Maisie managed a melancholy smile. 'She sure will. See you this evening, Madame D.'

Exhausted and more depressed than ever, Maisie slumped heavily into her car. She felt dizzy from want of sleep. As usual, she had lain awake the previous night, waiting to hear Charles's key in the front door. He was often late – two, three, even four o'clock in the morning was not uncommon, but at least he always came home. For all her indulgence, she was not stupid. Despite his excuses, his interminable business meetings, she knew he must be seeing other women. All the same, so long as the pretence could be maintained, she could force herself to bear it. Frenchmen, after all, were like that, or so she had been told. Mistresses and lovers were part and parcel of *la vie et la culture françaises*.

For all these reasons Maisie had somehow managed to ignore Charles's infidelity for years. In many ways, deep down, she even took the blame for it. Perhaps if she had given him children things would have turned out better. Even so, his cavalier behaviour cut her to the quick. She felt so compromised, she was even starting to despise herself. So long as Charles had the courtesy to play the game, she never made a fuss. A façade, at least, allowed some modicum of self-respect. But what now? Last night's performance was a new departure, a fall rather than a slither down the slippery slope. She only wished she had the guts to deal with it.

She turned the key in the ignition and the silver-grey BMW purred into life. Never frenetic, at that time of morning the avenue Foch was positively peaceful. Maisie pulled out and moved off towards the Bois de Boulogne. It was a wonderful morning, the sky clear and blue, a slight nip in the air, but today she was in no mood to notice or enjoy it. Today, her mind was such a jumble of emotions, she barely knew what she was doing. The powerful car accelerated effortlessly as she moved up into fourth. Unblinking, she stared in front of her. The sun on the windscreen, the hum of the engine, somehow she felt strange and disembodied. Gradually, it began to seem as if the machine were driving itself.

Quite where the little girl came from, Maisie would never know. Petite, blonde and dressed in a red woollen coat, she must have darted out into the road in pursuit of her ball. By the time Maisie noticed, it was almost too late. She braked hard. The car screeched as, desperately, she struggled with the steering wheel. She held her breath, vaguely aware of the smell of burning rubber. Then, as if in slow-motion, the car swerved across the road and straight into the oncoming traffic. For a split second, the silence was absolute.

Then she heard it. The excruciating sound of crunching metal and shattering glass catapulted her back to reality. Suddenly she could hear the child screaming. Maisie's mouth turned dry with terror. A woman started screaming too, and then an angry man. Soon the noise was unbearable. A crowd began to gather and everyone wanted his say. Maisie covered her ears with her hands and felt something warm and sticky. Suddenly she felt quite sick. She must have bumped her head in the collision. Dazed and helpless, she watched as the droplets of blood trickled down the side of her face and on to the black leather upholstery. Desperate for some fresh air, she struggled to open the door and almost fell out into the road.

'Are you all right, Madame?' A well-dressed gentleman with a Jack Russell terrier seemed to have taken charge. He saw the gash on Maisie's temple and handed her his handkerchief.

'Yes, thank you.' She tried to staunch the ugly wound. 'The child – is she . . .?'

'Don't worry, she's fine.' The man led her across to the pavement where she collapsed on to a bench.

Her stomach lurched as she surveyed the Citroën she had just ploughed into. 'Is anybody else hurt?'

He shook his head. 'It's a miracle, Madame, but no.'

By now, the driver of the Citroën was gesticulating wildly. 'My car!' He pointed to the pieces of wreckage scattered all over the road. 'That stupid bloody woman! What on earth did she think she was doing?' A small group gathered around him, trying to calm him down, but he continued to shout angrily at Maisie, who buried her head in her hands.

It was then that the police car arrived, its siren wailing loudly. Two burly *agents* jumped out and, in a supercilious Parisian manner, proceeded to inflame passions further. Eventually, after what seemed like an interminable list of questions, one of them drove Maisie home. 'It was an accident.' He shrugged as he helped her into the car. 'At least no one was hurt.'

Maisie could not bring herself to respond. The thought of what might have happened made her blood run cold. She must get a grip. She must not allow herself and her emotions to be buffeted around like this. If she continued down this path, she would soon be a liability to herself and everyone around her. She rallied her resolve. As soon as she saw Charles, she decided, she would issue him with an ultimatum. It was high time she put an end to this charade. She would not be used, undermined and exploited any more. Gently she dabbed her bruised and throbbing temple. A ferocious migraine had already taken hold.

The house was empty when Charles returned at around ten o'clock that morning. In a rare gesture, he had decided to take Yolande to the airport and the traffic on the way back had been dreadful. He showered and changed before phoning the Gautier office.

'Do you wish to speak to your father?' his secretary enquired. 'I've seen him around this morning. He's here with Mademoiselle Gautier.'

'She's calling herself Jay, nowadays,' snapped Charles. Even the idea that Laura shared his name filled him with irritation. 'And, no, in that case I don't wish to speak to him.'

'Will you be in later on today, monsieur? There are some letters here for your signature.'

'Yes. I have a lunch appointment at one but I'll drop in at the office around four. In the meantime, if there's anything urgent I'll be at home all morning.'

The recording machine clicked off as Charles replaced the receiver. Every call to his study, no matter how trivial, was taped.

He knew some people might call that paranoid, and perhaps it was, but he could not have cared less. Over the phone, people often made promises of which they had to be reminded. Sometimes they even admitted things which could later be used against them. Those were the kind of calls that Charles always stored. The rest he generally scrubbed.

He sat down heavily in his chair. There was no doubt that January and February had been exceptionally bad months. Not for the company, of course. Charles's face set hard. Thanks to his efforts and despite a world-wide recession, the House of Gautier was doing very nicely indeed. But company profits were not *his* profits, that was the trouble. That was the reason why he had to hang on until his father died. Then, and only then, could he even things up. He sifted through the wodge of bills. He had had no luck at the tables that month and his gambling debts were horrendous. And then there were the horses . . .

Gambling and horses. Why did *real* excitement have to be so damned expensive? He heaved a sigh of frustration. Last night had been an aberration: he should never have stayed over with Yolande. However nauseating, he had to keep Maisie sweet – at least for the time being. Malleable though she was, she could not be pushed too far. In the end, she was bound to snap. No, the goose must be persuaded to lay another golden egg, just enough to tide him over until his own plan could be hatched.

By the time Maisie reached home she was feeling ghastly. The sight of Charles's car in the driveway did nothing to improve her state.

'I think you ought to call a doctor,' said the *agent* as he helped her to the door. 'You never know with head injuries. You may have slight concussion.'

She shot him a grateful smile. 'I'll see how I feel, but thanks anyway. You've been extremely kind.'

Despite her screaming headache, she marched straight into Charles's study, determined to force a show-down. Charles lifted his head and, without really looking at her, switched on his most dazzling smile. 'Hello, Maisie. Been out shopping?'

Her face grey with pain, she brought her fist down hard on his desk. 'Don't try and fob me off!' she shouted. 'Where the hell were you last night?' And with that, she fainted.

When she came round, some thirty minutes later, Maisie found herself tucked up in bed in her nightclothes. Hovering over her stood Charles, his face carefully etched with concern.

'How are you feeling, darling?' He brought her hand to his lips and kissed it.

Maisie's head was swimming. 'The car. It's a write-off. I . . .' She struggled to find the words.

'Sssh!' He sat down beside her on the bed. 'I know. I got the details from the police.'

'It wasn't my fault.'

'Of course not, and anyway, it doesn't matter, just so long as you're all right.' He continued to hold her hand. 'Now, tell me how you're feeling. That's some bump you've got on your head.'

Her eyes were full of tears. It was years since he had shown her so much attention. 'I'm fine. I've just got a bit of a headache, that's all. I'll be OK for tonight.'

He shook his head gravely. Concern for the well-being of the patient, he reckoned it seemed like the best approach. 'Well, we'll have to see about that. I've called in Dr Lebrun. He'll be here as soon as possible.'

'I don't think I—'

'No. We *must* have a medical opinion.' A touch of authority mixed with that concern: Charles was really relishing his role. 'In the meantime, just close your eyes and get some rest. I'll be here if you need anything.'

Maisie could feel her resolve evaporating by the second. She felt so weak and pathetic. Summoning her few remaining shreds of determination, she forced a final rally. 'Last night . . .?'

But Charles was waiting for her. 'Those bloody Hong Kong Chinese!' His tone was one of pure exasperation. 'You think you've got a deal with them, then they start nit-picking over trivia.' Softly he stroked her cheek. 'I'm so sorry, darling. It never even occurred to me that you'd wait up.'

Her eyelids flickered shut again. It was as if her last ounce of willpower had suddenly drained away. She did not know if

Charles was telling the truth, in fact, deep down, she suspected that probably he was not. All the same, so long as there was an element of doubt she was prepared to take his word. With futile and deluded bravery, she would fight to keep the fragile peace in what she had learned to call a marriage.

Charles smiled to himself as he rearranged her pillows. He could see he had her on the run. Poor Maisie, she was so pathetically gullible that he almost – but only almost – felt sorry for her. He stared down at her tired, battered face. No, he told himself, suppressing that scintilla of pity, there was no point in feeling sympathy. Life was a game for the selfish and strong. The rest simply picked up the tab.

Exhausted and still in shock, Maisie was soon dozing again. Charles wandered around the bedroom he so rarely visited nowadays and picked up a magazine, one of the shoal Maisie always kept on her bedside table. Lying down beside her on the bed, he started to leaf through the pages. 'Green Scene – You and Your Environment'. He snorted in contempt as he skimmed through the article. Endangered species, pollution, alternative energy sources – all these were losers' problems. Money, profit and progress, now, they were concepts he could understand, that was winners' vocabulary. Maisie's eyes fluttered open. Desperate for some human warmth, she reached out to touch his elbow. He put down the magazine and rolled over to face her. Their lips were only inches apart. Now was the time to guarantee his debts. He took her gently in his arms and kissed her long and hard. 'This company's taking up too much of my time,' he said, surfacing for breath. 'When this deal is out of the way, I'm going to take things easier. Today has made me realize just how much you mean to me.' He kissed her again, more tenderly this time and she could feel her headache receding.

'I know I've failed as a mother,' she mumbled, her voice uneven, 'but if you'd only let me, I'd do my best to be a wife.'

The doorbell rang as lingeringly he kissed the tips of each one of her fingers. 'That must be the doctor.' He jumped up, grateful for the interruption. 'I'll bring him up and then I'll phone and cancel my lunch appointment.' The smile remained frozen on his face.

'But, Charles, you mustn't—'

He put his finger to her lips. 'What does business matter when something like this has happened?' It was a calculated risk. Today's lunch was one he genuinely could not afford to miss. With Maisie so softened up, however, he reckoned the gamble was an odds-on winner.

'You mustn't do that,' she remonstrated duly. 'There's no point wasting your time hanging around here all day. I'll only be asleep.'

Charles's face relaxed. Now he knew he could afford to argue. 'Are you sure?'

'Positive. But promise me you'll be home early this evening?'

He kissed her lightly on the cheek. All right, let her think she had the upper hand. It was a small enough price to pay.

'Of course. But if you're not well enough for the party, we'll just stay home and I'll cook for you myself.'

CHAPTER EIGHT

S ammy Sandton looked across at his new wife, Daphne, and
thought himself a very lucky man. The frosted bouffant
hair-do, the long immaculately lacquered nails, that natural
authority with the waiter ('I'll have a crème-de-menthe *frappée*,
please, *garçon*, and *une assiette* of dry roasted peanuts') everything
about her reeked of what Sammy knew was class. From the
moment he had first clapped eyes on her, almost three years ago,
he had known that this woman could add something to his life.
Unlike Elsie, Sammy's wife of fifteen years, Daphne had style,
Daphne had sex appeal and, more important still, Daphne had a
husband in Hendon (a pharmacist in flares) from whom she was
desperate to escape.

It had taken some time – and not inconsiderable alimony – to
get rid of the first Mrs Sandton. Eventually, however, Sammy
was free to marry the woman of his middle-aged dreams. His
mother, who, despite his offers of Californian condos, still
refused to budge from her two-up-two-down in the East End,
remained deeply cynical. Daphne, she maintained, was a gold-
digger and even if Sandton & Sons' stuff was only nine carat, she
would eventually mine him dry.

An only child, Sammy hoped and prayed that his beloved
mum would change her mind. In the meantime, however, the
delicious and indefatigable Daphne more than compensated for
the rift. True, she was expensive, but Sammy could well afford
it. High-street jewellers for almost twenty years, Sandton & Sons
owned prime sites all over the British Isles. The jewellery they
purveyed was cheap and cheerful, the turnover impressive and

the marketing impeccably pitched. The week after Lady Diana Spencer's engagement, for example, Sandton's were selling Taiwanese replicas of the famous sapphire and diamond ring. 'Make the Little Lady a Princess for under Fifty Quid', ran the advertising slogan and the punters turned up in their droves. At every annual sales conference, Sammy would proudly announce that, despite everything, even Andrew Morton, the royal rubbish was still shifting.

Jewellery, however, had never been Sammy's real passion. It was his unerring flair for property that had made him a millionaire. On the eve of the 'eighty-nine property crash, he had decided to go liquid. Then, in 'ninety-one, with the real estate market well and truly in the doldrums, he repurchased his former properties at bargain basement prices. In three years he had made an absolute killing. For Sammy Sandton nowadays, money was no object. But as Daphne had told him the day he presented her with her very own platinum American Express card, money was not everything. Forty-seven years of age, Sammy was now determined to learn about the finer things of life. And Daphne, who had O levels in art and craft, was precisely the woman to teach him.

It was Daphne, for example, who had insisted on staying at the Crillon, in one of its palatial suites overlooking place de la Concorde. Left to his own devices, Sammy would have stayed at his old favourite, the Georges V, but Daphne would have none of it. It was one of those chain hotels, she had sniffed, flicking through her brochure. And, besides, who wanted to stay in an hotel run by people who had motorway cafés? As usual, Sammy had given in and let her have her way. Surveying the splendour of Les Ambassadeurs, the restaurant housed in what was originally the *grand salon* of this regal mansion, he had to admit that Daphne always knew best in such matters. The wine waiter served their pre-prandial drinks. For some months a cocktail waitress, in 'an exclusive Marbella bar', Daphne reckoned she knew what was what about alcohol and was still quite partial to a nice long crème-de-menthe *frappée*. It had, so she informed Sammy, a certain *je ne sais quoi* that your average punter would not appreciate.

Far less adventurous, and in deference to the champagne family who ran the hotel, Sammy had ordered a bottle of Taittinger. The waiter poured him a glass and moved swiftly out of sight. 'Cheers, love,' said Sammy, winking as he raised his glass. 'Here's to us and a second honeymoon in gay Paris.'

Daphne tittered coyly. 'Oh, Sammy, you are a one.' Ever so nice, she sipped her drink through the straw she had requested.

Sammy devoured her with his eyes. It was one of the things he loved best about her. In the bedroom, she was the dirtiest little tramp he had ever been lucky enough to encounter. But outside she was such a lady. Elsie had always been a jellied eels and port sort of woman. In a place like this, she would have stuck out like a Sandton silver-plated decanter in the display window of Gautier's, New Bond Street. But Daphne, with her pert little bottom and brand-new silicone boobs, was a different proposition. You could take the new Mrs Sandton anywhere.

'Will I do?' she purred, patting an imaginary crease around the cleavage of her black woollen sheath dress.

Sammy slavered into his champagne. She would have done a lot better upstairs, prone and naked, in among the mirrors and the marble of that extraordinary bathroom. Perhaps, if he played his cards right over lunch with this Gautier bloke, she might give him just that for afters. 'Fabulous, doll. Old Charlie boy won't know what's hit him.'

Daphne's heart fluttered together with her heavily mascaraed lashes. She had only met Charles Gautier once before, at the Sandtons' Monte Carlo residence, Mon Repos. Suave and charming, to her he epitomized everything a Frenchman ought to be. Soon after, she had purchased herself a set of language tapes. 'Conversational French in twenty-eight days', the accompanying blurb had promised. Over and over, she played them on her Walkman as she did her early morning fitness exercises. She had even taken to practising her vowel sounds in the mirror. That 'u' sound, she found, was particularly difficult but came out quite well if she tried it while strengthening her pelvic floor muscles. After six months, she felt sufficiently confident to start dropping a few bons mots into the conversation. She felt sure that Charles would notice.

It was Daphne who first caught sight of him, nodding affably to a waiter here, exchanging brief pleasantries with a business acquaintance there as he made his way across to the table. Daphne felt a sudden flutter in the pit of her stomach. Tall and distinguished with thick shiny black hair, Charles personified everything Daphne was striving to achieve for herself and her husband. Charles Gautier simply oozed class, something her dear Sammy, for all his many attributes, was distinctly short on. Daphne caught her husband's eyes, keenly observant, following Charles's every movement. Underneath the table, she searched for his hand and, having found it, interlaced her fingers in his. He was a dear soul, she thought, smart, gutsy and energetic. Certainly, there was the raw material there to take him right to the top. All he needed was a bit of moulding, a bit of help and encouragement to push him in the right direction.

Daphne was no fool. She had read enough success stories in the Sunday tabloids to know how such things were done. A few well-focused and publicized charitable donations, a regular contribution to the Conservative Party and a knighthood would not be out of the question. If she had her way, and so far a besotted Sammy had never resisted, she would soon knock the residual East End edges off him. Sir Sammy and Lady Sandton. Unconsciously, Daphne straightened her back. Now, that really *would* be one in the eye for the dreaded ex-husband in Hendon.

Under the table, Sammy squeezed her hand in affectionate complicity. She flinched and made a quick mental note. He really must get rid of that huge knuckle-duster he always wore on his right hand, a twenty-first birthday present from his mother. She knew he was deeply attached to it, but all the same it had to go. A gentleman's jewellery, she had read in one of those upper-class glossy magazines, should be restricted to a pair of cufflinks and, if appropriate, a signet ring bearing the family coat-of-arms. Daphne made another mental note. On her return to England, she would set about buying the Sandton family a suitable chunk of heraldry.

'Charlie, my old mate, it's good to see you.' Sammy stood up to welcome his guest to the table.

'*Enchanté.*' Charles smiled, shaking him by the hand.

Daphne also noticed an almost imperceptible little bow. So elegant, she thought, so very Continental.

'Our Daphne's been like a cat on a hot tin roof,' continued Sammy, merrily. 'She couldn't wait to come to Paris to meet you again.' He gestured towards his wife who blushed, irritated. She would have to have a word with him about his upfront manner. A little blasé nonchalance, she had learned, was far more upmarket.

'*Ma chère* Daphne.' Charles took her hand (thank God she had been to the manicurist that morning!) and lightly brushed it with a kiss.

'*Enchantée*, Charles,' she whispered, her blush now one of sheer pleasure. So romantic, she thought, to have your hand kissed. Far more romantic than that bonk outside on the balcony in Beaulieu which, to date, had been the height of her romantic experience with Sammy. Suddenly she began to feel quite faint.

'A glass of fizz, eh, Charlie?' asked Sammy amiably, lurching to grab the bottle from the ice bucket. Charles caught sight of the horrified sommelier, but nodded anyway. Sammy Sandton did things *his* way, and Charles admired him for it. The world Charles inhabited was full of genteel folk with perfect manners and *beaucoup de savoir-faire*. In his experience, such people rarely had either the guts or the wherewithal to achieve their hearts' desires. Sammy, on the other hand, was quite a different animal. Charles had run a check on him and liked what he discovered. An astute businessman and now a self-made millionaire, in his youth Sammy had been a successful amateur boxer. If and when this deal went ahead, there was bound to be a fight. Charles looked at his host's lean, powerfully built frame and recognized a winner. Just as well, he concluded. It was futile entering into negotiations with someone too wimpish to follow through.

Charles raised his glass to his host and hostess and proposed a toast. 'To our mutual satisfaction.'

'To our mutual satisfaction,' they echoed, Sammy smiling politely, Daphne far more enthusiastically.

The point did not escape Charles's attention. Right from the very beginning it had been Daphne who had made all the running in their relationship. His chance meeting with the

Sandtons in Monte Carlo had immediately been followed by an invitation to their expensively and execrably decorated house. Of course, it was he, Charles, who had first floated the idea of Sandton & Sons taking over Gautier. The two companies, he had suggested, half drunkenly over Armagnac, would be a perfect fit. It was Daphne, however, who had jumped on the idea. Sammy, far more sceptical, had merely promised to look at the possibilities. That was over six months ago and since then the two men had kept in close touch. Charles saw the Sandtons' decision to come to Paris as a very positive development.

Lunch passed agreeably enough. Daphne pushed a small salad around her large plate and talked incessantly of her 'regime'. Sammy, ever watchful of his powerful physique, ate grilled sole and mange-touts with no boiled potatoes. Only Charles, increasingly obsessed with food, did real justice to the extensive menu: a serious helping of *foie gras* followed by roast duckling plus trimmings, all finished off with a small mountain chain of cheeses. Sammy noted his guest's eating habits with interest: in his experience, overeating was a sign of either stress or frustration. Throughout the meal, he surreptitiously studied the thickening girth which Charles's expensive, well-cut suit might have hidden from a less observant eye. Certainly, thought Sammy contentedly, the middle-aged Charles bore little resemblance to the lithe, athletic Adonis he used to read about in his youth. Yes, it had been worth all those City scoundrels' inflated fees to get the dope on Charlie. Information, after all, was power. 'Never go into a fight without first getting to know your opponent.' That was the only piece of advice his old boxing coach ever gave him. He had found the same held true in business. Sammy had done his homework thoroughly. Now he knew precisely where Charles's weak points lay.

'I think,' declared Daphne after coffee, 'that it's high time I went to *poudroyer mon nez.*'

Charles winced inwardly as he shot her his most dazzling smile. How he wished this woman would stop mangling the language of Racine and concentrate on doing what she did best – mangling her own.

'*Ma chère* Daphne.' He stood up and helped her from her

chair. 'It's quite incredible. I had no idea you were bilingual.' He
smiled as much to himself as to her. After conning Maisie for so
long, duplicity was becoming second nature. Perhaps, he mused,
there was something of the legendary Renard in him, after all.

Daphne fluttered her long black eyelashes, genuinely
pleased. Those language tapes, those interminable hours of
practice had certainly paid off. '*Merci*, Charles.'

'Brilliant, isn't she?' enthused Sammy, beaming. His gaze,
Charles noticed, never once left his wife's *décolletage* as she moved
sinuously around the table to kiss him. It was a lingering kiss,
full on the lips, a caress quite uninhibited by the disapproving
looks of a restaurant full of people. Charles watched as she bent
over, her skin-tight sheath dress clinging to the cleavage of her
pert little buttocks, rising to display the tops of her black silk
stockings attached to frilly lace suspenders. For a split second he
imagined her writhing beneath him in wild, abandoned pleasure.
Judging by Sammy's slavering infatuation, she must be quite
something in bed.

B.A.F., thought Charles. It was his own private system for
categorizing women. Women like Daphne were '*bonne à foutre*',
'good for a lay.' Women like Maisie, on the other hand, belonged
to a far rarer and more useful species: 'B.P.L.', '*bonne pour liquide*',
'good for cash'. It was an unsophisticated system, but Charles
could not remember any woman of his acquaintance who did not
fall into one of those two categories.

'In fact,' cooed Daphne, stroking Sammy's cheek, 'I think it's
probably time I went upstairs for my siesta. I'll leave you two
gents alone to talk business.' She picked up her clutch bag and
turned to leave. 'See you later, darling.' She winked meaningfully
at Sammy. 'And *au revoir*, Charles. I hope we'll be seeing you
soon at Mon Repos.'

Charles inclined his head in one of those elegant little bows
he knew she so adored. Why not pander to her? After all, the
silly bitch was turning out to be his major ally.

Sammy's demeanour changed as soon as his wife had disappeared from the restaurant. Charles felt the transformation
immediately. It was like the unexpected onset of frost after a
warm summer's evening. Gone the sloppy, schoolboy glances

and the fatuous small talk, Sammy Sandton moved straight to the point. 'As you know, Charlie boy, I've had my lads take a look at your outfit.'

'Of course.' Charles studied the perfectly laundered tablecloth with sudden interest. A Frenchman to the marrow, he did not take easily to this gratuitous familiarity. 'Charlie boy'? 'Outfit'? Perhaps this was the way they did business in the East End of London. All the same, he wished this parvenu would learn a little respect for his betters. At least his appalling wife deferred to class when she encountered it. 'And I hope you like what they came up with.' His voice was casual and confident, betraying nothing of his contempt.

'Very interesting.' Sammy nodded as he poured himself another cup of coffee. The waiters, by this stage, had decided to give up. 'You're a bright boy, Charlie.' Without asking, he refilled Charles's cup. 'Some of those property deals you've pulled off, I'd have been proud of them myself.'

'Thanks.' Charles smiled across at his host. Patronizing clown, he thought, increasingly irritated. 'But as you're probably aware, there's rather more to the House of Gautier than a series of prime real-estate sites.'

'Oh, yeah,' replied Sammy. 'I know all about your fancy firm and your fancy name. But take my word for it, Charlie,' his jaw set hard, 'I don't give a toss about status. The likes of me didn't make our dough worrying about crap like that. Sure, Daphne has set her heart on this deal and nothing would give me more pleasure than to give that little lady what she wants. All the same, sunshine, if the figures don't stack up, there's no way I'm going to play.'

For the first time during their lunch, Charles began to loosen up. The figures, he knew, really *did* stack up. He, personally, had made sure of it. 'That's what I'd expect', he sipped his coffee slowly, 'from an operator as shrewd as you.'

Despite himself, Sammy smiled. Whatever he might say, it was nice for an East End boy to be courted and flattered by the likes of Charles Gautier. It meant he had arrived. 'I'm particularly impressed by the success of your accessory business,' continued Sammy, the smile evaporating instantly as he returned to the subject of business. ' "Les Petits J" de Gautier have done wonders for the cash flow of your operation.'

Charles bit his lip as a sudden pang of jealousy gripped his chest. Launched in 1971, the Petits J de Gautier range of trinkets had been aimed at the mid-market purchaser. Right from the outset, the range had proved a winner, helping Gautier to achieve 15 per cent growth in the seventies, 27 per cent in the eighties, and by 1991, contributing more than half of the company's billion-pound sterling sales. Far from undermining Gautier's cachet of affluence and luxury, however, the new range had simply succeeded in extending consumer appeal. Les Petits J de Gautier, with their relatively low labour costs and their extremely high profit margins, were now the mainstay of the company. It was a fact that had never ceased to aggravate Charles. However many people he fooled into believing that the original idea was his, deep down he had to admit that the concept had been Caroline's.

Charles shrugged, very Gallic. 'They've served us very well. Sadly, the market for really important jewellery is shrinking all the time.'

'I know.' Sammy's accountants and merchant bankers, the highly paid advisors he generally referred to as 'the lads', had been running their slide rules over every corner of the Gautier operation. 'But if, and I do say *if*, we were to take over Gautier, we'd leave Les Petits J alone.'

'I thought you said you weren't concerned with status,' quipped Charles and immediately wished he had not.

Sammy flashed him a look that would have curdled milk. 'It *doesn't* concern me, Charlie boy,' he said deliberately. 'And, like I said, I'm buggered if I'll pay through the nose for it.'

Charles felt a sudden chill down the length of his spine and resumed his inspection of the tablecloth.

Sammy swallowed his by now tepid coffee in one swift gulp. 'Now let me tell you something,' he said, suddenly all smiles. When an opponent was flat out on the canvas, there was no point in punching him any more. 'At Sandtons we need to go upmarket. People want quality nowadays. There's no longer the profit in crap.'

Charles nodded obligingly.

'Obviously,' continued Sammy, 'we're not talking tiaras, but the Petits J line is round about where I'd like to be positioned.'

'I see.' Charles was feeling better by the minute.

'If our two operations merged, I could save a packet on labour and distribution costs. I've got contacts in Thailand and Hong Kong who could be whacking out Les Petits J at a fraction of the price.'

Charles said nothing. An undisciplined extension of the brand, a plethora of products on the market was bound to be counter-productive. The way Sammy was talking, the time-honoured name of Gautier would swiftly be diluted beyond repair. Charles mulled the prospect over and found, almost to his surprise, that he did not give a damn. *'Après moi le déluge.'* The thought actually gave him pleasure. On the defensive for too long, he felt he now had to make a move. 'So, you think a deal is possible?'

'Ask the lads in London, Charlie. They'll tell you Sammy Sandton is always ready to deal. The point is, sunshine, when *precisely* are you?'

Like a swift, unexpected jab to the head, the question left Charles reeling. Sparring with these bar-room bruisers, he was learning, was a completely different game. He pulled himself together. 'I've always tried to be straight with you.' Charles moved into his most sincere look. 'And as I told you in Monte Carlo, I can't do anything while my father is still in charge. My hands are tied until . . .'

'Until the old codger drops off his perch. So how long are we talking about?'

Despite his own feelings of animosity, Charles felt oddly annoyed to hear his father referred to in such terms. 'He's eighty years old today.'

'Only eighty! Christ almighty, my old mum's almost ninety and still down the pub every night.' Sammy tapped his garish knuckle-duster fondly. 'What a trooper! Then there's her bingo twice a week. They broke the mould when they made my mum. There's no flies on her, I can tell you!'

For once in his life, Charles almost began to feel ashamed. 'According to the doctors, my father doesn't have very long.'

Sammy nodded, matter-of-fact. 'It's nothing personal against your dad – hell, I've never even met the bloke. But I've got to know where I stand.'

He poured himself another coffee and mulled over the facts so far. According to Charles, Gaston would never accept the idea of his beloved company being taken over. Snobs and old-fashioned sticks-in-the-mud, all his life, Sammy had been battling against such Establishment types. In his book, they had called the shots for far too long. Now he was growing impatient. The takeover of the House of Gautier would turn him into a world-class player, a serious punter to be respected. That made the whole thing a simple equation. The sooner the old man snuffed it, the better it was for him.

He looked up and smiled engagingly. 'So, then, Charlie boy, until the fateful day, you and I will keep in touch.' He drained his coffee in a gesture which seemed to mark the end of the meeting.

Charles was not slow to take the hint. Delighted with the progress achieved, he conveyed his regards to Daphne and graciously took his leave. Sammy waved for the bill and, while waiting, retrieved a picture postcard from his pocket: a photograph of the Eiffel Tower. He felt sure his mother would like it. Whenever he went abroad, he always sent her a card. He had been sending them since, as a ten-year-old Scout, he had been dispatched on a day trip to Calais. 'Dear Mum,' he wrote in a bold hand, 'Paris is really lovely. I wish you'd let me bring you here one day. Lots of love, Your Sammy.' Swiftly, he stuffed the postcard back into his pocket as the waiter appeared with the bill. With these Froggie waiters, you could never be sure. Perhaps the bloke read English.

The waiter gave him an unctuous smile as he picked up the generous tip. Sammy barely noticed. Already his thoughts were wandering upstairs to where a freshly bathed and perfumed Daphne was waiting, naked, for him.

CHAPTER NINE

Laura stared hard at herself in the dressing-table mirror and willed the burgeoning spot on her chin to disappear. It was just her luck! The very night she wanted to look her best, this stubborn pink blemish had suddenly popped up. She fished around for some concealer in her tattered make-up bag. A blusher, a set of two contrasting eye shadows, a semi-congealed mascara, it was not an impressive collection. Apart from the odd touch of lip gloss in the winter, she rarely had recourse to cosmetics: a flawless complexion was something else she seemed to have inherited from her mother. That was, she thought, until the night it really mattered.

She pulled out an ancient Max Factor Pan-Stik and went to work with her one and only sable brush. Not bad, she thought, studying the end result with an artist's critical eye. This evening, her mass of fine blonde hair had been cajoled up into some semblance of a French pleat. With such a wonderful dress to wear it seemed only right to make the effort. Laura sighed. Try as she might, she had not quite managed the sophisticated look she was hoping to achieve. Stray wisps shot out all over the place, framing her beautiful blue-eyed face in what looked like a fuzzy haze of light. Far from drop-dead chic, she looked more vulnerable than ever. No matter, she decided. She gave her head a helpful shake and a few more tendrils tumbled down. For all his talk of equal opportunity and women's liberation, Robert seemed to prefer the helpless female look.

Robert de la Marotte. She reached for her bottle of Guerlain's Shalimar, her only real student extravagance, and splashed it on with a vengeance. Behind her ears, on her wrists, around her cleavage, as Frenchwomen said, anywhere and everywhere a gentleman might be inclined to kiss. Not that Robert de la Marotte seemed to notice anything much, mused Laura disconsolately. A talented young actor, she had first seen him playing Meursault in a fringe production of Camus' *L'Étranger*. The part, she had swiftly come to realize, could have been written for him. A radical left-winger, he made no secret of his contempt for the bourgeoisie and their posturing. Laura looked anxiously at the expensive piece of couture hanging on her wardrobe door. Fuss and formality was not her style and it most certainly was not Robert's. For the hundredth time that evening, she wondered whether she should have invited him after all. How would he cope with the inevitable trivia and small talk of a party? Would he be bored? Would he throw one of his scenes? The crowds of butterflies in Laura's stomach fluttered around more wildly still.

She zipped herself into the red silk dress and, almost despite herself, felt better. The fabric clung to her tall, slim body, accentuating her firm breasts, tiny waist and narrow hips. She twirled, catching her reflection in the full-length mirror of her wardrobe. In such a dress, it seemed downright sinful to be miserable. Her thoughts turned at once to Maisie, still recovering in bed, and her elation soon turned to guilt. She had spoken to her earlier that afternoon, and was not convinced that her injuries were as minor as she continued to insist. She sat down on the bed and dialled the familiar number. Odd, she thought, as she waited for the call to be connected, Maisie was such a careful driver, she had never even scraped her car before.

'*Allo*, Gautier.' Laura recognized Charles's voice on the other end of the line. Tonight he was clearly in mellifluous mode. She grimaced. The smarmy bastard! Maisie had let nothing slip, but every instinct told her that somehow Charles must be to blame. Their conversation was short and not excessively sweet.

'Who was that?' shouted Maisie from the bath.

'No one.' Charles continued to fasten the studs of his evening shirt. 'Only Laura.'

Maisie bit her tongue. She did not want to wreck their newly made truce. All the same, she wished he would stop being so off-hand about Laura. 'You should have called me.' She heaved herself out from among the luxuriously perfumed bubbles and reached for a fluffy white bath sheet. By now, her headache had almost disappeared but she was still feeling slightly dazed. She glanced in the mirror. The gash on her head was looking less angry, and if she brought her hair down across her forehead she could camouflage it for the evening. She sat down heavily on the wicker chair and started to rub herself dry. Her legs, long and slim, were still in marvellous shape. Flat and taut, her stomach was the result of frequent, perhaps excessively frequent, exercise classes and her breasts, never large, remained firm and round. Despite her age, she was still an enviably attractive woman. Charles's greatest strength, as he was well aware, was his ability to make her doubt it.

She emerged from the bathroom to find him sitting on her bed and tying his bow-tie. A warm glow, unrelated to her rub-down, began to suffuse her body. It was ages since he had changed in her bedroom. How handsome he still looked in his tuxedo. True, he had put on weight but, in the subdued bedroom lighting, her eyes could still see the dashing young beau she had once fallen in love with.

'Was it anything important?'

'I'm sorry?' Charles raised a quizzical eyebrow.

'Laura's call.'

'Oh, that.' He struggled to fasten his cufflinks. 'No, nothing. She just wanted to make sure you were still coming.'

'Poor kid!' Carefully, Maisie started to brush her hair. 'I'd promised to go along early and give her moral support. I guess she must be feeling nervous.'

He dropped a cufflink on the floor and bent down to pick it up. 'Nervous about what, for God's sake? Surely, the caterers have done everything that needs doing?'

She smiled wanly. It felt like her head was swimming again. 'It's not that side of things that's bothering her,' she confided. 'It's this actor boyfriend of hers, Robert de la Marotte.'

He pricked up his ears. 'Really? So our little Laura's got the hots for him, has she?'

Maisie nodded. 'The trouble is, she's worried he might not

feel at home tonight. I'd promised to introduce him to people, you know, make sure he was OK. But now I really don't feel up to it.'

Charles stood up and moved towards her. 'Of course you don't, darling, but you mustn't let that bother you. I'll take care of young de la Marotte.'

'Would you?' She shot him a look of deepest gratitude.

'It's the least I can do.' As he kissed her on the shoulder, his lips felt soft and warm against her skin. Maisie felt a sudden tremor down the length of her back. Her dizziness forgotten, she let the towel slip to the floor. Charles felt his erection growing harder by the second. He knelt before her like a supplicant, begging for forgiveness. It was a well-worn strategy but, so far, it had always worked. 'You know I love you, Maisie.'

She leaned down and kissed the top of his head. 'And I love you too.'

Charles totted up his most pressing gambling debts. That last trip to the casino at Monte Carlo had been an absolute disaster. He moved forward to kiss her nipple. 'Darling, would you . . . I mean . . . are you feeling up to it?'

'Never better,' she whispered and, one by one, began to undo his diamond studs.

Alone in his dressing room, Gaston Gautier pinned the small red ribbon on to his jacket. Presented to him by his old friend Charles de Gaulle, the Légion d'Honneur was the one decoration he invariably wore. Britain's Military Cross, France's Croix de Guerre and a plethora of others were kept under lock and key in the safe. Sometimes Gaston would take them out and recall the comrades who had received each honour alongside him. He closed his eyes and patted his ribbon with pride. The old comrades were fewer on the ground nowadays; of Gaston's own Resistance cell, only two others still survived.

The jeweller, the Jew and the scribbler: the three young men had made the strangest of bedfellows. Gaston closed his eyes and conjured up his fellow cavaliers. An avant-garde Jewish film producer, Serge Birnbaum had featured high on the hit list of the occupying Nazis. Gaston smiled to himself as he recalled their first outing together – an audacious attack on a German officers' Christmas party.

'For my wife,' the jeweller had muttered as he detonated the initial bomb.

'For my race,' Serge had added drily.

Far less serious-minded, Daniel Baudon had always been the joker in their pack. A fearless anti-Fascist and a writer, he had gone on after the war to make a fortune with his scabrous satirical magazines. Nowadays, *Le Pou qui Tousse* was considered compulsory reading amongst the intelligentsia of Paris and the *Gadfly*, recently launched in Britain, seemed to be meeting with equal success. Low behaviour in high places, thoroughly researched and well sourced – that, according to Daniel, was still the fail-safe prescription for a fortune.

Gaston reached for his tablets, poured himself a glass of water and swallowed two. This bloody heart complaint, it was a constant cause of annoyance and frustration. Somehow the prospect of illness and old age filled him with far more fear than the Gestapo ever had. Until the palpitations started, he had never considered the prospect of death, not even during his closest shaves. Having cheated the Grim Reaper for so many years, the celebrated Renard had almost begun to believe in his own indestructibility. The old man shook his head. Such was the ignorance and arrogance of youth – and such was the unalloyed bliss of it!

Gaston poured himself another glass of water and, this time, sipped it slowly. Eighty years old today. Whatever happened now, he knew he had had a decent run. He had known intense happiness and profound sorrow. He had risked his life for his country and his compatriots. And above all, he had carried on a proud tradition, creating things of beauty and of value for countless generations to come. He picked up Laura's jade box and studied it with renewed pleasure. As long as the House of Gautier produced marvels such as this, he knew his name would live on for ever.

Memento Mori – that was the problem with war, the survivors remembered nothing. If Gaston had learned anything over the years, it was that heroism in itself was no guarantee of immortality. War, death, destruction – of late, he had even taken to wondering whether all the sacrifice had been worthwhile. He smiled, despite his growing melancholia. Perhaps cynicism was just another symptom of old age. But somehow the society he and his comrades had fought for had failed to materialize. Nowadays, people seemed so alienated, so unconnected. The social cohesion for which he had risked his life seemed an ever-receding mirage. It was hard, sometimes, not to feel utterly depressed.

He struggled to pull himself together. These black moods seemed to close in on him so frequently nowadays and he knew he must shrug this one off. The emeralds of Laura's box seemed to wink up at him in the lamplight and he felt suddenly ashamed. What right had he, of all people, to feel depressed? There was so much that was good in his life. He stroked the box lovingly. There were always the artists and craftsmen, there were always the Lauras of life. Even if it *was* true, even if the world was becoming increasingly depersonalized, these makers of small precious objects would still provide the solace of individualism, the poetry of the physical. There would always be a place for beauty, even in the most brutal of worlds.

Cheered at the thought, Gaston checked his hair in the mirror and continued to count his blessings. He had a daughter he adored and a son . . . A sudden shadow crossed his face. Well, he had a son who was capable and astute. Gaston drained his glass of water and tried to be objective. For all his many faults, there was no doubt that Charles had proved himself an excellent steward of the company's interests. And Charles *was* right. He, Gaston, could not expect to go on for ever. It was time to make the necessary arrangements. He would have to get on to his lawyers.

A sudden knock at the door interrupted his train of thought.

'Are you ready yet, Papa? You seem to be taking ages.'

'I'm sorry, my dear. Please, do come in.'

His face lit up as his daughter entered the room. Flushed with apprehension and excitement and resplendent in red, she looked the very image of her mother.

'You look superb!' he exclaimed and kissed her on the cheek.

Laura giggled self-consciously. 'Madame D says she doesn't even recognize me. Mind you,' she lowered her voice conspiratorially, '*I* hardly recognized *her*.'

'Don't tell me she's forsaken her black?'

She nodded. 'Unheard of, I know, but tonight she's in midnight blue. Very fetching. What's more, she's wearing your brooch.'

'Not the diamond rose?' His black mood quite forgotten, Gaston was almost jaunty.

'Yes.'

'Well, fancy that! It's only taken her twenty years!'

He smiled at his own little joke as Laura took him by the arm. 'Come on,' she said, 'let's have a quiet drink together before the multitudes arrive.'

'Just one minute, young lady.' Gaston disengaged his arm and walked across to his old, mahogany dressing table. He opened one of the drawers and pulled out a gold-tooled red leather Gautier box. '*Donnons-donnons*,' he said and handed it to her. 'I want you to have this.'

'But it's *your* birthday, not mine,' she argued.

His eyes twinkled with pleasure. She was so similar to him in many ways, happier to give than receive. 'Please,' he urged, childishly impatient. 'I want you to open it.'

Laura flicked open the lid and stared, wide-eyed, at the bracelet which nestled against the jet-black velvet. Made of platinum and set with calibre rubies, round cut, and baguette diamonds, it was one of the most dazzling pieces she had ever seen. Slowly she shook her head. 'Sorry, Papa, I just can't accept. I don't feel I've done anything to deserve it.'

'Stubborn as ever,' he tutted. 'Since when did you have to *deserve* my affection? Come on, let me put it on for you.'

For a moment she considered withdrawing her hand, but it seemed too ungracious and ungrateful. Reluctantly, she allowed him to fasten the bracelet around her narrow wrist.

He studied it with pleasure, quite oblivious to her dilemma. 'There, at last that's found a home.'

Entranced, yet still slightly awkward, she looked at it in the light. Gradually, she felt her resistance evaporating as the sparkling rubies worked their charms. 'You made this yourself, didn't you?'

He smiled, ruefully. 'Over twenty years ago. I made it for your mother, but she left before it was finished.'

The admission was so poignant that her remaining objections simply collapsed. 'I'll *try* and deserve it,' she said, at last.

'You already do,' he replied.

By the time Maisie and Charles arrived, the party was in full swing. Towering above the throng of politicians, artists and businessmen, Gaston moved with his usual ease, dispensing Clos du Mesnil with a flourish.

'Maisie,' he shouted, making his way across to them. 'How are you, my dear?'

'She's fine,' answered Charles, casting his eyes around. The great and the good of Paris made a very impressive gathering. There were so many useful people to talk to – he knew he must park Maisie somewhere quickly.

'Monsieur *le ministre.*' He waved to a dapper little man holding court near the window. He must have a word with the old rogue. What he did not know about offshore tax havens was simply not worth knowing.

Gaston studied his daughter-in-law's face before kissing her. Despite her accident, Maisie was looking extraordinarily happy and relaxed. He wondered anxiously whether she was still in shock.

'I'm OK.' Warmly, Maisie returned the old man's embrace. 'All the same, I'd be grateful if you'd find me a nice quiet spot to sit down. The doctor's told me to take things easy.'

'Maisie!' While talking animatedly to Robert, Laura suddenly caught sight of her friend. Leading the young actor by the hand, she started to make her way towards her sister-in-law. A tall man, lean and ascetic-looking with a cadaverous face and huge dark eyes, interrupted their progress.

'So, young Laura! Have we no time, nowadays, for old family friends?'

'Monsieur Baudon!' Delighted, Laura embraced her father's former Resistance comrade.

'Tut, tut!' Baudon's eyes twinkled with mischief and intelligence. 'Monsieur Baudon, indeed! You make me sound like some ossified Establishment figure.' He pointed to the minister. 'Mind you, there's no shortage of them here tonight.'

She shook her head, mock-horrified. 'You shouldn't be so rude about my father's illustrious guests.'

'Not *the* Daniel Baudon?' interrupted Robert, visibly impressed. So far, this evening had been nothing but surprises.

'The same.' Daniel took a low, exaggerated bow and, in so doing, butted a former minister in the groin.

'Baudon!' exclaimed the horrified Gaullist, doubling up in pain. An article in *Le Pou qui Tousse*, listing some interesting details of this gentleman's overseas deals, had once helped remove him from office. Now, here was the perpetrator of the piece, adding further insult to injury. 'Don't tell me *you* were *invited* here?'

'Not only was I invited', Daniel shot him the most contemptuous of glances, 'but I declined.'

Laura struggled to keep a straight face as the disgraced politician shuffled off in a huff. Open-mouthed, Robert stared at Daniel, the hero of his adolescence, the most feared and notorious of all Parisian iconoclasts.

'I'm honoured to meet you, Monsieur,' said Robert, to Laura's intense relief. All her worries and apprehensions had been groundless, after all. Robert was really enjoying himself.

'I'll risk leaving you two together for a moment,' she beamed, her eyes trained now on Maisie. 'But, Daniel, for once in your life please try and behave and don't go subverting my friend.'

Settled in the large leather armchair in Gaston's study, Maisie sipped her apple juice. 'You're making me feel quite guilty,' she chided, as Laura organized her cushions. 'I wish you'd just leave me and go and enjoy yourself.'

'But I *am* enjoying myself.' Laura placed an occasional table next to the chair. 'There, that's for your drink. Do you feel like something to eat?'

'Not really, though I must say the caterers have done a wonderful job.'

Laura nodded. In the dining room, the huge eighteenth-century table heaved with all manner of exquisite delicacies. *Foie gras* and stuffed quail, king prawns and lobster, rare roast beef and tender, ever-so-slightly pink lamb – even Madame D had been moved to voice her approval. 'Everyone seems to be enjoying themselves, even Robert.'

'Now I see.' Maisie smiled up at her friend. 'So that's why *you* are enjoying *yourself*.'

Laura blushed. 'I think I'm falling in love with him. He's such an idealist, so principled, so wonderfully unmaterialistic. Sometimes he makes me feel so embarrassed, the way you and Papa just shower me—'

'Ah, Maisie, there you are.' A vision in shimmering pink silk interrupted their conversation. Looking like a woman half her age, Betsy Lamielle erupted into the study. 'I've only just heard,' she continued, unfastening her Chanel cape and dumping it unceremoniously on the floor. 'How are you feeling, honey? Don't tell me one of those dumb French macho drivers cut you up. I'll get that lawyer of mine on to him.' She turned and enveloped Laura in a huge bear hug. 'Boy, you're looking wonderful tonight, isn't she, Maisie? Come on, tell me, who's the lucky guy? It sure ain't *Optrex* making your eyes shine that way.'

Laura's gaze followed her admiringly as she sat down on the sofa. No wonder Maisie called her Hurricane Betsy! With that kind of energy, there were few who would dare to stand in her path. Deftly she extricated herself from the imminent third-degree. 'Would you like me to fetch you a glass of champagne?'

'No. You just run along. Send me one of those cute tight-assed little waiters. Don't worry about Maisie – she's just fine here with me, aren't you, honey?'

Maisie nodded helplessly. When Betsy took control of things, there was little else to do.

Laura rejoined the throng in the drawing room, stopping for a moment to dispatch the best-looking waiter to the study. Automatically, her eyes seemed to focus on Robert, still deep in conversation with Daniel. She watched as Serge Birnbaum, now a celebrated film producer, moved across to join them.

Her father sidled up beside her. 'And the latest report from the front?' Clearly enjoying himself, Gaston took Laura's empty glass from her hand and refilled it from his magnum.

'Oh, my goodness!' She giggled as the bubbles tickled the tip of her nose. 'I'm feeling quite giddy already.' She continued to sip her champagne all the same and gestured towards the increasingly raucous trio in the corner. 'Robert seems to be having a whale of a time.'

'Good! I told the old comrades to make sure he was all right. Who knows, Serge may even be of some use to him.'

If it wasn't for the bottle, she might have flung her arms around his neck. 'You're an angel.'

'We may be old men,' he winked, skittishly, 'but we still do our best to please.'

'Champagne, Madame.' The young waiter placed the elegant, fluted glass on the table next to Betsy.

'Thanks.' Despite her breezy manner, she was concerned about her friend. It was not the accident that bothered her. She had soon established that Maisie's injuries were genuinely minor. But the sudden euphoria, the almost bovine serenity – she had witnessed these symptoms far too often before. That bastard Charles! He had obviously been making up to her. Poor Maisie, she always fell for the same routine. God knows how much she would let him sting her for this time.

'More apple juice?' The waiter picked up Maisie's empty glass. She shook her head.

'No thanks.'

'I think that's all for now,' said Betsy, almost curtly. She must have a few minutes alone with Maisie before someone else came in. She beamed at the handsome young waiter. 'And please, be a honey, will you, and close the door behind you.'

As soon as he was gone, she started in earnest on her friend. 'I don't mind admitting, I'm worried about you.'

Maisie cranked up the well-worn recording. 'But I keep telling you. It was only—'

'Forget about the accident. That was only a warning. I'm telling you, honey, what you need is a break, a good long break away from Charles.'

Maisie's brow furrowed as she felt her headache returning. 'Perhaps I was a little hasty the other day. Charles and I have been doing some talking – I reckon we can work things out.'

'Maisie, Maisie, when will you ever learn? The whole of Paris knows why Charles is under pressure—'

'I won't let you talk—'

'I'm sorry, and if I wasn't your friend I wouldn't take the liberty of speaking to you like this. But I can't stand back and watch what's happening to you.'

'But I know we could be happy if only . . .'

'If only what? What price happiness . . . huh? How much did three weeks' happiness cost this time?' She stopped abruptly as Maisie burst into tears. 'Look, I'm sorry,' she said, pulling an Irish linen handkerchief from her evening bag. 'But this see-saw of a relationship is killing you. You need time to stand back and look at things objectively.'

Maisie mopped her eyes. 'But the trouble is I love him. I know he really needs me.'

'OK.' Betsy's voice was conciliatory. In this state, she knew it was useless trying to make Maisie see sense. Two months away from the source of the problem, she reckoned, and she would begin to see things differently. 'But whatever you say, you *do* need a long vacation. If Charles really cares about you, he'll understand.'

'But I don't have time for a long vacation. There's my charity ball in March. April, we have our art auction. May, I'm due to open the new wing of the John P. Appleford Foundation. Then June's my garden party. July, there's Laura's degree exhibition . . .'

Betsy gave a dismissive wave of her hand. 'Stop right there!

Sounds like it's high time you took some time off for *you*.' She took a fortifying sip of champagne. Saving people was thirsty work! 'Now look here,' she continued, relentless, 'you might end up hating me for this, but I'm prepared to take that chance. I've already gone ahead and booked the tickets. Come August, you and I are doing Egypt and the Nile.'

Maisie's face blanched. 'I feel I'm letting you down', she stammered, 'but this evening Charles promised—'

'No!' Betsy almost barked. 'Whatever he promised, you know as well as I do that he'll change his mind. Anyway, it's useless to argue. You're coming with me and that's final!'

With slow deliberation, Maisie folded the handkerchief into a perfect square and returned it to its owner. There were times when the warmth of Betsy's friendship felt like the inside of a blast furnace. And yet, deep down, she knew that Betsy had her best interests at heart. For that, she was prepared to forgive everything.

'You win,' she said at last, with a sketchy parody of a smile. 'Just mark me down as the latest hurricane victim.'

'And so you see,' Serge Birnbaum was concluding, 'we're always looking for interesting new talent.' He handed Robert an expensively embossed visiting card. 'Give me a ring – I'll tell my PA to expect your call. You must come and have lunch with me early next week.'

Still struggling to believe his good fortune, Robert slipped the card into his pocket. What an evening! Daniel Baudon and Serge Birnbaum – two of the most influential men in the whole of France! And to think he had expected to be bored rigid all evening. He looked across at Laura's father, still dispensing champagne, and silently gave thanks to him. All this must have been his doing. Of course, as a dyed-in-the-wool socialist Robert still believed in equal opportunity and all that it implied. But, on occasion, he decided, the old-boy network might not be quite so iniquitous, after all.

'Gentlemen, gentlemen.' The three men turned to find

Charles, trying to muscle in on their group. 'My word, Serge, you're looking well. I saw your latest film – what was it? – *Destruction?'*

An unobtrusive man, short and corpulent, Serge eyed his friend's son disparagingly. *'Desolation.'*

'Yes, that's it – *Desolation*. It was wonderful, really wonderful. I think it's the best thing you've ever done.'

'Actually,' replied Serge, po-faced, 'it was without doubt the worst.' Despite his enduring affection for Gaston, he had never taken to Charles. Laura was a very different proposition. There was not a man in Paris who would not have been proud to have her as a daughter.

'Perhaps that's why it was your biggest success to date.' Nonchalant as ever, Daniel lit up a Gauloise. Charles, he knew, could not abide cigarettes. That was precisely why he did it.

'I'm sorry—' Charles coughed loudly into his handkerchief.

'Terrible chest complaint you've got there!' Slowly he exhaled a small grey cloud of smoke through his large, flared nostrils. 'You really ought to see a doctor.'

'Serge, Daniel, you two old reprobates. It seems like you've been avoiding me.' Having imbibed freely all evening, Gaston was beginning to feel quite merry.

'The Three Musketeers,' said Serge, raising his glass.

'All for one,' replied Daniel, lifting his own.

'And one for all,' added Gaston, solemnly hoisting his magnum. The three former comrades burst into loud and bibulous laughter.

Gaston turned to Robert. 'You must forgive our inanity, young man. Who knows how many more birthdays we have left to celebrate?'

'Please, don't apologize. I'm having the time of my life!'

'Excellent!' Gaston slapped the actor heartily on the back. He seemed a nice young man – not good enough for his darling Laura, of course, but then again, would any man ever be? 'Have you eaten?'

Robert shook his head. He had been far too occupied to feel hungry. 'No, not yet.'

'I can see that this pair of hardened drinkers have been

leading you astray.' Gaston turned good-naturedly to his son. 'Charles, why don't you take Robert in to supper? We'll be along in a minute, but right now, we have some serious libelling to do.'

Over in the corner, a slightly tipsy Italian countess was pontificating to Laura. 'Of course, the Siamese have always thought pearls unlucky. Such stuff and nonsense, I always say! Look at this!' She grappled for a minute among the frills of her white lace blouse and fished out a magnificent baroque pearl pendant.

'It's remarkable,' said Laura in all sincerity. This, she always thought, was the greatest drawback of her trade. The ugliest people often ended up with the most beautiful things. Perhaps, she reasoned, it was merely some form of natural justice.

The countess nodded. 'A hundred and fifty grains, you know. I've worn it for the last thirty years and just look at me, fit as a fiddle, never a day's illness. So what, I'd like to know, is so unlucky about pearls?'

Laura noticed the countess's fat, squat, oily husband ogling a pretty waitress. There were, she thought cynically, some curses worse than death.

'Mind you, the ancient Egyptians used to believe . . .' The countess was off again.

Desperate for an excuse to move on, Laura was thrilled to see that Harry Blumstein had just arrived. 'Do forgive me, Countess. Another guest – I must go and make him welcome.'

'Of course, my dear.' Myopically, the countess turned to resume her conversation with the Brancusi on the console.

'She's extraordinary, isn't she?' enthused Robert, catching a glimpse of Laura as Charles led him off into the dining room.

'Who?' Charles glanced back over his shoulder, afraid that some female talent might have escaped the broad sweep of his attentions.

'Your sister, of course.' Robert swayed uneasily on his feet. He was feeling deliciously drunk. Charles handed him a gold-rimmed china plate.

'Laura? Oh, yes, she's a bit of a goer, all right. So you're her latest, are you?' He helped himself to a crayfish and a generous dollop of mayonnaise.

'Her *latest*?'

Charles could see the colour draining from Robert's cheeks. He nodded cheerfully. 'I mean her latest *Parisian* amusement.' The plate slipped from Robert's fingers and shattered on the parquet. Unperturbed, Charles picked up an oyster and popped it into his mouth. 'Of course, a girl like Laura needs constant entertainment. Actors, waiters, hairdressers – I honestly don't know how her fiancé puts up with it.'

'Her *what*?'

Charles could see Robert's knuckles, clenched white around his glass. 'My dear boy,' his voice oozed sympathy, 'don't tell me she didn't tell you?'

'A *fiancé*?' Robert's face was ashen. 'But how long has she been engaged?'

'Six or seven months. Of course, she hasn't got round to telling Father yet, so I suppose it's still unofficial.'

Robert was actually shaking. 'But how do you know?'

Charles shrugged in a gesture of utter exasperation. 'The poor boy rang me up from London the other day in a terrible state. He said he thought Laura was two-timing him with someone here in Paris. What could I say? I said that I'd have a word with her and that there was nothing to worry about.'

Robert smashed his glass down hard on the table. 'The devious little bitch!'

Charles placed a restraining hand on his arm. 'Now then, I wouldn't go making a scene, if I were you. We've tried everything, you know, therapy, counselling, everything, but it seems she just can't help herself. Her mother was exactly the same, you know, a promiscuous little cheat.'

Robert looked totally poleaxed. Now he thought about it, it seemed to make sense. Everyone in Paris knew the story of Caroline Jay.

'Trust me,' continued Charles, 'you're better off without her.' He summoned a passing waiter who came forward to offer champagne.

'No, thanks.' Robert covered his glass with his hand. 'I'm leaving. But before I do, there are just a few things I'd like to say to Laura.'

'Don't,' said Charles quickly. 'She'll deny everything and we don't want her throwing a wobbly, do we? Not in front of all these guests.'

A look of sharp self-interest crossed Robert's handsome face. Laura might be a lying little bitch, but Serge Birnbaum was clearly fond of her. 'No, I suppose not.'

'Quite right!' That look had not been wasted on Charles. These bloody socialists, in his view they were all the same. There wasn't one of them who couldn't be bought. It was just a question of finding their price. 'You must come and have a drink with me some time,' he concluded, smiling warmly. 'The director of the Comédie Française is a very good friend of mine. I know you two would get on like a house on fire. I'll invite him along as well.'

'You're not going already?' Alarmed, Laura had spotted Robert making his way towards the hall.

'Yes.' His brusqueness took her by surprise.

'But I thought you were having such a good time?'

'So I was.'

He made to continue on his way but she caught him by the hand. 'It's just as well I'm used to you. Anyone else might find this rude.' She smiled at him engagingly. 'Promise you'll phone me tomorrow.'

Roughly he pulled his hand away. 'I'm busy all day tomorrow.'

'Then I'll phone you in the evening.' She went to kiss him on the cheek but he moved before she could reach him.

'Goodbye.' His voice, she thought, was oddly restrained. He turned on his heel to leave.

'Laura, Laura, have you heard the news?' Excited, Gaston pushed his way through the host of guests still milling around in the drawing room. Like a small tug behind a large ocean-going liner, a far less demonstrative Harry Blumstein followed in his wake. Desperate to establish what was bothering Robert, Laura was about to follow him into the hall. Now, it seemed, whatever it was would have to wait until tomorrow.

'No, Papa,' she glanced pointedly at Harry, 'but I think I've got a fair idea.'

'What a birthday present!' Gaston clasped Harry around the shoulders. 'The Star of Heaven – and so soon! I knew you'd come up trumps!'

Harry coughed discreetly. 'It's not exactly a gift, you know!'

Laura's eyes searched his.

'Don't even ask!' he replied to the unspoken question. 'The price even frightens me!'

'Money!' By now, Gaston was boisterous with bonhomie. 'At my time of life, why worry? The Gautier Collection now has its Star. That's all that really matters.'

Laura hugged her father. Despite her misgivings, such enthusiasm was infectious. 'How did you track it down?' she asked.

Harry tapped his nose with his forefinger. 'Secrets of the trade. But I can at least tell you that it's in Tel Aviv and I'll be collecting it personally from the—' A sudden shadow crossed Harry's face. Gaston shot him a thunderous look.

'What's the matter?' Laura was immediately aware of the tension. 'Collect it personally from whom?'

Harry stared at his friend in mute apology. He had promised to keep the secret and now he had gone and given the game away. It must have been the champagne.

'From the widow.' It was Gaston himself who broke the news. 'I'm afraid the owner has just died.'

'How?' It was a question she hardly dared to ask.

'In a car crash.'

By now, she had turned quite pale. 'Oh, my God!' She grabbed her father by the sleeve. 'It's a warning, I just know it is. Please, Papa. Don't go through with it.'

Gaston's jaw set hard. 'I've never been superstitious and I don't intend to start now.' Resolutely upbeat, he replenished their glasses with champagne. 'To the Star of Heaven,' he said, all smiles once again, 'and the Gautier Collection.'

Laura looked ruefully at Harry who raised his hands in a gesture of resignation.

'The Star of Heaven,' they chorused bravely as Laura voiced a silent prayer.

CHAPTER TEN

Cold, damp and drizzly, London seemed even gloomier than ever. Struggling upstairs with her suitcase, Laura turned the events of the previous few days over and over again in her mind. What on earth could have happened to Robert? His behaviour made no sense whatsoever. He had not called, nor returned any one of the dozen or so messages she had left on his answering machine. She tripped on a jagged edge of torn linoleum and caught her shin on the corner of her case. That was all she needed. A nice big blue-black bruise to round off the trip completely. Of course, the visit had not been unremittingly ghastly. Up until the party it had been wonderful. She rubbed her throbbing shin and continued up the stairs. What had she done to upset him? Whatever it was, she felt he could at least have found time to ring and say goodbye.

The case seemed to gain in weight with every step she took. That wretched man had ruined Paris for her! Not even an evening at the theatre and dinner with Gaston and Maisie at her favourite restaurant, Joel Robuchon, had succeeded in lifting her spirits. What should have been the most wonderful long weekend had left her tired, despondent and depressed. What on earth was he playing at?

She could hear the phone ringing as she reached the top of the stairs. Robert! Her heart missed a beat. It just had to be Robert and he was bound to have some logical explanation! She opened her front door and, dumping her bags in the hall, raced straight into the sitting room.

'Hi, honey. You got home safe? Everything OK?' Maisie's voice sounded deeply anxious.

Laura made an effort to conceal her disappointment. 'I'm only just back but the place seems fine – despite the wide-open windows!'

'You're not sounding too hot.'

'I'm sorry. I was hoping it might be Robert, that's all.' The tears rolled down her cheeks and on to the telephone wire. In Paris, with Maisie and her father around, she had managed to maintain some semblance of control. But now, back home alone in London, she felt desperately low.

Maisie's protective instincts made her sound fierce. 'Any guy who behaves like that is not worth worrying about. I'd forget about him if I were you.'

Suddenly something in Laura snapped. 'Why don't you just leave me alone and start taking your own advice? I'm tired of being told what's good for me. It's *my* life I'm trying to live.'

Inured to Laura's tantrums, Maisie ignored the outburst. 'You mustn't let this get you down.' Her voice was calm and soothing. 'Especially not at this stage. There's far too much at stake.'

'I know.' After her brief flash of temper, she felt ashamed of herself. 'And I'm sorry for what I just said.' She sounded thoroughly dejected again, as if the spirit had been knocked out of her.

'Now look here,' said Maisie, very directive, 'I've just been speaking to Harry Blumstein and I've told him to organize a delivery.'

'But, Maisie—'

'It's nothing – just a couple of interesting stones for you to get to work with.'

Laura sighed in weary frustration. It seemed impossible to make Maisie and her father understand. She had to be allowed to make her own mistakes and to stand on her own two feet. 'Look, I know you mean well, but I don't want—'

For once, it was Maisie's turn to sound irritated with her. 'You don't want *what*? Help? OK, then, let's call it something else. Let's call it a business proposition. I'll work out the return I want.'

'You always say that, then you never let me pay—'

'Just listen to me, will you?' There were occasions, all too infrequent in Laura's book, when Maisie could sound really ferocious. 'You've got to stop acting so goddamn prissy. You want to produce stuff that'll knock them dead at the degree exhibition?'

'Of course.'

'Sure you do, but to *do* your best you've got to *use* the best. So please, honey, if you won't do it for yourself, then do it for your father. Who knows how long he's got left with us?'

Maisie could have kicked herself. In her efforts to overcome Laura's recalcitrance, she knew she had overstepped the mark. There was a moment's silence at the other end of the line. When at last she spoke, Laura's voice sounded tired. 'I know you all mean well. But I can't bear to be thought of as a parasite like . . .' She hesitated for a second.

Maisie helped her out. 'I know. Like Charles.'

'Yes – like him. It never occurred to me that self-reliance might look selfish. Do you know, I've never even asked myself what Papa *really* wants?'

Maisie spotted the danger signs. She moved quickly to close the deal before Laura was back in the doldrums. 'So you accept my little surprise?'

'How can I say no?'

'Quite right. You can't. Besides, work's the best therapy for a broken heart.'

'And how can I ever thank you?'

'Easy.' Maisie's voice was soft again. 'By being what you are – the best in the bloody business.'

By the time she had unpacked her suitcase, Laura was feeling immensely better. The idea of Robert still gnawed but, despite everything, the prospect of Maisie's package filled her with excitement. She sat down at the table with a notepad and began to sketch a few ideas. For some reason – perhaps the proximity of her father's birthday – the signs of the zodiac kept recurring in her thoughts. Deftly she sketched a lion, then a bull and finally a ram. No, she decided, ripping out the pages, such animals would be too solid for what she was trying to achieve. A scorpion . . .

Laura's face brightened immediately. With its two formidable claws, segmented body and curled stinging tail, it was the perfect shape for a bracelet. Deftly she drew the outline, dreaming of the materials she would most like to use. It would have to be yellow gold and diamonds, she decided at last, cunningly articulated to fit neatly around a wrist.

Immersed in her work, it was a good three hours before she noticed the evening closing in. She got up, pleased with the afternoon's endeavours, to draw the curtains. Outside, a light rain spat and splashed against the windows. For a moment, she stood and watched as the tiny rivulets of water zig-zagged, wind-blown, down the panes. The droplets, it seemed, were like tiny jewels, refracting the rays of the street light below into every colour of the spectrum: red, orange, yellow, green, blue, indigo and violet. Violet. Laura remembered her glorious sugilite stones, still hidden beneath the sink. A collar of gold, pierced by dramatic splashes of violet light – what a fabulous necklace they would make! She swished shut the curtains and returned to her note-pad. The next time she glanced at her watch, it was almost eleven o'clock. To her surprise she realized she had not thought of Robert all evening.

It was only as she was running her bath that the thought suddenly struck her. Backbencher! How could he possibly have slipped her mind? It was always the way when she started to work. Everything else went by the board. It was late, but Jenny never went to bed before one in the morning. Laura decided to give her a ring.

She knew something was the matter as soon as her friend picked up the phone.

'Oh, God,' stammered Jenny, 'you're back.'

'Of course I'm back. I'm sorry if I gave you the impression I was emigrating for good.' She waited for a reply, but none came. By now, her sixth sense was working overtime. 'What's the matter?'

'Something awful's happened.' Jenny's voice sounded shaky. 'I'm not sure how to tell you.'

'Not Backbencher?' Laura felt her hands begin to tremble.

'I'm afraid he's escaped.'

Laura sat down heavily on the bed. 'Escaped? In this weather! The poor bird won't last a week.'

'It's all my fault,' wailed Jenny. 'I used to let him fly around in the drawing room for a bit of exercise. He seemed to enjoy his little outings. Then yesterday morning, one of the builders forgot to shut the door. Backbencher upped and offed.' She burst into tears. 'I reported it to the police.'

'Any joy?'

'No. In fact, they seemed to think it was all a bit of a joke. Some clever dick even invited me down to the station to help with an Identikit picture.'

Laura bit her lip. 'There's no point getting het up about it,' she said, more or less convincingly. 'I'll see you in college tomorrow.' She put down the phone without further ado. Jenny's blubbing was all she needed!

Some week-end! she thought, and pulled a tuft from her candlewick bedspread. A Bolshie boyfriend, a big black bruise and now her friend and companion flown. Reaching for a box of Kleenex, she pulled the bedcovers up over her head and allowed herself the luxury of a sob.

Ten minutes later she had had enough. Self-pity was all right in small doses, but it had never been her strong suit. She rolled out of bed and wandered back into the bathroom where a tubful of warm water still beckoned. She topped it up from the hot tap and added a few drops of Guerlain's Shalimar essence. Slipping off her ancient towelling bathrobe, she hopped into the gloriously fragrant water and was soon miles away, dreaming up original and ever more dramatic ideas for her brilliant new scorpion bracelet.

God knows how long whoever it was had been buzzing at the front door downstairs! Aroused from her reverie, Laura jumped out of the bath and quickly swathed herself in a towel. Who on earth would come visiting at this time of night? She wrapped another towel around her hair, turban-style, and squelched wet-footed towards the Parlaphone. The clock in the sitting room chimed twelve. Shit! thought Laura, irritated. It was bound to be Jenny, no doubt bearing a penitential bottle of Chardonnay and determined to drown *her* sorrows.

'Hello. Who is it?' The shampoo in Laura's ear made the voice difficult to decipher but it sounded like Jenny's. Without thinking, she pressed the button which opened the bottom door to the building.

Laura waited outside her flat as a hunched, bedraggled figure clunked its way up the stairs. Suddenly, in the half-light, she caught sight of the figure's profile. 'Mother!' Aghast she stared at the woman who now stood dripping all over her hall. 'What on earth are you doing out on a night like this without even an umbrella?' She felt irritated at her own line of questioning. Rational behaviour had never been her mother's forte.

Caroline shook the folds of her mackintosh. Around her feet, the drips had already formed a small puddle. 'I know it's late, but may I come in?'

Laura ushered her into the sitting room and turned on three bars of the electric fire. 'Here, you'd better dry off. Why didn't you phone me first?'

Caroline threw her coat over a chair and huddled close to the fire. 'We only arrived this morning.'

Already Laura had given up. A logical answer from Caroline was as likely as manna from heaven. 'We?' She shot into the bedroom and pulled on an old nightdress.

'Yes, Ralph and I.'

She returned to the sitting room and began to rub her hair dry with a towel. 'I see. Just thought I'd better check.' It was a cheap gibe and she knew it, but with Caroline she could never be sure. The memory of one particularly excruciating prize-day flitted across her mind. Drunk as a lord, done up like a tart and with a twenty-year-old toy-boy in tow, her mother had made her the laughing stock of her entire boarding school.

'But Ralph's gone.' If Caroline noticed the sarcasm, she did not react to it. 'He's had to shoot off to Newmarket to look at some two-year-old fillies.' She sneezed loudly. 'At least that's what he says.' Her eyes wandered off across the room. Laura knew precisely what they were after.

'Care for a mug of cocoa?' she asked pointedly.

Caroline's lips twitched into some semblance of a pout. 'You wouldn't have anything stronger?'

'Afraid not.' It was a lie as Laura knew she would recognize. All the same, there was no point in encouraging her. Judging by her speech, she had had quite a few already.

Caroline shrugged, resigned. 'All right, then. Cocoa it is, but make mine a strong one, would you?'

Laura pottered into the kitchen and put a saucepan of long-life milk on to boil. A sudden pang of hunger reminded her that she had eaten nothing since the disgusting in-flight meal on the plane. She opened the cupboard and rummaged around. Like the contents of her wardrobe, her food cupboard yielded a singularly uninspiring selection. A bag of dried pasta shells, a few tins of sardines in oil, a can of baked beans and a mildewed packet of mixed herbs. Laura spotted a half-eaten packet of chocolate digestive biscuits lurking towards the rear and grabbed them. She arranged them on a plate, munching a broken one in the process. The kitchen was absolutely freezing. She looked down at her slipperless feet, turning blue on the white linoleum. Still damp, her hair stuck in clammy strands to the back of her neck. She shivered and, warming her hands over the gas ring, peeped around the door at her mother, who was stretched out languorously in front of the fire. Camouflaged by the sombre half-light, the tell-tale signs of her drinking – the bags, bloodshot eyes and sickly pallor – were almost invisible. Laura continued to study her in silence. With her fine, gamine features and her lithe slender body she was still a remarkably beautiful woman.

The milk hissed and fizzed as it started to rise and boil over. Quickly, she removed the pan from the heat and extinguished the gas flame. However much she might want to deny it, the woman in the sitting room looked like her. She poured the milk on to the cocoa, already measured out in the mugs. Her hands, she noticed, were shaking. The thought of such a strong resemblance filled her with absolute dread.

She returned to the sitting room, put the tray on the floor and sat down next to her mother. Outside, the wind was gusting stronger now and the rain beating hard against the windows. Both shivering, the two women moved even closer to the warm glow of the fire. Laura handed her mother a mug, and felt decidedly odd. She could not recall anything quite so cosy in their entire relationship. For a while, neither dared speak, loath to break this unexpected intimacy.

'I didn't think you travelled much nowadays,' ventured Laura at last.

Caroline continued to stare into the fire. 'I don't. This trip was a last-minute decision – at least as far as I was concerned. With Ralph, it's different, of course. It seems like every day of his life is organized years in advance.'

Laura ran her fingers through her hair in an effort to get rid of the knots. 'How are you two getting on?' It seemed like an odd sort of question, the sort a proper mother ought to be asking *her*.

'So so.' Caroline pulled a face. 'As ever, Ralph has his promising young fillies – not all of them equine, I'm afraid.' A flicker of a smile played around her lips. Despite the alcohol, she still retained some vestiges of humour. 'As for me, well, there used to be the odd fling to relieve the boredom of it all. But now, I just . . . well, I just . . .' She resumed her study of the fire.

'I read in the papers that Ralph's doing very well.' Laura was determined to move the conversation to safer ground. The events of the last few days had left her drained. She had no patience for a lengthy discussion about Caroline and her drink problem.

'Oh, yes,' Caroline's eyes remained fixed on the luminescent bars. 'They say he's one of the best trainers in the world nowadays. Even the oil sheikhs have started using him. He reckons he's got a winner for this year's Epsom Derby.'

'But that's wonderful!' enthused Laura.

'And a few for Royal Ascot.' Caroline sounded distinctly less impressed. 'And the Prix de l'Arc de Triomphe, you name it, all the biggies. Oh, yes, good old Ralph's a major performer. He no longer needs me or my money.'

Laura could not resist it. 'You mean the money Papa gave you.'

'Whatever.' Caroline made a vague gesture with her hand. For once, she was in no mood for an argument. 'Anyway, the point is, nobody needs me now.'

If it had been said with the slightest hint of self-pity, Laura would have steeled herself to ignore it. As it was, the statement was bald and objective, a simple assessment of the facts. She looked up at her mother, still engrossed in the fire, and wished she could find the charity to contradict.

'That's why I came to London,' continued Caroline. 'I needed to talk to you.'

'But you really should have phoned. I could easily have been away. In fact, I only got back from Paris this morning.'

Caroline nodded slowly. 'Your father's eightieth birthday.'

'You remembered?' Laura looked genuinely surprised. She turned and for the first time that evening, the two women's eyes met. Instinctively, Laura looked away again, unable to maintain the connection. There was something too disturbing about the sight of naked pain.

'Of course. I even phoned.'

Laura was on the attack again. 'How could you? We never—'

'I know,' Caroline interrupted. 'The trouble is, I've never had the courage to wait for your father to reply.' There was a silence. 'I phone you too, Laura,' she continued, her voice soft and tender. 'Quite often, in fact, but only when I know you're sure to be at college.'

Laura fortified herself with another chocolate biscuit. She felt as if the conversation was slipping out of her control. It was the same old story. Whenever her mother seemed to be making some kind of sense, her mind veered off into orbit.

'At least that's a cheap time to call,' she joked, trying to defuse the tension.

For once, however, Caroline was not to be diverted from her purpose. 'The truth is,' she insisted, adamant, 'that I've been too frightened to talk to you. I've been frightened to admit to you how deeply ashamed I am.'

Confused by this sudden revelation, Laura affected to study the pile of the carpet. 'It's OK,' she stammered. 'All that was a long time ago.'

With a sudden bound, Caroline was on her feet, towering over her daughter. 'No, it's not OK!' she shouted, suddenly animated. 'I've been walking up and down the pavement for the last three hours, staring up at your windows and trying to muster the guts to come and tell you how I feel.'

Laura determined to keep calm. If experience was anything to go by, her mother would rant drunkenly on for a few minutes before collapsing into tears. The next day, she would remember none of it.

'I've been unhappy since the day I left your father,' Caroline continued. 'You must believe that I loved him. And now I know that he was the only man who genuinely loved me.'

It was too much! Despite her best intentions, Laura could no longer hold her tongue. The pain and hurt of an entire lifetime erupted deep within her. 'Oh, sure!' She leapt up to confront her mother. 'So you loved him and he loved you. Two eminently good reasons to leave us, I suppose.'

'You don't understand!' Caroline grabbed her by the shoulders. Laura winced, surprised by the force of her grip. 'And I don't blame you. I've only begun to understand it myself.'

Laura pulled herself free and noticed her mother's eyes, frighteningly, hypnotically lucid. She felt trapped by the force of that gaze.

Caroline continued, more calmly, 'I couldn't help it. At the time, I felt the whole thing was stifling me.'

'Who? What was stifling you?'

'Gautier – the history, the traditions – I don't know – everything about it. And then there was your father, doting, protective. I know he loved me, but I felt like a bird in a gilded cage. When you came along, I felt even more tied down. I knew I just had to escape.'

'And Ralph?'

Caroline shook her head, suddenly weary. 'Poor Ralph – he was just an excuse. The whole thing was purely physical. We never really understood one another – not the way your father and I had done. By the time I realized, it was all too late.'

'But you *could* have come back. Papa would have forgiven you.'

'Would he, though?' Caroline's gaze returned, unfocused, to the fire. 'That thought has tormented me since the day I left. But I felt the cut was too deep, the scandal too terrible.'

'You're wrong!' Laura felt like kicking herself. Despite her best intentions, here she was, having just the argument she wanted to avoid. 'He's still in love with you.'

Caroline brought her knees up under her chin. 'It's all water under the bridge now, isn't it? And, besides, it's not the reason why I'm here.'

The clock on the mantelpiece chimed two. Laura curled up in the bean-bag. By now she had given up any hope of a good night's sleep. She would let her mother talk.

'I don't want you to make the same mistakes as I did,' continued Caroline, moving in closer to the fire.

'That *would* be difficult, wouldn't it?' Laura's voice dripped sarcasm.

'Oh, really?' returned Caroline, very sharp. 'That may be what you think, but you're starting to make them already.'

Laura could feel her cheeks tingling with anger. 'Well, let's hear it then, from the world's leading expert, a few words of sound advice.'

Caroline's eyes were pleading. 'Say what you want, but listen to me. I've got to make you understand.'

There was something so desperate in her manner, that Laura found she had to obey. 'OK,' she sniffed, 'you've got fifteen minutes. Then I'm turning in for the night.'

Caroline collected her thoughts. 'It's difficult to know where to start, but I'll begin with the House of Gautier.' Her voice became suddenly urgent. 'Believe me, Laura, however talented we are, it's far more important than all of us. I only realize that now. Your father gave me so much confidence, I thought I was good enough to fly off on my own.'

'But you *were* good!'

'Yes,' Caroline smiled wryly, 'very good. But, then, when I was out there on my own, without Gaston and without Gautier, I discovered how insignificant I really was.'

All at once, Laura saw the inevitable looming. She decided to pre-empt it. 'Forget it. You won't convince me to go and work for the company.'

'But, Laura—'

'No! Not yet. When I look back, I want to know that my success was *mine*.'

'I'm not talking about that!' Caroline banged her mug on the arm of the sofa. 'I'd be the first to admit that the big independence routine is fine – at least, for now. But your father won't be with you for ever, you know. And when he goes, you mustn't believe that Gautier will always be there, just waiting for you to tip up.'

The cold hand of fear gripped Laura's stomach and gave it a sudden tweak. The spectre of her half-brother seemed suddenly to fill the room. 'Do you think that Charles . . .?'

'Who knows what that bastard will do!' She was on her feet again. 'All I *do* know for certain is that he's capable of anything. Do you know, he once told your father that I tried to seduce him?'

Laura's face turned ashen. 'You didn't—'

'Don't be so ridiculous!' Caroline's eyes blazed. 'In fact when I first went to Gautier, he tried to seduce *me*. He never forgave me for turning him down.'

Laura's head was reeling. 'But what can he do to me? Papa intends to split the company fifty-fifty between us. There's nothing he can do to stop it.'

'God knows what he'll dream up but, believe me, he'll stop at nothing to deprive you of your rightful place at Gautier. He just can't bear the fact that your father loved you – and me – more than him.'

By now, Laura's back was rigid with tension. She sat bolt upright in the bean-bag. 'But what can I do?'

Suddenly, after all the fury, Caroline collapsed back on to the sofa. 'I'm afraid I don't know. It all depends on what that troublemaker comes up with. I'm simply here to warn you. Never take for granted the things you love. I did, and lost them all.'

It was some minutes before Laura managed to speak. There was so much to say but tonight the right words failed her. Only banalities came. 'Where are you staying?'

The question sounded trite and inadequate, but Caroline seemed to understand. 'The Portobello Hotel. Ralph loves it there.'

'I'll drive you back. Hang on a minute, I'll go and get my coat.'

She pulled herself up from the bean-bag but Caroline made no effort to move. 'Do you mind if I stay here?' she asked tentatively. 'I'll be all right in the morning, but right now, I need a friend.'

Laura's face relaxed into a smile. 'If that's what you want. I can sleep here on the sofa.'

'No, I'll take the sofa. You take the bed. You've got a hard day ahead tomorrow.'

Laura brought a spare pillow and a duvet from her bedroom and handed her mother a new silk nightdress.

'Thanks.' Caroline ran her fingers across the expanse of oyster silk. 'Another Maisie special?'

'I'm afraid so.'

'Thank God for Maisie!'

For one awkward moment, they stared at one another in silence. It was Caroline who mustered the courage to make the first move. She threw her arms around her daughter's neck and hugged her very hard. 'I love you, darling,' she whispered. The tears were streaming down her cheeks.

'And I love you too, Mummy.'

They stood there for some minutes, just holding one another. Mummy, thought Laura, strangely content. For the first time in her life she had used that most tender of all words.

Exhausted, Laura slept like a log, only coming round to the insistent bleep-bleep-bleep of her alarm at seven the next day. She opened her eyes and stared blearily around. A gap in the curtains revealed another dark and rainy morning. British winters, she groaned inwardly. It was enough to make anyone depressive. She flicked the snooze button and rolled over again. Just ten more minutes, she promised herself, snuggling down into the womb-like warmth of her bed. She always felt that these were the most delicious moments of the day, stolen from that twilight zone located between sleeping and consciousness. She allowed her mind to float unfettered along its secret labyrinths. Had she dreamt it or had she really seen her mother? Unconsciously, she drew in her arms and curled up into a tight, defensive foetal ball. Odd! The dull ache that used to live in the cavity of her chest had disappeared. And in its place, a wave of lightness had suddenly flooded in.

The alarm managed once again to bleep its way into her

dreams. She hit the snooze button and jumped swiftly out of bed. To hesitate any further, she knew, would mean the morning lost. She pulled on her dressing gown and wandered into the sitting room, half knowing what to expect. Sure enough, her mother had already disappeared, leaving her night-dress and bedclothes folded neatly in a pile. Laura stooped to pick them up. It was better like this, far better. Morning-after-the-night-before sessions were always flat, no matter with whom they were shared.

She meandered back to the bedroom, stopping by the table to read the message her mother had left on the notepad. Written in Caroline's distinctive hand, it said simply, 'The scorpion design is really good. Remember I love you, Mummy.'

Outside, the wind dropped and suddenly the rain abated. Laura watched the shards of watery sunshine as they penetrated the clouds, illuminating the grey slate roofs of the houses opposite. She hummed happily to herself as she put the kettle on to boil. This morning, she decided, she would walk to college. It was then that the sun broke through completely, bathing the street below in its off-white, wintry warmth. She turned on the radio. The place seemed strangely quiet without Backbencher's constant chatter. 'Nothin's worryin' me,' – she sang along to Burt Bacharach's ever popular 'Raindrops Keep Fallin' On My Head'. She made her tea and, still singing, waltzed off into the bath-room. Today, she felt as if she could walk on air. The icicle of resentment in her heart had finally melted away.

CHAPTER ELEVEN

The vein in Charles's neck began to pulse alarmingly. 'Do you mean to say,' he roared, 'that you refuse to do this for me?'

His face white with anger, Maurice stared back unflinching at the son of his friend and employer. That one look said it all. How could such a bullying philistine be the Gautier son and heir? 'I thought you'd have known,' he said quietly, gesturing towards the package of ivory which Charles had just placed on his bench. 'But your father doesn't agree with it and, for that matter, neither do I. No, M'sieur, you're quite right. I will not work with ivory or, for that matter, with tortoiseshell or any materials from endangered species.'

Over by the door, someone dropped a pair of tweezers. The tiny implement hit the floor with a clatter, the noise reverberating around the vaulted ceiling of the workshop. The craftsmen of Gautier looked at one another in silence. It was always the same whenever *le fils* (as they disparagingly referred to Charles) made one of his rare appearances. They could tolerate him so long as he stuck to his office, constructing his deals and studying his balance sheets. Such things he understood. But down here in the workshop they ensured he was never made to feel welcome.

Charles could sense the growing antagonism in the room. Why was the old fool being so ridiculously stubborn? He could gladly have shaken him. All the same, he rationalized, Maurice *was* the best craftsman in the company and this bloody casket *had* to be made! Charles gritted his teeth. It was just so typical of Daphne Sandton! Of all the materials to choose from, she just had to go for ivory! Irritated, he glanced at the monstrous pile of the stuff gleaming on Maurice's bench. God knows how or where the doting Sammy had acquired it! Daphne, he had explained to Charles, was 'now going in for cream'. Her new interior designer had told her that it was *her* colour and she had just redone the mansion in Bishop's Avenue accordingly. Now she had set her heart on an ivory casket for the coffee table in the middle of her drawing room. Custom-made by Gautier, Sammy was determined she should have it as a present for their wedding anniversary. He would fill it with Godiva chocolates and just knew she would be thrilled.

Charles could not recall the full details of the conversation. He had rung Sammy to discuss business, not to hear the second-hand sweet nothings of besotted middle age. All the same, Daphne was his major ally in the projected Sandton takeover. If Daphne wanted ivory then, by God, ivory she would have!

Charles studied his adversary's lined and leathery face and decided to change tack. 'Look, Maurice,' he said soothingly, putting an arm around the old man's shoulders, 'I agree with you. It's appalling the way these poor creatures have been hunted almost to extinction. You know, I sit on the committee of our "Save the Elephant Fund".'

'In that case,' replied Maurice, removing Charles's arm from his shoulder and returning to his work, 'you ought to be ashamed of yourself.'

Charles struggled to control his temper. Who the hell was running this company? Himself or a bunch of geriatric environmentalists? 'You're quite right.' He forced the features of his face into some semblance of a smile. 'But there's nothing we can do about the tragic creatures who gave us this.'

Maurice glanced at the offending pile. 'No, I don't suppose there is.'

Charles sensed a possible opening. 'That's why I want you to create something beautiful with it,' he concluded triumphantly. 'To ensure that those wonderful animals haven't died a pointless death.'

The silence in the room was almost tangible. Carefully, Maurice rewrapped the off-white segments in the paper in which they had arrived and carefully knotted the string. 'Here,' he said at last, handing the parcel back to Charles. 'I must say, M'sieur, I hadn't appreciated the depth of your sensitivities. Perhaps you and your committee would like to give this abomination a decent burial.'

The entire workshop erupted into laughter. Incandescent with rage, Charles turned to glare at these so-called artists he knew despised him. Let them mock, he thought as he stormed, tight-lipped, out of the room. They were safe so long as his father was alive, and then . . . white-knuckled, Charles clutched the parcel to his chest . . . then he would have the last laugh on every bloody one of them.

Upstairs on the second floor, the meeting in the boardroom had been convened for eleven o'clock. By twenty past ten, the participants had already started to trickle in. Legal and financial advisors to the House of Gautier, they had all been personal friends of Gaston for over twenty years. Nowadays, their annual meeting was more like an old boys' reunion. Reports would be read, profits applauded and future strategy outlined. It was an eminently civilized affair, with business neatly rounded off by an exquisite lunch. There, conversation would develop along far more intimate lines, deaths of old friends, births of new grand-children – it was a rare opportunity to laugh and gossip and was savoured by everyone. Everyone, that was, with the exception of Charles.

By the time he arrived in the boardroom, it was one minute to eleven. Still fuming over his encounter with Maurice, he had spent the next hour on the phone to the Gautier workshop in Hong Kong where, with the help of the local manager, he had managed to find a craftsman prepared to make Daphne's ivory casket. What a monumental waste of time! Charles dumped his pile of documents on the table with such force that the water tumblers rattled.

'Ah, Charles, there you are.' Encircled by a group of chattering colleagues, Gaston was in high spirits.

Sourly Charles surveyed the scene. 'I think we'd better get

down to business,' he replied, looking ostentatiously at his watch.

Gaston was instantly apologetic. 'Of course. I'm sorry. I know you're very busy. I'll get things moving right away.'

Within minutes, Gaston and Charles were seated at opposite ends of the mahogany table with the other six participants ranged on either side between them. After welcoming his colleagues, Gaston asked his son to deliver the annual report. As usual, it was delivered with few notes and in a brisk, no-nonsense style.

'And so,' concluded Charles, some thirty minutes later, 'despite the worldwide recession, Gautier's profits for the year are still remarkably healthy. I have no reason to doubt that this trend will continue.' He signalled to his secretary who began to distribute a bulky, plastic-coated document. 'I'm sure, gentlemen, that you'll find everything covered by this report. However, if there are any questions, I'd be happy to deal with them.' Pleased with his own performance, Charles sat back to study the faces around the table.

'Congratulations,' said Gaston, barely bothering even to flick through the document. 'You've done a wonderful job.'

'This series of inter-company loans . . .?' a querulous voice piped up. The board members turned to look at its owner. A small, ferret-like man with a long, aquiline nose and gold-framed *pince-nez*, Victor Desquand was the company accountant.

'Just a few short-term financing problems,' replied Charles, flashing him a dazzling smile. 'But as you can see, they're all settled now.'

Victor nodded slowly, but still seemed unhappy. He had known Charles since his childhood and had never much cared for him. True, Gautier *fils* had turned out to be a brilliant businessman – the figures spoke for themselves – but he was forever cutting corners and Victor disapproved. The problem was that it was difficult to say or do anything. Gaston would hear nothing against his son and, when all was said and done, the House of Gautier *was* a family business.

Charles poured himself a glass of water. Trust that nit-picking little bastard to delve into all the details. Of course, he had 'borrowed' money from the company in order to finance his gambling debts. But once Maisie had come good, he had paid it back, every last centime of it. He downed his water in one swift gulp. How dare these useless old cronies subject him to such an inquisition? It was *his* company, after all.

A few far more desultory questions followed, which Charles fielded with consummate ease.

'But about the authorization for these loans?' insisted Victor.

'I'm sure you'll find that everything there is in order,' interrupted Gaston, beaming broadly at everyone around the table. Victor clenched his teeth, wishing he had the information and energy to follow through with his hunch. He was sure that Charles was up to something, but he was damned if he knew what. In his time, he had seen the wizards of creative accountancy at work, camouflaging corruption and confusion with an impressive gloss of hyperactivity. This, however, was something different. Here there was nothing to hide. The company, Victor knew, was in genuinely good shape, almost too good. There were none of the usual loose ends to tie up: no deals pending, negligible monies owed or owing. It was altogether too neat a package. Deep down in his accountant's bones, Victor felt uneasy. In his experience, packages tied up so very neatly were about to be dispatched.

'And I'd like to thank Charles, once again, for our excellent results.' Gaston led the round of applause which rippled gently around the room. Relieved, Charles began to collect his papers. If past years were anything to go by, the rest of the meeting would be devoted to the trivia of Any Other Business: help for the widow of a former employee fallen on hard times, details of Gautier scholarships awarded to underprivileged children – it was just the sort of paternalistic nonsense which made Charles want to vomit.

'Now, gentlemen,' continued Gaston amiably, 'at last we come to the *real* reason for this meeting.'

Startled, Charles dropped his wodge of papers, knocking over a carafe of water in the process. He pulled out a monogrammed handkerchief and began to mop up. The *real* reason, he wondered. What the hell was the old fool on about?

Gaston scanned the table. 'As you are well aware, none of us is getting any younger and nowadays I find myself travelling increasingly.'

'A regular Passe-Partout,' quipped Harry Blumstein. 'Around the world every eighty days or so.' There were murmurings of mild amusement at which Gaston shrugged, good-naturedly.

'I'm only making up for lost time, my dear Harry, most of it lost arguing prices with you.'

Now it was Harry's turn to shrug. 'Business is business, you know.'

Charles drummed his fingers on the table. If only his father would get on with it! That was the trouble with this company: it was stuffed to the gills with friends. In Charles's book of business, there were no such things as friends, only a series of temporary alliances. That, as he knew from his dealings with Sammy Sandton, was the way to get things done.

'The point is,' said Gaston, 'that I've decided to change my will.' Charles squeezed the handkerchief so hard that the water trickled down his wrist and on to his cuff. That bitch Laura, he thought, what the hell had she been up to?

'On my death, the Liechtenstein trust which owns the House of Gautier will still be split equally between Charles and Laura.' One by one, the fingers of Charles's hand began to relax. 'But I intend to bequeath my private collection to London's Victoria and Albert Museum.'

Charles was beginning to feel quite sick with relief. True, his father's collection, comprised of old Gautier pieces inherited or bought back at auction, was worth a small fortune. But he could live with that decision. Running around the world, painting and collecting seemed to keep his father happy, and that kept him out of Charles's hair.

'I think that's a splendid idea,' said Charles, almost too enthusiastic.

'I'm glad you approve.' Gaston looked genuinely surprised. Altruism had never featured strongly in the lexicon of Charles's mind. 'Especially as I've just made a substantial addition to the collection.'

'Substantial?' Charles feared he just might have been had. 'How big is substantial?'

Gaston paused for a second. 'Very big. Harry has acquired the Star of Heaven on my behalf.'

The room fell silent as the implications of the announcement sank in. Of the eight men in the room, seven were wondering about the curse which supposedly attached to the diamond. The eighth, as ever, was contemplating money.

'And how much did that set you back?' asked Charles, still stunned. The Star of Heaven – part of a collection to be given away – he wondered how many more ways his father would invent to deprive him of his inheritance.

Gaston looked at Harry who, as usual, simply shrugged. 'Around fifty million pounds – cheap at the price, I'd say. The stone is incomparable.'

Charles glowered at his father who understood at once. The pleasure of the moment was utterly destroyed. 'I was hoping you'd agree.'

'Why bother asking me?' Charles's face was mottled with anger. 'I just work here, a sort of salaried dogsbody.' He stood up to leave. Around the table, the Gautier advisors wriggled uncomfortably in their chairs.

Gaston leapt to his feet. 'But I didn't think you'd be interested . . .' It was then that the wheezing began.

Harry poured his friend a glass of water and waited for him to drink it. It was outrageous to witness, but he had seen it so many times before: Gaston Gautier, avenging angel of the French Resistance, reduced to a gibbering idiot by this wretched son of his. 'Sit down, Charles,' ordered Harry angrily, 'and show some bloody respect.'

Charles resumed his seat and did his best to look contrite. If he played this one properly, he decided, he might even end up on top. 'I'm sorry, Father,' he apologized. 'If you want this stone for your collection then, of course, you must have it. I'd just be happier if you confided in me once in a while.'

It sounded like a plea for intimacy, at least to a grateful Gaston.

Gaston was soon breathing normally again and, to everyone's relief, Madame Goffinet appeared to announce that lunch was ready in the dining room upstairs. 'If there's no other business . . .' rasped Gaston, his eyes wandering up and down the table.

Charles raised his hand, excessively polite. 'There's one slight matter, Father. It's just a point of good order, really.'

'Please. Go ahead.'

'It's hard to talk about such eventualities—' Charles coughed, embarrassed, 'but since you've raised the issue of your will, there's something I'd like to say.'

Anticipating trouble, the six trustees of the family trust groaned inwardly. Just when it was time for lunch!

'Naturally, Father, I'm delighted that the company is to be shared equally between myself and Laura.'

Stunned, Harry Blumstein nearly fell off his chair. He could hardly believe that Charles was not going to object after all.

'Laura and I have had our differences,' continued Charles, all smiles, 'but tell me which siblings haven't.' There were murmurs of general agreement around the table. 'What worries me is that Laura is only twenty-two. She's still young and impetuous and so far she's never shown any real interest in the financial side of the company.'

'I'll vouch for that,' said Gaston beaming, but the expression on Charles's face wiped the smile from his own.

'What I'm trying to say, Father, is that if anything happens to you, it's going to take me some time to teach her all the ropes.'

'Charles is right,' agreed Victor, very businesslike. Despite his personal antipathy towards Charles, there was no doubt that he ran the House of Gautier exceedingly well. Laura, as everyone knew, was an artist and a dreamer. It would take some years for her to learn how the company was run.

Eminently deferential, Charles inclined his head in Victor's direction. 'I knew you'd understand. The point is, Father, that I can't be obliged to defer to Laura's wishes while she's still so inexperienced. As we all know, she's adorably stubborn,' he smiled indulgently, 'and, in today's climate, I often need to move quickly. Without that flexibility, I have to warn you, this company would grind to a standstill.'

From the looks on the faces present, Charles knew he was

winning his argument. Grey-haired old men, all of them over seventy, it was a safe bet that none of them really believed in the subtler nuances of female emancipation. Only his father, it seemed, was less than completely convinced. It was time, Charles decided, to play the Caroline card.

'I must also add', he continued, 'that Laura is a very beautiful woman and rich, beautiful women often attract the wrong sort of men. I don't want to find myself arguing the future of Gautier with some fly-by-night adventurer.' Charles watched with pleasure as a shadow of pain crossed his father's features.

When, at last, Gaston spoke, his voice was weak and low-pitched, like that of an invalid. 'What are you suggesting?'

'A simple precaution, Father, that's all. I'd just like to ensure that, until Laura is thirty, I continue to make all the decisions relating to the company. After that,' Charles grinned boyishly, 'I'm sure we'll find some amicable *modus operandi*.'

Gaston looked first at Harry and Victor and then at the four other trustees. For one second, Leon Bourgeot, an eighty-three-year-old Liechtenstein lawyer, demurred. Deep down, he doubted that any woman could be responsible at so early an age as thirty. In the end, however, he decided to go along with the rest as they nodded their silent agreement.

'I'll have the relevant papers drawn up as soon as possible,' Gaston concluded.

Charles beamed at his father from the other end of the table. 'Thank you,' he said, with a gracious inclination of the head. 'You don't know how much this means to me.'

Gathering his papers for the third time that morning, Charles felt like pinching himself. For months he had been wondering how to neutralize Laura's potential influence in the company. Now everything, it seemed, had been handed to him on a plate. That one seemingly insignificant concession, accepted on the nod, meant virtual plain sailing towards the Sandton deal. There was now only one more obstacle standing in his way. He looked up to find Gaston rising with difficulty from his chair. With a shrewd gambler's guess, Charles gave him six more months at most. Triumphantly, he replaced his documents in his black leather briefcase before escorting his father up to lunch.

'I don't know if Maisie mentioned it to you,' said Gaston, as he and his son walked slowly up the stairs – Gautier, Paris, had never had a lift – 'but I'm sending Laura on a holiday.'

'How nice.' Charles thought of all the places where he would like to send his half-sister.

'The trouble is, I've been so busy, I've done nothing about money. Could you organize a transfer?'

'Just leave it to me. You've got enough on your mind. How much would you like me to send?'

'Well, you know your sister. She's off to the mountains, somewhere between Pakistan and Afghanistan. I've said I don't want her to go slumming it, so perhaps we'd better make it around five thousand pounds, just to be on the safe side.'

Charles smiled broadly. 'I'll get it organized first thing this afternoon.'

Gaston gave his son's arm a sudden, grateful squeeze. 'Thank you,' he whispered.

Charles guided him into the oak-panelled dining room and seated him at the head of the table. Sitting down himself, he took a quick look at the embossed, gold-tasselled menu which invariably accompanied such occasions. *Canard à l'orange* – excellent – that was his favourite dish. He poured himself a glass of wine and, settling back happily, thought of all the disasters that might befall a woman travelling alone.

CHAPTER TWELVE

Laura gazed out of her hotel bedroom window and towards the beckoning foothills of the Himalayas beyond. March in Peshawar, she decided, might just qualify for heaven on earth. Flying in over Attock the previous day, she had marvelled at the epic beauty of the scenery below. Surrounded by mountains, the Vale of Peshawar looked like a huge grey bowl with a green bottom and three chips missing from its rim. Laura had held her breath. The legendary Khyber, Kohat and Malakand passes – this really was the stuff that artists' dreams were made of.

Situated along the border between Pakistan and Afghanistan, the North-west Frontier province had always fascinated her. Her previous two visits, one during an intensely hot, dry summer, the second in the freezing fog of a bitterly cold winter, had done nothing to diminish that passion. Neither the cruel changes of climate nor the frequent setbacks and discomfort could ever detract from its appeal. Up in the mountains, where the air was pure and the clarity dazzling, Laura had found a sense of peace and beauty impossible to describe. Here, a thousand miles away from Western civilization, she knew she was truly at home.

The sound of the phone ringing interrupted her train of thought. She lurched for the receiver, desperate to hear the news. No, apologized the man from the car hire firm, he was terribly sorry, but her Land-rover would not be available until tomorrow morning at the earliest. Was she sure she did not wish to take a guided tour? An experienced driver would take her anywhere she wanted and have her back by nightfall. The mountains, she must know, were full of smugglers and bandits; they were not safe for a woman alone.

For the tenth time in their brief business relationship, Laura thanked the agent for his concern but insisted she would wait for her Land-rover. Amused, she heard him sighing down the other end of the phone. In his book (the Koran, she assumed at an educated guess), young ladies did not rock around the country-side unescorted and driving powerful cars. She picked up her room key, sunglasses and handbag and made her way down to the foyer. If she could not make it up into the mountains, she might as well spend the rest of the day exploring the city.

Situated at the foot of the Khyber Road, the Pearl Continental Hotel boasted the degree of homogenized luxury that such establishments are expected to provide. Leaving the security of its air-conditioned portals, Laura felt a sudden lightness in her step, as if she had finally shaken off the last vestiges of the West. Comfortable and expensive, the Pearl had not been her own choice of hotel. She would have been perfectly happy at one of the cheaper flop-houses around the Khyber Bazaar, but her father had insisted. The Land-rover had also been his idea. Nothing, he had stressed to her during their last telephone conversation, but the safest and the best. Eventually Laura had agreed. It seemed ridiculous to play the independent woman routine when Papa was footing the bill.

Already, the bright spring sunshine was warming the air. Laura inhaled deeply as she strolled down Sharah-e-Pehlavi towards the bustle of the Khyber Bazaar. Wobbly *tongas*, motor rickshaws, careered alarmingly along the road, exclamations of *'Inshallah'* springing readily to the lips of passers-by. As a jeans-clad European, Laura was used to the locals' inquisitive and often disapproving stares. In this part of the world, women obeyed the laws of *purdah* and, at this hour, few were out and about in the street. Those who were went quietly and modestly about their business. Laura studied them with interest. Some were almost invisible inside the white *burqqa*, the classic women's garment of the rigid Muslim fundamentalists. Others had opted for the *chaddar*, the sheet wound around the head and body, barely revealing their eyes. Thoughtfully, Laura fingered her long-

121

sleeved cotton shirt. The embryo of a little plan had already developed in her mind.

She meandered along, trying to shake the ubiquitous dust from her feet as she went. Perhaps, on reflection, open-toed sandals had not been such an inspired idea. High up in the sky above, kites and crows swirled and whirled, looking for potential breakfast. Light-hearted and light-headed, Laura felt like singing. Already thoughts of exams and London seemed light years away and Robert de la Marotte a distant, almost forgotten memory. She had worked so hard for the previous few weeks, determined to be well ahead before leaving on vacation. Justifiably proud, she now felt she had earned her break. The scorpion bracelet, recently finished, was being hailed by her professor as a master-piece. And the sugilite necklace, close to completion, was the most exciting and dramatic piece she had ever created. Laura pricked up her ears to catch the strains of a distant *muezzin* as he called the faithful to prayer. As she sauntered onwards, it seemed like walking back in time.

The sights, smells and sounds of the Khyber Bazaar soon assailed her every sense. There were a few tourists, mostly ageing, long-haired hippies still in search of where it was at. Some seemed to think that they had found it in *neswar*, a green paste made of wood ash, tobacco and cannabis or opium. Others had opted for the local *paan* or betel nut, to be chewed and spat out in disgusting bright red gobbets. Those who had been there, done that and were now after something harder would find heroin at a price. Pakistan, much to the impotent distress of its authorities, had overtaken the Golden Triangle of Thailand, Burma and Laos as the world's chief source of supply. Thanks to endemic smuggling, there seemed to be no shortage of it here.

Ignoring the conversational overtures of her spaced-out com-patriots, Laura wandered on. Why waste time on hopeless Europeans when the most glamorous of all mountain peoples were everywhere around? She stopped for a moment to stare, unashamedly, at the teeming mass of local tribesmen. Predomi-nantly Central Asian in physical type, many were sharp-featured and fair-skinned. She pulled out her sketch pad and allowed her imagination free rein as she drew. Members of the world's largest tribal society, the proud Pathans were shrouded in adventure and romance. Their very names – Yusufzai, Mohmand, Afridi, Bangash, Khattak, Mahsud, Wazir – were steeped in military history. Indomitable tribesmen, impossible to govern and easy to respect, they had remained uncowed by Alexander the Great and by Britain and her empire. Even now, they continued to live by their own code of honour, a code far more binding than the strictures of any national legislation. As they swaggered, some truculent, others merely haughty, around the market, Laura tried to capture their inalienable sense of vitality and independence.

She replaced her sketch pad in her bag and continued on into the market. A few mangy dogs tried to scavenge, their tails tucked tight between their legs to avoid the odd impatient kick. Two men, one with a rifle slung casually over his shoulder, argued about a carpet, their threats and conciliations spliced with shrugs, spasms and many gestures of the arms. Laura listened, intrigued, to the harsh clusters of consonants which accompanied their negotiations. She had learned a few words of Urdu, the national language of Pakistan, but up here that was seldom used. She concentrated for a while, but managed to understand nothing. They had to be speaking Pushtu or Pukhtu, she decided, and left them to their argument.

A small boy carrying a brass tray full of tea-cups zig-zagged across her path. The idea of refreshment was appealing but Laura decided to wait. She knew she would be offered *qawa*, delicious green tea with cardamom and lemon, as soon as she stopped to consider a purchase. Barrow boys selling fruit and street vendors cooking snacks vied with one another for her attention. She caught the waft of frying meat and contemplated a *chappli kebab*. A spicy 'beefburger' mixed with tomato and eggs and served on unleavened bread, it certainly smelt delicious. She dawdled for a moment before marching on, the advice of her father still ringing in her ears. She had not come all the way to Central Asia to run the risk of food poisoning!

Backtracking on herself to avoid the hubbub of the bus terminus, she was soon engrossed in the maze of stalls and alleys which filigreed outwards towards the Inner and Old City. From carpets she copied the geometric patterns of the Islamic world.

From brassware, she sketched the floral and foliate motifs influenced by Perso-Turkic invasions. With time and imagination, her own creative ideas would evolve from this eclectic mass of raw material. A brightly coloured jewellery stall attracted her attention. Chokers, bracelets and ear-rings, many Moghul in inspiration, lay juxtaposed with coarsely moulded silver collars of rustic provenance. The vendor held out a stranded necklace of red and blue beads, but Laura shook her head. By way of wordless communication, she pointed to her watch. The day, it seemed, was slipping away and she had yet to orchestrate her plan.

At first, the man seemed taken aback when Laura pointed to what she wanted. He was used to Europeans and their idiosyncrasies but, even by their standards, this seemed very odd. He had been pleased when, after some haggling, she had bought the red velvet satchel. With its gold appliqué arabesques and the mirror-work flowers so common in Pathan ceremonial waistcoats, it seemed like the sort of thing a beautiful, young European woman ought to have. But this! The wizened old man looked quizzically at Laura who nodded her insistence. After much sighing, he removed the long khaki shirt and drab baggy trousers from their hanger.

'*Salwar kameez*,' he tried to explain. She nodded politely and measured the trousers against her leg. The man looked increasingly bothered, racking his memory for the scraps of the English he had learned whilst fighting for the British Army.

'Very plain,' he recalled the words triumphantly. 'Much too plain.' He cast around for something more feminine and came up at last with a long, white diaphanous scarf. 'Pretty,' he said, handing it to her. 'More pretty thing for lady.'

'No thanks.' Laura gave him the shirt and trousers. 'The man's clothes are what I need. Now, please, could you tell me how much?'

By the time Laura returned to her hotel, it was past five o'clock in the evening. A spot of lunch under a shady tree at Dean's Hotel, some gentle sightseeing, it seemed that the day had just flown. Wearily she climbed up the steps, only to hear the indefatigable *muezzin* bashing out his stuff once again.

'Maghrib,' explained the doorman, as he helped her with her

shopping. She nodded. The fourth of the day's five statutory prayer times, there were days when Christianity did not seem too demanding, after all.

Manning the reception desk, Muhammad returned her key with a flourish. 'And a message for you, Mrs Jay.' He handed her a folded memo. In her hurry to open it, Laura fumbled and dropped her room key on the floor. 'Land-rover ready,' read the message. 'To be delivered to Pearl Continental at 6 a.m. tomorrow.'

'Everything all right?' enquired Muhammad, gesturing to a passing porter to pick up Laura's room key.

'Just wonderful.' She beamed at him as she gathered together her parcels. 'Thanks for the message. Oh, and please, I'd like an early morning call at five o'clock tomorrow.'

Muhammad did not recognize the slim, young man who pitched up at his desk early the next morning. Dressed in a nondescript *salwar kameez*, a large, floppy turban and a pair of square-toed, local *chappals*, he looked as if he might be a local guide.

'Good morning, Muhammad,' trilled the young man. 'Looks like another wonderful day. Has my car arrived?'

Surprised by the accent, Muhammad took a closer look. '*Accha!* Mrs Jay! I didn't realize it was you.'

Laura felt suitably gratified. Her strategy was working, after all. A lone man would not attract the same degree of attention as a woman travelling on her own. 'Good, I was hoping you wouldn't.'

'*Accha!*' Muhammad looked completely confused. He handed Laura a large buff envelope. 'Yes, your car is waiting outside. The documents and keys are in here. Will you be back this evening?'

'I expect so,' she said brightly, ignoring the anxiety in his voice, ' but don't worry if I'm not.' A porter arrived with assorted canvas packs and a rolled-up sleeping bag. 'I think I've catered for every conceivable eventuality.'

Muhammad frowned. He had spent some time in London, learning about hotel management, and knew something about the ways of headstrong Western women. All the same, the

Himalayas were quite a different proposition from Mayfair or New Bond Street.

'You know, you ought to take a guide. My brother-in-law—'

'Thanks, but I've been through this one before. I'll be perfectly all right.' She twirled gaily on the ball of her foot. 'Especially in this gear.'

His face grew even darker. 'Even so. There are smugglers and bandits up there. You really should—'

'Look,' interrupted Laura, 'the whole point of being in the mountains is to be there *on my own.*'

'If you insist . . .'

'*Inshallah!*' said Laura before sweeping out, the scurrying porter in her wake.

She drove west out of the city, up towards Landi Kotal and the Khyber Pass. She had no idea how far she would get today, neither did it matter. Freedom! A powerful car and her own space – that was all she really wanted. The urban sprawl soon petered out into an affluent residential area. In the large, well-tended gardens traces of early morning dew still clung in glistening globules to the blossom. Laura moved down into third gear and, opening her window, breathed in the perfumes of a Peshawar spring. Memories of the freezing barrenness of winter and the summer's dust seemed to belong to a different life. Now, fruit and nut trees were springing into bloom. Apricots, pears, plums and peaches, almonds, walnuts and pistachios, lychees and loquats, oranges and lemons, cherries and mulberries all flashed by in a glorious riot of colour. Neatly trimmed banana-plant hedges and shaded vegetable gardens seemed to create a patchwork quilt effect. Laura internalized the picture, watching as, gradually, the houses became less frequent and their gardens gave way to large fields of wheat, maize, rice and potatoes. Soon, even they disappeared and at last the Land-rover was climbing into the brown-grey foothills of the Himalayas.

A lone green parrot fluttered past but Laura felt that nothing, not even the memory of her adored Backbencher, could dampen her soaring spirits. Half a mile ahead, she could see a caravan of camels, followed by a herd of goats and a few stubborn, straggling sheep. A few of the camels carried nomads' tents,

lashed tightly to their backs. Others bore large packs of household equipment bouncing and dangling down either side. A tiny
child balanced precariously atop one camel's large brown hump,
but the rest of the tribespeople appeared to be on foot. The
powerful Land-rover soon caught them up and Laura felt like
waving as she passed. On seeing the women cover their faces,
however, she soon decided against it. Over in the distance, a white
bullock drawing a wooden plough trailed his clouds of grey-
brown dust behind him. Ten minutes later, even that had faded
into the distance and at last she was alone in the mountains.

She drove on until around eleven o'clock, when the hunger
pangs started to rumble. Pulling off the narrow dirt road, she
cast around for a suitable parking spot and soon found one in the
shade of a boulder. After locating her flask and a satchel of
provisions, she sat down on an old tartan rug for a swift *al fresco*
snack. Ravenous now, she tore off a piece of *naan-kebab* and
hacked herself a chunk of *paneer*. The humble home-made cheese
tasted exquisite. She lay back, munching happily, and contemplated a clear blue sky. Up here, even tastes seemed purer and
sharper, every sense so much more receptive. She rolled over,
opened the flask and poured herself a cup of ice cold *lassi*. What
bliss! They could keep their three-rosetted restaurants in the
Guide Michelin, this was the best meal ever!

Somewhere in the azure distance, a hawk glided and
swooped in a joyous exhibition of aerial acrobatics. Laura stood
up and sauntered over to the Land-rover to retrieve her sketch
pad and camera. A top-of-the-range Nikon, the camera was yet
another example of Maisie's unstinting generosity. Catching sight
of herself in the wing mirror, she rearranged her turban, still
slightly askew after her languorous stretch on the ground.
Ebullient, she wandered on, stopping now and then to photograph the snow-capped mountains and their myriad rock forma-
tions. Stark and angular against snatches of cotton wool cloud, a
bird of prey would occasionally catch her eye. Ideas for patterns
and shapes, designs and colours were swiftly noted down in her
sketch pad. The hours drifted by as she dawdled on, oblivious to
everything but the grandeur of nature and her own sense of
spiritual exaltation.

The first chill wind took Laura by surprise. Dressed only in her dowdy cotton clothes, she shivered and looked at her watch. Three o'clock! She must have been walking for well over four hours. A large black cloud loomed ominously on the horizon, blotting out the warmth of the sunshine and turning the epic landscape grey. Suddenly, her teeth began to chatter. She replaced the lens cap of her camera and started to retrace her steps towards the Land-rover. Soon, the cold fingers of panic started to claw their way into the pit of her stomach. Now that she actually looked, she realized that the narrow, snaking road was no longer in sight. Shivering, she pulled her thin shirt more tightly around her. Hell! She might have strayed miles off the beaten track. The sun peeped out for a moment, casting a confusion of shadows across her path. She began to feel frightened, no longer certain of which direction she should take. As if for added warmth, she clutched her camera and sketch pad close to her chest and started to run as fast as she could. It was then that the heavens opened.

Like tiny ice floes, the droplets of rain began to trickle down her neck. Panic-stricken, she quickened her pace, berating herself for her own stubborn and irresponsible behaviour. Damp now, the sketch pad clung clammily to her shirt. She stuffed it inside, desperate to protect its contents. Lined and craggy, the rocks seemed to be pulling faces at her, laughing at her predicament. A sudden bang in the distance made her jump with terror. She landed awkwardly, slipping as she missed her footing and falling heavily to the ground.

Trembling with shock, she forced herself to sit upright and pulled up her trouser leg. Already her left ankle was ballooning hideously. Terrified, she tried to move it. The pain was excruciating. Her yell, an amalgam of fear and frustration, seemed to echo for miles around. She held her breath for a second, but the soft pit-pit-patter of the ever more insistent rain was the only response to her call. Her heart was thumping so hard, it felt as if it might crack her ribcage. Slowly, painfully, she crawled to the relative shelter of a clump of rocks nearby. Slumping exhausted against one age-smoothed boulder, she suddenly passed out.

She had no idea how long she had been there – thirty

minutes, an hour perhaps – before her eyes flickered open again. The rain, she could hear, had stopped but the wind was gusting far more fiercely than before. Again she struggled to move her ankle, but it was hopeless. The shafts of pain penetrated upwards, making her whole leg throb. She sneezed, and every bone in her body seemed to ache. What a nightmare! Again she closed her eyes, only to find her father's warnings and Muhammad's pleas swirling round and round in her head. Her hands shaking, she tried hard to pinch herself. She must remain conscious . . . remain conscious . . . her mind rambled off again.

Perhaps she was imagining it. Screwing up her eyes, she willed them to focus properly. There, not five yards away, a lone horseman seemed to be staring down at her. Laura's blood ran cold as the blurred image focused into reality. Her heart palpitating wildly, she tried to return his stare. What a redoubtable figure he made! Resplendent in his Pathan tribal garb, with a voluminous green turban and baggy khaki trousers, the man wore bandoliers slung casually across each shoulder. Then, she noticed it. In his right hand he was carrying a Lee Enfield rifle, the sniper's favourite weapon.

She covered her mouth with her hands in an effort not to scream. At best a smuggler, at worst a bandit, it was impossible to know how this man might react to the discovery of her true identity. He shouted to her in Pukhtu and then, when she failed to respond, in Urdu. Uncomprehending, Laura shook her head. In one swift, fluid movement, the man dismounted and bounded towards her with the grace and agility of a wild cat. She looked up to meet the glint in his extraordinary pale blue eyes. Her head began to swim. Perhaps the pain was causing her to hallucinate, but with his finely chiselled features and light brown skin, he looked like the most handsome man she had ever seen. Mute with apprehension, she pointed to her ankle. He knelt down beside her, gently removing her sandal to reveal a set of perfectly polished toe-nails. Laura groaned. That had torn it! Now her little charade was well and truly up. The Pathan stared up at her quizzically before breaking into the most magnificent smile.

'Chanel's spring collection, I assume,' he said at last, in perfect Oxford English.

For Laura, the next few minutes seemed to flash past in a dream. The man whistled to his horse, which obediently trotted over. A brightly coloured blanket was soon produced from the saddle bag and wrapped tightly around her shoulders. Her teeth still chattering, more from relief than cold, she attempted to stammer out her semi-hysterical explanations.

'I've seen your car,' said the Pathan, when at last she calmed down. 'It's only about a mile away. Do you think you're up to riding?'

Laura nodded and struggled to get to her feet.

'No, you mustn't move.' His voice was deep and velvety, authoritative yet kind.

The next moment, she felt herself being swept up into his arms. Trembling, she put her hand around his neck, wondering if this was delirium. Lean and powerful, his body was warm against hers. Her skin began to tingle as suddenly her whole aching frame relaxed. As he lifted her on to his horse, she thought she could detect the vaguest hint of Guerlain's Vetiver. He swung up effortlessly behind her and reached forward for the reins. Sinking back, semi-conscious, into his arms, Laura wished they could keep riding for ever.

The Pathan's name, she discovered as they drove slowly back towards Peshawar, was Sharif Khan. The son of wealthy local landowners, he had been educated in England at Winchester and Oxford. Now he spent his time commuting between London and the mountains of the frontier. 'To preserve my sanity,' he smiled, revealing the most perfect set of teeth, 'and because I'm trying to make a film about this place.'

Laura's eyes lit up. 'What kind of film?'

Sharif glanced in the wing mirror. Loosely tethered to the back of the car, his horse was following meekly. 'A film about this land, its people and our culture . . .' his jaw set suddenly hard '. . . before Western civilization and its values get in and destroy us for ever.'

Laura sniffed. 'You make me feel like a barrel of toxic waste.'

He turned to look at her, his eyes full of mischief. 'It's nothing personal. Besides, a few irresponsible explorers don't count! Let's just say that radio and television have done more to undermine our society than the Moghul and British empires put together!'

'So you're making a documentary?'

He shook his head. 'Far too dry. People would ignore it. No, this film of mine is a love story.'

She was feeling sufficiently restored to attempt a little banter. 'With a deep and meaningful sub-text thrown in for good measure?'

He grinned, pleased to note that she had stopped shivering. 'But of course! Traditional values under attack. The effects of Western materialism on tribal communities – all smash-hit-at-the-box-office stuff!'

Laura prodded her ankle, which had turned an interesting shade of blue. 'I see why you needed the romance! Does it have a working title?'

'I've decided to call it *Tor*.'

'*Tor*?' She looked at him inquisitively. 'I'm afraid you'll have to explain.'

His grin grew even broader. 'Now that really *is* a long story.'

'That's all right.' She pointed to her ankle. 'I'm not rushing off anywhere.'

His whole physiognomy seemed to change as he spoke. Her throbbing ankle quite forgotten, Laura watched, fascinated, as he described the Pathans' inalienable code of honour. It was as if the suave, sophisticated film-maker had given way to another, far more vital, more passionate spokesman. *Pukhtunwali*, Sharif explained, was a way of life, a set of tribal customs which held more force than any national legislation. First came the rule of *melmastia*, hospitality to be offered freely to all visitors, even enemies, without anticipation of reward. Next was *badal*, revenge wrought in the wake of quarrels. According to Sharif, these usually involved gold, women or land (*zar, zan, zamin*), but the bloodiest of all always centred around women.

'Pathan women are cherished by their menfolk,' he continued. 'We see it as our duty to protect them, and any affront to their honour is severely punished.' His eyes settled on his Lee Enfield rifle. 'That's why rape is almost unknown up here. Our women know they are safe.'

So do caged canaries, she thought, but decided to keep that one to herself. 'It sounds like you're always fighting about something,' she ventured, heading for less dangerous territory.

He shrugged his shoulders, amused. 'When Pathans aren't fighting a common enemy, they're generally fighting themselves. In Pukhtu, we have the same word for enemy and cousin.'

'And *tor*?'

'*Tor* means black. When revenge involves a woman's honour, we call that *tor*. In serious cases, only bloodshed can wipe out the shame.'

Laura shuddered. 'Sounds very enlightened!'

'Up here it's the only way. For everyone's sake, rape, adultery and illicit relationships must be severely punished.'

'You make it sound very harsh.'

'It *is* harsh. Offenders are often killed by their own nearest male relatives in order to avoid a vendetta.'

Laura looked aghast. 'But that's hideous.'

'Perhaps, but the alternatives are worse. Look at the West, with its disintegrating family structures. We just can't afford to let that happen to us. Our entire society would die.'

She stared out of the window, deep in contemplation. *Pukhtunwali* – to a young, emancipated European woman, the whole concept sounded so alien. All the same, she mused, the values it espoused, honour, family and tradition, were her father's values, the values he had tried to instill in her.

'Your film,' she piped up at last, 'I hope it'll be a huge success.'

He gave a sudden, self-deprecating laugh. 'It's bound to do well in the States,' he joked. 'It's full of heroin and violence.'

Despite their slow progress, the lights of Peshawar were visible all too soon. Between talking, joking and a little gentle leg-pulling, the hours had simply sped by. Laura glanced at her watch and then took it off to shake it. 'What a bore! It must have stopped. Any idea of the time?'

'About six o'clock,' replied Sharif, his eyes still firmly on the road.

'How can you tell without looking at your watch?'

'I'm not wearing one.'

'Don't tell me,' she gibed, good-naturedly, 'your one-man crusade against Western consumerism!'

'Nothing so noble, just a habit. You'll never catch any self-respecting sniper with a watch. Watches glint in the sun, you see. That gives the game away.'

'Sharif Khan – Wykehamist and sniper!' She collapsed into giggles. 'What am I to make of you?'

Skittish now, she reached down for her sketch pad and began to draw his profile. How she wished her hands would behave themselves and stop shaking. It was quite ridiculous. The heating in the Land-rover was more than efficient and her clothes had long since dried out. As the lights of the city drew closer, she could feel her heart grow heavy. An enigmatic mixture of East and West, this man was totally beguiling. She showed him the results of her endeavours.

'Very good.' His voice was calm and measured.

Blushing furiously, she fished around for a biro and pretended to make some notes. 'This is all for my travel diary,' she said. 'So just for the record, tell me, how would you describe yourself?'

Sharif fell silent for a moment, his gaze focused on something beyond the gathering gloom. 'Are we being serious now?'

She nodded. To her, such a man was uncharted territory, a phenomenon she was eager to understand.

'Then perhaps I'll rely on the wisdom of the great Wali Khan and say that I'm a Pathan, and have been for thousands of years. Then I'm a Muslim, something I've been for about thirteen hundred years. And last of all, I'm a Pakistani, which I've been for only the last forty years or so.'

She scribbled feverishly. 'But your education,' she prodded, 'your accent, your sense of humour – they'll all so very English public school. Hasn't any of that rubbed off?'

'But of course!' The reflection of his face grinned back at her impishly from the mirror. 'Why else do you suppose I'd be out in the mountains, picking up pretty boys?'

CHAPTER THIRTEEN

At the hospital it transpired that Laura's ankle was not broken, just badly sprained. Having strapped it up tightly, the doctor advised pain killers to be followed by a good night's sleep. He studied her clothes with vague suspicion. And perhaps, he added pointedly, a few days' rest and recuperation, away from the rigours of mountain climbing.

Laura nodded gratefully and, as directed, tried walking around the consulting room. The pain was not half as bad as she had expected. She thanked the doctor for his help and hobbled off into the waiting room where Sharif was flicking through an ancient copy of the *National Geographic*.

'What did he say?' he asked, springing to his feet.

Laura rubbed her chin, noncommittal. 'It's nothing much,' she said, determined to play things down. 'Just a bit of a sprain. The doctor reckons I'll be as right as rain by morning.' She prayed that he might take the bait.

'Good.' He offered her his arm and she felt the remaining strength draining out of her weary legs. 'Then perhaps tomorrow you'll let me show you around the city.'

Her heart was beating faster by the minute. She struggled desperately to sound cool. 'Would this be an example of the legendary Pathan hospitality?'

'But of course.'

'Then I suppose I must accept.'

Arm in arm, and very slowly, they hobbled out of the hospital.

*

'Tomorrow morning, then. Ten o'clock,' said Laura, as he delivered her to the foyer of the Pearl Continental. She paused for a second. In London she would not have thought twice about inviting him in for dinner, but here that might seem very forward. Sensing her dilemma, he gallantly provided an excuse. 'I really must go and water my horse.'

She smiled gratefully as he helped her across to reception. After one quick glance, the man at the desk ignored them, and dealt instead with another resident.

'Ahmed!' Sharif's voice was sharp.

The man turned and at once, his entire attitude seemed to change. Offers of a wheelchair, a porter and a chambermaid were all swiftly made. Embarrassed, Laura declined, but by now the man was grovellingly apologetic.

'His father used to work on one of our family estates,' explained Sharif as he shepherded her into the lift. 'I'm afraid some things around here are still a bit medieval.'

The lift doors opened and Laura tumbled inside. 'Like knights on white chargers?' she whispered and watched until he disappeared from sight.

Her mind still buzzing with excitement, Laura burst into her bedroom and collapsed on to the bed. She lay there for some time, thinking, dreaming, smiling, promising her aching body somehow to haul herself up and take a much-needed shower. Eventually, she pulled off her mud-stained clothes and hobbled across to the dressing table. There, in the drawer, she found a large plastic laundry bag with which she covered her bandaged foot. She shuffled across to the bathroom and lurching under the shower, turned the jet on full. What utter bliss, she thought. The tiny needles of hot water penetrated to her scalp, washing away the patches of colour left by her cheap green turban.

Drying off, she searched for the small bottle of *Arnica* amongst her homeopathic kit. 'To prevent swelling and bruising,' she read on the label, and instantly took two. She was still chewing the chalky white tablets when the phone rang.

'Laura?' A distant voice bounced back on itself, reflected from some far-flung satellite. Laura settled down in an armchair, dying for a gossip. Disturbed by the news of the accident, however,

Maisie was soon clucking anxiously. 'You sure you don't want to come home?'

'Come home! You must be joking. I've just met the most amazing man!'

There was a pause at the other end of the line. 'That's one of the reasons I was phoning you. I was at the theatre last night with Betsy and who should I bump into but Robert de la Marotte.'

'And what did the bastard of the year have to say for himself?' Laura could not have sounded less concerned.

'Well, it was all a bit awkward really, but it seems someone told him you were already engaged.'

'*Me? Engaged?*' Laura gave a hollow laugh. 'Who on earth would have put an idea like that into his head?'

There was another pause. When Maisie spoke, her voice was cold with rage. 'He says Charles told him.'

'But why on earth . . .?' Laura's mouth fell open. 'What an absolute shit!'

'I know. We've just had the most terrible argument. He says he did it for your sake. He says he didn't want a sister of his tied up with some no-hope leftie actor.'

'And since when has he been so concerned about my happiness and welfare?'

Maisie ignored the obvious. 'I've spoken to Robert since and, believe me, he's mortified. He's desperate to talk to you and make amends. Shall I tell him where he can reach you?'

The image of Sharif, magnificent and macho, presented itself to Laura. Would such a man have believed Charles's tittle-tattle without first consulting her?

'No,' she replied, very cool and precise. 'In fact, you can tell him that I never want to see him again.'

'But he's so upset,' argued Maisie, 'and you know how plausible Charles can be—'

'*Never!*' insisted Laura. Her mind floated back to the mountains and she smiled contentedly to herself. '*Badal.*'

'I'm sorry?'

'*Badal,*' she repeated softly, 'it means it's his turn to suffer now.'

As she put down the phone, her thoughts returned once more to the enigma of Sharif Khan.

After leaving the hotel, Sharif untethered his horse from the Land-rover and set off down the road. Despite the lateness of the hour, he needed time to think, and decided to take the long route home. As he trotted on down the Mall, towards the Company Bagh and Mackeson memorial, his mind wandered to the extraordinary girl he had rescued earlier that day. He closed his eyes for a second and tried to conjure up her image. Her mouth, her eyes, that ridiculous turban – he thought he had never met anyone quite so wilful or enchanting. Over in the distance, the violet-tinged mountains formed a circle of jagged peaks around the plain. He smiled as he rode past the cricket ground, recalled the many wickets he had taken and the centuries he had scored.

The house where his widowed mother still lived lay on the outskirts of the city. A well-designed bungalow with white-washed walls and fanlight windows, it stood in the middle of rolling lawns, shaded by banyan trees. After attending to his horse, he sauntered into the house to see his mother. Khatija sat, a frail yet bright-eyed figure, embroidering in her quarters.

'You're late this evening, Sharif.' It was a simple statement, yet she made it sound like a reproach.

'Yes.' As a male in Peshawar society, he knew it was never incumbent to explain.

'So, then,' she returned to her needlework, 'that film seems to be keeping you very busy.' Again, it was like a criticism. Illness had made her tetchy.

He decided to try to humour her. 'That's a beautiful embroidery.'

'I hope to finish it for your birthday.'

'Don't remind me! Nowadays birthdays make me feel old.'

She fixed him with a stare. 'At your age, your father was married to me. We already had a son.'

He knew all too well where this was leading and deftly changed the subject. 'I hear the estate manager has not been well. I'll have to find someone to deal with things – that is, until he gets better.'

'It's *you* who should be dealing with things, my son. You are the head of the family.'

Despite her frailty, she could be a daunting woman. When one opening closed, she spotted the next. 'I'm quite aware of my responsibilities.' He struggled to make allowances for her failing health and age. 'I'm sorry, Mother, it's been a long day. I just came in to say good night and to make sure you were all right.'

Khatija pulled herself up in her chair. 'I'll be all right the day you settle down, Sharif. Until then I do nothing but worry.'

He smiled and respectfully kissed her cheek. 'I'm going to have to leave again soon. Let me go with a happy memory.'

Relenting, she looked up at him and smiled. 'Remember you have a mother who is very proud of her son.'

Quietly he closed the door behind him. He must have been mad, he told himself, even to have considered mentioning Laura.

Despite a sleepness night, Laura was up at seven o'clock the next day, raring to get going. Pushing aside the pairs of figure-hugging jeans, she opted for an embroidered Kashmir kaftan. Loose and comfortable, it looked just the sort of garment of which Sharif might approve. Besides, she thought, carefully camouflaging her bandaged ankle, she might as well make a virtue of necessity.

Downstairs in the dining room, a bunch of loud-mouthed British yobs were shouting orders at the waiters. She looked at them and shuddered. In their pastel-coloured shell-suits, reversed baseball caps and five o'clock shadows, these were precisely the sort of Brits whose passports ought to have been stamped NO EXIT in large red letters. She sat down and hid quietly behind a menu, praying they would ignore her. Fortunately, they seemed happy in their own company, whingeing on about everything from 'funny food' and 'crappy climate', to 'diarrhoea density' and 'thieving locals'. They were, it transpired, a film crew, shooting a car commercial in the mountains. Every so often, like mindless football hooligans, they would stop complaining and start chanting their advertising slogan: 'The International Traveller,' they chorused, 'Feel at Home Anywhere'.

Laura was just finishing her toast when Sharif appeared at her table. For a split second, she failed to recognize him. Dressed in beige slacks, an open-necked shirt and a pair of Gucci loafers, he looked suave and sophisticated, quite different from the dashing horseman who had rescued her the previous day. As they made to leave the dining room, Laura heard one of the crews muttering something about 'wogs'. From the look on Sharif's face, she knew that he had heard as well. He said nothing, but walked across to their table and simply glared at them. Laura watched, fascinated, as they seemed to shrivel in their shell-suits. Devoid of their bluster, they were nothing, crumpled heaps of second-class humanity. She studied them with loathing. And to think such creatures believed their very whiteness conferred superiority!

Outside, the sun was shining as Laura and Sharif walked slowly to the car park. 'I think you'll find my car more comfortable.' He opened the door of a blue Mercedes sports car and graciously helped her inside. Gingerly she stretched out her legs. 'Are you really the same Sharif I met yesterday?'

'No.' He turned the key in the ignition. 'Yesterday I was working. Today I'm having fun.'

Being with him was the most potent pain-killer of all. She hardly noticed her throbbing ankle as together they meandered around the Andar Shehr, the Inner City of Peshawar. Dazzlingly bright inside, the plethora of jewellers' shops displayed their wares with the help of lights and mirrors. Intrigued, she studied the range of gold and silver jewellery, occasionally stopping to make a sketch. At last, they arrived at a tall house, where the owner welcomed Sharif warmly.

'Not that anyone could fool you,' said Sharif, as he helped Laura negotiate the stairs, 'but you can trust Wafiq implicitly. My family has been doing business here for over three generations.'

The upper room was like an Aladdin's cave, full of sacks of precious and semi-precious stones. Laura browsed for over an hour, emerging with a magnificent selection of rubies and sapphires.

'What will you make with them?' asked Sharif, sipping his fourth complimentary cup of tea. She let them slip through her fingers, a stream of multicoloured light.

'Right now I've no idea,' she laughed, 'but one always comes along.'

In Shinwari Plaza, they admired the antique silver jewellery set with ivory, amber, lapis lazuli, cornelian, turquoise and malachite. For Maisie, Laura bought a fine silver locket from Turkestan, and for her father, a glorious Afghan rug.

'Look,' said Sharif, pointing out the tiniest flaw in the weave. 'It's done on purpose. It's supposed to avert the evil eye which is attracted by perfection.'

Next, they visited the mosque of Mahabat Khan, where each said a prayer to his own God. At Chowk Yagdar, the Speakers' Corner of Peshawar, they stopped to listen to a rabble-rouser vilifying those rich Muslims who avoided the *zakat*. 'It's a special Islamic tax,' explained Sharif, as they continued on their way. 'Here, wealthy people are meant to give two and a half per cent of their income directly to the poor.'

They wandered on towards the leather market, where Laura had fun trying on hats made from curly Karakul lamb skins. She took photos of Sharif, posing beside the Moghul Gateway of the Gor Khatri, a warriors' grave built by Shah Jehan's daughter. At Meena Bazaar, he returned the compliment, taking snaps of her as she watched women embroidering in gold and silver thread. In Banjara Bazaar, the gypsies' quarter, Laura insisted on having her fortune told and laughed when she was told of a handsome stranger who would suddenly appear in her life. Another old gypsy woman offered the couple magical love potions, but Laura shook her head. If the giddiness she was feeling was anything to go by, she had no need of artificial stimulants.

They walked through the grain and cloth markets, stopping briefly at Honest Ali's to admire his brass and copperware, before arriving at the bird market. All about, partridges, quails, parrots and doves were fluttering in captive frustration. Immured in a minuscule cage, a pair of song birds chirruped out the story of their sorrow.

'Poor things,' murmured Laura, suddenly subdued.

Sharif caught sight of her face, furrowed with concern and within seconds he was off, bargaining with the stall-holder. Words followed by notes were swiftly exchanged. 'Here,' he said, returning with the cage. 'Now their destiny is in your hands.'

She looked up at him, her eyes sparkling. 'Do you make a habit of rescuing things?'

'Only things worth rescuing.'

She blushed furiously and fumbled to open the cage door. 'You won't mind, then, if I set them free?'

His face broke into the most glorious of smiles. 'It's just what I expected!'

For a moment, the two song birds continued to hop around in the confines of their prison. The concept of this unexpected freedom, it seemed, was too difficult for them to grasp. At last, one of the birds poked his tiny head out of the cage and perched, still unsure, on the threshold of liberty. Laura and Sharif watched, spellbound, as he began to twitter excitedly to his mate. Soon she was at his side, and for a while the two were deep in animated discussion. At last, they reached their decision and together soared off singing joyously to the sky.

'You must be tired,' said Sharif, when the two black specks had finally disappeared from sight.

Laura shook her head vigorously. She was desperate for this perfect day not to be brought to a premature end. 'Not in the slightest. Do you think we could see the Street of Storytellers before it's time for lunch?'

'If you're feeling up to it.' He glanced briefly at his watch.

The corners of her mouth twitched slightly. 'No sniping today, then?' she quipped.

'Do you make a habit of noticing things?' he replied.

His jet-black hair shone like granite in the sunshine. Today, his Western-style clothes seemed to hug his sinewy body. 'Only things worth noticing,' she said.

As usual, Qissa Kahani, the Street of Storytellers, was packed with travellers from India, Afghanistan, Turkestan and China, all drinking tea and swapping tales as they had done since time immemorial. The whole place seemed alive, colourful and buzz-

ing, like an English flower garden on the afternoon of a warm
summer's day. Entranced, Laura sketched a few of the characters
in evidence: a pale, vague-featured Chinese with a perfectly egg-
shaped head; a fierce Mahsud, with a long, drooping moustache
and hair hanging down to his shoulders beneath his headcloth; a
distinctly flat-faced Mongolian; and a blond-haired, snake-hipped
young Englishman who was clearly in a world of his own. At
one end of the street, a wizened old man in a skull cap was
holding court to a throng of eager listeners. Set deep in bony
sockets, his eyes glistened red like fiery cabochon rubies.

'What's he saying?' asked Laura, wondering whether age or
wind-blown sand were responsible for that colour.

'He's telling the tragic tale of Hir and Ranjha,' whispered
Sharif. 'Doomed love, it's the backbone of Panjabi romantic
literature.'

She frowned beneath her fringe. 'I'm not sure I like the sound
of that, but I suppose I'd better hear it anyway.'

Comfortably ensconced at the Peshawar club, Sharif
recounted how Ranjha, the handsome flute player, first met and
fell in love with the beautiful Hir. 'But then,' he continued, after
a sip of lime soda, 'Hir is forced to marry Saida, the man she's
betrothed to but hates. She resorts to trickery to be reunited with
Ranjha and eventually her marriage to Saida is declared invalid.'

'Nothing too tragic yet.' A mischievous smile flittered dangerously about her lips.

Sharif was quick to notice. 'No, but then her wicked uncle,
Kaido, decides that she's brought shame upon the family and has
her poisoned. When Ranjha arrives at her grave, he's so distraught, he collapses dead with grief.'

For a minute, she stirred her *chota peg* in silence. 'I hate tragic
endings,' she said, at last. 'How about you?'

Sharif smiled. 'Some of the best stories ever told have ended
up that way. *Romeo and Juliet, Gone with the Wind, Anna Karenina,
A Tale of Two Cities, Beau Geste* – I could go on for hours.'

'So is *your* film sad?' she asked, suddenly earnest.

He watched as a droplet of condensation trickled slowly
down the side of his glass. 'You'd probably think so, but that's
because Westerners place such emphasis on personal happiness.'

She flicked a stray hair from her face. 'Don't you?'

He turned to look for a waiter.

'Don't you?' she insisted.

He swivelled around and caught her eyes, staring straight into his. 'It's too lovely a day for an argument.' He yawned and leaned back in his chair.

'How do you know there's going to be an argument?'

'Because you've started it already.'

'You rotter!' Laughing, she threw her napkin at him. It landed on the floor. As he handed it to her, their fingers touched for the briefest of moments. Suddenly, his eyes clouded over.

From that point on, the meal continued in virtual silence. After the easy jollity of the morning, they felt suddenly awkward, like animals in a strange environment wondering where the boundaries lay. Determined not to appear too forward, Laura struggled to hide her feelings. It was hopeless. The barely touched chicken curry gave her away all too eloquently. Across the table, Sharif pushed food half-heartedly around his plate.

'I'm going away tomorrow,' he said, quite brusquely. 'We'll be filming in the mountains for the next three weeks at least.'

'I see.' Laura felt her stomach churning. She had another fortnight's holiday left, but she was desperate not to seem pushy. 'I'd love to come and watch.' Astonished, she heard the words tumbling out and immediately felt like kicking herself.

He looked across at her, still doubtful. 'But are you *really* interested in what I'm trying to do?'

Laura wondered whether she had heard him aright. 'Interested? But of course I am.'

'This isn't just misplaced gratitude?'

She felt her heart soar as effortlessly as the song birds. It was all she could do to stop herself from reaching out to touch him. 'Don't be so ridiculous! I want to come because I want to understand.'

His face broke into the broadest of smiles as he relaxed back into his chair. 'In that case, we'll have to do our best to explain.'

*

The next two weeks were the most frenetic Laura had ever experienced. Shooting on location, just outside Darra, Sharif was like a general running a complicated military operation.

'But I thought this was a low-budget production!' She tried to tot up the scores of script-writers, hairdressers, make-up artists, wardrobe assistants, technicians, cameramen, actors, actresses and extras milling around outside their trailers.

'You'd better believe it,' quipped Milt, an assistant director who claimed once to have worked with Warren Beatty. 'Five minutes of *Heaven's Gate* would've paid for this entire shemozzle.'

Sharif's schedule was killing. Up at four each morning, he would begin his rewrites of the script. By seven, he was ready to brief his crew before going over any difficult parts with his actors. Then, depending on weather conditions, they would film until lunchtime, returning after a short break to continue until the light faded. 'It wouldn't work,' Milt assured Laura, 'if they weren't all scared shitless of him.'

By evening, there were innumerable ends to tie up, rushes and 'dailies' to study, shooting schedules to organize.

'At least Sharif don't have no stars to keep happy,' opined Milt to Laura one evening over a surreptitious sundowner. 'Those mothers are the real grief in any goddamn film!'

Laura drank in the atmosphere, happy with the few snatched hours she and Sharif shared together each day. At night, she slept alone in her trailer (out of convention, she would have been the first to admit, not choice), and dreamed of Sharif's characters and plot. Occasionally, an idea would cross her slumbering mind and in the morning they would discuss it. He was a good listener, open to suggestions but, as Laura noticed, the final script was always his.

Eventually, she found herself both living and dreaming the film. After two weeks, she knew every snippet of dialogue, every twist in the narrative by heart. After reading and rereading the script, she had a far greater insight into Sharif and, more important still, the ideas and values he was trying to promote. She respected and admired him but, to her increasing consternation, wondered how such a film would pay its way.

The day before she was due to leave, Laura and Sharif decided to go out for a ride. By now, her ankle was completely restored and she felt the pressing need for a rigorous bout of exercise. It was a glorious morning, the peace of the mountains a welcome curative after the hustle and bustle of the film set. Only a troop of minivets, cheeping and stirring in the leaves, disturbed the absolute silence which enveloped them. They rode on together for some time, both apparently deep in thought.

'I'm afraid I've been neglecting you.' He reined his horse back to a walk. This morning he was again in full Pathan regalia and, for some reason, that put her on edge. Perhaps, it was the way he oscillated so easily between the two cultures. Certainly, whenever she thought she was beginning to grasp him, he seemed to slip away again.

'I don't mind. You've been busy.' She guided her mare into step. For a while they rode on, letting the fresh mountain air work its miracles on their tired and cluttered minds. Sharif stared straight ahead, his face immobile, his eyes, like those of some ancient guru, focused on something out of sight. To watch, she could never have guessed at the turmoil within him. For once, he was struggling to say what was on his mind.

'I'll miss you.' He whispered the words as if to the winds. She stiffened in her saddle. Tomorrow she would be back in England. She could not afford to let things drift.

'When will you be coming back to London?'

He patted his horse which whinnied happily in the sunshine. 'Sooner than I expected. We're way over budget. I'm going to have to raise some extra finance.'

She felt suddenly cold, despite several layers of jumpers. 'Is that the *only* reason?'

She saw his long, nervy fingers tighten on the reins. 'No. You know I must see you again.' He turned suddenly to look at her. 'But I've got to square with you. The film's in deep trouble and we're right out of cash. I'm not sure that I can save it.'

'But the film is brilliant – it's daring and innovative . . .'

The folds of his *salwar kameez* flapped gently in the breeze. 'Thanks. I appreciate that. But you know as well as I do what it's *really* about. I'm sick of media imperialism. I'm tired of the values of dominant Western culture being constantly stuffed down our throats!'

'You needn't get so angry with me!'

'I'm not angry with you, but I *am* angry! How can *we* fight back? Who wants to hear what *we* have to say? The West controls the media and the media controls the world.' He laughed harshly. 'There's no need nowadays for wars and crusades – they just destroy us with MTV.'

To her dismay, Laura could feel the discussion spinning out of her control. 'But we can all learn from one another,' she interjected feebly.

'Oh, really? What has the West to teach us? It's destroyed all its own structures. There's nothing left now but a vacuum.'

Suddenly Laura felt angry too. 'We're not *all* bad!' she shouted. It was precisely what she had been dreading. Now their relationship would be over before it even touched first base. The hell with it! She could not just sit back and allow such blanket criticism. 'Let's start with living standards, shall we?' she continued. 'Not to mention health, education – oh – and while we're at it, women's rights. I don't think you can teach us too many lessons in those departments, can you?'

'Capitalism,' he snorted. 'Capitalism and its so-called enterprise culture! All right, so there have been some benefits, but what has it really meant? Individualism at the expense of society. Materialism at the expense of care. Yours is a culture obsessed with youth and looks. A culture where divorce, suicide, crime and murder are the reality behind the gloss. It's a culture based on nothing but hypocrisy and lies.'

Her head was reeling from the vehemence of this unexpected philippic. By now her dander was really up. She could not stop herself. 'So you think you hold the monopoly on everything that's good. Well, let me tell you something, Sharif, when it comes to courage and compassion there's none of you can hold a candle to my father!'

Suddenly he was calm again, his voice very weary. 'I'm sorry. I've worked so hard on this project and now it's evaporating before my eyes. My film, my vision – perhaps it was madness to think I could do it – I just don't know any more.' He laughed, a hollow, self-deprecating laugh. 'What exquisite irony. And now I must go to the men with money to produce an indictment of their system!'

Laura chewed her thumb-nail thoughtfully. 'I think I may be able to help.'

'I can't accept—'

'Oh, do shut up for a moment. I'm not suggesting a charitable donation. This would be strictly business.'

He smiled at the reproof. The idea of this dreamer and hard-headed business seemed somehow very ill-matched.

'I can't promise anything,' she continued, ignoring his smirk, 'but I *can* explain what you're doing to someone who might be useful.'

Sharif's ears pricked up. Suddenly he was interested. 'I'll organize copies of the script and rough cuts.'

She urging her mare into a canter. 'Please do, but then don't call us, we'll call you.'

He spurred his horse on to catch her. 'Come on, tell me who it is.'

Like a golden mane her hair streamed out behind her. 'A friend of the family,' she shouted and flicked her mare into a gallop.

He raced to catch up with her. 'Sounds very positive.'

'Perhaps!' Her laughter tinkled like silver bells on the winds. 'There's only one problem for you as a Muslim. This family friend's a Jew!'

CHAPTER FOURTEEN

Busy as usual, Serge Birnbaum was delighted nevertheless to accept a call from his favourite honorary niece. She seemed in high spirits, brimming over with energy and in an excellent frame of mind for her final term at college. As she chattered on, France's most celebrated film producer nodded his head benevolently. If only he had a daughter, he mused. Even when they married, daughters never really left. His three sons, now scattered all over the world, only seemed to phone when they were in need of money. *Eh, bien*, at least they phoned. Serge gazed fondly at the framed family photograph that graced his desk. Children! They broke your heart, then they ruined your bank balance. If only he had a dozen of them!

'So will you take a look at it, then?' Laura's voice, strangely insistent, brought him back to earth again. Snippets of her breathless monologue – romance, adventure, honour and revenge – trickled into his consciousness. *Merde alors!* What had he let himself in for? The greatest story ever told, the film to end all films – he had heard it all a thousand times before. All the same, he mused, lighting his first Monte Cristo of the day, Laura *was* Laura and he *did* have a meeting in London in two days' time. He agreed to take a look at the rough cuts at a private cinema in Soho and invited her to dinner afterwards. She thanked him profusely and assured him that he would not be disappointed. Serge smiled as he replaced the receiver. Of course he would, he told himself, but what the hell! Laura was the most attractive young woman in London and, besides, he owed his life to her father.

Two evenings later, Laura found herself nervously sipping champagne in Soho's Gay Hussar. She knew it was Serge's favourite London restaurant and had taken the wise precaution of booking one of the quieter tables upstairs.

'Well,' she urged, pink-cheeked, 'what do you think of it?'

'I'm afraid to say . . .' as he poured himself another glass of Bollinger, she could hear her heart thudding loudly, '. . . that I'm very impressed.'

She felt like jumping for joy. 'I knew you'd like—'

'I'm not saying there isn't a lot needs doing to it, but you're right, it does have potential. This friend of yours . . . Sharif?'

Her eyes grew wide with enthusiasm. 'You *have* to meet him. He's so wonderful, I know you'll just love him. Right now he's doing everything himself, writing, producing, directing – everything. Just like you did at the beginning. But now he's desperate for help. He needs someone of your experience to pull the whole thing together.'

'Not so fast, young lady.' She looked suddenly deflated, like a punctured balloon. He gave her hand an avuncular pat. 'No one goes into a multi-million-dollar venture with a complete unknown without doing some preliminary homework. First of all, the story.'

'You're worried about copyright?' She was immediately back on form. 'No problem. Sharif wrote the whole thing himself.'

Serge pulled out a Gautier memo pad – one of the little luxuries that all Gaston's friends seemed to possess. 'I see. And how did he come up with the idea?'

'You have to go there to understand it all.' She gulped her champagne rather too quickly. 'I mean, their code of honour and all that.'

'Yes, but the drug-smuggling plot?'

149

'Oh, that's easy. Up on the Frontier gun-running and smuggling have always been endemic. Everyone's at it, but the Afridis have always been the best.'

'And that other tribe,' Serge scribbled as he talked, 'what are they called again?'

'The Shinwaris – they're the businessmen. They run the mountain laboratories which convert the opium into cocaine. Then they get the Afridis to smuggle it out of the country. It's a highly profitable relationship.'

'So in the story everything's going fine until our tall dark Afridi hero falls for the Shinwari girl?'

In her excitement, Laura's words were tumbling out. 'Yes, but when their affair is discovered, the whole operation is placed in jeopardy. Rana has to be killed by her brother for bringing shame on her family. And her lover, Asif, must be killed by *his* brother, Mustaq, to avoid a feud developing.' She held out an empty glass. 'It's all there, if you read it, in the dossier I gave you.'

Serge reached for the bottle and poured them both more champagne. Her enthusiasm was infectious. 'Hero and heroine dead,' he muttered approvingly. 'I'm sure we could push it as a modern-day *Romeo and Juliet*.'

A sudden cloud crossed Laura's face. 'Oh, but it's so much more than that. Sure, it has romance and adventure and tragedy and all the right ingredients. But behind all that, there's a bigger message.'

'You mean, when Mustaq blows up the laboratories?' He turned the page of his pad and continued writing. 'We could go to town on the special effects.'

'But you must understand,' she frowned, 'this is the most important part of the whole film. It's where Mustaq suddenly realizes that the cocaine trade is all wrong. Two young people have just been shot. Their families are devastated. Mustaq rides up into the mountains and for the first time thinks about the millions of other families torn apart by drugs. In the end, he takes what he now knows is the only honourable course of action. He destroys the operation that's already destroyed so many.' She paused, her face flushed with a mixture of animation and champagne.

Serge's fine, spidery scrawl had filled a dozen or more pages. 'It's great,' he said at last, snapping shut the burgundy leather memo pad. 'Or, at least, it *could* be great. "A return to immutable values" – I like it – we might even start a fashion.'

'So you'll help?'

The old man stroked his chin. 'I'm not promising anything, but why don't you go ahead and fix a meeting between me and your friend?'

Laura leaned over and kissed him hard on the cheek. A passing guest glanced knowingly at the couple. Elderly man and pretty young girl – it looked like the same old story.

'Hold on!' laughed Serge, slightly embarrasssed. 'I've yet to see if I like this fellow.'

Ebullient and slightly tipsy, Laura kissed him again. 'In that case,' she said, knocking back the final few drops in her glass, 'it's already in the bag.'

Two weeks later Serge flew out to Peshawar and was met at the airport by Sharif.

'Laura tells me you're doing everything in this film.' The old man studied the aquiline profile as they drove off towards the hills.

Sharif smiled wryly as he moved his Suzuki pick-up truck into fourth. 'Not *quite* everything.'

Staring out of the window at the snow-capped Himalayas, Serge puffed contentedly on his cigar. 'If you ask me, the only thing you're not doing is precisely the one you ought to be.'

'I'm sorry?'

'Starring in it.'

Sharif smiled awkwardly. 'I'm very flattered.'

'Flattery's never been my style.' Serge leaned back in his seat. 'Tell me, are you happy with the actor who's playing Mustaq?'

'I see you've read the script.'

'Read it? After Laura's sales pitch, I felt obliged to learn it by heart!'

The initial reserve was broken. The two men laughed together. Sharif rolled down his window, and breathed in the fresh, cool air of the foothills. 'She's a very special person – and as for Mustaq, no, I'm not wild about the way he's shaping up.'

Serge pulled nonchalantly on his cigar. 'Then drop him!'

'Drop him?' Sharif sounded horrified. 'But the project is way over budget already. I can't start reshooting his scenes.'

Serge shrugged nonchalantly. 'Why not? He only emerges towards the end – you've barely used him yet. I'm telling you, you've got to get Mustaq right. The film sinks or swims with him.'

'But who am I going to find at such short notice?'

'I already told you.' Serge extinguished his half-smoked cigar in the ashtray. 'What's more, you already know the part.'

The two men found the Kohat Road and sped on towards the jagged blue-grey mountains and Darra. Although spring was well advanced, the lingering tendrils of morning mist and hoar-frost were still visible as they drove. Serge stared in fascination at the handsome, straight-backed tribesmen they met riding along the road. With their characteristic green turbans, and their voluminous khaki shawls drawn tightly around them against the chill, they seemed to belong to another world. Serge fought hard to contain his growing enthusiasm. Business was business, he told himself. He must not allow himself to get carried away. But already he could feel his fingers beginning to twitch. With him, that had always been the sign. He felt sure he was on to something.

Every now and then, the fields and canals would give way to an orchard, dazzling in its sudden glorious greenness. Outside a small roadside shop sat an old man, spitting out bright red betel juice as he contemplated an infinity of azure sky. The Suzuki climbed up higher into the foothills and the irrigated fields of the Vale of Peshawar slowly disappeared from sight. Herding sheep and goats, a group of gaily dressed girls suddenly appeared around a bend. Serge watched, intrigued, as hurriedly they pulled their black *chaddars* over their heads and turned their backs to the road. Ahead of them, perched on a craggy precipice, loomed a large, solitary house fortified with a watch tower.

'Feuds,' explained Sharif, as they passed through the gloomy gorge. 'We're not far from the village of Zarghun Khel. That's real gun-runners' territory.'

They stopped briefly at the so-called Darra Bazaar to watch the fabled Afridi gunsmiths at work. Lying in the narrowest part of the pass, the cliffs on either side seemed almost vertical. Serge looked all around him and shivered. Even at midday, it was almost impossible to see the sun.

At once Sharif sensed his disquiet. 'We're OK. They know me around here.'

Despite his anxiety, Serge drank in the murky atmosphere. 'Wonderful,' he enthused, 'this place is just wonderful. Cold, dark, threatening – we'll shoot a scene up here for sure.'

Loud voices followed by a shot, ricocheting loudly off a nearby wall, made Serge jump. Sharif took him by the arm. 'It's always the same. They're testing their guns in the main street.'

Serge marched on bravely. 'Let's go take a look. You people, you're extraordinary! I've got to try getting inside your heads.'

The lean, grey-bearded man in the gun shop welcomed the two visitors courteously. A lunch of mutton pilau was swiftly arranged and they all sat down to eat. Serge thought he had never tasted anything quite so delicious. Normally he never bothered with lunch but already the mountain air seemed to be working wonders on his appetite. After innumerable cups of tea, the man agreed to show them around his workshop. He pointed out the drill presses, lathes, grinders and borers. The steel, Serge noted with astonishment, was still being cast in sand and the rifling all done manually. 'Hand guns, rifles, even field artillery,' explained Sharif, 'if you ask them, they'll copy anything you want.'

Over in the corner, a small boy was counting out a huge bundle of rupees. Intrigued by the child's dexterity and competence, Serge looked on amused. 'So everyone gets involved in the family business? I could get to like you people.'

Sharif nodded. 'We believe that children learn best by copying their elders. Here, youngsters will probably start at four or five,

doing simple jobs like sorting screws. By the time they're adolescents, they'll know the business inside out.'

Serge patted the child's head approvingly. 'A return to family
values,' he murmured, and made another mental note.

By the time they reached the camp where the film crew was
located, Serge had made up his mind. He just *had* to salvage this
project. The idea seemed almost incredible. A Jew, working hand
in hand with a Muslim? Until today, he would never have
believed it possible. Co-operation, he mused, already dreaming
up the hype. He made a note for their future publicists. War,
hate, violence, degeneracy – all these been done to death. This
joint venture would break *new* ground. If he got it right, *Tor*
could be *the* film of international understanding. Serge could feel
his fingers twitching again. Honour and understanding . . . boy,
could he weave some publicity around that!

He showered and changed before making his way across to
Sharif's trailer where he was met by a mixture of the most exotic
smells. 'Don't tell me!' He sniffed appreciatively. 'You even do
the cooking around here.'

'Only very occasionally and for very special guests.' Sharif
returned to his array of herbs and spices – saffron, cardamom,
sesame, garlic, ginger, turmeric, chillies, roasted poppy seeds –
and added a few judicious pinches to a simmering pot of *bhuna
ghosht*. 'I find it helps me relax.'

Serge plonked a bottle of single malt whisky on the table. 'I'm
afraid nowadays I need this to relax. I don't suppose I can interest
you . . .?'

Sharif shook his head and handed his guest a tumbler. 'Not
for me, thanks, but feel free to help yourself. I'll be another
fifteen minutes.'

Dinner, when it arrived, was gargantuan. Chicken, mutton
and fish dishes garnished with onions, raisins, cashew nuts,
pistachios, almonds and tomatoes – it all looked simply mouthwatering. Ravenous again, despite his copious lunch, Serge
tucked in with pleasure. 'So this is what you call Pathan hospitality?' He helped himself to another serving of *machli ka salan*. A
combination of fish and curry – he found it quite delicious. 'What

a day! A whole new universe of experiences. It's been a revelation.'

Sharif continued to sip his *lassi*. 'We like our guests to feel welcome.'

'And do you kill many with your kindness?' He loosened his belt and allowed his corpulence to sag.

Sharif noticed and smiled. Despite their differences, he had genuinely taken a liking to this indefatigable Jewish dynamo. Wiry and sprightly despite his age, Serge Birnbaum exhibited an undying *joie de vivre*, a rare intelligence and an acute interest in everything around him. It was no wonder that his films had more than a dozen Oscars to their credit.

'Nothing so devious,' he replied. 'A true Pathan will look you in the eye before he shoots you.'

Serge laughed and poured himself another whisky. 'You'd better watch yourself in Hollywood. There, people specialize in stabbing one another in the back.'

'Hollywood?' Sharif looked suddenly downcast. 'I can't even think as far as paying my crew.'

Serge smiled, a slow, gentle smile. 'Why don't you just leave finances to me? I reckon I can pull in a few markers.'

Sharif's pale blue eyes glinted in the gas light like Ceylonese sapphires. 'You'd do that for *me*?'

'No.' Serge sat back in his chair, sated and relaxed. 'I'd do it for *any* good idea I thought deserved an airing.'

'So you agree with what I'm trying to say?' Sharif sounded surprised.

Serge savoured his whisky. 'You know, we Jews and Muslims, we're not so very different. We're both Semitic religions. We all believe in the simple virtues, humility, compassion and concern. None of us is really at home with modern, secular values.'

'But the West has come to terms with the Jewish people. Nowadays you're accepted and successful.'

'Don't try telling me anti-Semitism doesn't exist.' Serge's tone was mordant.

'Of course not, but it's been pushed underground. We're the

new Jews. Nowadays, it's hip to hate Muslims. Look at the way we're portrayed in the media. Corrupt, fanatic book-burners. The Communist bogey-man has disappeared and suddenly Islam is the new threat.'

Serge paused to study the amber liquid swirling around in his glass. 'I survived the holocaust,' he murmured, 'but the rest of my family was killed. During that time I saw people, ordinary, hard-working people, people who used to be our neighbours, brainwashed against us. Now I see it as my job to show men and women everywhere the truth about each other. I want them to realize that whatever their colour, race or creed, there are fundamentals we all share. I want people to relate, Sharif, I want them to connect.'

Suddenly Sharif found himself hugging the Frenchman. It was as if he had just found a mentor and an *alter ego* all rolled into one. 'So you *do* understand,' he said, the vaguest lilt of emotion in his voice.

Serge's eyes were rheumy. 'Understand? This is the film I've been waiting years to make. Honour, chivalry and tradition – all the values we've almost lost. It's high time someone made a stand.'

They talked on, deep into the night. Opening his heart and his briefcase, Sharif divulged everything there was to be known about the film. Serge could see that the finances were in a fairly parlous state, but nothing he could not handle. Since his first box office hits in the early sixties, backers for a Birnbaum film had never been short on the ground. Gradually, they ironed out the finer details of the plot and Sharif was finally persuaded to assume the hero's part. Time flashed by. Like a disobedient schoolgirl sneaking surreptitiously home, the silver-grey dawn crept in over the mountains.

After their night of deliberations, Serge looked quite exhausted. 'And I'll deal with distribution.' He yawned. He had long since given up on the Gautier memo pad and had started using a dictating machine. 'If we package this right, it should sell everywhere, even in Eilat.'

Sharif rubbed his eyes, fighting to keep awake. 'And the soundtrack?'

'You're right. It needs some powerful music . . . something between *Lawrence of Arabia* and *Chariots of Fire*. I'll do some phoning when I get home.'

'And I was thinking, perhaps a theme song too.'

Serge paused to drain the last of his Scotch. 'I know just the man,' he whispered almost to himself. 'The only question is, how we lure him out of retirement.'

CHAPTER FIFTEEN

Alone in his custom-built gymnasium, Scorpio had just completed his early-morning circuit. He sauntered across the light oak parquet floor and into the sports equipment room. It was full of kit, all neatly arranged and recently serviced: skis and tennis racquets, golf clubs and diving gear. The place was a testament to one man's quest for physical health and fitness. He checked his blood pressure, which was normal, and his weight, which was hovering around a hundred and eighty pounds. Not bad, he smirked to himself in the full-length mirror. Not bad for a bloke of six foot three now approaching his forty-seventh birthday. Lined and craggy, the face of a thousand hangovers smiled back at him approvingly. To Scorpio, the reflection still came as something of a shock. Gone now the stranger who used to peer at him, slit-eyed and fuzzy, whenever he managed to drag himself out of bed. This was the new-look Scorpio, the Scorpio that even Scorpio sometimes managed to like.

He admired his taut, hard stomach in the mirror. No, it was certainly not bad for a guy whose previous four birthdays had been spent in the Betty Ford Clinic. He took a quick slug at the punch-bag hanging lumpenly in the corner. Hell, it felt good. If only he could do the same to so many of the so-called friends and associates he had come across over the years. Suspended from its hook, the punch-bag swung heavily to and fro. Scorpio waited until it came to rest before delivering a swift flurry of murderous punches straight into its canvas torso.

'This one for my mate, the coke dealer. And this for the crook who arranged that record deal. And this for that bastard pro-

moter—' A right hook, then a left, then another right, each blow
seemed to intensify the ferocity of the next. At last, he stopped
and bent to pick up a towel. After every narcotic in the business,
it felt good to be high on nothing but your own adrenalin.

He wandered across to the indoor pool and dived in. The
water was cold and revivifying, just the way he liked it. His mind
focused on breathing technique, he started his thirty-length stint,
but a loud wailing sound outside soon shattered his concentration. Desperate for company, his mad mutt Clancy, half Irish
wolfhound, half Labrador, was bashing his tail frantically against
the glass. 'Lunatic dog!' exclaimed Scorpio affectionately, and
heaved himself out of the pool. He draped himself in a towel and
opened one of the large french windows. The huge grey-black
dog bounded in, almost laying him out flat.

'Calm down, calm down!' Scorpio laughed as he fended off
the barrage of devoted licks and slobbers. 'Are you looking for a
swim?' Clancy's paws were round his master's neck, pinning
Scorpio to the wall. 'Just stop it, you daft dog.' He fought to
extract himself. It was worse than being mobbed by fans.

All of a sudden he ducked, leaving the animal standing
momentarily on two legs. 'Can't catch me,' he yelled, diving
headlong into the pool. Grinning from ear to ear, the mongrel
took a flying leap into the water and paddled after him.

'You're in good nick, old son,' shouted Scorpio, from the far
end of the pool. Two brown eyes, a pink tongue and a large black
nose were visible somewhere in amongst the spray. 'But can you
catch?' He threw a small red ball up towards the glass-paned
roof. The dog glanced up and plucked it out of the air as it fell
towards the water. Delighted with himself, he paddled on and
returned it to his master.

Scorpio patted his faithful friend's soaked and spiky head.
What a difference from the emaciated creature he had rescued
from the Battersea Dogs' Home almost five years before! Large,
lost and ludicrous, the dog had then reminded Scorpio irresistibly
of himself.

'We're going to get well together,' the ailing rock star had
promised, as his chauffeur-driven Bentley whisked them back to
the Sussex mansion. He would never forget the way that stray

dog had stared back at him. Perhaps it was the methadone but to Scorpio a thousand years of wisdom seemed to inform those large brown eyes. The dog had appraised him carefully before coming to a decision. Nuzzling up against his new master, he had licked him quite deliberately on the nose. That had set the seal on their relationship. The rehabilitation of Scorpio, the dog seemed to know, was now largely in his paws.

Scorpio took the ball from Clancy and flung it high into the air again. Ecstatic, the dog splashed off to retrieve it as his master looked on, amused. They had come a long way together but, in Scorpio's case, it had been a long, slow and very painful haul. One day at a time, the counsellor at Alcoholics Anonymous continued to remind him, just one day at a time. He pushed off from against the blue mosaic wall and swam a full length under water. Never in his life had he felt so fit and well, so full of zest and energy. All the same, clean living did not come easily to a man who had almost managed to drink and drug himself to death. He had wrestled with the Lucifer of self-destruction and won, but now there was a new, far more perilous challenge to confront. The days, it often seemed to Scorpio, were so very, very long.

'Scorpio! Scorpio!'

The voice of Flo, his personal assistant, reverberated around the pool room. He surfaced immediately, as if summoned by his sovereign. 'Good morning,' he shouted, shaking the water from his ears. 'And how's my favourite girl today?'

Already Clancy had clambered out of the pool and was shaking himself, spraying Flo in the process.

'Get off with your bother!' she shooed, trying hopelessly to shield herself from the dog's dribbling devotion. 'Clancy, you dreadful old eejit, you're ruining my outfit.'

Scorpio smiled. However hard she tried, Flo never sounded anything other than mellifluous and kind. He sprang nimbly up the steps and reached for his towel. Clancy danced merrily between them, excited as a puppy. Since his first day in the Scorpio household, the dog had known instinctively that Flo was very good news indeed. Sixty years old, bright as a button and as straight as a die, the small buxom Irishwoman was an odd choice for a rock star's personal assistant. She had arrived in Scorpio's life just a few weeks before Clancy – wafted in like Mary Poppins, he used to say, to sort the whole mess out. Before her, a seemingly endless succession of dolly-bird secretaries had processed their way through his office and bedroom, most of them itching to get their neatly manicured hands on his multi-million-pound fortune. Scorpio squirmed with embarrassment whenever he looked back. Fortunately, in looking back, there was little he recalled.

'I didn't realize you were here.' He looked up at the pool clock and saw it was only a quarter to eight.

Flo flicked the spray from her grey cashmere twin set and rearranged her single row of pearls. 'Well, here I am and a good thing too. You haven't forgotten, have you? You've a meeting today with all your grandees. I've paperwork to do before then.'

He rubbed his hair with a towel. 'You're a star. And I really do think it's time you accepted a rise.'

'Away with you! I'm paid well enough already. Now, did you return Serge Birnbaum's call?' Scorpio looked suddenly sheepish.

'No, actually, I didn't get around to it.'

Flo fixed him with what she hoped might pass for a look of opprobrium. 'Sure and that's a very poor show. The man's supposed to be a friend of yours and he called five times yesterday. Now, you promised me you'd ring him back.'

The icon of an entire generation stared awkwardly at the floor. He hated upsetting Flo. A mother-figure, a mate and a protector, this woman had steered him lovingly out of the nadir of his life. There was nothing she did not know about him and, with all the sex, drugs and rock 'n' roll he had lived through, there had been some fairly gruesome stuff. To the starchy-looking spinster from Skibbereen, however, it made not the blindest bit of difference. Flo was the first person Scorpio had ever met who wanted nothing from him. To her, he was simply the son she had never had. All she wanted was his happiness.

'I'm sorry,' he said, shamefacedly. 'I know I promised, but I guess I was frightened to.'

'So you're worried he'll be asking you to do something?' Her half-hearted stab at disapproval turned immediately to concern.

Scorpio nodded. 'I'm not up to it, Flo. Or, at least, I can't be sure that I *am* up to it. Who knows what might happen if I let the pressures build up again?'

Flo's unlined face evinced a protective smile. 'Leave it with me.' She patted Clancy whose long damp tail was beating a tattoo on the back of her legs. 'I'll say you've no intention of coming out of retirement and I'll send him your kindest regards.'

Scorpio could not shed the feeling of depression that gripped him over breakfast. Blankly he stared at the three platinum and six gold discs which lined the walls of the garden room. Almost hidden amongst the jungle of statuettes on the sideboard, his once cherished Oscar seemed now to be sneering at him. He downed his freshly squeezed orange juice and started to count out his morning dose of minerals and vitamins. As usual, Clancy sensed his master's mood and lay lovingly at his feet.

'It's no use,' sighed Scorpio, as Flo appeared at the door with the day's mail and diary.

'Now then, dear,' she said soothingly, sitting down at the table and pouring herself a glass of juice from the heavy cut-crystal jug. 'You're doing very well, you know. Why don't you phone Marcia and invite her out to dinner this evening?'

'I'm afraid Marcia and I are history.' He spread butter on a slice of wholemeal toast then scraped most of it off again.

'What a shame. She seemed like such a nice girl.'

Scorpio looked decidedly unconcerned. 'It was getting heavy – the old "marry me or else" routine. I told her the "or else" suited me fine and that she could keep the Lagonda.'

'I'm sorry.'

'I'm not. Anyway, Clancy didn't take to her and I reckon he knows best.'

Cocking his ear at the sound of his name, the mongrel barked his agreement.

Scorpio finished his balanced and calorie-counted breakfast whilst Flo went through the mail. 'We'd better get a move on,' she said, sorting the various missives into piles. If she was trying to sound brisk and businesslike, it was only for her dear boy's sake. When he fell into one of these moods, it was imperative to keep him busy. The continuing avalanche of fan mail was dealt with by his publicist, but there was still a host of invitations, requests and begging letters to be answered every day. Flo and Scorpio had developed a simple routine. A 'yes' and a cheque to most of the requests, a 'no' to the invitations.

Worried, she glanced up at him briefly. Poor darling, for all the multi-millions, he still looked so very lost. There had been a time when peace, quiet and solitude were necessary for his rehabilitation, but now, in his efforts to avoid temptation, she felt Scorpio was in danger of becoming a recluse. He rarely went out in public and large groups of people unnerved him. For a man who had gloried in performing to packed concert arenas all over the world, it was an incredible transformation.

Flo felt her gentle Celtic heart melt as she watched him downing his kelp. She could only guess how he must miss the roar of the crowd and the buzz of life at centre stage. To his credit, he had done everything he could to obviate the boredom of retirement. Since kicking his assorted addictions, he had tried everything – psychoanalysis, yoga, meditation, Alexander technique, Rolfing, EST – everything to keep the demons of destruction at bay. His love of art and antiques had never wavered, not even during his darkest moments, and recently he had become concerned in environmental issues. Flo was happy to promote his every interest, however wacky. The vacuum left by Scorpio's music had to be filled. It was his only hope of salvation.

'There's another one here from that dreadful woman!' she said, determined to cheer him up. Scorpio rewarded her efforts with a watery smile.

'Well, that don't narrow down the field a whole lot,' he replied, in a passable Clint Eastwood drawl.

'Mrs Sammy Sandton – you remember, Sandton's, the high-street jewellery people?'

Scorpio groaned. 'Oh, no, not her. What does she want this time?'

Flo readjusted the half-moon spectacles on the end of her nose. 'Well, it's an invitation to sing at her gala dinner for Dyslexic Aborigines—'

'Give me strength . . .'

That was enough. Flo marked 'NO' in large red capitals across the formal invitation. 'There's also a hand-written letter attached.'

'Go on,' urged Scorpio, skittishly. 'Mrs S is always good for a laugh.' Flo cleared her throat and began.

'"Dear Scorpio,
I hope you do not mind me writing to you like this but, at last we have something in common. It has arrived at my cognisance that our interior designer, Yves, whom is currently engaged in the amelioration of our Bishops Avenue establishment, was implicated in your recent refurbishments. I have always thought that design is so very important, having once myself personally been chief *vitrine* display *artiste* in Sandton's Oxford Street Branch."'

Scorpio's eyes moved heavenwards. Flo struggled not to giggle.

'"My husband, Sammy, and I would love you to come to dinner to see what Yves is creating *chez nous*. Perhaps you could communicate some dates which might be of ultimate convenience to you.
   Yours sincerely,
   Daphne Sandton."'

Flo looked up to find a massive grin illuminating Scorpio's face. 'Send the Dyslexic Aborigines a grand from me.'

'And Mrs Sandton?'

'Tell Mrs Sandton I'm out of the country and, in any case, I'm fasting!'

By the time they had ploughed through the heaps of letters, Scorpio was sunny again. Today's mail bag had cost him over fifteen thousand pounds but giving, at least, made him feel useful.

'One final thing,' said Flo, attaching a yellow sticker with a scribbled 'Send £2000' to the corner of a 'Save the Rainforest' request. 'It's from the Royal College of Art, an invitation to their degree exhibition in July.'

Unsure of his reaction, she had deliberately left this one until last. A student at the Royal College in the sixties, Scorpio had never managed to finish the course. At the time, it hardly seemed to matter, swept up as he was in the glamour and glitz of the pop world. Recently, however, he had taken to brooding over past mistakes and failures. Flo knew that dropping out of college featured high on Scorpio's list of 'cock-ups'. Having worked so hard to raise his spirits, she prayed this would not now send them plummeting.

For what seemed like an eternity, Scorpio turned the suggestion over in his mind.

'Do you know what,' he said at last, 'I think I'd like that. Young artists, new talent – yes, it could be very interesting.'

Delighted, Flo made a note in his diary before tidying her sheaves of paper into various plastic trays. She looked at her watch. A solid gold Gautier and a source of constant joy, it had been a Christmas present from Scorpio. 'Five to ten,' she said, picking up her work. 'The lads will soon be here. I'll tell Bridget to organize coffee for them and a pot of herbal tea for you.'

'Herbal tea!' Scorpio smiled and shook his head wistfully. 'And to think I'm so clean nowadays I even get high on that!'

It was a case, as the lads agreed, of the mountains coming to Muhammad. Four times a year, they were invited to see Scorpio at whichever of his four houses he happened to be in at the time. From May to September, it was usually the Sussex mansion, October to January, the villa in Cap Ferrat. Depending on the big man's mood, February to April might mean Aspen or Gstaad. The summonses arrived as regular as clockwork and no one with an eye to business had ever been known to turn one down.

Scorpio welcomed his guests warmly and made a point of dispensing the coffee himself. Mike Lang, the rock star's accountant for over twenty years, glanced anxiously across at him and waited for the spill. This time there was none. The big man, to his eternal credit, had shaken off the shakes. Mike wandered around the newly revamped drawing room and declared himself impressed. On the walls, the Renoir, Chagall, Poliakoff and Klein were appreciating by the day. Scorpio had always gambled that fine art would out-perform blue chip. Cunningly hung, Italian giltwood mirrors reflected the delicate Savonnerie carpet on the floor. Mike sipped his coffee contentedly. He had been a bright boy, old Scorpio, at least as regards his art investments. Even in the days when he was high as a kite, he had never once made a mistake.

On the mantelpiece, above a raging log fire, Scorpio's latest acquisition chimed ten. Signed by Jean Gautier, the bronze musical clock was his pride and joy in a large and enviable collection. 'Don't you just love it?' asked Scorpio, entranced.

'It explains one hefty withdrawal I was meaning to ask you about.'

'Come on, Mike, loosen up, money's made for spending.'

The accountant winced. This was not a philosophy his client's pension fund managers could always be made to agree on. He decided to change the subject. 'Anyway, Scorpio, the place is looking fabulous. I suppose that interior design bloke must have taken you to the cleaners.'

Scorpio shook his head. 'Yves? I kicked that charlatan out after forty-eight hours. What a Hottentot! A real cream leather and tiger skin man.'

'Just like a certain flat I seem to recall in Clapham.'

Scorpio's eyes twinkled at the recollection. 'Hell, that's like an age ago.'

'It sure does. Remember that moth-eaten old tiger skin of yours? There was so much vertical jogging on that poor beast, we wore straight through him to the floorboards!'

Scorpio struggled to keep a straight face. 'Humping ourselves senseless on an endangered species! What right-off bastards we were.' Turning, he caught sight of his reflection, slim, fit and clean-shaven in the mirror. He still felt like an imposter. Suddenly he laughed out loud.

> 'Mirror, mirror, on the wall,
> Was *I* the shit who had a ball?'

'Scorpio, the catalogue you wanted.' Small, neat and dapper, Alexander Duchène had acted as Scorpio's art advisor for fifteen years or more.

'Don't tempt him,' tutted Mike, alarmed at the size of the tome. 'His insurance premium is bad enough already.'

Alexander sniffed loudly. 'What is an insurance premium to a man of profound susceptibilities?'

'Thanks.' Scorpio flicked through the pages. 'There are a few Gautier pieces coming up I'd really like to bid for.'

Mike's face turned positively pale. 'But this place is a museum already. The way the economy is going nowadays, people who can stay liquid.'

Abner Levy, Scorpio's agent, joined them by the fire. Just returned from Barbados, he found May in England decidedly chilly. 'It's OK,' he said, reaching up to pat his client on the shoulder. At five feet seven, Abner stood somewhere around the level of Scorpio's armpit. 'You want clocks, you buy clocks. That re-release deal I've just done will slay you. Fifty million dollars guaranteed and if you could see your way to a few promotional concerts . . .'

The look on Scorpio's face stopped him in his tracks. Abner shuffled closer to the fire and warmed his chubby hands. 'What the hell! It was worth a try. Who gets anywhere in this life by never asking questions?'

Admiring the Brancusi head on the console, Miranda Bentley could not help overhearing the conversation. Terrifyingly well educated and at home in six languages (including, as Abner had once remarked, fluent hype and bullshit), Miranda was Scorpio's latest in a long line of publicists and press agents. She owed her contract with Scorpio to Abner and felt obliged to help him out.

'He's right, you know, Scorpio,' she said, wafting across to the group. 'Your fans are desperate to see you again.'

'Just one concert,' piped up Abner, fortified by the support of this tall, raven-haired beauty. 'Let's say Wembley – you used to love playing Wembley.'

'A few in-depth interviews for the heavies – I guarantee sympathetic coverage – and a couple of "I've been to hell and back" sessions with the tabloids. That's all you'll need to do. Then the hype feeds off itself.'

'It'll triple your record sales,' urged Abner.

'I could get Snowdon to do the shots.'

Scorpio brought his fist down hard on the mantelpiece. Abner jumped almost as high as the musical clock.

'How many times do I have to tell you people?' Scorpio's voice was ominously quiet. 'Miranda, I pay you to keep me *out* of the papers, not to get me *in* them. The last thing I need is that bloody rat pack sniffing around again, dabbling their mucky fingers into the stuff of my soul. Do I make myself quite clear?'

Miranda wiggled her toes in her hand-made Italian shoes. 'I'm sorry.'

'And, Abner, I'm not interested in the geriatric circuit. You won't catch me rocking around in a corset and a rug . . .'

'But, Scorpio, that's just it! You're in great shape. You even got your own hair.'

Scorpio tried glaring at him, then melted. It was impossible not to admire the man's tenacity. 'Look,' he said more gently. 'I know you're the best in the business and I'm grateful for what you've done. But please, no more talk of live performances. I just can't face the idea.'

There was an embarrassed silence while the housekeeper cleared away the coffee-cups.

'I reckon it's time to get down to business.' Scorpio ushered the group into the dining room. 'You're all very busy people and I don't want to detain you too long.'

Bright and beautiful with yellow silk striped wallpaper and a large eighteenth-century English table, the dining room looked rarely used. Nowadays, Scorpio hardly ever entertained at home and full-scale parties were a thing of the past. Mike took his seat at Scorpio's right hand. For all its style and elegance, he thought, the entire house was curiously soulless. It was all a far and heartrending cry from the long-gone days of Clapham. He handed Scorpio a typed agenda and hoped his old mate was happy.

The items of the agenda were dispatched within the hour. Dollar volumes, grosses, territories, unit sales, no detail of his two-hundred-million-pound fortune was too abstruse for Scorpio's agile mind. Mike marvelled at his client's grasp of finance, investment, and planning. The former rock star was a natural. It seemed he knew instinctively when and where to make a move. His pension manager gasped as he explained how, the previous month, he had turned a cool half million in some arcane futures deal. With a clear head and time to think, he was now making more money than ever. Abner scribbled a few share tips on the back of his agenda. Perhaps that was the root of the problem, he mused. There was no real motivation now to sing.

Flo sidled silently into the room and whispered in Scorpio's ear, 'Your tennis coach is waiting outside. Shall I tell him you've cancelled out?'

Around the table a dozen faces looked on anxiously. Cohorts of the Scorpio empire, they prayed the big man was satisfied with their efforts on his behalf. Working for him was a sinecure none of them could afford to lose. His success had bought their houses and their cars. It had put their children through public school. It paid their alimony.

'Tell him I'll be with him in fifteen minutes.' Scorpio flashed her an impish grin. 'Perhaps, in the meantime, you'd like to practise your double back-hand on him. I'm told you're a bit of a demon.'

'Away with you now,' said Flo, and marched briskly off to the tennis court.

'I think that just about wraps it up, doesn't it?' Scorpio smiled, scanning the room. No one moved a muscle. 'In that case, I'd like to thank you all for your continued diligence and wish you a safe journey home.'

The sigh of relief was almost audible. Around the table, people began piling notes and documents back into their expensive briefcases. Abner Levy prevaricated for a while but finally elected to say nothing. He had spoken to his old friend, Serge Birnbaum, on the phone this morning, and the idea was interesting. All the same, it was clear that Scorpio was still out of bounds and even Abner knew when to stop pushing.

After two hours of strenuous tennis and a lunch of chicken and salad, Scorpio retired to his study to leaf through his latest catalogue. He gave Flo instructions to hold all calls before relaxing into the squelchy comfort of his favourite armchair. Within minutes he was miles and centuries away. He uncapped his fountain pen and began to mark the lots in which he was interested. A gold *cloisonné* enamel and jewelled box by Gautier. That would look wonderful on his dressing table. A diamond, pearl, black onyx and opal pendant necklace, also by Gautier. His niece's twenty-first was coming up and this was far too beautiful to miss.

Overcome by a sudden wave of loneliness, he snapped the catalogue shut. Perhaps if he had married and had children, things might have turned out better. As ever, his thoughts turned to Rosemary – the one girl out of the countless hundreds he had genuinely loved and cared for. Quiet, gentle and bookish, she had been in a different league from the hordes of groupies who had constantly besieged him. Desperate to maintain his hard-earned wild-boy image, the PR people had warned against marriage. Too bourgeois, they had argued, the fans would never wear it. It was another lost opportunity for which Scorpio now berated himself. Rosemary had grown tired of waiting and, one day, said goodbye.

The catalogue slipped from his lap, hit the floor and fell open at one page. Scorpio stared down at the fabulous Gautier necklace which seemed to be gleaming up at him. Created for the Maharajah Scindiah in 1875, it was composed of ten rows of creamy baroque pearls. Its clasp, a large oval diamond, was set in platinum and surrounded by an openwork motif of rose-cut diamonds and pearls. A thing of beauty, a joy for ever. Scorpio closed his eyes. How much of his music would survive the test of time? None, he reckoned, and rightly so. Music of its time, it had been instant and disposable. Free love, fast food, a quick buck – those were the values it had shared. He could feel the depression setting in again, like a big black rain-bearing cloud. He opened his eyes to find the Maharajah's diamond twinkling knowingly at him. Hundreds of thousands of years old; it seemed to know it would continue until the very end of time. Scorpio marked the necklace with a cross. Such beauty was a glimpse of true immortality. If only he had someone to share such beauty with.

CHAPTER SIXTEEN

By the time July breezed along, Laura was feeling quietly confident. In the two months since her return from the Frontier, her work had taken on a fresh enthusiasm, her ideas a new and naturalistic approach. Some of Maisie's diamonds ('the relative's rocks', as she affectionately referred to them) had been transformed into a glorious snow leopard brooch. Studded with the Peshawar rubies and sapphires, a fabulous, prowling tiger of yellow gold now stalked her drawing room. After the countless hours at her work-bench, she should have been exhausted, but nothing was further from the truth. As she assured an ever-anxious Maisie every time they spoke, she had never felt so well and happy, so totally revitalized.

As the degree exhibition drew closer, her social life contracted dramatically. The time not devoted to college was spent at home, studying hard and waiting for Sharif's calls. He rang whenever he could, the operator-assisted line hiccuping with unearthly bleeps and crackles. Serge, it transpired, had done a marvellous job in raising additional funds and now his artistic contribution to the film was proving equally useful. Relieved of financial pressures, Sharif was sounding more and more optimistic. Two days before the exhibition he called her, full of the latest developments.

'I've written in this new character called Meera,' he enthused. 'She was Serge's idea to start with. He reckoned Mustaq ought to be passionately in love with someone and we should give him a fiancée.'

Curled up on the sofa, a warm summer breeze wafting in

through the french windows, Laura lay sketching Sharif's fine strong face.

'At first I couldn't see it,' he continued, 'but, in the end, he convinced me he was right.'

'Sounds like good old Serge.' Lovingly she began to trace Sharif's extraordinary eyes.

'We've filmed the explosion scenes – I saw rushes this morning. They really look terrific.'

A sudden twinge gripped the pit of Laura's stomach. 'I hope you used a stand-in.'

'No need to.' His tone was dismissive. 'Serge took care of everything. I was never in any danger.'

She felt the twinge growing stronger. 'And now?'

'Now we'll slot in the relationship between Mustaq and Meera. I've written this wonderful love scene . . .'

'I see.' Now the twinge was more acute, a small sharp stiletto twisting in a wound.

'Then the scene after Meera's family have forced her to dump our hero. It's great stuff, the best I've come up with so far. Even Serge says he cried when he read it.'

'Doomed love – it seems to be your forte!' Thousands of miles away, he failed to catch the caustic edge in her voice.

'And Serge found the most beautiful actress to play Meera,' he rambled on, elated. 'She's wonderful – everyone adores her! Serge says this is the love story that will *really* make the film.'

By now, the twinge in her stomach had become an unbearable pain. 'Serge says, Serge says, Serge says! I'm sick to death of Serge. I wish I'd never put you two together.' A moment's silence followed.

When, at last, Sharif spoke, he sounded quite taken aback. 'Whatever's the matter with you?'

Immediately, she felt ashamed by the vehemence of her outburst. 'I'm tired,' she lied, trying to choke back the tears. And how about jealous, she asked herself, with anxious and lonely thrown in?

'Look,' his voice unguent, velvety, 'I know you've been working hard – we both have – but I'll soon be back in London. I think it's time we had a serious talk.'

She sniffed and wiped her nose. Tears and tantrums, she knew she was being ridiculously possessive. Such histrionics were guaranteed to put any man off. 'I'm sorry.' The words jumped out. 'I was being stupid, that's all. It must be exhibition nerves. I hadn't realized I was so uptight.'

The silence which followed seemed interminable. She thought he might even have put the phone down. 'Sharif, Sharif?' Her voice was desperate. 'Are you still there?'

'Yes, of course I am.' His tone was calm and measured, the joyous exuberance gone. 'Don't apologize. I've tried not to say anything, but I'm feeling on edge myself. I can't stop thinking about . . .'

She gripped the receiver so hard that her fingernails bit into her palm. Serge and his wonderful bloody actress! She could hardly bear to listen to what he was struggling to admit.

'. . . about you.'

She felt the pain dissolve like a shard of ice in fire. Her sketch pad fell to the floor. 'Do you really mean that?'

His words reverberated back. 'On my honour.'

Caught in a sudden shaft of sunlight, the jewel-studded tiger on her table burst into multicoloured flame. There was so much in her heart that she wanted to say, but the telephone seemed far too impersonal. She resolved to wait until she saw him again. She could wait for a long time now. 'Give my regards to Serge,' she said, 'and be sure to take care of yourself.'

The degree exhibition of the Royal College of Art was the high spot of the academic year. For its graduating students, it provided a unique opportunity to impress doting parents and, more important still, prospective employers. Determined to lend moral support, Gaston and Maisie arrived in London the day before the event and checked in at the Berkeley. Quiet and discreet, despite its proximity to the hubbub of Knightsbridge, the Berkeley had always been Gaston's favourite London retreat. A recent convert from the Connaught, Maisie was delighted with the unobtrusive service and the large indoor swimming pool at the top of the building. Taking an early morning dip on her previous visit, she had been only mildly surprised to find Dustin Hoffman and Henry Kissinger swimming alongside one another. As Gaston maintained, the Berkeley was for the *truly* famous, for those who no longer sought publicity.

'You're quite sure you don't want to join us for dinner?' Just ensconced in her luxurious, lemon-wallpapered suite, Maisie was already on the phone to Laura.

'No, thanks all the same. I'll phone Papa and explain, but I need to be on my own tonight.'

'You sure you're OK?' probed Maisie. Oddly serene and tranquil, Laura sounded as if she might have OD'd on tranquillizers.

'Never felt better. How about you?'

'We'll talk about me tomorrow when *your* big day is over.'

'You're not mad at me for jacking out this evening?'

'Of course not,' Maisie forced a smile. 'It gives Gaston and me the chance to talk about you behind your back.'

'You rats!' Laura laughed, such a joyous, uninhibited, carefree laugh that Maisie felt relieved.

'Get yourself a good night's rest tonight,' she ordered, 'and slay them all tomorrow.'

Maisie lay back on the king-sized bed and stared vaguely up at the ceiling. After some minutes, she reached across to pick up the phone again, and booked dinner for two at eight. Some life, she mused, resuming her supine position. Dinner with her father-in-law and another night on her own in a large, lonely bed. There had to be more for her than this. She had not seen Charles in weeks. He was away on business, or so he said, but goodness knows what he was really up to. After the brief respite following her accident, their relationship had sunk back into the doldrums once again. Her head lolled back on to the snowy softness of the pillow. She was sick of conning herself. Charles was a complete and utter bastard and there was no longer any point in pretending otherwise. Stretching out, she kicked off her high-heeled shoes. Attractive and horribly expensive, they had been killing her all day. She twiddled her liberated toes with pleasure.

'What a relief!' She sighed out loud to herself and suddenly began to smile.

The next morning, Laura got up early, dressed and, after a snatched breakfast of Ryvita and tea, hurried off to college. It was the sort of cloudless summer's morning which, in England, heralds a scorching afternoon. Making her way through Kensington Gardens and down towards Kensington Gore, she stopped briefly to watch a few young children sailing their boats on the pond. The softest of breezes, barely a ripple on the surface. Across the water, the children's laughter seemed muffled, buffered by an atmosphere of stillness and of heat. She moved on, a spring in her step, wondering whether such carefree joy was seemly on this her day of reckoning. She had barely slept a wink all night, and yet she felt fresh and invigorated, ready to conquer the world. A squirrel scuttled past, his puffball tail wafting after him like a cloud of grey-white gossamer. Wandering on, she bent to pick a buttercup, glistening like a small golden button on a dark green loden coat.

'He loves me, he loves me not.' One by one she pulled off the petals, watching as, slowly, they swirled and whirled to the ground. 'He loves me.' The last petal fluttered upwards, merging with the light. Suddenly she began to sing, a folk song she had learned long ago as a child.

> 'Sur le pont
> D'Avignon,
> On y danse
> On y danse . . .'

The sun felt deliciously warm on her face. She left the gardens, crossed the road, and continued on to college.

Confident though she was, Laura had never expected the amount of fuss her pieces generated. Journalists from *Vogue*, *Harpers & Queen* and *Elle* were all in raptures, busily scribbling notes on this exciting new talent and making arrangements for 'major colour features'. The man from *Connoisseur* magazine was equally impressed and spent a good hour interviewing her about her training, work and background. Laura's friend Jenny winked as she passed and gave the thumbs-up sign. It was common knowledge in class: *Vogue* and *Harpers* were good for the ego, but *Connoisseur* meant real commissions.

Laura was so busy talking that she failed to notice the strange hush that had descended on the hall. 'And so you see,' she continued, oblivious, 'I decided to use the sugilite as an experiment with colour . . .' Her voice trailed off. The journalist, she realized, was no longer hanging on her every word. Instead his eyes were focused on the tall, elegant figure which had suddenly appeared beside him.

'I do apologize,' said the newcomer, 'I didn't mean to interrupt.'

Laura looked up to find a kind, well-worn face smiling down at her. She racked her brains. The man looked vaguely familiar, but she was damned if she knew where she had seen him before. Well-spoken and expensively turned out in an Alan Flusser suit and what looked like an MCC egg-and-bacon-striped tie, he could have been a successful barrister or a merchant banker. Certainly, she decided, sizing him up, some pillar or other of the Establishment.

'Scorpio.' The whisper became a murmur and the murmur graduated into a buzz. Sensing a scoop, every one of the journalists present scuttled across to where the reclusive rock star was standing.

'Sorry.' A large burly man with a squashed nose and a loud check jacket materialized from nowhere. 'The gentleman ain't here to give interviews. This is a private visit. Now, ladies and gents, *if* you wouldn't mind . . .'

Scorpio's minder had arms the size of a small JVB and the body of a baby bulldozer. No strangers to the odd free-for-all at the Paris couture collections, the assembled group of journos nevertheless intuited defeat. They raced off to phone their respective offices, asking for reinforcements. Phalanxes of fearless paparazzi were immediately dispatched. However blurred, even a snap of Scorpio would be better than nothing. It had been months since the press had managed to catch him out and about.

Laura gulped as the hero of her adolescence stared awkwardly around him. Back home in Paris, somewhere at the bottom of her chest of drawers, lay an old scrapbook, yellowing with age, which chronicled Scorpio's every concert.

'I do hope I haven't ruined your interview.' He smiled, delightfully bashful.

Laura shrugged. 'He'll be back. They'll all be back. I suppose I ought to thank you for all the publicity.'

He picked up one of her visiting cards. There were stacks of them dotted around the table. 'Laura Jay,' he read, and popped the card into his breast pocket. 'From what I can see, you'll be getting quite enough of that without me.' Suddenly his eye fell on the scorpion bracelet shining bright against black velvet. He whistled appreciatively. 'Wow, this is beautiful! Do you mind if I take a closer look?'

She watched as he caressed the piece with his long, sinuous fingers. The nails on his left hand, she noticed, were clipped very short. Much longer, those on his right hand were neatly manicured.

'So,' she concluded, 'you still play the guitar?'

He looked up, clearly amused. 'Well spotted. Yes, I do, but only for myself nowadays.' He laid the scorpion across his sleeve. 'This is stunning. Is it for sale?'

She shook her head. 'Sorry, but a lady from the V and A saw it first thing this morning. She wants to buy it for the museum.'

He stroked the scorpion's glistening head before handing it back to its mistress. 'Too bad. Mind you, I don't suppose I could have worn it myself, at least not with my MCC tie.'

'Honey . . .'

Above the general noise and chatter, Laura could hear the familiar inflexions. She glanced over to see Maisie and her father making their way across the room

'We decided to come a little late,' explained Maisie, half glancing at the good-looking stranger towering beside Laura.

Deferring to the man with a quaint, old-fashioned bow, Gaston turned to embrace his daughter. 'Yes, we thought we'd better let you find your feet before we came along to pester you.'

Scorpio coughed, aware of his intrusion into what was obviously a family reunion.

'I have your card.' He extended his hand to Laura. 'I hope you won't mind if I give you a call. I'd like to commission something – a scorpion ring, perhaps.'

As he turned on his heel to leave, he was aware of the attractive American woman staring fixedly up at him. The thought struck him like a jab to the solar plexus. This dark-eyed, slightly sad-looking lady was the spitting image of Rosemary, the only girl he had ever loved.

'My dear young man,' interrupted Gaston. 'I'm afraid my daughter is forgetting her manners. Let me introduce myself.' He proffered his hand. 'Gaston Gautier.'

Scorpio's mouth fell open.

'And this is my daughter-in-law, Maisie Appleford Gautier.'

The rock star's gaze seemed to come to rest quite naturally on Maisie. Laura looked on, intrigued. They might have been old friends.

'I'm very honoured to meet you, sir,' said Scorpio, tearing his eyes away from Maisie. He gestured towards Laura's exhibits. 'Now I can see where the talent comes from.'

The slightest shadow crossed Gaston's face. 'It's from her mother's side as well.'

'Of course.' Scorpio shook his head, annoyed at his own absent-mindedness. 'The J line. I've got several of the earlier pieces in my collection.'

Laura noticed Maisie fumbling in her clutch bag. She retrieved nothing and snapped it shut again. Her hands were trembling.

'Everything OK?' asked Laura.

'Me? Sorry. Oh, yes, fine, thanks.' She blushed and then, noticing her scarf caught in the clip, opened the bag and dropped it. The entire contents – purse, mirror, comb, lipstick – tumbled out on to the floor. Immediately, Scorpio was down on his hands and knees, helping to collect them. Her face turned a deeper shade of crimson. 'Thanks. I'm so clumsy today. It must be nerves for Laura.'

Scorpio's fingers lingered gently on her palm as, one by one, he handed back the items. She slipped them back into her bag. 'I saw you once,' she blurted out. 'Live at Madison Square Garden. You were fantastic. It's years ago now, when I was first . . . when I was first married.' Her voice seemed to taper off.

To his surprise, Scorpio felt a warmth he had not experienced in years. Despite the obviously expensive blue silk dress, this woman exuded a sense of loneliness which he understood too well. A sudden thought crossed his mind. He turned to Gaston. 'I don't want to interfere with family plans, but are you doing anything this evening to celebrate your daughter's triumph?'

Laura noticed Maisie's eyes, bright with anticipation. She decided to pre-empt her father's almost inevitable response. 'No,' she said quickly, 'we don't have anything planned.'

Scorpio's anxious face creased into a beaming smile. 'Then perhaps you'd care to join me for dinner?'

Gaston looked dubious. 'I'm not sure—'

'We'd love to,' replied Laura.

Scorpio turned to Maisie. She was now studying the baize tablecloth as if it were the Bayeux tapestry. 'And, of course, if your husband's free . . .'

'He's not – I mean he's not here – in fact, he's away – in the Middle East, I think.' She ordered her mouth to stop talking. She knew she must sound an absolute fool.

'What a shame,' said Scorpio softly. He scribbled his address on the back of one of Laura's cards. 'Why don't we make it eight o'clock? I'll look forward to seeing you all.'

The Neanderthal minder, Bruce, sidled up to his employer. 'Hell's bells, Scorpio, there's such a bunch of bloody photographers out there, you'd think you was Princess Di. You want me to go and rough a couple up – just for old times' sake?'

Scorpio blanched. 'No! And with three convictions for GBH, the last thing you need to do right now is deck another journo.'

Bruce sighed, crestfallen. It was not the same since Scorpio had given up touring. In those days he had punched paparazzi all over the world. Now there was real job satisfaction!

On the main door, a few beleaguered janitors fought to stave off a growing barrage of photographers and press. Frustrated,

Bruce was now shadow-boxing. 'Look, boss,' he continued, a swift jab here, a quick upper-cut there, 'I been on the dog to the driver. He'll be round the back by now. You hack off quiet, like, and I'll hang around and distract the reptiles for a while.'

Scorpio raised his eyes to heaven in a gesture of utter hopelessness. 'Who needs it?' he groaned theatrically. 'A minder who needs minding.'

The racket outside had become so loud, it permeated the exhibition hall.

'Are you going to be all right?' asked Maisie, anxiously.

Scorpio touched her arm. Her eyes, he noticed, were large and limpid, her features as delicate as a child's. 'Don't worry. Bruce and I have been in worse scrapes than this and lived to tell the tale. I hope this nonsense hasn't changed your minds about dinner tonight . . .?'

'Of course not,' retorted Maisie so loudly that both Laura and Gaston stared.

'Good,' said Scorpio, grabbing his recalcitrant minder by the arm. 'Then I'll see you all this evening.'

In all her years as Scorpio's personal assistant, Flo had never heard her employer sounding so genuinely excited. Even on the car phone, his elation bubbled through. 'So you'll be four for dinner,' she repeated, pleasantly surprised. Try as she might, Flo could not remember the last time Scorpio had organized a formal dinner party. Nowadays, social acquaintances were never invited into the privacy of his home. Business contacts might be called in, but these were always dealt with on a purely professional basis.

'Yes. Could you go and talk to Bridget and organize a menu?'

'Of course, dear.' In her office, Flo sat scribbling short-hand notes on a pad.

'I want it to be something really special, I'm not sure what. I'll leave that up to you.'

Flo nodded happily as she wrote. Bridget, the housekeeper, would be thrilled at the news. A wonderful cook, she often felt frustrated at the frugal nature of Scorpio's daily diet. A dreary amalgam of cereal and salad, it was hardly designed to push her culinary potential to the full.

'And then would you go down into the wine cellar and pick out whatever's necessary. A few bottles of Clos du Mesnil to kick off with – I remember reading somewhere that it's Gaston Gautier's favourite fizz.'

Flo caught the hint of awe in Scorpio's voice. Gaston Gautier, she knew, was one of his all-time heroes. Few people were in on the secret, but Scorpio's last hit song, 'Those Beautiful Things', had been dedicated to Gaston.

'And flowers,' continued Scorpio, 'I want flowers every-where. Lots and lots of roses.'

'I'll ask the gardener—'

'No, I want this to be really special. Call in Moyses Stevens and get them to do the arrangements.'

'Any particular colours?' There was a moment's silence. Speeding along the motorway, he conjured up an image of kind, doleful eyes and a gentle, diffident smile.

'I should imagine pinks and mauves.' The phone line crackled as Scorpio's car and voice both disappeared into a tunnel.

It was a glorious July evening. A brief shower of rain had left the garden fresh and fragrant, the rose petals glistening in the mellow, early-evening light. By seven forty-five, Scorpio was feeling decidedly jumpy. For the umpteenth time, he checked the champagne which was chilling on ice in the drawing room. He wandered around the house, rearranging a flower here, an ornament there. He wound up all his clocks – it would not do to have Gaston insulted by an errant Gautier timepiece – and ensured that they chimed in harmony. He sat down and flicked through a Sotheby's catalogue, but it was no use. He was finding it impossible to concentrate.

Puzzled by his master's mood, Clancy became increasingly manic in his efforts to gain attention. He jumped up and licked Scorpio's face all over, impervious to the quantities of Eau Sauvage after-shave with which the object of his affections had doused himself.

At last, Scorpio gave up trying to ignore him. 'Come on, boy.' he said. 'Let's go and check on the trout in the lake.'

Clancy wagged his tail, ecstatic, and followed him into the garden. The smells of wondrous cooking emanated from an open kitchen window. Scorpio inhaled them deeply, wishing the knots in his stomach would disappear and leave room for what was to come. He caught sight of Bridget, bustling happily about her kitchen. Pleased with her employer's initial interest, the old housekeeper had soon grown tired of his interminable queries and finally ordered him out from under her feet.

He picked up a fluorescent orange ball and flung it high into the air. With a leap and a yelp, Clancy was after it, racing down towards the pond, twisting and turning in the air like some madcap canine Maradona. Over in the distance, the slightest of breezes played across a field of brilliant yellow rape. Scorpio watched, spellbound, as it rose and fell, a sea of liquid gold. Panting, Clancy returned with the ball and, looking up adoringly, waited to be stroked.

'Good dog!' He gave the dog an affectionate pat and threw the ball again.

As the car purred up the long, tree-lined driveway, the clock on the village church chimed eight. Leaving a bewildered Clancy staring after him, Scorpio sprinted across the lawn to welcome his guests. Both Maisie and Gaston were in high spirits, thrilled with the amount of praise that had been lavished on their protégée's work. Laura, by contrast, looked a little tired, happy yet quite obviously drained after the excitement of the day.

'I'm so pleased you could make it.' Scorpio took Maisie by the arm. He was just about to usher everyone towards the house when Clancy bounded across. Miffed at his exclusion from this unexpected party, he leapt up against his master's back and sent him flying across the driveway.

'For God's sake!' Scorpio fell heavily on to the gravel, 'You mad—' He picked himself up, expecting the usual flurry of slobbering canine kisses, but for once none came. Clancy, it appeared, had discovered a new object for his unbounded adulation. Forelegs on her shoulders, the animal was now nuzzled up to Maisie's neck, busily licking her chin.

'Get down at once,' Scorpio ordered. He turned apologetically to Maisie. 'I just can't believe it – he never takes to strangers.'

'It's OK, he isn't bothering me.' She patted the dog on the head. 'In fact, I think he's wonderful – aren't you, boy?'

It was all Scorpio could do to stop a besotted Clancy from following her into the house. She looked prettier than ever, he thought, almost ethereal in her pink and mauve silk dress. Coming into the entrance hall, she stopped to admire the huge display of roses on the table. 'Pink and mauve,' Scorpio smiled. He chose a particularly pretty pink one from the vase and handed it to her. 'My very favourite colours.'

'Mine too,' she murmured softly and brought the velvet petals to her lips.

To Scorpio's enormous relief, Bridget had excelled herself. The dinner of asparagus, saddle of lamb and summer pudding was truly exquisite and the wine and conversation flowed. After some prompting and rather more Château Latour, Gaston relaxed and began to regale the party with tales of the early Maison Gautier. High on a mixture of good company and simple Perrier water, Scorpio listened, awestruck.

Stories of emperors, queens and courtesans – Gaston spanned centuries of history and gossip with effortless eloquence and wit. 'Lanthèlme,' he continued, sipping his wine, 'now she was one of the most beautiful courtesans of the Naughty Nineties.'

After a few glasses of champagne, Laura was looking more perky. 'Wasn't she the one who fell overboard into the Rhine?'

'Or jumped,' chipped in Scorpio, eager to impress. 'In fact there was even talk of foul play at the time. The rumour was that her lover was desperate to get rid of her.'

Gaston shrugged. 'It was never proved. Myself, I always reckoned it was simply the suicide of an unhappy woman. When her lover took up with someone else, she was utterly distraught.'

Scorpio could hardly contain himself. 'Do you know, I bought something of hers just recently. A gold and black enamel vanity case. It's a Gautier, of course.'

'Would you mind if I took a turn in the garden?' The blood had suddenly drained from Maisie's cheeks. She was trembling like a leaf. 'I'm afraid I'm feeling rather dizzy. It must be all the wine.'

Scorpio was on his feet at once. He helped Maisie from her chair. In seconds, Gaston was also at her side. 'I'll come with you,' he said.

Pipped at the post, Scorpio looked rather glum. He put his hand over Maisie's. 'But I'd like . . .'

She shook her head, embarrassed at all the fuss. 'A few minutes of fresh air, and I'll be perfectly fine. Please Scorpio, don't break up the party on my account. Stay here and talk to Laura. She's been jotting down designs for you all the way from London.'

Defeated, he watched as Maisie took Gaston's arm and wandered out into the garden. Once they were safely out of earshot, he poured Laura another glass of wine. She was feeling quite giddy and garrulous as she leaned forward across the table. 'She's got to dump that bastard.'

Scorpio looked taken aback. 'You mean your brother?'

'My *half*-brother. What a shit! He does nothing but cheat on her and spend her money. The whole thing's wearing her down.'

A small inner voice told him that this was none of his business. He was used to ignoring such voices. 'Why doesn't she just divorce him?'

She began to fold her starched napkin into a flower. 'She thinks about it, then vacillates. She's been vacillating now for as long as I can remember. Maisie makes Hamlet look like Indiana Jones.'

His brow puckered into a frown. 'They say a bad relationship is like a drug addiction. You know it's probably killing you but it's difficult to kick.' He paused, then smiled, slightly sheepishly. 'Would you mind if I invited her out to dinner?'

Laura felt an uncontrollable urge to laugh. The whole notion was too ridiculous! Scorpio, the legendary tearaway, the notorious womanizer, asking for her permission to invite Maisie out on a date. 'I'd count it a personal favour,' she giggled, 'and, for that matter, so would Papa.'

The meniscus of Laura's wine had slithered down to the bottom of her glass. As he topped it up again, Scorpio caught sight of the notepad, jutting out of her hand-bag. 'My scorpion ring! Do you mind if I take a look?'

Quickly she shoved the pad back into her bag. 'Yes, I do! These designs aren't good enough yet. For you, I need to do something spectacular.'

'I only hope I can afford it.'

She seemed suddenly to sober up. 'I can tell you here and now, Scorpio, this ring will not cost you a penny.'

'Don't be so daft. I'm a rich man and you're a struggling artist. As a matter of principle, I must insist on you ripping me off.'

'Not one penny.' She mouthed the words very slowly.

'Something else then? A swap?'

She gave a slightly wobbly nod. 'I'll swap you for a song.'

'A song? But I haven't written—'

'Sssh.' The effects of the alcohol were seeping through again. 'I want you to write a song for me – or, at least, for a friend of mine.'

Scorpio stared longingly at the bottle of Château Latour, then reverted to his water. 'I'm sorry, I'd really like to help but I haven't written anything since . . .'

'Since you dried out?'

A shaft of pain shot across his face. 'Yes. I don't know what it is. I guess I'm frightened of failure. Before, nothing bothered me. I was too out of it to give a toss. But now it's different. Now I'm not sure I can come up with the goods.'

In a flash of semi-inebriated insight, Laura saw the small, insecure and desperate child who was camouflaged as Scorpio. Reaching out, she caught his hand and held it tight in hers. It was too late, perhaps, to save her mother. Caroline, it seemed, had lost the will to fight. Scorpio, however, was a different

185

proposition. Freed from the demons of drugs and drink, he had now to start a new life, believing in himself. 'Please,' she begged, 'will you at least let me tell you why we need it?'

She looked so beautiful in the candlelight, so earnest and so young. 'You strike a hard bargain,' he said wistfully, 'but how can I resist?'

When Maisie and Gaston returned, some fifteen minutes later, Laura was still going strong. A tale of honour and love, of chivalry and courage, the script of *Tor* came tumbling out with barely a pause for breath. 'And then Serge Birnbaum—'

'Serge Birnbaum?' interrupted Scorpio. The penny suddenly dropped. 'So that's why the old devil's been after me. He's working on this film as well.'

'Sure, and he's the best there is. So are you.' Laura's voice was suddenly weary. She had done everything she could to win him over. Now, at the end of a long hard day, she felt completely drained.

'Please.' Maisie's voice was soft and gentle, almost inaudible. 'Please, Scorpio. You'd attract so much publicity to the venture. You could make this film for them.'

For a second, he stared at her. 'What could any man do against the pair of you?'

Laura let out a whoop of joy and flung her arms around his neck. 'Wait till I tell Sharif!' she cried. 'This is the best news I've had all day!'

Embarrassed, Scorpio began to brush down his ever so slightly ruffled coat. 'I'm not guaranteeing fireworks,' he added cautiously. 'It's been a long, long time.'

The rest of the evening sped by. Lost in admiration at Scorpio's collection, no one even heard as a car rolled off down the drive. Oblivious of time, it was well past one o'clock when the Gautier clan made its farewells and meandered slowly back to London. Before long, Laura was asleep in the back, snoring contentedly. Bright-eyed and light-headed, Maisie could not stop herself from chattering. Gaston smiled contentedly. He had never heard his daughter-in-law sounding quite so adolescent. He decided it suited her.

After dropping off a sleepy Laura, they made their way back

to a still and silent Berkeley. Still wide awake, Maisie wandered around her suite, humming merrily to herself. Suddenly she noticed a small parcel, illuminated by the lamp at the side of her bed. Her fingers trembled as she unwrapped it. The gold and black enamel case which had once belonged to Lanthèlme glistened in the lamplight. Nervously, she flicked open the lid. Inside were two rose petals, one pink, one mauve, and a message which read 'Don't jump.'

CHAPTER SEVENTEEN

It was the day Daphne Stanton had been waiting for, the culmination of twenty years of relentless social climbing. Even now, she could barely believe her luck. A five-page, full-colour, no-depth piece in *Right-ho!* magazine. It was everything she had ever dreamt of. Already, she hoped, there would be mutterings of envy amongst the ladies of her Save the Planet Gala Ball Committee. 'Mrs Sammy Sandton shows us around her lovely home' – she could already see the headline. The time, the effort, the fortune spent on Le Bijou, at last, everything was worth it. As she teased her hair in the mirror, her sun-bed bronzed face smiled back at her. Mrs Sammy Sandton had finally arrived.

Photographer in tow, Flick Harrison drove slowly up the Sandtons' half-mile drive. Green and luxuriant, the lawn had been watered and weeded to unnatural perfection. On either side of the pink-gravelled driveway, the hedges had been clipped and shorn into variegated animal shapes, a duck, a dog, a giraffe and an elephant. Flick shuddered and drove on. Nothing, she noticed, had been left either to Mother Nature or to chance. Pruned and trained, the roses grew obediently around a green and white gazebo. With the help of a cunningly concealed pump, an artificial waterfall tumbled into a man-made moss and lily pond. Even the carefully distressed stone fountains seemed to tinkle in coerced harmony.

After the garden, the house came as no surprise. 'Christ,' gasped Sid, hauling his shoulder-bag of photographic equipment out of the boot. '*Gone With The Wind* meets *Dallas*. Did you ever see such a shambles?' He checked his light meter and took a few preliminary shots.

Stubbing out her cigarette in an already overflowing ash-tray, Flick stared at the amalgam of colonnades and porticoes and low-rise ranch-style extensions. 'I thought we'd seen it all with what's-his-name.' She sighed. 'You remember, that heavyweight boxer.'

'You mean the swirly-carpet bloke?'

'That's the one.' She shuddered at the recollection of pinks and aquas. 'But this is a different league.'

Sid replaced his lens cap and put the camera back in his bag. 'Whatever you're thinking, just button your lip, and remember to keep a straight face. I'll shout you a beaker when we're through with Mrs S. Looks like we're both going to need one.'

Daphne had thought it more impressive to have her maid answer the door. 'Filipinos!' she groaned theatrically as Flick and Sid were ushered into the drawing room. 'Maria, I asked you for coffee – coffee and biscuits – bis-cuits – here, in the drawing room, ten minutes ago. Now go and fetch some for everyone, *tres personas*, or whatever. Go on, snap, snap. Off you go.'

She smiled apologetically as the young woman scurried out of the room. 'Staff nowadays – don't you just wish they'd learn the language?' She gestured expansively around the room. 'Miss Harrison, Mr Tyler, welcome to Le Bijou. I know you must have seen far grander places, but this is home to us.'

Flick adjusted the glasses she had worn to camouflage the previous night's hangover. 'It's, well . . . what can I say? It's a monument, Mrs Sandton.'

Daphne preened visibly as Flick rummaged around in her satchel, looking for her tape recorder.

'I think we'll start here, shall we?' Daphne sat down on one of the white leather sofas and arranged her fuchsia silk frock around her. 'Then I can tell you all about my charity work while you're having your cup of coffee.'

Ten minutes and two cups of coffee later, Daphne was still wittering on. 'You see,' she said, leaning forward earnestly so that Sid might catch the full extent of her cleavage. 'I'm a carer, I can't help it, I always have been. A carer and a conservationist. Prince Charles is so right, don't you think? And that mentor of his, yes, Sir Laurent van der Perrier, I've read all of his books, you know.'

Surreptitiously Flick turned off the recorder. 'If we could take a look around the house?'

'But of course.' Daphne sprang to her feet. 'It's just been renovated. My dear husband Sammy, he's such an artist, you know, being in the jewellery business, he told me to spare no expense. *Nihil nisi opprobium*, he said, that's Latin for *carte blanche*.' Daphne paused for a moment, delighted at her own *bon mot*.

Sid was beginning to feel decidedly nervous. Despite her sunglasses, he could see Flick's eyes staring fixedly at the ceiling. It was always a dangerous sign. 'A quick shot, Mrs Sandton,' he spluttered, fiddling with the focus. 'Over there, perhaps, on the zebra skin.'

'Or here, maybe,' suggested Flick, suddenly wreathed in smiles. 'Next to this fabulous ivory casket.'

Delighted, Daphne wafted across. 'It was made for me specially, you know, by the House of Gautier.'

'Fascinating!' Flick turned her recorder on again. 'Remind me, what was it you were saying a minute ago, about your work for conservation?'

Two hours later, Flick and Sid sat ruminating over a couple of Bloody Marys in Hampstead's Spaniards' Inn.

'And those spotlights on the paintings!' Sid added a dash of Worcestershire sauce to the viscous red mixture.

Ravenous, Flick was munching her way through a packet of salt and vinegar crisps. 'Oh, yes. We must make sure that no one misses the signature! I ask you. Why don't they just forget the picture and frame the cheque instead?'

'And the dining room!' he wheezed, lighting up another cigarette. 'Black and aubergine PVC!'

'With the ashes of Daphne's dad in an urn on the mantel-piece!' She rewound the tape to the appropriate juncture on her recorder.

'Father was a man near to God,' trilled Daphne's voice. 'A carer just like me.'

'Bollocks!' coughed Sid. 'We all knew Daphne's dad. The nearest he ever got to God was his string of crematoria.' He was laughing so hard, he nearly tumbled off his bar stool. 'A carer – oh, give me strength! Whenever there was a pile-up on the M1, old Reg would throw a party.'

Flick ordered another round of drinks and rubbed her blood-shot eyes. 'I can't do it, you know, Sid. I can't go on making the likes of Daphne Sandton into role models for the rest of us.'

He put a comforting arm around her shoulder. 'Course you can. It's only a bit of fun. Besides, these people do no harm.'

'They're harming *me!*' she snapped, more than slightly drunk. 'They're gnawing away at the few shreds of integrity I reckon I still might possess.'

'Come on, old girl, you're tired, that's all.'

'Sick and tired! Fed up to the back teeth with the Daphnes of life and all their bloody nonsense. I'm going into the office this afternoon and I'm handing in my notice.'

'But, Flick,' Sid's weather-beaten gargoyle face assumed an expression of concern, 'you can't . . . I mean . . . why don't you wait until . . .?'

'It's too late. My mind's made up. Besides, I've been offered a job on the *Gadfly*.'

'The new satirical magazine?'

Her long blonde fringe bounced up and down as she nodded enthusiastically.

'Are you taking it?'

'I most certainly am!' Jauntily she raised her glass. 'To the truth,' she said, suddenly quite serious, 'or, at least, to a better class of bullshit!'

By his wife's fifth call, even a besotted Sammy Sandton was finding it difficult to sound interested. 'Of course, sweetheart.' Seated in his office behind his large, green-leather topped desk, he rolled his eyes heavenward for the benefit of his sales director,

Ray. 'The photographs will be just great. The fuchsia frock? The one you bought in Paris? Of course it was right. You must've looked just smashing.'

He lit a cigarette and handed one to Ray. 'Save the Planet – no, of course I haven't forgotten the gala dinner.'

Ray winced. Another East-End boy, he had known Sammy all his life, and his father before that. Gala dinners and charity balls, old Sammy senior would be turning in his grave. Like Sammy's first wife, Elsie, he had been a pork pie and jellied eels fan. He would have had no time whatsoever for Daphne and all her high-falutin' nonsense.

Swivelling in his chair, Sammy caught the look of disapproval etched on Ray's lined and leathery face. He covered the receiver with his hand. 'Good PR,' he whispered apologetically. He had known his sales director far too long not to know what he was thinking.

Ray drew deep on his cigarette. 'Yeah, but as your old dad always used to say, "Does it pay the gin bill?"'

Sammy shuffled uncomfortably in his chair. 'See you this evening,' he said, doing his best to truncate the call.

Daphne, however, was not an easy woman to truncate. Her relentless high-pitched whine was still audible to Ray across the room. Sammy's voice grew quieter and quieter. 'Of course I do. Lots and lots. Oh, all right, then.'

Ray looked away as his employer planted a loud wet kiss upon the mouthpiece.

'Women!' Sammy smiled sheepishly as he replaced the receiver. He thought for a second and decided to take it off the hook again. Ray said nothing. There were times, disturbingly more frequent nowadays, when he thought Sammy was going soft in the head. Sammy senior had put his finger on it. 'When a bloke trades in the old model for a much younger wife, you can bet he's a goner in business.'

'The Sandton's Christmas catalogue,' ventured Ray, returning to safer ground. 'We've had some very competitive tenders. Myself, I reckon the crowd from Telford look the best.' He pushed a sheaf of papers across the desk. Immediately, Sammy took out his pen and started scribbling numbers on the back of his cigarette packet. Ray looked on approvingly. All the clever dicks he came across with their snazzy lap-top computers and their pocket calculators, when it came to business pure and simple there was not one of them who could hold a candle to Sammy and his fag packets.

'Get on to the Telford mob right away,' he ordered. 'Tell them to lop another ten per cent off these prices and the job is theirs.'

Ray looked horrified. 'But, Sammy, these prices are already rock bottom. They'll never—'

Sammy smiled a slow, humourless, flint-eyed smile. 'Of course they'll accept. We're in the middle of the biggest recession this country can remember. Let's thank God for discounts and good old Norman Lamont.'

Ray leaned back in his chair. Cold, calculating, heartless: this was the Sammy he knew and loved, the pre-Daphne-gala-dinner Sammy. He pulled another wodge of papers out of his briefcase and handed them to his employer. Sammy flicked through the Sandton's Special Christmas Selection with obvious satisfaction. Nine-carat-gold ankle chains, three-coloured-gold Russian slave bangles, cubic zirconia engagement rings and crystal-heart drop earrings. He beamed across at Ray. 'You've done a great job. This sterling silver St Christopher pendant, complete with presentation box, all for under a fiver – it's perfect, just perfect. You know, there's no one understands our punters as well as you do.'

Ray grinned, happy to accept the praise. 'No one except yourself. That English Football Association signet ring was a stroke of genius. They'll be going like hot cakes – and with a five hundred per cent mark up and all.'

For a split second, Sammy wondered how many English Football Association signet rings he would have to sell to cover Daphne's most recent Renoir. He soon gave up. For once, the cigarette packet could not cope. The numbers involved were stratospheric. The sound of Ray's voice brought him back to earth.

'And the special purchase Yugoslavian cut-glass decanters? I have to know for certain before going to print. Are we flogging them or not?'

Bartered in Bosnia for a consignment of non-European Community regulation corned beef, the job lot of decanters was a tribute to Sammy's inalienable sense of profit. It was unfortunate, however, that Daphne had come to hear of them before Sammy could do a turn. Now she was insisting that their provenance was doubly checked. 'Daphne says . . .' Sammy flicked an imperceptible speck of dust from his sleeve. 'Daphne says we'd better make sure they come from the right side – Serbs or Croats, I can't remember which. I'd better check it again with her.'

Ray's face turned bright red. 'Politically correct *decanters*?' he exploded. 'For Christ's sake, Sammy, we're not Lambeth bloody Council.'

It was at that moment that Sammy's bubbly young secretary popped her head around the door. 'Sorry to disturb you, Mr Sandton, but your phone's not answering. I thought I ought to tell you Mr Gautier has just arrived.'

'Charles Gautier!' Ray looked as if he had just been winded by a large bag of wet sand. 'What's a bloke like that doing here in your office?'

Sammy started shuffling papers. He had never been good at lying to his mates. 'Daphne's gala,' he muttered and turned to his secretary. 'Denise, would you show Mr Gautier in? Ray's just about to leave.'

Ray rose slowly to his feet. After all his years with Sammy, it hurt to be dismissed so summarily. Charles Gautier and Sammy Sandton. He felt his head beginning to swim. The questions that such a meeting raised filled him with alarm. Miserably he stuffed the Sandton's Special Christmas Selection back into his briefcase. 'I don't know what's going on here but, whatever it is, I don't like it.'

Sammy could not bring himself to look his old friend in the eye. 'What are you on about? This is a purely social call and, anyway, it's got nothing to do with you. Daphne and Charles do a lot of charity work. They have quite a bit in common.'

Ray knew all he needed to know about Charles Gautier. It was the stuff of gossip columns. 'The only thing that pair have in common', he spat, 'is a genius for spending other people's dosh!'

The vein in Sammy's neck stood out alarmingly. 'Get out of

here!' he shouted, throwing a heap of photographs across the room. They scattered all over the floor. 'Get out of here and never – do you hear me? – if you want to keep your job – *never* speak about my wife that way again!'

Ray was shaking, alarmed by the vehemence of Sammy's response. He bent down and, one by one, began to collect the photographs. 'You should know by now who your friends are. I'm only looking out for you, Sammy. Like your father used to say—'

Sammy rammed home his drawer with such force that the entire desk shook. 'I don't give a toss what my old man said. Or what you have to say. And don't think that I don't know what you and all the other parasitical bastards in this company are saying behind my back. Well, you can all fuck off for all I care. Daphne's the best thing that ever happened to me. Now get out of here before I *really* lose my temper.'

Ray was still trembling when he stumbled, ashen-faced, back into his office.

'Are you all right?' His soft-hearted secretary, Gladys, had been with him for twenty years.

'I'll be OK,' he wheezed, fumbling for his Ventolin inhaler. 'Damn this bloody asthma.'

Gladys rose, a C&A-sponsored Venus, from behind the mountain of paperwork on her desk. She guided Ray into his office and made him lie back in his chair. 'Has his nibs had one of his tantrums?' She poured him a glass of mineral water which he drank in grateful silence. Gladys was furious. 'I don't know what's happened to him since he married that little tart. Gone off his rocker, I reckon. No wonder Kylie left – you can't treat a secretary like that, forever shouting and screaming. Ideas above his station, that's the trouble nowadays. Kylie used to say he'd end up making a laughing stock of himself.'

'Not our Sammy,' wheezed Ray loyally. 'Sammy's still the smartest businessman in England today. There ain't no way *he* could ever make a laughing stock of himself. It's his bitch of a wife who'll do that.'

*

Charles was ushered smiling into Sammy's office. 'My dear Sammy,' he gushed, shaking him warmly by the hand. Sammy pulled back ever so slightly. He was always half afraid that this greasy Frenchman might try kissing him. 'And how is the beautiful Daphne?' At his mention of her name, Charles noticed Sammy loosen up.

'She's wonderful, just wonderful, and looking forward to seeing you at home this evening. No big fuss, you understand, just a few close friends, an intimate little *soirée*.' Sammy could have kicked himself. He felt an absolute prat. No self-respecting East-Ender would be caught dead talking about 'an intimate little *soirée*'! Intimate little *soirée*, indeed! He was even beginning to sound like Daphne. If he didn't watch it his high-street cred would really be down the pan.

'*Formidable!*' enthused Charles, pulling up a chair and wondering how much he would have to drink in order to survive an evening with the appalling Daphne Sandton. 'I do hope Daphne will be pleased. I've organized a few Gautier gifts for her gala dinner auction.'

'She'll be over the moon,' replied Sammy, genuinely sincere. It was not the money involved that mattered. It was the ability to call in markers. That, as Daphne always maintained, was what *genuine* status was all about.

'I've promised to meet a business associate at Heathrow in two hours' time.' Charles glanced briefly at his wrist-watch. 'But I wanted to drop by personally, just to see how things are shaping up.'

The smile vanished instantly from Sammy's rugged face. '*Shaping up?* Sunshine, as far as I'm concerned, Sandton's have been ready to move for months. It's *you* we're waiting for!'

As Charles moved forward, he felt something crackle under the leg of his chair. He bent down to retrieve it. Marked Sandton's Super Christmas Saver, it was the photograph of a pair of gold-plated spitfire cufflinks, 'attractively priced at nine pounds ninety-nine including VAT'. He placed the wrinkled photo on Sammy's desk. 'I know, and I've been feeling very guilty towards you.' He did his best to look remorseful. 'I'm quite aware that you've been selling stock, going liquid, doing everything you can to be ready to move. That's why I'm here, Sammy, to give you my personal assurance. Before the end of the year, I honestly believe that the House of Gautier will be yours.'

Not for the first time, Sammy wished this deal imbued him with slightly more enthusiasm. Of course, Daphne had set her heart on it so done the deal would be. All the same, he felt uneasy. Hard businessman though he was, he was beginning to feel that there was something not quite right about waiting for a man to die. Especially, his atrophied conscience whispered to him, when that man was a Resistance hero.

'And your sister?' ventured Sammy.

'My *half*-sister.' Charles's fleshy lips transformed themselves into a sneer. 'That's all taken care of. She has no voting rights in the company until she's thirty.' The sneer grew more cynical still. 'She's twenty-three next birthday.'

'She wouldn't try to pull something – you know, to stop the deal going through?'

Charles laughed a hollow, mirthless laugh. 'Laura? She's a child. Besides, she hasn't got the guts for a fight. No, we needn't worry about her. Once she's paid off she'll walk away, just like her tramp of a mother.' He got up to leave. 'I know you're a busy man, so I'll be getting along. It's been good to touch base with you again.'

As they waited for the lift outside the office, Sammy tried hard to raise his own spirits. 'So it's simply a question of hanging on?'

The steel doors slid open to reveal an expanse of orange acrylic carpet. Charles stepped into the lift. 'Try to be patient,' he said, as the doors moved together. 'Everything comes to those who wait.'

Laura and Maisie had spent the whole morning trawling the shops of Knightsbridge.

'Please, Maisie,' urged Laura, already loaded down with gifts, 'you've got to stop. I can't possibly let you buy me anything else.'

'Nonsense,' laughed Maisie, pulling Laura towards the cosmetics department at Harvey Nichols. 'It was high time you had a few decent summer outfits. I'm tired of those old jeans and shirts you always wear. And some pretty lingerie – every woman needs pretty lingerie, the less sensible the better. When I think of that mangy old T-shirt you've been sleeping in!'

Astounded by Maisie's extraordinarily high spirits, Laura followed meekly.

'Yes, madam?' Ignoring a few potential but prevaricating customers, a sales assistant made a bee-line for Maisie. Laura suppressed a smile. It was as if sales assistants everywhere could see the words 'Unlimited Funds' written in large letters on her face. 'My friend here', Maisie smiled in Laura's direction, 'needs the complete works.'

Face immobile behind a carefully co-ordinated moisturizer, base and powder, the lady coughed politely. 'The complete works, madam?'

'Yes, I've thrown her make-up bag away. You should have seen it. Yuk, yuk, yuk. So now she needs to start from scratch and we'd better get a move on. She's just about to be very famous.'

Laura stared fixedly at the perfume testers. It was a toss-up whether to die of shame or burst out laughing. She had never known Maisie behave like this. Giggling, joking, laughing out loud, she was behaving like a teenager. She sprayed a puff of Shalimar on her wrist and held it to her face.

'I do so love this stuff.' She sighed.

Maisie leaned over to take a sniff. 'It sure is great on you. We'll have the whole range of that to start with.'

The assistant could hardly believe her ears. 'The whole range? But madam, the perfume alone starts at—'

'Whatever.' Maisie took out a platinum American Express card and handed it to the woman. 'Like I said, she needs the *business!*'

Laura shook her head, embarrassed, but then decided to give in. Maisie, of course, had been a shopaholic for as long as she could remember. But before it had always seemed as though she were shopping out of loneliness and depression. Today was different. Today, for the first time either of them could remember,

Maisie was shopping for sheer fun. It seemed churlish to spoil her pleasure.

Weighed down under the mass of packages, the two women staggered out of the department store and down the road towards the Berkeley. Laura giggled as she juggled with her impressive new collection. 'Where on earth am I going to store all this? I'm going to have to move flats.'

Maisie stopped for a breather. 'I don't think I'm going to make it to the hotel.' She caught sight of herself in a display window and collapsed into gales of laughter. 'What's become of me? The daughter of John P. Appleford the First – a bag lady!'

Her laughter was infectious. Laura put down her bags on the pavement and wiped her streaming eyes. 'You're hopeless. I know it's only a three-minute walk but I'm going to hail a taxi.'

As usual, the lunchtime traffic in Knightsbridge was horribly congested and moving at a snail's pace. 'Taxis!' huffed Laura as another occupied cab crept past. 'Just like men. Never there when you need them!' Expecting some gay riposte, she turned towards her friend, but Maisie was just standing there, rooted to the spot.

'What is it?' Laura's eyes followed in the direction of Maisie's gaze. Not a foot from where they were standing a black cab was idling, stationary in the traffic. Sitting in the back, locked in a passionate embrace with a woman, was Charles.

Laura felt an uncontrollable urge to gag. She let her heap of parcels crash to the pavement and put her arms around Maisie's haute-coutured shoulders. 'I'm sorry,' she mumbled, 'this is horrible, really horrible, but you had to know for certain sooner or later.'

The cab moved off down the road, in the direction of Park Lane. Maisie trailed it, unblinking, until it disappeared from sight. 'It's OK,' she said at last, her voice calm and controlled. 'Deep down, I guess I've always known that he never loved me. The only consolation is, I know he can't love anyone.'

A vacant cab hove into view and Maisie flagged it down. Still shaking, Laura picked up her packages and bundled them into the back. During the short trip to the hotel, she studied her friend's profile carefully. Poised and cool, Maisie seemed quite at ease, far less upset than she was herself. In fact, thought Laura, as the cab pulled up outside the hotel, she looked positively dignified.

'My two favourite ladies!' Waiting in the lobby for Laura and Maisie, Gaston already had a bottle of Clos du Mesnil on ice. 'Come, we're celebrating.' Too impatient to call for a waiter, he poured each of them a glass of Krug's most celebrated champagne. 'To my dear friend Harry Blumstein!' he said, holding his glass aloft.

'The Star of Heaven!' Laura's face was pale. 'You mean, it's already been delivered?'

Gaston chatted on, oblivious to her. 'Harry's bringing it to our London office in the morning. It couldn't have worked out better. I've just received a fax from Charles . . .'

Maisie stiffened slightly, but Gaston did not notice. He seemed completely wrapped up in a world of his own. 'Or at least from his secretary. I tried to contact him earlier, but it seems he's still tied up in Hong Kong. No matter. He'll be flying in to join us first thing tomorrow.'

Gaston was so excited that he failed to catch the look on Maisie's face. Laura made to say something but Maisie put her finger to her lips and she nodded in silent understanding. Why spoil her father's elation? For his sake, she would have to put its curse, and the curse of her wretched half-brother, out of her head. At least for the space of a day.

Thoughtfully, Maisie sipped her champagne. 'Gaston, I think I'll organize a small celebration, if that's all right with you.'

'A *real* family get-together, yes, that would be very nice.'

She circled the rim of her glass with her forefinger. 'And if you wouldn't mind, I'd like to invite a friend.'

The old man shot her a quizzical look. She blushed like an adolescent.

'I don't know if he's free,' she continued, 'but I'd like to ask Scorpio along.'

Gaston took the bottle from the ice bucket and reached across to top up her drink. *'Nothing* would give me greater pleasure.' His eyes twinkled with something akin to mischief as he raised his glass to her.

CHAPTER EIGHTEEN

In an effort to annoy him, Yolande rolled over and lit a cigarette.

'Everything all right?' Charles got out of bed and waltzed off into the bathroom.

'No, it bloody well isn't,' she shouted, but the bathroom door was already closed.

She got up and started to collect the pieces of her Air France uniform which lay scattered across the floor. It had been precisely fifteen minutes since she and Charles had booked into their sumptuous suite in Park Lane's Dorchester Hotel. Fifteen minutes! Yolande drew deeply on her untipped Gauloise and stared idly out of the window. It irritated her to hear him singing loudly to himself in the shower.

'At least one satisfied customer!' She opened her suitcase and pulled out an écru silk *peignoir*. Shivering now, she put it on and wrapped it tightly around herself. Despite its warmth, her teeth were chattering. She dived back underneath the bedclothes and pulled her knees up to her chin. 'I did it *my* way!' Charles's voice reverberated around the marble-tiled bathroom. She reached out for the cigarette she had left burning in the ashtray beside the bed. There was no point pretending. She felt used and dirty, like a disposable and now disposed-of paper handkerchief. This afternoon's love-making had been particularly depressing, more cold and clinical than ever. With nothing but a glass of champagne for foreplay, Charles had penetrated her with a hungry disregard, climaxing swiftly before her soft, supple body had even had time to relax and leaving her sore and angry. She stubbed out the cigarette hard in the ashtray and thought of François, the young pilot with the tanned body and adventurous fingers, whom she had just left behind in Morocco.

Charles emerged from the shower, swathed in a large white towel. He turned on the television with the remote control and zapped from channel to channel. 'I shouldn't be too late tonight.' He stopped to look at a tennis match. 'Great shot! Did you see that? That woman Seles can really play.'

She leaned across, grabbed the remote control and angrily turned the television off. 'What do you mean? Where the hell do you think you're going?'

He looked at her, vaguely surprised. 'Didn't I tell you? I'm sorry, darling, I'm expected at the Sandtons' for dinner.' He bent down to kiss her toes.

Furious, she pulled her foot away and secreted it under the bedclothes. 'So this evening you're out with the Sandtons and tomorrow with your father. Just let me try and guess why I've been dragged all the way over here to London.'

'Chérie,' he said soothingly, sidling up beside her, 'a little patience, that's all I ask. Right now, I've got to play up to these people, but it'll all be worth it. Soon I'll be able to tell the lot of them to take a running jump.'

'Some ambition!' she snorted, flinging back the blankets. 'There's a flight for Paris early this evening. I may as well be on it.'

He sprang up to bar her way as she made for the bathroom. 'Please, don't go. I need you here with me.'

'Fine.' Her mouth was set in a hard, tight line. 'In that case I'm coming to dinner with you.' She tried to dodge past him, but he caught her by the waist and pulled her towards him.

'Please,' he implored her, his eyes suddenly desperate, 'you can't possibly come. Daphne likes to play happy families – besides she can't cope with female competition. She'd go mad if I turned up with someone as beautiful as you.'

'Daphne Sandton!' Yolande struggled to free herself, but his grip was too tight. 'You've said yourself she's just a silly little bitch. What do you care what she thinks?'

He pulled her even closer. 'Look, this whole takeover deal

depends on Daphne. Owning Gautier is *her* dream, something *she* wants. Sammy could take it or leave it. And from what I've seen, he'd probably leave it. That's why I've got to keep Daphne sweet.'

'Daphne, Maisie – I'm sick to death of hearing about all the women you have to accommodate! How about accommodating me for a change?' Tearing herself away, she pushed past him into the bathroom where she dissolved into floods of tears.

Charles flopped down wearily on the bed. Keeping people satisfied, it was such an exhausting business! Suddenly it struck him. He got up and walked across to his jacket, slung across the back of a chair. Hidden in the inner pocket was a gold-tooled burgundy-leather box. He took it out and opened it. Sparkling green against black velvet was the most fabulous square-cut emerald ring. He lifted it from the box. An heirloom from her mother, it was one of the many jewels Maisie had not bothered to wear in years. He held it to the light and studied it with dispassionate approval. It was a perfect specimen, worth at least thirty thousand pounds even in a bad market. He sighed as he replaced it. What a pity! He had been intending to sell it to pay off some of his more pressing gambling debts. He had reckoned that she would never notice and, even if she did, he could always convince her she had lost it. Charles felt a sudden wave of panic. Whatever it cost, he would have to placate Yolande. Once Gautier was sold and his family cut adrift, he knew he would need her more than ever. The prospect of a future without her warm, soft body was too lonely to contemplate.

He tapped gently on the bathroom door. 'Yolande?'

'Go away.'

'Please, Yolande, please come out. There's something I want to say to you.'

'There's nothing left to say. I'm having a bath, then I'm leaving for the airport. I'm tired of hanging around.'

'OK.' He pretended to cave in. 'But before you do, there's something I want to give you.'

'You already did. A pain in the neck. Now leave me alone in peace.'

'Yolande.' He paused. 'I want . . .' The words seemed to stick in the back of his throat. 'I want you to marry me.'

A long silence followed. She must be thinking, he decided. At least that bought him time. 'When this wretched deal is out of the way, when I can afford to dump Maisie, then the two of us can get married.'

Suddenly, the door opened and there stood Yolande, naked and dripping. 'You really mean that?' She moved towards him, her body slender and languorous. Charles let the bath-towel slip from his waist. It slithered to the floor.

'Here.' He took her left hand and placed the ring on her third finger. 'I've been meaning to do this for months.'

Yolande stared, wide-eyed, at the glorious emerald. Then, smiling slyly, she knelt down and drew the tip of her tongue along the length of his erection. Charles groaned as gently she kissed the very tip of his penis. 'And I,' she whispered, 'have been meaning to do this.'

If there was one thing Charles did not need that evening, it was dinner with the Sandtons. Staring out through the tinted windows of Sammy's chauffeur-driven Bentley, his thoughts were on Yolande, happy, exhausted and now sleeping peacefully in their bed at the Dorchester. It was extraordinary, he mused, to witness the effect a ring had on a woman. That afternoon, Yolande had done everything a man could reasonably and, perhaps, even unreasonably expect. There were prostitutes in Pigalle not prepared to go so far. He smiled at the recollection. The prospect of his retirement was looking better all the time.

'Is the air-conditioning too cool for you, sir?'

Awoken from his reverie, Charles stared at the back of the chauffeur's head. 'No thanks. It's fine.'

'Mr Sandton don't like it. He likes his windows open, says he thrives on petrol fumes.'

Charles perked up at once. Chatty employees were often mines of useful information. 'Have you been with Mr Sandton long?'

'Fifteen years next May. Before that, my cousin drove for him. Mr Sandton's always had a driver, says if a bloke's doing business, his mind ought to be on the deal, not on how he's going to get there.'

'He's done very well for himself,' ventured Charles, accentuating his normally slight French accent.

'He's a first-class bloke,' said the chauffeur enthusiastically. 'And I don't say that because I'm an East-End boy myself, though it's true we do stick together. Of course, you'll always find a few knockers, but it's jealousy in the main.'

Charles pricked up his ears. 'But his company results are excellent. Why should anyone complain?'

The car purred effortlessly along the edge of Hampstead Heath.

'Mr Sandton's clean as a whistle now, but he's been a bit of a lad in his time.'

Charles leaned forward, suddenly very familiar. 'Trouble with the police?'

'Oh, no.' The chauffeur seemed genuinely amused. 'Getting nicked is a mug's game. Sammy Sandton was always too clever for that. Besides, he never did anything strictly illegal – leastways, not according to my cousin.'

'Gambling?'

'No, that's a mug's game an' all. No, in the old days Sammy was into a bit of – how'd you call it? – barter trade. When the Yanks slapped sanctions on all them Commies, Sammy used to, like, move things around for people. He used to say he was doing his bit for international understanding.'

'Really?' Charles laughed amiably in an effort to encourage the man. 'And what sort of "things" did Sammy move around?'

'Nothing, like, immoral,' replied the man quickly. 'I mean, Sammy's basically a decent geezer. He'd never touch hard drugs or guns. But, like, he'd buy penicillin in the States and ship it on to Holland. Then he'd get the boxes relabelled and forwarded to China with a load of duff documents. In return, the Chinese would send a pile of silk to Europe and Sammy would collect payment in dollars in East Berlin. It wasn't really what you'd call sanctions-busting, more humanitarian aid.'

'Very laudable,' nodded Charles, without the slightest trace of cynicism.

'Then one day some posh City punter tries to double-cross Sammy. They still talk about it, you know, down the pubs in Brick Lane. The bloke ended up in intensive care, a broken leg, a few smashed ribs, a completely reorganized boat race.'

Charles did not know what kind of a boat race that might have been, but he thought he probably had the picture.

'He behaved like a real gent, though,' added the driver, fulsome, 'a regular bloody hero. He even sent the bloke's missus flowers.'

The car rolled up the Sandtons' driveway and glided to a halt. The driver jumped out and opened the back door. Charles checked the bouquet he had brought for Daphne, before looking up at the man. 'Has anything similar happened since?'

'Only once.' The chauffeur's voice was hushed. He did not want to run the risk of being overheard here. 'Last year, some ponce at Ascot upset Mrs S.' He smiled proudly at his passenger. 'They tell me he's still in traction.'

'Charles, how wonderful to see you again!' Shimmering in electric blue satin, Daphne welcomed her guest at the door.

He smiled and bent to kiss her hand. '*Ma chère* Daphne,' he gushed, presenting her with the flowers, 'you look dazzling this evening!'

'Too kind.' She handed the flowers to the maid who was hovering anxiously in the entrance hall. 'Put these in *agua*, will you, Maria? Come, Charles, everyone's just *dying* to meet you.'

With a swish of satin, she led him into the drawing room where the Sandtons' other 'intimate' friends were already assembled. Manfully, he maintained his gleaming ersatz smile as Sammy ran through the introductions. A country vicar and his mousy wife, a peer of the realm and his long-suffering spouse – Charles gritted his teeth.

'Did I tell you? We're in next month's edition of *Right-ho!* magazine,' Daphne gloated happily as Sammy dispensed the drinks.

Freed for a few minutes from his hostess's attentions, Charles surveyed the unholy hotch-potch of animal skin and leather.

Restored Regency juxtaposed with green plexiglass and chrome; Renoirs, Klimts, Picassos, all slapped together without the slightest concern for either size or colour. He swallowed hard. He himself boasted no aesthetic pretensions, but in all his life he had never seen anything quite so gross or ostentatious. Every picture, every sculpture, every bibelot had been spotlighted so that nothing stood out. He scanned the room but soon discovered there was not a single book to be found. For the briefest of moments, his conscience began to prick him. So these were to be the new owners of the House of Gautier. He picked up his tumbler and, as usual, found that guilt dissolved in Scotch.

To his horror, the dining room was even worse. Covered in black and aubergine PVC, the walls shimmered like a coal-face in the candlelight. The black velvet curtains, held back with enormous gold tassels, did nothing to alleviate the claustrophobic atmosphere of the room. For the first half-hour, the conversation around the table was equally funereal. There was only one thing for it. Charles decided to keep on drinking.

'That's why we're so pleased to have supporters like Daphne and Sammy in the parish,' oozed the Reverend Michael Ellwood, whose church spire appeal had taken a decided turn for the better since the Sandtons had purchased their Kent estate.

Daphne's gaze was distinctly off-focus. She tried to dab her mouth with her napkin but hit her nose instead. 'I think,' she began unsteadily, 'I think it's so important for one to play one's role in the community, wouldn't you agree, Arthur?'

Lord Marple of Sallyworth turned his rheumy eyes to his hostess and did his best to suppress a burp. Throughout dinner, he had positively gorged himself, taking second helpings of everything and drinking copiously. 'Quite so, my dear. Quite so. Miriam and I have devoted our lives to helping the community. "Putting something back", I call it. Too many folk nowadays are takers. As I'm forever telling their lordships, we are the helpers, the hole-pluggers, the tar which keeps the galleon of society afloat.'

A picture of unresolved anger, Miriam Marple smiled, a

pinched, thin-lipped little smile. Viciously, she squashed a raspberry with her fork and watched as it oozed red. It was bad enough being married to a ranting hypocrite but, as everybody knew, Lord "Putting Something Back" Marple was the biggest kleptomaniac in town. In Jermyn Street, there was one gentleman's shop from which he regularly emerged with two or three hundred pounds' worth of shirts stuffed surreptitiously up his coat. Nothing was ever said, of course – that was not the Jermyn Street way. Only this morning, however, Miriam had received yet another invoice to cover her husband's idiosyncratic shopping habits.

'But it's also right that society should reward its helpers.' Daphne's words were seriously slurred.

'I don't think that tonight's the—' One look from his wife and Sammy was stopped in his tracks.

'We're all friends here,' she continued, unabashed. 'And I know Arthur has always said that people should speak their minds—'

'I most certainly have. Indeed—'

Ignoring his interruption, she soldiered on. 'So the point is, what I want to know from you is, when is my Sammy here going to get his knighthood?'

Charles stared hard at his dinner plate and, for the first time, noticed the crest and motto at the top. *Auro Argentoque Fidemus*. He drained his burgundy. 'In Gold and Silver We Trust'. That just had to be Daphne's idea. He glanced up and caught the look of contempt etched on Miriam's pale, patrician face. He turned to find Lord Marple trying his best to sound placatory.

'Well, my dear, it's never really that simple . . .' He could feel his gout flaring up again.

'Look here. Now I'm going to tell you something for a change.' Daphne's voice was loud and querulous. She reached over for the bottle and poured herself another glass of wine. 'Sammy's done everything you said, ten million pounds to charity and a packet to Tory Party Central Office. Not to mention your own directorship of Sandton's. I should think by now—'

'Daphne,' Sammy looked anxiously around the table, 'I think it might be a good idea if we all took coffee in the drawing room.'

It was not long before the Reverend Michael and Mrs Ellwood made their excuses and departed. Lord and Lady Marple followed shortly afterwards. As their cars roared off down the drive, Daphne turned suddenly maudlin. 'You're not abandoning us too, are you?' She gripped Charles by the arm.

Sensing an opportunity to score Brownie points with Sammy, the Frenchman shook his head. 'Of course not.' He smiled, settling down with a large Cognac. 'The evening is yet young.'

Two miniature French poodles escaped from the kitchen and bounded yapping into the room. 'Monet, Manet,' wailed Daphne and burst into tears. She picked up one of the pooches and hid her face in its clipped, pink-tinted coat. 'Mummy's been a very silly girl.' Her mascara ran in gritty, black rivulets down the side of her pancaked cheeks. 'Mummy's been a naughty girl. She's gone and let Daddy down!'

'It's OK, darling.' Sammy put the dog down on the floor and lifted her up in his arms. 'I know you've had one hell of a day and you've been an absolute star.' He kissed her tenderly and then carried her upstairs. The dogs followed him, yelping at his heels.

Alone in the room, Charles's eyes began to roam until they came to rest on a chess set. Individually cast, the figures were crafted in gold and silver and beautifully enamelled. One side had been made to represent the Duke of Wellington's army, the other Napoleon's. He went over to admire it. Even Daphne, it seemed, was capable of the odd lapse into good taste. He picked up the silver Duke of Wellington and studied the piece intently. Scratched on the side, there appeared to be the tiniest of signatures. He held it close to the light. 'Caroline Jay'. Like a hot coal, the piece seemed to sear the tips of his fingers and he dropped it. It hit the table with a loud clatter.

'Do you play?' Sammy entered the room nonchalantly, as if nothing had happened.

Caught off-guard, Charles looked up and smiled. 'Occasionally. Much less often nowadays.'

Sammy poured himself a Cognac and sat down opposite. 'We used to play all the time when we were kids, me and my brother Kevin. He was always the bright one, Kev, he always used to whop me. Come on, I'll give you a game. I need to clear my head.'

He held out his hands with a player concealed in each. Charles chose Napoleon's army leaving his host with Wellington's.

'I bought this for Kev the day I made my first million.' After some thought, Sammy moved a pawn. 'It's a Caroline Jay – well, you'd know that, wouldn't you? Cost me a small fortune, it did, but it was worth it for our Kev.'

Charles said nothing, but slowly moved his knight.

Sammy sipped his Cognac and stared down at the board. 'He returned it to me the day I divorced my first wife.' His voice was oddly uneven. 'I still look after him, of course. He's still my brother. But nowadays we're not really mates any more, not like we were in the old days.'

'Families,' sighed Charles sympathetically, 'who needs them?

Sammy clenched the edge of the table. 'You don't understand! I really loved my brother. Despite everything, I suppose I still do. But not half as much as I love Daphne. I'd do anything for her.' The pieces rattled ominously on the black and white marble board.

'Take those wankers this evening. Thank God, they're an easy pay-off. A bigger company car for Marple, a fund-raising garden party for the vicar. But I won't have them racing off, telling tales about Daphne and making her look a fool. Whatever it takes to protect her and make her happy – do you understand? – I'll do *whatever* it takes.'

The game continued for an hour in silence, each man immersed in his thoughts. It was Charles who broke the conversational stalemate. 'Our deal. You know I'll act the moment I can.' He pulled back his queen in defence. 'I realize my name will be mud in Paris but, I swear, I won't let you down.'

'You'd better not!' As if from nowhere, Sammy conjured up a bishop, then smiled at his guest in triumph. 'Checkmate!'

By seven the next morning the maid was already clearing away the debris. Despite the perennial, placid smile, she was feeling desperately tired. In the six months she had been working for

Mrs Sandton, she had not yet had a free day to herself. This morning, however, the madam was still fast asleep when she delivered her early morning lemon juice. Maria's varicose veins were throbbing. One day, she hoped to save enough money to have them stripped. On her salary of twenty pounds a week, however, that was going to take some time.

After collecting the glasses and hoovering the carpet, she stopped for a moment's breather. The previous night's chess game stood as it had ended on the board. Maria knew a little about chess. She could still remember those days outside in the sunshine, when she used to play it with her son. She wiped her eyes with the corner of her apron. There had been no choice. The little boy had been left behind with her mother in Manila. Out of her meagre earnings, Maria repatriated fifteen pounds a week.

She stared at the beautiful chess set without envy. Back home, such a thing would feed a family for a couple of years. She tried not to think of that as, carefully, she began to put the pieces back in their original places. It was then that something struck her. At first, it looked as if Wellington's army had emerged victorious from the fray. But now she studied the deployment of his pieces, there was something very strange. Both of the good Duke's bishops were positioned on white squares.

CHAPTER NINETEEN

It was the proudest day of Harry Blumstein's long and eminently successful life. The competition had been ferocious and the negotiations far more complicated than he had ever anticipated. This morning, however, as he handed over the Star of Heaven to his old friend, Gaston Gautier, Harry could not help feeling an enormous surge of pleasure. For over fifty years, he had dealt in diamonds, some steeped in history, others worth many millions of pounds. But today's transaction was something different. Today he, Harry Blumstein, had become part of a legend, a figure in the terrible history of this extraordinary stone.

Gaston looked around the oak-panelled boardroom of Gautier's London branch and his eyes grew misty. Situated in New Bond Street, the offices of this elegant store had housed countless refugees during the course of the Second World War. General de Gaulle himself had spent many hours in this very room, discussing strategy and arguing politics. Gaston choked back the tears. De Gaulle had behaved so badly to his former friends and allies. Now it was time to make amends. The Star of Heaven would be *this* Frenchman's way of thanking the British people.

Twelve forty-five and still Charles had not arrived. Maisie looked anxiously at Laura. The small celebration had been scheduled for midday. As usual, the indefatigable Harry had appointments to keep and was soon due to leave for Antwerp. As the shagreen clock in the boardroom chimed one, Laura took her father to one side. 'I'm afraid there's no news of Charles.'

Gaston looked downcast. 'His plane must be late. When does Harry have to leave?'

'Any time now. Why not say a few words before he does? You know how much these things mean to him.'

Tapping an ancient gavil on the oval mahogany table, Gaston cleared his throat. 'There will be no speeches today,' he said, afraid of his own emotions. 'All I'd like to say is how happy I am to welcome you, my friends and family, and to share this moment with you.' He felt a sudden lump rising in his throat and continued in a whisper. 'I've always wanted the Star of Heaven and now, thanks to Harry Blumstein, it belongs to me at last.'

He held out the diamond in the palm of his hand for his guests to see. From all over the room there were murmurs of amazement. Scorpio, who was standing next to Maisie near the window, let out a gasp. 'What a beauty!'

'It's magnificent!' As Laura reached out, a sudden shaft of sunlight caught the diamond, refracting off its myriad facets and setting it aflame. She blinked. The stone was like a living creature, possessed of energy and soul. 'May I?' she whispered. Gaston nodded and she took the stone from his hand. She stared at it, unable to utter a single word. It was small wonder that men had cheated and murdered for this dazzling, fiery creature.

'So now you understand.' He kissed the crown of her head. 'Now you really understand why I simply had to have it.'

'I wouldn't go getting too attached if I were you, Laura dear.' Almost an hour late, Charles swaggered across the boardroom, helping himself to canapés *en route*. As he plucked the diamond from her hand, its fire seemed to flicker and die. 'Well, well, well, the Star of Heaven. Not good for one's health, they tell me, though, Father, I must say, you're looking very fit.' He motioned to the waitress who brought him a glass of champagne.

'*Santé!*' He swivelled round on his heel, smiling broadly, until his eyes came to rest on the good-looking stranger, sipping water and standing a trifle too close to Maisie. The smile froze for an instant. Then, brushing the fleeting suspicion from his mind, he turned his attention back to his father. 'Congratulations!' Insolently, he tossed the diamond up and down a few times before dropping it into Gaston's breast pocket. 'I've no idea how much it cost or how the hell we're going to pay for it. But don't let that worry you, not today. Today, let's all drink and be merry.'

214

Everyone fell silent. The few ancient Gautier employees invited to the reception exited swiftly from the boardroom. Harry Blumstein hugged his old friend and, almost in tears, left immediately for the airport.

Scorpio moved forward but Maisie grabbed him by the elbow. 'Please, don't,' she begged. 'I'll deal with this.'

'Deal with what, my dear?' All smiles again, Charles swung round to confront his wife. He gestured dismissively to the stranger, still by her side. 'And what's this we've picked up on our rounds? A bit mature, wouldn't you say, for the average toy-boy?'

Scorpio felt the muscles tighten in the back of his neck. Lean and fit, he was across the room in no time, his fists clenched, his face white with anger.

'Please, Scorpio.' Gaston caught hold of Scorpio's forearm. 'It's all right. No insult intended. It's only my son's sense of humour. Come, Charles, you must be very jet-lagged, I'm sure you need a rest.'

Charles stared at the lithe, handsome stranger and felt as if he had been hit by a girder. Scorpio was one of Gautier's most important clients. He grasped him warmly by the hand. 'Scorpio! I've always been such a fan! Do you know, my wife and I have followed you for years, haven't we, Maisie, darling?'

Scorpio studied Charles's face intently. Although his eyes were pale and cold, his lips were full and sensual. His dislike for the man increased.

'Just a slight misunderstanding,' continued Gaston apologetically. 'I know we should have waited for you, Charles, it's no wonder you were cross.'

Bewildered, Scorpio turned towards Laura in search of some rational explanation. She simply raised her eyes to the ceiling in a gesture of pure frustration.

For all of thirty minutes, Charles was the very essence of attentiveness and charm. Gaston's health, Laura's exhibition, Maisie's well-being – suddenly these were all matters of the utmost concern to him, until, as the clock struck half past one, he said, 'I'm afraid I must dash.' He had promised to meet Yolande for lunch and was already running late.

215

'You're not leaving?' Gaston looked deflated.

'I'm sorry, but I'm on the afternoon flight to Bonn. That wretched franchise is causing more headaches than it's worth.'

Laura glanced at Maisie who was staring fixedly at the floor. Arrogant as ever, Charles mistook her silence for upset and, tilting up her chin, tried to kiss her proprietorially on the lips. Instinctively, she jerked her head away. A glimmer of surprise ran fleetingly across his face, but he was too preoccupied to delve. He knew Yolande would be furious if he kept her waiting. He said his farewells and left.

'If you two wouldn't mind,' Laura gave Scorpio a gentle dig in the ribs, 'I'd like to have lunch alone with Papa.'

Scorpio took his cue. 'Well, Maisie, it looks like we're *de trop*. Would you like to come with me to Lord's?'

'Lord's?' Surprised, Maisie sounded even more Texan than ever. '*You* belong to the House of Lords?'

Laura began to giggle. 'For goodness sake, *Lord's*, the *cricket* ground. He's inviting you to the cricket.'

'Cricket?' Maisie wrinkled up her nose. 'That weird English game with pin-ball scores. The one that goes on for ever?'

'I've always wanted—' began Gaston enthusiastically, but Laura stopped him with a stare.

'I promise you you'll just love it,' she urged. 'They say the English invented cricket when they stopped believing in God.'

'That's true,' added Scorpio smiling, 'it's supposed to provide us with some notion of eternity.'

'I'll come.' Maisie picked up her clutch bag and took Scorpio by the arm. 'But let's duck the lessons on eternity, shall we? It seems like I've lived through that already!'

The Bentley drew to a halt outside a large, wrought-iron gate and the driver waited for his instructions. 'You can meet us back here at six,' said Scorpio, helping Maisie from the back of the car. 'If they won't let you park, just cruise around, somewhere near the Grace Gate.'

Inside the cricket ground, a roar went up, so loud it could be heard in the Regent's Park mosque. Scorpio quickened his step.

'A wicket! Come on, Maisie. Let's get a move on. That must be fourth man down.'

He led her to a lift beside some open metal stairs and urgently pressed the button. 'This is the new Mound Stand.' He gestured to the massive white construction above them as the stainless steel doors swung open. 'It was financed by J. Paul Getty Junior, the billionaire philanthropist.'

'Well, I never.' Maisie stepped into the lift. 'My father was a great rival of his father's, you know. They were both in the oil business together.'

The lift deposited them near the top of the stand and they made their way along a corridor, past a row of light grey doors until they came to one marked 'Scorpio'. The waiter in the box was most deferential. 'Good afternoon, sir. How nice to see you again after all this time. Only two for lunch, I've been told.'

Maisie took a seat on the balcony and stared out on to the sea of bobbing heads below. 'I thought you were supposed to be a recluse.'

Scorpio pulled out a pair of opera glasses and trained them on the scorebox opposite. 'So I am and, believe me, Lord's is the best place on earth to be a recluse. Paul Getty, Mick Jagger, Michael Caine – we all come here and no one pays us the slightest bit of attention. Shot, sir!' He applauded loudly as the ball went soaring over the boundary.

For some minutes Maisie watched the white-clad players moving in arcane patterns all over the grass. Accustomed to the rules of baseball, this game made no sense to her whatsoever. The crowd even cheered as the striker knelt and swept the ball *behind* him.

'Foul!' she exclaimed. Scorpio shook his head, amused.

'Not in cricket. Hitting behind is perfectly OK. That was a brilliant stroke.'

Batsmen, bowlers, wickets, overs, Maisie felt as if she had been beamed up into a parallel universe. 'I'm beginning to feel like Alice in Wonderland. Could you please explain the rules?'

'Sure.' Scorpio let his scorecard drop to his lap and tentatively took her hand. 'But I have to warn you, it'll take about a lifetime.'

Lunch and tea came and went and still he was explaining.

'I'd never realized it was so complicated.' Maisie's head was reeling. 'Do you play this game yourself?'

'I used to, when I was at Eton.'

She raised an eyebrow. '*You* were at *Eton*?'

'Until they kicked me out. Possession of cannabis, amongst other things. My father nearly killed me.' He picked up his scorecard again and scribbled in a leg before wicket.

'You must have been a tearaway.'

Scorpio shrugged. 'Not really. Just lost and insecure, looking for something, I guess.'

'And did you ever find it?'

The crack of perfectly timed leather on willow echoed around the ground. The crowd voiced their unanimous approval as the ball rocketed through the covers. Scorpio jumped to his feet. 'Hundred up! Well played, sir.'

She waited for him to sit down again. 'Well, did you?' she insisted.

'I don't know,' he grinned back at her sheepishly, 'and even if I did I don't remember. I was too spaced out at the time.'

The afternoon session sped by and at five o'clock Scorpio ordered champagne for Maisie and Perrier for himself. At last she managed to steer the conversation away from cricket and on to Scorpio himself. 'Didn't you ever fall in love?' she asked, as he filled her glass.

'Only once – a girl called Rosemary.' He watched as the stream of bubbles sped swiftly to the top of her glass. 'In fact, she looked a lot like you.'

Maisie stared at the bowler, coming in from the Nursery End. 'What happened to her?'

'She got tired of hanging around and ran off with my accountant.'

She turned her attention to the slip cordon. 'Were you . . .' She paused. Prying into the life of an almost perfect stranger! She could hardly believe her own behaviour. 'Were you very upset?'

'Devastated.'

She reached out to touch his hand. 'I'm sorry.'

'So was I.' His fingers wrapped themselves around hers. 'He was the best double-entry bookkeeper I ever had.'

A huge cheer went up and a group of fielders converged, excited, around the bowler.

'That's out!' shouted Scorpio, jumping up. 'Wonderful ball, turned and lifted, totally unplayable.'

The entire crowd rose as the century-scoring batsman, his bat held aloft, made his way back to the pavilion. To her surprise, Maisie found herself on her feet, applauding next to Scorpio. Suddenly, he was aware of her body, warm and comfortable against his own. A sudden tingle ran down his spine and he felt a desperate urge to kiss her. Resisting the temptation, he gestured towards the batsman. 'He had a good innings,' he murmured, 'but it's always the unexpected one that rolls you over.'

The shadows on the outfield grew longer as the afternoon wore on. On the top of the pavilion, the flags fluttered gently in the early evening breeze. Scorpio thanked the waiter and dismissed him for the day.

'You play a good defensive game,' he said, turning his attention back to Maisie.

'I'm sorry?'

'There you go again. Perfect blocking tactics. A right little Geoffrey Boycott!' He lifted the champagne from the ice-bucket and poured her another glass. 'You've heard all about me this afternoon. Now, I want to hear about you.'

She shivered slightly in the breeze and pulled a light wool shawl across her shoulders. 'There's nothing much to tell. My father was John P. Appleford the First – you've probably heard of him?'

Scorpio nodded. 'Who hasn't? I've seen the Appleford museums in Dallas and New York. He must have been a fine man.'

'He was, and a self-made one. He started from nothing and clawed his way up.'

The cricket seemed a thousand miles away, the noise of the crowd a distant rumble.

'So how did he become such a great lover of the arts?'

'He began by teaching himself. Then he started to collect. As he grew richer, collecting became a passion with him. Everything

219

– pictures, porcelain, manuscripts, jewellery – that's how I first met Charles.'

She seemed to shrivel at the very mention of his name. Scorpio moved closer, longing to put his arm around her as gradually her story unfolded. She had met Charles, so it transpired, in New York, at an exhibition of her father's jewellery collection. Suave and handsome, the young Gautier had made an instant impression on the young Texan heiress. Seven years her senior, the tall, slightly arrogant Frenchman seemed aeons away in style and sophistication. The slightly accented English, the charming way he kissed her hand, that almost imperceptible inclination of the head when she introduced him to her father, Charles was so totally different from any of the American boys the naïve Maisie had ever known.

At heart a simple red-neck Texan, John P. Appleford I was also deeply impressed. Apart from being the son of the celebrated Gaston Gautier, Charles displayed an encyclopaedic knowledge of Appleford's collection, which the oil magnate found deeply gratifying. Pieces from the great American jewellers of Tiffany, Marcus Trabert and Hoeffer, Seaman Schepps and from the celebrated houses of Fabergé, Cartier, Boucheron, Lalique, Van Cleef and Arpels and, of course, Gautier itself. Charles was at pains to tell Maisie's father of his boundless admiration.

The umpire drew stumps and the large crowd started to disperse. Maisie seemed barely to notice. A vaguely cynical smile stole across her lips as the memories came flooding back. Her father, she recalled, was so taken with Charles that he invited him to dinner. That had been the beginning. Three months later, after a well-chronicled whirlwind romance, Maisie Appleford and Charles Gautier were engaged to be married.

'I don't blame my father.' She sighed. Her fingers had turned blue with cold. 'He always wanted what was best for me. English nannies, French governesses, Swiss finishing schools, even a stint at the Sorbonne. He genuinely thought Charles was the perfect husband and, to tell the truth, so did I. Daddy didn't force me into anything. I was completely besotted.'

Scorpio could bear it no longer. 'But why?' He stared deep into her Labrador eyes. 'Why do you put up with him now? You and Gaston, you're both the same. You're each worth a million Charleses and yet you let him push you around.'

Her shoulders hunched forward. 'I guess we both feel guilty. Gaston, because he deprived him of a childhood. And me, because . . .' She stared at the figure of Old Father Time, gazing dispassionately across the ground, and fought hard to repress a sob. 'And me, because I deprived him of children.'

It was too late. Already the tears were cascading down her face. She started rooting in her bag.

'Here, use this.' Scorpio produced a monogrammed linen handkerchief and gratefully, she dabbed her eyes.

'I'm sorry. I didn't mean to blub. Things aren't as bad as all that any more. I've switched off the bits that really hurt.'

'That's a dangerous game.' Scorpio's eyes were dark with intensity. 'One day you'll wake up and find that nothing hurts any more, that you're no longer living, just existing.'

The sob, too long repressed, racked her slight, huddled frame. She looked vulnerable and tired. Overcome with tenderness, Scorpio took her in his arms and held her to him tightly. For only the second time in his life, he knew he wanted to care for someone else. 'I know.' His voice was kind and patient. 'I've been there myself, remember? Charles just happens to be your addiction. I intend to wean you off him.'

Gradually her body seemed to begin to relax and at last the tears subsided. She looked up at him, her eyelids red and swollen, her lipstick smudged over the edges of her rather too full lips. She looked a mess, but in all his life, he had never seen a more adorable sight. Moving forward, he kissed her eyelids gently, soothing away the tears. She tilted her face upwards towards him, and slowly parted her lips.

'You finished in here?' An ancient gargoyle of a groundsman clattered noisily into the box. Maisie and Scorpio jumped like two adolescents caught smoking behind the bicycle shed. Ignoring them, the old man started shovelling left-over scones and sandwiches into a large black plastic bag. 'I don't know,' he muttered to himself. 'The amount of stuff these people waste. Criminal, it is!' He bustled around, tidying and clearing, sweeping and swearing, paying no heed whatsoever to the occupants.

FRANCES EDMONDS

'Finished with this stuff, have you?' Without waiting for a
response, he dumped the champagne bottle into the refuse sack.
'Honestly! They say they come here to watch the cricket. Watch
the cricket, I ask you! Since when did anyone need champagne
to watch the bloody cricket?'

Maisie was still giggling as, hand in hand, she and Scorpio
left the ground by the Grace Gate. He hailed his chauffeur who
was cruising obediently outside. Like a pair of naughty children
they dived laughing into the back. Maisie glanced swiftly at her
haystack hairstyle and realized she did not care. She felt she was
twenty years old again, without a care in the world. As the car
drew closer to Knightsbridge, however, she felt the euphoria
begin to wane.

'Please,' insisted Scorpio. 'You can't leave on holiday! I'm
only just getting to know you.'

As the car pulled up outside the hotel, he ordered it to circle
again. Maisie's heart was sinking. 'You know I'd rather stay here
in London. But we're booked to fly to Cairo the day after
tomorrow. I can't let Betsy down.'

He looked totally crushed. 'So when can I see you again?'

'As soon as I'm back, if you still want to . . .' She felt silly
and utterly confused.

'I'll be waiting for you.' He kissed her hard on the lips and
then, probing gently, opened her mouth with the tip of his
tongue. She moaned softly. Scorpio, sunshine and champagne –
it was enough to make any girl faint!

Ten minutes later and looking as if she had just emerged from
a De Havilland wind tunnel, she surfaced and drew breath. 'I've
got to go,' she gasped. 'It's already eight o'clock.'

He looked at her, pleadingly. 'I'm sure Gaston and Laura
would understand. Please – have dinner with me.'

'I can't.' She sounded suddenly quite resolute. 'And it's not
their feelings I'm worried about. It's my own. I need some time
to think.'

Scorpio smiled, instantly contrite. 'Forgive me. I'm so afraid
of losing you, I'm going to end up frightening you off.'

She placed her hand quite naturally in his. 'No chance of
that,' she whispered, 'you're saddled with me now.'

222

The car finally stopped outside the hotel. 'My God!' Scorpio started fidgeting around in his briefcase. 'I almost forgot!' At last, he drew out a sheet of paper and a cassette and handed them to Maisie. 'Would you give these to Laura?' He sounded oddly bashful. 'Tell her it's the best I can do.'

'The theme song for *Tor*?' Her eyes sparkled bright with excitement.

He nodded sheepishly. 'I don't know if it's any good. You can tell her there's no hard feelings if they junk it.'

She flung her arms around his neck. 'I know it'll be just wonderful. I just can't wait to tell her. Serge and Sharif will be over the moon.'

He leaned across and gently kissed the tip of her nose. 'I'd be a fraud if I didn't square with you,' he whispered, 'but the truth is I didn't do it for them. I did it for myself.'

Maisie felt as if she must have floated up to her room. Once inside, she grabbed her Walkman and inserted the cassette. The machine clicked and whirred into action as she lay down on her bed. Powerful and resonant, Scorpio's voice soon began to permeate her consciousness. She closed her eyes and pictured him, singing to her and her alone.

A large warm tear rolled down her cheek and plopped on to the white linen pillowcase. Even without orchestration, with nothing but a guitar for backing, the song was simply beautiful. She rewound the tape and played all the verses once again. Everything was there, said and unsaid, in the cadences of that voice. Pain and yearning, endeavour and understanding, the song was the story of Scorpio's own life.

She flicked the OFF button as the final chords died away. Her heart was thumping wildly. A hymn to integrity and self-fulfilment, she vowed to make it hers as well.

CHAPTER TWENTY

Betsy could not get over the transformation in her friend. After the events of the previous few months, she had left for Egypt anticipating the worst. A kind-hearted woman, she was more than prepared to proffer a shoulder on which Maisie could cry her heart out. She had even packed a prayer book – an item she herself used rarely nowadays, but Betsy felt it might provide solace in Maisie's darkest hour of need. It was not long, however, before the widow realized that she was dealing with an entirely different woman. Even on the flight to Cairo, Maisie seemed extraordinarily happy and relaxed, brimming over with vitality and fun. Betsy was dying to know the reason. In their fortnight's holiday, she resolved to winkle it out. In the meantime, however, she simply ordered more in-flight champagne and decided to bide her time.

Recently opened, Cairo's Seraphim Hotel was a luxurious low-rise structure with prettily landscaped gardens and magnificent views across the Nile. As a base for their schedule of excursions, Maisie and Betsy both agreed it was ideal. Light airy suites, excellent service and wonderful food, it suited their requirements to perfection. The MacLeans, Betsy's friends and major investors in the project, turned out to be admirable hosts. Absent from Cairo, due to unexpected circumstances in the States, they had compensated by organizing the best of entertainment for their guests. Early one morning, the two Americans were wafted off over the Pyramids in a hot-air balloon. Shrines, ruins, tombs, courtyards, even the inscrutable Sphinx – everything was captured by an ecstatic Maisie with her brand-new camcorder. A two-day cruise up the Nile (complete with eccentric British archaeologist and plenty of gin) was also recorded for posterity. Mosques and museums, bars and bazaars, the days seemed to race by. Increasingly intrigued, Betsy was desperate for an opportunity to quiz her friend. Whatever it was, a euphoric and indefatigable Maisie was like a carefree teenager again.

As their first week drew to a close, the truth began to dawn: the persistent phone-calls, the daily bouquets of pink and mauve roses – it did not take a woman of Betsy's intuition to figure out what was going on. Late one evening, after a few too many glasses of wine, she resolved to take the bull by the horns. It was the second time over dinner that her dining companion had been called to the telephone.

'OK,' she began pointedly when Maisie returned to the table. 'What's his name?'

Under her light golden tan, Maisie's cheeks flushed pink. 'It's just a friend.'

'The same friend who's been ringing morning, noon and night – meal-times a speciality – since we got here?' Betsy continued to sip her wine: a few glasses of Chardonnay, followed perhaps by the occasional Cognac – Betsy's so-called 'Natural Remedies' – helped her to sleep soundly at night.

For a while Maisie said nothing. Instead, she stared intently at the barbecue which formed the focal point of the Seraphim Hotel's extraordinary dining room. Tricked out to look like an Arabian tent, the walls and ceilings were festooned with miles of flimsy purple silk which ballooned and billowed in the cross breeze. Two spits, each bearing a baby lamb, rotated non-stop over huge beds of glowing embers. The mouthwatering smell of sizzling herb-encrusted meat permeated the hotel's ground floor, wafting through the french windows, opened wide, and outside on to the terraces and swimming pool beyond. From time to time the chef would shave large, juicy slices of tender lamb with his sword-sized Sabatier knife. The fat oozed out, dribbling down on to the charcoal and sending up orange-blue flames which licked the rotating carcass.

'God, it's hot in here.' Somehow Maisie seemed to have forgotten the question. She slipped off her shawl and ordered another bottle of mineral water.

Tipsy though she was, however, Betsy was not to be deflected. 'Is it always the *same* friend?'

Maisie was immersed in the pudding menu. 'Yes, the same one.'

Underneath the table, Betsy kicked off her shoes. Despite the cross breeze through the restaurant, the heat was overwhelming. 'Do I have to drag it out of you, or are you going to tell me?'

'I don't know if I should tell you,' she answered, her eyes downcast. 'I'm not sure that you'll approve.'

Betsy loosened the belt of her green linen dress. Tomorrow, she promised herself, she would be back on the diet. Tonight had been excessive. She had wined and dined so well that already she felt sleepy. 'Whoever he is, I couldn't approve of him less than I do of Charles. Now, come on,' she insisted, 'do I know him?'

Maisie rubbed her chin. 'It depends. You might do. How's your rock 'n' roll?'

After a long hot day and all that wine, Betsy was beginning to feel quite tetchy. 'Have you caught the sun on your head? You're making no sense whatsoever.'

'I'm sorry.' Maisie looked genuinely contrite. 'I don't mean to tease. The trouble is, if you know who I'm talking about, you're bound to think I've flipped.' She fiddled with her earring. 'I think I'm in love with Scorpio.'

Slightly protruding at the best of times, Betsy's eyes seemed about to pop out of her head. 'You don't mean Scorpio – the rock star?'

Maisie nodded.

'The one who said he'd kept the Colombian economy going and that he'd done more booze than Liz Taylor?'

'I'm afraid so.'

'The one who was thrown out of the New York Yacht Club for peeing in the America's Cup?'

Maisie groaned. Deep down, she had known Betsy would

never approve. With Scorpio's reputation for madness and mayhem, who could really blame her?

Betsy's cheeks glowed pink. 'Why, I think that's the most exciting news I've heard in years. I'm so happy for you, honey.'

Open-mouthed, Maisie nearly fell off her chair. 'You mean, you . . .'

'I can still remember the night he threw up all over the British ambassador. Swell Republican, I thought!'

'He's a reformed character now.'

Maisie was desperate to play things down but Betsy would have none of it. She leaned conspiratorially across the table. 'Take my advice,' she whispered, her gaze unsteady. 'Live a little before it's too late. Shock a few people, take a few risks. It's the greatest advantage of being rich!'

Unable to sleep that night, Maisie turned Betsy's words over and over again in her head. Deeply conservative by nature, she had been shocked to hear the elderly widow verbalizing her *carpe diem* philosophy of life. She smiled wryly to herself. Nowadays the merry widow was certainly practising what she preached and few women in Paris were more contented. She put down the book she had been trying half-heartedly to read and switched off her bedside lamp. She stared up into the Stygian darkness, her mind still running wild. Divorce was such a messy business and Charles was bound to make a fight of it. Claims, counter-claims, intimate details of their personal lives – Maisie could feel her resolve weakening already. The good name of Gautier meant so much to her and to those she loved. She would give anything not to have it hauled over the prurient coals of so-called public interest. Maisie tossed and turned. Problems always seemed more difficult in the middle of the night. As a last resort, she even tried counting sheep. She knew she must try to get some sleep. Things always looked better in the morning.

It started as a mild tingling sensation at the back of her throat. Still half dozing, Maisie rolled over and fumbled for the glass of water she had left by the side of her bed. She drained it in one but the tingling persisted. She sneezed and rubbed her eyes which were stinging terribly. She sneezed again and was suddenly aware of the strange acrid smell which seemed to be lingering on the bedclothes. Struggling into consciousness, she reached over and switched on the light, then froze. Thick clouds of grey-black smoke had enveloped the entire bedroom. From where she sat, even the end of the bed was invisible. She jumped up and swiftly pulled on her dressing gown. As she tried to open the bedroom door, she was met by a hot blast of suffocating smoke billowing down the corridor. Terrified, she slammed it shut again and lurched coughing into the bathroom. From somewhere in the depths of her memory, she remembered a piece she had once read in a women's magazine. She turned on the cold water tap and filled up the sink. Then she soused a large white bath towel and wound it around her head.

By now her throat was burning painfully and the hot air scorched her nostrils. As she hurried almost sightlessly out of the bathroom, she fell against the dressing table. She could hear her handbag as it clattered to the floor. Instinctively she bent down to pick it up. Then she fought once more to open the door.

'Quick! Come with us!' a hand emerged from nowhere and grabbed her by the arm. She was aware of it trying desperately to pull her along the corridor. Stubbornly she stood her ground.

'Betsy, I must get Betsy.' Strong with fear, she tugged herself loose and staggered to Betsy's door. She tried it, but it was locked. She began hammering on it frantically. 'Betsy, Betsy!' Her voice was drowned in the bedlam of cries and screams which were everywhere around her. 'Betsy, please, wake up!' But there was no answer from the bedroom. Her hands bruised and bleeding, she tried throwing herself bodily at the door. As she hit it, a searing pain, like a blade of steel, shot up through her neck and shoulders.

'Betsy!' she shouted. 'Betsy, you've got to wake up. Please, Betsy, *open the door!*'

Another arm reached out from the smoke, and caught her in a vice-like grip.

'But my friend's in there,' she wheezed, trying hard to struggle free. 'We've got to get her out.' Suddenly, she slumped to her knees, exhausted. Her eyes ached, her shoulder throbbed and her head was beginning to swim.

'I reckon I'll have to carry her,' said someone.

Semi-conscious, she was dimly aware of muffled American voices. A burly man stooped to pick her up and slung her over his shoulder. 'Betsy!' She began to pound the man's neck with her tiny fists. 'I've got to get my friend out!'

With quiet deliberation, her rescuer let her slip to her feet. Then, standing her up against the wall, he slapped her hard across the face. Suddenly, Maisie's mind went blank. The next thing she could remember, she was safely outside in the hotel grounds.

The dried saliva of fear lay thick upon her tongue. Her head pounding, she sat huddled in the threadbare blanket a kindly nurse had given her. It was like being under partial anaesthetic. She could hear and see everything but somehow she was far too numb to feel. Firemen were everywhere, fighting a desperate battle to stem the blaze. The fire, she overheard, had begun in the restaurant in the early hours of the morning.

'A spark from the barbecue,' repeated one woman, still garrulous from trauma, 'and all those miles and miles of silk.'

With a wail of sirens, an army of ambulances ferried the most seriously injured to the hospital. Badly burned and screaming, people were being stretchered to helicopters. A tiny figure lay motionless on the grass, covered only by a sheet. Bent over it, an hysterical woman was clawing at her hair. The chaos was appalling. Desperate for news, angry residents surrounded hotel staff and demanded explanations. Wisely, the management elected to communicate through the medium of the police. The fire and smoke alarms, it appeared, had failed to go off. Already an American attorney was talking multi-million-dollar compensation.

Dawn broke, brilliant orange and yellow, to reveal the full extent of the disaster. Black-faced and exhausted, firemen combed the charred remains of the Seraphim Hotel, looking for further bodies. Twelve dead and as yet, unidentified, thirty-seven hospitalized, the police spokesman gave the interim figures to an instant influx of world press. Images of the inferno would soon be winging their way across the world. Her lips cracked, her eyes still smarting and bloodshot, Maisie walked falteringly along to an ambulance, searching for news of her friend. The doctor listened sympathetically to her story, then slowly shook his head. 'Betsy Lamielle. No, as far as I know, we've had no one of that name.'

She felt panic welling up inside her. She was about to say something when a policeman appeared and interrupted the conversation. 'You're looking for Mrs Betsy Lamielle?'

Her heart missed a beat. 'Yes.'

'In that case,' said the policeman, avoiding her gaze, 'I think you'd better come with me.'

CHAPTER TWENTY-ONE

Back in London, Laura opened her eyes and stretched contentedly. Already, the early-morning sunshine streamed in through her flimsy cotton curtains. She hopped out of bed and opened the bedroom window wide. Down below, the street was quiet, most of its residents still fast asleep. In the large beech tree outside her flat, a few hungry little sparrows came and went, foraging for breakfast. She wandered into the kitchen and found half a loaf of stale bread in the bin. Then she meandered back to her bedroom and spent the next ten minutes hanging out of the window, throwing gobbets to the birds. Her hair felt lank and heavy, the air clammy against her face. Lazily, she swept her fringe from her forehead. It was going to be another scorching August day.

She showered quickly and grabbed the most minimal of breakfasts. Two grissini and a mug of tea – whatever would Maisie say? Swiftly she pulled on an ancient tracksuit and extracted her cleaning equipment from the cupboard in the hall. This morning there was simply no time for the luxury of sloth. Dusters and Domestos, Windolene and wax, she was soon hard at it, cleaning and polishing as if her life depended on it. It was wrong, she mused, scouring the layers of grease off her cooker, to let things fall into such a state. All the same, she had been so busy of late, domestic neglect was inevitable. The new workshop in Blenheim Crescent had taken quite some time and organization. Revamped now with bare white walls and large open spaces, she was spending ten to twelve hours a day there. To her delight, commissions were already pouring in and every day she thanked her lucky stars and the journalist from *Connoisseur*.

She looked down at the tea-stained sink and grimaced. Thank God for rubber gloves! After sprinkling vast quantities of Vim all over it, she went to work with a Brillo pad. Talk about the sublime to the ridiculous! The previous day had been spent putting the finishing touches to Scorpio's fabulous new ring. Pleased with her progress, she took a breather from scouring and popped her head round the door. There it was, sitting on a velvet cloth in the middle of her gleaming dining table, her latest masterpiece. She went across the room, removed her rubber gloves and held it to the light. It was difficult to resist an enormous surge of pride and satisfaction. Crafted in platinum, the scorpion was perfect in every detail. The stinging tail, curled forward over the back, formed the ring in connection with the two front claws. It was, she knew, both beautiful and clever. She only hoped that Scorpio would like it.

She glanced at the clock on the mantelpiece and returned to the kitchen floor. What a mess! Ubiquitous grease and ground-in dirt, it looked as if it had not been washed in years. Getting down on her hands and knees, she set to with the scrubbing brush. Sharif's plane would be landing at ten o'clock and she still had shopping to do. She drew up a mental list – lamb, vegetables, fruit, bread – it would be just a simple dinner for two. Her imagination began to wander as she levered a piece of ancient chewing gum off the floor. Next, she pulled her best Swiss cotton sheets out of the tumble-dryer and shook out the few residual creases. She knew Sharif was supposed to be staying at his own flat, just off the Fulham Road. But a man could change his mind.

Immersed with her Ajax in the lavatory bowl, she did not hear the telephone at first. Eventually, however, its shrill, insistent ringing percolated through the stud partition wall. She dropped her brush and raced into the bedroom, her heart thumping. Perhaps his plane had touched down two hours early. With PIA, anything was possible. She picked up the receiver and was relieved to hear Scorpio's voice on the end of the phone.

'Laura—'

'You must be telepathic. I finished your ring last night. You wouldn't believe—'

'Have you heard the news?' He sounded as if he were at the end of his tether. Laura's blood ran cold.

'News? What news?'

'The Seraphim, Maisie's hotel in Cairo, I've just heard it on the *Today* programme – there's been a terrible fire.'

She felt her legs turn to jelly as she slumped down on the bed. 'Have you tried ringing?'

'Of course I have, but all the hotel lines are dead. I've even been on to the embassies, but they're constantly engaged. It's awful. I can't bear it. I think I'm going out of my mind.'

She found herself talking in a voice so calm it seemed to belong to someone else. 'I'll get on to Papa right away. He's got contacts in the Quai d'Orsay. They'll soon find out what's going on.'

'I told her I didn't want her to go.' Panic was making him sound irrational. 'I knew I should've stopped her. God, I really need a drink.'

Now it was Laura's turn to panic. For Scorpio's sake, however, she still managed to sound cool. 'I think the last thing we need right now is for you to go on a bender. Now, listen to me, Scorpio. I want you to lock your booze cabinet and give the key to Flo. Then I want you to go and take a nice long swim.'

Scorpio gulped, astonished at the quiet authority of her tone. The gutsy genes of the old Resistance hero must be somewhere there, after all. 'OK,' he conceded doubtfully, 'but promise you'll ring me the moment you hear anything?'

'I promise. Now go and expend some nervous energy. I'm sure we'll find Maisie's safe and sound.'

As she put down the phone, she flicked on the television. The images which greeted her did nothing to boost her ersatz confidence. Against the smouldering remains of the Seraphim Hotel, scenes of the most appalling chaos were still being acted out. Charred bodies, screaming children, frantic medics – the place looked like a bombsite. His face drawn and haggard, an official spokesman appealed for calm and assured the BBC's reporter that 'everything possible was being done'. Pressed on deaths and casualties, he remained resolutely vague. The police, it seemed, were still studying the residents' list. It was all a matter of time.

More worried than she could afford to admit, Laura dialled her father's number. The phone rang and rang, but there was no reply. She tried again. It must be nerves, she chided herself. In her hurry, she must have dialled the wrong number. This time, she let the phone ring for a full three minutes, but still there was no response. It was odd, very odd. Her father was usually at home at this time in the morning. Panicking now, she rang the Gautier office in rue de la Paix. At last she got through to Madame Goffinet who explained that her father had gone to Antwerp for the day.

Laura felt as if her head were a cauldron of molten tar. Frantic, she started ringing the French and American embassies in Cairo, Paris and London. At last, after two hours of sheer frustration, she was put through to an American diplomat in Cairo. The poor man did his best to talk while effectively saying nothing. Nervously she wound the telephone wire round and round her fingers. Despite his calm assurances, it was clear that he was also in the dark. He asked for contact numbers and promised to phone when he knew more. As she put down the receiver she began to feel quite sick.

Grasping now at straws, she tried Harry Blumstein's Antwerp office but the answering machine was switched on. She even called Charles's secretary in Paris but was told that he was somewhere in Madras. When the buzzer sounded, her nerves were so badly frayed, she almost dropped her mug. She picked up the Parlaphone and at the sound of Sharif's voice burst promptly into tears.

He bounded up the stairs and into her flat. 'I phoned you when we landed,' he started, 'but you were constantly engaged. I hope you don't mind—'

Without a word, she flung herself, sobbing, into his arms. It was not the way she had planned it. Her hair was filthy, her clothes torn and she smelt of domestic bleach. He held her close until the tears subsided then gently coaxed out the story.

Laura was inconsolable. As the day wore on, not even his presence could allay her gnawing fears. She jumped every time the phone rang and, on finding that it was only Scorpio, slumped back into a deeper depression.

'Maisie missing is bad enough,' she said as she joined Sharif on the sofa to watch the early evening news, 'but I'm worried about Papa too. He ought to be back by now.'

Sharif did his best to sound upbeat. 'We're bound to hear something soon. Right now, I think I'd better go and organize some displacement activity.' And with that he was gone.

He returned, some fifteen minutes later, laden down with plastic bags.

'I don't know about you,' he said, 'but I'm feeling ravenous.'

She did her best to raise a smile. 'I wouldn't make much of a Pathan, would I? Some hospitality you've had so far!'

He waltzed past her and into the kitchen. 'I'll let you off this once. Great *halal* butcher you've got just up the road. Now, where do you keep your saucepans?'

The smells of cooking were soon wafting through the flat. Eager to distract her, Sharif kept Laura occupied with a plethora of simple tasks. Under his instructions, she prepared a yoghurt marinade into which he chopped some lamb. She skinned tomatoes, peeled potatoes, separated cauliflower florets and chopped spinach for a delicious for a delicious *alu-gobi. Naan kebabs* had been located in a shop on Westbourne Grove. Laura surveyed the array of simmering pots and, despite herself, felt better. She glanced across at Sharif, engrossed in seasoning a *biryani*. 'You never told me you could cook.'

'Pathan New Man. We do everything, you know.' He smiled, his teeth white against his luminous brown skin.

'Do you really mean *everything*?' she said.

It must have been the strains of the day. Never, under normal circumstances, would she have been so forward, especially not with a man like Sharif. As he stared at her, she could feel her cheeks burning with shame, her mouth dry with trepidation. He put down the spoon and in one deft movement, removed the apron from around his waist. 'Perhaps it's time we found out.'

She sent a bottle of chillies flying as he took her in his arms. 'But what about the *sajji*?'

His eyes twinkled as he kissed her. 'About two hours, gas regulo five. That gives us just about time.'

He led her to the bedroom and pulled her closer to him. Their lips were almost touching. He kissed her gently and his lips were very warm. Then he kissed her eyelids and the corners of her mouth. 'Do you know what we're getting into?' His voice was soft, his eyes deep blue pools.

'Probably not.' She nuzzled against his chest as, slowly, he began to undo the buttons of her shirt. At last, she was standing naked before him.

'Are you sure?' he asked, his voice oddly nervous.

'Quite sure.' Her voice was steady. 'In fact, I was never more certain of anything.'

It was three hours later when the phone rang again and Laura was clearing away the dinner dishes. She hesitated, but already its intrusion had dispelled the euphoria of the evening. The apprehension flooded back as she picked up the receiver.

'I can't stand it any longer.' Scorpio's voice sounded thin and worn. 'I need to be with someone. Would you mind if I came over?'

'Of course not.' Her heart went out to him. 'You can even spend the night here if you want – that's if you don't mind slumming it.'

He paused. 'Are you sure Sharif won't mind?'

'Mind? Don't be silly. He's your number one fan. Come on, you can crash out on the sofa.'

As soon as Laura caught sight of Scorpio's twelve-string guitar, all thoughts of sleep were swiftly dispatched. 'I've been playing all afternoon,' he explained, 'trying to keep my mind off things.'

She padded into the kitchen and switched on the coffee percolator. If they were going to have to keep vigil, she decided, they might as well be *wide* awake. Relaxing in the sitting room, the two men chatted on as if they were life-long friends.

'So you really liked the song?' Scorpio strummed a chord.

Sprawled out on the sofa, Sharif was fighting hard against his jet-lag. 'It's perfect, just perfect. How can I ever repay you?'

Scorpio looked admiringly at the ring which he had found, gleaming on the mantelpiece. It now adorned his right hand.

'Laura already did.' The jewels of the scorpion's head flashed brightly in the lamplight. He shouted to her in the kitchen, 'You're a genius, you know, Laura.'

'But a romantic ballad,' insisted Sharif, 'that's such a new departure for you.'

'*I'm* a new departure for me.' Scorpio grinned and played a short sharp flurry of flamenco. 'I think I like the new direction better.'

'You'll never believe it, but Serge Birnbaum cried when he heard it.'

'The old rascal!' Scorpio smiled and tightened a string. 'Let me guess, it must have been all the way to the bank!'

Laura returned carrying a tray of coffee and biscuits. She handed a mug to Scorpio. 'Don't let me catch you taking the mickey out of an old family friend.'

'But he's right,' protested Sharif. 'Serge himself is quite open about it. Economics first, aesthetics second. He says it's the most important rule of film-making. That's why he's so thrilled. He says this song is going to give the film the ultimate promotional push.'

As the clock struck eleven, Laura tried her father again but still there was no reply.

'He must be staying over in Antwerp,' she reasoned half-heartedly and poured herself more coffee.

Scorpio glanced at her pale, drawn face and racked his brains for something to revive their flagging spirits. He turned suddenly to Sharif. 'That script of yours was brilliant.'

'Thanks.'

Scorpio scratched his earlobe. 'It's just that the ending bothers me.'

Sharif raised a quizzical eyebrow but he continued regardless.

'I mean, couldn't you and your woman just go off together and sod the rest of them?'

Sharif drained his coffee and leaned up slowly on one elbow. 'It wouldn't have worked.'

'I don't see why not. The punters adore happy endings.'

'No, I mean it wouldn't have rung true. The characters are Pathans.'

'And Pathans don't believe in love?'

'Of course we do. But not like you. Here in the West it often seems that love is the only thing that counts.'

Scorpio resumed his gentle strumming. 'And isn't it?'

Sharif was sitting up straight, his jet-lag completely forgotten. 'There are other imperatives. Honour, for example.'

Scorpio stopped playing abruptly. 'So you'd trade personal happiness for an abstract concept?'

'We're not talking about abstract concepts. We're talking about a philosophy of life. If my character failed to do what he knew he must, he'd never be happy, not even with the woman he loved.'

The lines of Scorpio's face were set in an earnest frown. 'It's funny, isn't it? I spent my live rebelling, breaking down the conventions – things I reckoned didn't count. Then one day I woke up and there was nothing left, just a vacuum filled with all the dope and drink I could possibly lay my hands on.'

Sharif nodded vigorously. 'It's the malaise of the West. Here, everything – even the very concept of society – has been challenged and undermined. All that's left is an obsession with the trivial and the immediate.'

Scorpio mulled this over for a moment. In the end, he thought he agreed. 'And you and your Pathans?'

'That's where we're so different. In our culture, we still have *absolute* values and beliefs.'

'And that's why you wanted to make this film?'

'Yes.' Sharif's smile was vaguely self-deprecating. 'I had to capture it on celluloid before we're all as lost as you.'

It was then that Sharif noticed Laura, fast asleep and curled kitten-like on the sofa. He picked her up and carried her into the bedroom. He laid her on the bed, then bent down and kissed her tenderly. Her forehead was puckered with worry, her mouth drawn into a thin, tense line. Sharif stroked her bedraggled hair and thought of the headstrong, cross-dressed girl he had come across in the mountains. He touched her cheek. She looked so vulnerable, he thought, so sad and beautiful, a female pierrot.

'Don't worry.' He pulled the duvet up over her shoulders. 'You've got me to help you now.'

Laura slept fitfully, her repose disrupted by recurrent images of leaping flames and fire. She awoke confused, unsure of the boundaries between reality and dream. In the sitting room, she could hear two male voices singing softly in unison. She rolled out of bed and stood in silence by the doorway. The singing stopped for a moment.

'Much better!' said Scorpio, scribbling furiously on a notepad. 'During that scene at the end, where the two lovers part, we'll whack in this extra verse.'

Sharif's eyes were dancing. 'Right. Now let's try the whole thing from the start.'

Soft and haunting, the music seemed to rise, expand and fill the room. The two voices melded perfectly, Scorpio's warm and sonorous, Sharif's plaintive and resonant.

Laura felt the hairs prickling on the back of her neck. The harmonies were wonderful. It was as if these two men were soul-mates, drawing on a bottomless well of unspoken yet shared experience.

The final strains died away, leaving her immobile as she watched them. Love and honour, courage and fortitude – here was everything Sharif had ever taught her about his people and their way. She felt a warm tear trickling down her cheek as, quietly, she closed the door.

CHAPTER TWENTY-TWO

In the middle of the night, the Bois de Boulogne seemed oddly, eerily quiet. Dazed and still shivering, Maisie mouthed instructions to the young diplomat who had been dispatched to meet her at the airport. The man drummed his fingers anxiously on the steering wheel. The American ambassador himself had taken a personal interest in the case. It was he who had ordered the private jet to bring this woman back to Paris. The man glanced up at his rear view mirror. In the back seat, a slight, dishevelled figure in an ill-fitting dress stared blindly into the gloom. The young man shuffled awkwardly. He had seen the pictures on television and guessed that this poor woman was probably in shock. The young man clicked his knuckles. Wars and famine he could cope with. He was fluent in high-profile tragedy-speak. But one woman and her personal grief – for him, that was unknown territory.

'Are you sure you're warm enough, ma'am? I can always turn the heater on if you'd like.'

Maisie looked up, vaguely aware of a voice. 'We'll soon be there,' she murmured distractedly, 'it isn't very far now.'

She resumed her staring. Black and twisted, the trees outside looked like so many charred and tortured corpses. She clenched her hands and her nails dug hard into the soft pink flesh of her palms. The memory of Betsy's body would haunt her always. That was the last thing she could remember – being asked to identify Betsy's body. She wound down the window. Cold though she was, she was desperate for air – anything, just *anything* to blow away the stench of burnt flesh.

'Are you OK, ma'am? Do you want me to pull over?' The young man's voice was tinged with concern, but Maisie never heard it. Her mind was still in the Cairo mortuary where the body she had been shown was too disfigured to identify. The image returned, seared for ever in her consciousness: a small, shrunken skeleton, lumps of carbonized flesh still hanging from the bones; a tiny eyeless skull staring up at her in amazement. She leaned out of the window and retched from the bottom of her stomach. A thin green line of bitterest bile slid slowly down the door.

She wiped her mouth on her sleeve and rewound the window. Betsy, so full of life and so intent on living it to the full, how could that mangled, alien carcass ever have been her? Maisie hugged herself round the middle. The mortuary, the sobbing, hysterical people – the images came crowding back. Desperately, she tried to fight them off but, in the darkness, one particularly insistent vision kept returning. The ring! She rubbed her still stinging eyes. The gleaming ruby engagement ring was the one her friend always wore. And that, in the end, was all that remained of Betsy Lamielle.

Maisie did not remember passing out on the mortuary floor. The next thing she knew, she was in a hospital bedroom, demanding to see the American ambassador. The name of Appleford worked wonders. The ambassador, it seemed, had once been the beneficiary of an Appleford scholarship to Yale. Two hours later, despite her doctor's protests, she was on the plane back to Paris.

The young man coughed politely. 'It's the next road on the right, isn't it?'

She struggled to pull herself together. 'Yes. That's it. I'm the first house on the left.'

As the car made its way up the driveway, the young man noticed a solitary landing light puncturing the darkness of the mansion. More concerned than ever, he helped Maisie up the steps to the front door.

'Are you sure there's someone at home?'

Her response was staccato and toneless, like a robot on automatic pilot. 'The housekeeper – she's from Normandy – she doesn't believe in waste.'

He rang the bell and they waited in the porch. Another landing light went on, then another, then the vast entrance hall was suddenly illuminated. The housekeeper looked cautiously through the fish-eyed spy-hole before disarming the alarm system. It seemed like an eternity before she finally opened the door. She almost fell upon Maisie. 'Madame, thank God you're safe. I've been sick with worry. Your sister-in-law has been phoning all day. None of us knew what was happening.'

Relieved to find someone on whom to offload his responsibility, the young diplomat swiftly took his leave. Maisie watched in silence as the car swished off down the driveway. The night air was warm and humid, but her teeth still chattered loudly. Anxiously, the housekeeper tried to shepherd her into the hall. 'You must go to bed immediately. I'll fetch you a hot-water bottle and some brandy. Then I'm going to call the doctor.'

'No!'

The housekeeper jumped. Madame looked too weary for such a degree of vehemence.

'I *don't* need a doctor and I *don't* need a drink.'

'Some hot milk, perhaps?'

Sensing the woman's genuine concern, Maisie relented a little. 'Go back to bed. I can see to myself. I'm perfectly fine on my own.'

She wandered into the drawing room and switched on all the lights. Then, she flopped down into an armchair and, for some minutes, stared blankly into space. A watery smile danced fleetingly across her lips. Human beings were so impossibly perverse. She had not smoked in years and yet now, the survivor of a holocaust, she was desperate for a cigarette. She heaved herself up and made her way to her husband's office. Charles hated smoking with a passion, but he always kept supplies of cigars and cigarettes at hand for favoured clients. It was so typical of him, she thought, as she pushed open the door. There was no principle he was not prepared to sacrifice in the interest of increased profits.

She turned on the side lamp and scanned the room for the gold and lapis lazuli box he used for cigarettes. At last she spotted it on his desk, half covered with sheets of paper. She opened the box, intrigued at the surrounding mess. It was so unlike Charles to leave his desk in such a state. A neurosis for secrecy if not tidiness meant that everything was generally cleared away. She lit the cigarette and inhaled deeply. The smoke hurt her throat, scorched raw from the fire, but she continued to puff away none the less. Never before had she pried into Charles's personal affairs. Until now, she had always felt that such behaviour was beneath her. She coughed long and hard. As far as her husband was now concerned, *that* Maisie died in Cairo.

The nicotine fed into her system and gradually began to revive her. She began to sift through the papers on the desk and noticed that the initials S.S. seemed to crop up everywhere. She frowned, unable to work out what they stood for, and continued with her reading. Columns of figures, additions, subtractions, conversions into various currencies – none of it made any sense. Increasingly puzzled, she leaned back, closed her eyes and blew smoke rings into the air. The figures involved were astronomic. What on earth was going on?

A sudden loud click startled her out of her reverie. On the desk, near the bank of telephones, an answering machine whirred into action.

'Hello, Charles. Sammy Sandton here . . .'

Maisie pricked up her ears. S.S. – Sammy Sandton. Why was a cowboy like that phoning Charles?

'I didn't want to ring you in the office for obvious reasons.' There was a loud guffaw. 'But I just wanted to let you know that I'm here at the Mandarin in Singapore until Sunday. By the way, where the hell are you? Anyway, for your info, the funding is now completely in place and old Sammy's itching to go. Daphne's head over heels with your new boutique here. She says she can't wait until Gautier is really hers!' There was another loud guffaw. '*Hers!* Women – what would we do without them? Anyhow, give us a bell if you touch base before Sunday. If not, I'll catch up with you next week.'

Stunned, Maisie rewound the tape and played the message again. No, she assured herself, she had not been dreaming. Outrageous though it might seem, Charles and Sammy Sandton were concocting a deal. Shaking, she ran through the columns of figures that before had seemed so meaningless. By now, her heart was beating so hard she thought her ribs would crack. Soon, the pieces of the jigsaw started falling into place.

'You bastard!' She stubbed out her cigarette so hard that the filter tip snapped off. Charles, it appeared, had it all worked out. As soon as he could, he intended to relinquish control of Gautier to none other than Sammy Sandton.

A searing, migrainous pain attacked the left side of Maisie's skull. Frantic now, she began to rummage through the drawers of Charles's desk. Evidence! She knew she had to have more evidence. Her mind racing, she pulled out sheaf after sheaf of papers. She scanned them quickly but, to her growing distress, found nothing incriminating. Maisie rammed home one drawer and pulled out another. Charles was too clever by half, but even clever people sometimes made mistakes. She emptied an envelope full of documents on to the desk and began to sort through them. She knew she had to find proof that would convince even Gaston. If only he could be made to believe her, there was still time to stop Charles and his scheme.

Breathless, she tugged at the top drawer but discovered it was locked. For a split second, she hesitated. It was as if she were standing outside herself and looking in, observing the manic behaviour of a stranger. A silver paper-knife, a gift she had once given Charles, lay gleaming in the lamplight. She picked it up and, with a strength born of anger and frustration, savagely attacked the lock. The mechanism soon gave way and the surrounding wood splintered into a shower of tiny fragments. Oddly indifferent to her own act of vandalism, she pulled out the drawer and tipped its contents on to the desk. A large, yellowing envelope remained stuck in one of the corners. As she yanked it out, a letter fell to the floor. She picked it up and opened it. Suddenly she felt her fingers grow numb. The letter was addressed to Charles from Professor Duval, France's leading expert on infertility. Maisie sat down and, taking a deep breath, began to read his report.

The letter slipped from between her fingers and wafted down to her feet. She tried to retrieve it, but her body refused to move. It did not matter. The contents of that report would live with her for ever. She stared blankly at the wall. According to the Professor, the conclusions of extensive tests had revealed that Charles was suffering from 'an almost non-existent sperm count'. Maisie bit her lip. For twenty years he had managed to keep the secret of *his* infertility from her. For twenty years he had made her feel guilty and inadequate – a failure as a woman and a wife.

Outraged, she picked up the paper-knife and flung it across the room. It caught the edge of a silver-framed photograph and brought it crashing to the ground. She walked across to where it had landed and, with her heel, ground the picture further and further into the thick pile of the carpet. Beneath the pressure, the shattered glass ripped and tore at the photo. She glanced down at the damage. Of the set-piece image that was her wedding day, all that remained was a heap of shreds.

A phone on Charles's desk rang with a sudden shrillness. From the flashing red light, Maisie could see that the general house number, not Charles's private line, was being accessed. Curious, she walked towards the desk to answer it. It was still the middle of the night. Who on earth would be calling at this hour?

On the other end of the line was Gaston's housekeeper who was making no sense whatsoever.

'So your son's car broke down,' repeated Maisie, struggling to make sense of the babbling, 'and you've only just arrived home.'

'I shouldn't have gone,' wept Madame D, 'but Monsieur insisted I should take a week's holiday, but I should never have left him on his own. He's so much weaker nowadays.'

Maisie felt her pulse quicken. 'For heaven's sake, what's happened?'

'Monsieur is gone. They've taken him away to the hospital and I wasn't even here. Oh, Madame, I'll never forgive myself.'

'Which hospital?' Maisie was suddenly wide awake.

'St Cloud.'

'What happened? A fall? One of his turns?'

'The neighbours told me it was a heart attack.' Madame D started crying again. 'They say he was unconscious when he left.'

Maisie's head was throbbing. She told Madame D to have a

brandy and try to get some sleep. Next she phoned the hospital and was put through to the intensive care unit. The doctor there was relieved to hear from her. He told her that Gaston had been admitted two hours before. The hospital was now trying to contact relatives.

'Is it *that* serious?' Maisie's voice was hoarse yet clear.

'I'm afraid so,' replied the doctor. 'He hasn't regained consciousness since he's been here. Could we leave it to you to inform the family?'

'Of course.' Her throat was dry, her chest felt tight and she was feeling dizzy again. 'Then I'll be straight over, just as soon as I've made the calls.'

Laura was only half asleep when she heard the telephone ring. Hurriedly she grabbed the receiver. At the sound of Maisie's voice, she burst into tears of joy.

'I'm fine, honey, fine.' Maisie's voice was a peculiar monotone, struggling to find conviction.

'We've all been so worried. Oh, Maisie, thank God you're safe. It's been awful. Papa's been out of Paris – I couldn't even talk to him.'

There was a short pause on the line. 'There's bad news. I'm afraid Gaston's been taken into hospital.' Already Laura was out of bed and standing upright. 'Is it his heart?'

'Yes. I think you'd better get over here as soon as possible.'

'I'll be on the first flight out.' A sudden sharp pain rent her chest. She doubled over, breathless. 'I'm sorry, Maisie. Right now, I can't really speak.'

'It's OK, honey. I understand. Look, let me organize your reservations.'

'Don't be silly. You're hassled enough and, besides, I've got Sharif and Scorpio here.'

The very mention of Scorpio's name seemed to lift a burden from Maisie's shoulders. 'Let me speak with him, will you, honey? Then go try catch some sleep.'

Scorpio's relief soon evaporated as a clearly distraught Maisie relayed the details of Charles's plans. Ensconced on a bean-bag in the sitting room, he gestured to Sharif to close the adjoining bedroom door.

'I don't want to go worrying Laura,' continued Maisie, 'at least, not yet. If Gaston pulls through, there won't be a problem. I reckon I've got enough on Charles to make him change his will.'

'But what if he doesn't pull through?'

'It doesn't bear thinking about.' She fell silent for a moment. 'Will you do me a favour?'

'Anything.'

'Laura's sounding real low. Would you mind taking her to the airport?'

'I'll do better than that,' he replied earnestly. 'I'm coming along myself.'

'Me too,' added Sharif.

Scorpio nodded his approval. 'Yes,' he continued, 'and Sharif's coming too.'

'Good.' Maisie was sounding more controlled. 'Laura's going to need all the support she can get.'

Scorpio shook his head in silent admiration. Strong, brave, selfless Maisie, it was high time someone supported *her*.

CHAPTER TWENTY-THREE

B ack at the hospital, the luminous green line flickered feebly on the screen. Exhausted but far too worried to sleep, Maisie maintained her bedside vigil. Gaston had not stirred all night. His face, grey yet unlined, seemed strangely at peace. She studied the plethora of wires, drips and tubes attached to his motionless body. Around the hospital room, the latest in cardio-vascular technology bleeped out its dispassionate message. She stared at the screen, knowing that no device on earth could ever answer the question even now at the forefront of her mind. Was it really possible that a diamond could be cursed?

Stiff from sitting, she stretched her legs, then got up and walked to the window. Pulling back the blind, she watched as a blue-grey Parisian dawn rose swiftly over the rooftops. She glanced back at Gaston, praying that he might open his eyes and ask her to let the sunlight in, but his lips did not move. She returned to his bedside and smoothed back his silver-grey hair. The tears pricked hard behind her eyelids. She closed them tight and began to pray. 'Please, God, let him get better. He just *has* to get well again. You can't let Charles . . .' She stopped herself mid-sentence. Even if God did exist, something she had grave doubts about right now, there was no point in telling Him what He could and could not do. A long-forgotten line of scripture came swimming back into her consciousness. 'Let Thy will not mine be done,' she whispered, 'but please, God, let both of them coincide.'

Smart and rather daunting in her starched white apron and light blue frock, the ward sister entered the room with the brisk efficiency of a professional. Maisie looked up and, to her surprise, found she was carrying a tray of coffee and croissants. Suddenly she felt ravenous. For the last few days eating and drinking had been expunged from her daily routine.

'Some breakfast for you, Madame.' The nurse placed the tray on a table near the window. She washed her hands and started checking the drips and monitors stationed all around. Expressionless, she made notes on the clipboard at the bottom of the bed. Maisie watched intently as she sipped her cup of coffee.

'Any improvement?'

The woman smiled encouragingly. 'He's stable. He's suffered a massive coronary, but he's very strong for his age.'

'Is there any chance he'll be able to speak to us soon?'

'I'm sorry,' replied the nurse, 'there's no way of knowing. He's still a very sick man.'

'His daughter should be here any time now.' Maisie glanced anxiously at her watch. 'I feel sure he'll recognize her voice.'

'I hope so, but we mustn't overburden him with visitors. My instructions are "immediate family only".' Briskly she started to straighten the sheets. 'In fact, I've just had to send someone away.'

Maisie's coffee cup rattled on its saucer. 'Not Scorpio?'

The sister looked at her as if she were hallucinating. 'Scorpio – you mean the rock star?'

'Yes.'

The nurse resumed in the tone she reserved for cases of senile dementia. 'You've been through a lot, Madame. Perhaps we could ask the doctor to prescribe a course of tranquillizers—'

Irritated, Maisie cut her short. 'For goodness' sake, I'm perfectly well. I've got to know who that was.'

Sniffily, the sister fished around in her apron pocket and pulled out a piece of paper. 'A gentleman by the name of Daniel Baudon. I must say, he was acting very strangely. He kept saying it was all his fault.'

Maisie jumped up, knocking over the tray in the process. It fell to the floor with an ear-splitting clatter, but still Gaston did not move. 'When was this?'

'Just a few minutes ago . . .'

Already Maisie was off, racing down the corridor. Impatiently she waited, but the lift seemed to take an age in coming. It stopped at every level and finally refused to budge from the floor above. Furious, she cast around for the emergency staircase and ran helter-skelter down to the entrance hall. It was there that she caught sight of Daniel as he was about to disappear through the automatic doors. 'Daniel! Daniel!' she wheezed, completely out of breath. He turned at the sound of his name. His cheeks were hollow and he looked in more pain than his friend in intensive care. He hurried across the highly polished hospital floor and almost fell upon Maisie.

'I should have known something like this was bound to happen.' He gestured towards the cafeteria. 'Come on. I need a tisane to calm my nerves.'

The hospital cafeteria was as clean and soulless as the hospital itself. Sitting opposite one another across a bright white melamine table, Maisie and Daniel made a sorry-looking couple. Grubby, dishevelled and still wearing her baggy borrowed frock, the American heiress could easily have been mistaken for a penniless pan-handler. The irony was not lost on Daniel whose sharp eyes never missed a trick. He leaned forward across the table.

'I met Gaston on the plane to Antwerp the other day.'

'Yes.' Maisie sipped her tea. 'Laura said he was out of town.'

He rubbed his chin. He had not had time to shave that morning and the stubble was annoying him. 'I've been meaning to speak to him for some time now, but the time has never seemed right.'

There was a bowl of sugar lumps in the middle of the table. Maisie picked them out one by one and began to construct a pyramid. 'Believe me, I *do* know what you mean.'

Daniel coughed, embarrassed. 'There's no point pretending that I ever liked your husband.'

'Join the club.'

He looked vaguely surprised. He had never expected such complicity from Maisie. 'The arrogance I could live with. We all made concessions because of his mother. But I could never accept his behaviour towards Gaston.' He drew a deep breath. 'Or, for that matter, towards you.'

She continued building in silence.

'For years, *Le Pou qui Tousse* has been an invaluable source of information. Sleaze and corruption in high places – there's nothing I don't know.' He stared out of the adjacent window.

Maisie studied her completed pyramid and then, with a sudden swipe of her hand, brought the entire structure crashing down. 'If you're trying to spare my feelings, don't. Nothing about Charles can upset or surprise me any more. I've decided to divorce him and now I want to know the truth.'

Daniel put his wrinkled hand over hers. 'I'm so sorry, my dear.'

'There's nothing to be sorry about.'

'Only the fact that you should have done it twenty years ago.' Slowly he sipped his tisane. 'I've had dirt on Charles since he started in the business. Illicit diamonds, shady deals – not to mention his private life.' He glanced at her for signs of distress, but her face gave nothing away. 'The real problems started a few months ago, when I set up the *Gadfly* in London. We've got some very hot people on that magazine. Their sources are first-rate.'

'I've read it,' she said, 'and I must say it's addictive.'

'Thanks. We do our best.' His smile was vaguely sardonic. 'Anyway, one of our investigative reporters, Flick Harrison, has been working on a story. Last week, she came up with her final report. At first I couldn't believe it.' He lowered his voice. 'But Flick had all the supporting evidence. It seems that Charles is trying to hand Gautier over to that philistine Sammy Sandton.' He sat back waiting for Maisie's reaction but, to his surprise, she barely moved.

'I already know.' Her voice was crisp and calm. 'I found out late last night. But what about Gaston? Do you reckon he has any idea?'

Suddenly Daniel's head drooped forward into his hands. 'I'd been meaning to tell him about the story before we ran it in the *Gadfly*. When I met him on the plane, it seemed as good a time as any.'

'How did he take it?'

The tears were glistening in Daniel's eyes. 'The way he always takes bad news – cool, calm, unruffled, just like the old Renard.'

'And do you think he believed you?'

'He had no alternative. I showed him all the evidence. We've even got sworn statements from the Sandton employees who raised the cash for the deal.'

Maisie ground a sugar lump to powder on the table. 'He's *got* to pull through,' she said, her voice toneless. 'He's got to stop this happening.'

'But I can't help thinking that if I hadn't told him—'

'Nonsense! If Gaston's ill, it isn't your fault. We know who to blame for that.' She stood up brusquely and, after embracing the old man, promised to keep him posted on further developments.

His face was grim as he pulled on his ancient Burberry raincoat. 'You know I'll do anything to stop that bastard – anything at all.'

They walked together back into the hall and Maisie watched as, straight-backed, Daniel left the building. For a few minutes she stood there, mentally marshalling her allies. Then, all at once, the doors swooshed open and there, haloed in the sunshine, stood Scorpio. She raced across the hall and fell, limp with relief, into his arms.

Upstairs they found Sharif already sitting in the waiting room. 'Laura's gone straight in,' he explained, and introduced himself to Maisie.

The ward sister walked past, wheeling a trolley, and did a double take. Open-mouthed, she stared from Scorpio to Maisie then back to Scorpio again. 'Is there anything I can get you?' Her eyes were trained unblinking on the icon of her rebellious adolescence.

Scorpio eyed the trolley mischievously. 'Well, now, how about a nice little cocktail of methadone and Mogadon – just for old times' sake?'

The woman tittered nervously and trotted off down the corridor.

'I'm so glad you two are here,' said Maisie, collapsing gratefully on to a chair.

'Why don't you lie down?' Scorpio pointed to an *ad hoc* bed in the corner. 'You might even manage some sleep.'

She shook her head. 'There's no time for that – at least, not now. Let me fill you in on events.'

Laura sat next to her father's bed and tenderly held his hand. His long, artist's fingers were surprisingly warm and supple. She only wished they would respond to hers. 'Papa.' Her voice was tremulous. She leaned forward to kiss his forehead. 'Papa, it's me, Laura.' She gripped his hand more tightly and his eyelids began to flicker.

'Laura?' Slowly he opened his eyes and stared blearily up at her. 'Laura, my dear, thank God you're here.'

She flung her arms around his neck and kissed him hard. The drip in his arm swung to and fro. She checked herself, alarmed. 'Perhaps I ought to tell the staff that you're awake?' She peered anxiously at the alarm button at the side of the bed.

'Please don't!' his eyes were desperate. 'They'll only pump me full of sedatives and I have to talk to you.'

Shaken by the thin, feeble voice, Laura clasped his hand with renewed urgency. She glanced around at the barrage of life-support equipment and felt suddenly afraid. The black rubber suckers on her father's chest seemed like monstrous parasites, intent on draining him of life. 'You must rest,' she insisted, pulling up the blanket. 'We can talk later, when you're feeling stronger.'

Gaston caught her wrist with an unexpected force. 'But you don't understand! Charles . . .'

The green line on the monitor zig-zagged furiously up and down. Laura stroked her father's forehead and contemplated ringing the alarm. 'Don't worry,' she said. 'I'm sure Charles will get here just as soon as he can. His secretary is already ringing round. She's sure to track him down.'

Gaston's head lolled slightly to one side. 'I trusted him,' he murmured. 'Shouldn't a man be able to trust his own son?'

With increasing consternation, she looked at the graph being traced out on the monitor. '*Papa*, you mustn't go upsetting yourself. Please, you must rest.'

Suddenly Gaston clenched his fists and, with a dreadful groan, forced himself up on to his elbows.

'*Papa!*' Her voice was shrill with alarm. 'Please, stop it. I'm going to call for help.'

'No!' The order seemed to echo round and round the spotless, white-walled room. 'This is important. You must call my lawyers at once.'

'Please, *Papa*.' She was shaking all over. 'You *must* calm down. I'm going to call the doctor.'

Maisie was anxiously pacing the floor as the emergency team raced past. A few minutes later, Laura appeared at the waiting-room door. 'He says he wants to see his lawyers,' she sobbed. 'There was nothing I could do to calm him down.'

Sharif shot Maisie a meaningful look. She raised her index finger to her lips. 'It's going to be all right.' She put her arm around Laura's heaving shoulders. 'Your father's as strong as an ox.'

Scorpio's platinum ring glistened as, slowly, he scratched his chin. 'These lawyers, tell me, do you know where to get hold of them?'

Laura looked up, surprised. 'They're mostly in Geneva. But why—?'

'Scorpio, please, don't even think of it!' Maisie's tone was adamant. 'Even if you managed to round them up, Gaston's in no fit state to deal with them.'

Laura's head was swimming – a combination of fear, fatigue and anguish, she felt as if she was going mad. 'Will someone please tell me what the hell's going on? Why on earth do we need the lawyers?'

'Mademoiselle Gautier.' Po-faced, the ward sister poked her head around the door. 'Please, we'd like you to come quickly.'

At a sign from the consultant, the members of the emergency team left Gaston's room in silence. Trembling, Laura searched the eyes above the green mask for the answer to her question. 'He's in no pain,' said the consultant kindly. 'He's just suffered another serious attack and I'm afraid he hasn't got long.' He sidled out of the room and quietly closed the door.

Alone now with her father, Laura sat down on the edge of the bed. Most of the drips and wires had been disconnected. His eyes fluttered open as he reached out for her hand. 'You'll have to be strong,' he whispered, 'strong enough to stop it.'

She nodded, uncomprehending. This was no time to be asking questions. 'Of course, Papa. Of course, I will.'

He smiled contentedly. 'That dossier in my office . . .' His voice trailed off into nothing.

'The design dossier?'

Gaston's eyelids flickered feebly. 'I want you to have it. Remember, Laura, it's important. Our family, everything we stand for – I confide all that to you.'

She could feel his fingers growing weaker by the second. 'I'll do my best not to let you down.'

A sudden shadow crossed his face. By now his voice was barely audible. 'My private collection is going to the V and A – that's all been organized. But the Star of Heaven must go there too. Please, will you sort that out?' A watery smile spread fleetingly across his lips. 'I never got round to dealing with it myself. I don't suppose old Renard ever believed he was going to die.'

Distraught, she buried her head in the pillow next to his. With a shaking hand, Gaston reached out and lightly touched her hair. 'I love you,' he whispered as he closed his eyes, 'you're the only child I truly loved.'

CHAPTER TWENTY-FOUR

I t seemed that Charles Gautier had disappeared off the face of
the earth. Discreet as ever, his secretary tried all the usual
numbers, but even thirty-six hours after his father's death, he
was still nowhere to be found. As the hours ticked by, Maisie
became increasingly anxious. After seeing Laura safely to Gaston's apartment, she returned home, refusing to go out in case
the phone rang with news of her husband's whereabouts. A
worried Scorpio insisted on keeping her company. As they sat
together in the drawing room, he begged her to see a doctor.

'I keep telling you, there's too much to do!' She jumped up
from the sofa and started pacing around the room.

'But you aren't doing anything here.' His eyes followed the
pale, gaunt figure as it collapsed again on to a chair. 'All you're
doing is driving yourself completely up the wall!'

'I'm sorry.' She looked so crumpled that he wished he had
held his tongue. 'I couldn't care less where my so-called husband
is. But, for Gaston's sake, I have to consider the family. Gaston
Gautier was a national hero. Whatever anyone thinks about
Charles, he has to be here for the funeral.'

'That bastard killed his father just as surely as sticking a knife
in his back.'

She sighed wearily. 'There'll be plenty of time for recriminations later. But let's at least have a civilized burial before the
fighting's allowed to start.'

The french windows in the drawing room had been thrown
wide open. Frustrated, Scorpio sauntered outside into the garden
and stared up at the cloudless blue sky. Behind him, a restless

scratching sound soon distracted his attention. He turned, and there, not three feet away from where he was standing, a rare red squirrel was burying nuts by the roots of a gnarled old oak tree. 'Come quickly.' He was happy for an excuse to lure her out into the sunshine.

'What's the matter?' Like a mole, inured to the darkness, she blinked as she emerged from the house. He pointed to the squirrel and her face relaxed into a smile.

'That's much better!' He put an arm around her waist and felt her hips protruding like two razor blades. Protectively he pulled her closer. 'My God, you're nothing but skin and bone. At this rate, you'll disappear completely.'

Her emaciated body seemed to tense again as he spoke. 'Someone's got to watch out for Laura. Charles will have her tied up in knots in no time at all. And she's in no fit state to fight him—'

Scorpio put his finger to her lips. 'She'll be OK, believe me. Sharif and I were discussing it last night at the hotel. There's no way we're going to let Charles get away with this deal.'

Maisie watched the squirrel as he scurried around, busily hiding his winter reserves. Slowly she shook her head. 'The trouble is, none of us has any real idea of what he's been up to all these years. God knows what he's managed to stash away or how much Sandton has offered him for his stock.'

The couple fell silent as they contemplated the potential strength of the opposition. Arm in arm, they ambled down the garden and into the small orchard at the perimeter of the property. It was cooler there, underneath the spreading apple trees. Scorpio stooped to pick up a few semi-grown windfalls. Then, with a strong right arm, he sent them skimming across the wall.

'I don't care what deal they've concocted and how much money is involved. All I know is, we're going to stop them.'

She flopped down exhausted on a beckoning green bench. 'That's what I keep telling myself but, right now, I'm not sure I believe it. Charles is streets ahead of us. How can we stop him in time?'

He sat down beside her and grasped her hand in his. 'Now's

not the time to start talking of defeat. You've been so brave for yourself and Laura. You're feeling tired, that's all.'

A glorious Red Admiral butterfly sailed effortlessly past their faces. Maisie followed it with her eyes until it soared off, up, up into the azure sky and disappeared out of sight. 'I'm tired of being brave,' she murmured. 'Sometimes there seems a lot to be said for simply walking away.'

Scorpio chewed his lip. He knew all about depression, the ups and downs, the mood swings. What Maisie now needed was firm direction. It was what his therapist called Tough Love. 'You may say it's none of my bloody business,' he said abruptly, 'but I'm not going to stand by and let that happen.'

She looked at him in surprise. 'Why should the House of Gautier mean anything to you?'

'It doesn't, but *you* care. It matters to *you*.' He leaned over and stroked her cheek. 'Besides, that bastard Charles has done enough damage already. It's time someone sorted him out.'

He twisted the scorpion ring from his finger and placed it in her hand. 'Here, I want you to have this.'

Filtering through the branches, a narrow ray of sunshine fell plumb upon the ring. Glistening in the light, the chiselled creature seemed to spring to life. 'I don't understand. Laura made this for you.'

Scorpio made a big play at swatting a passing fly. 'I know. So at least, like this, we're keeping things in the family.'

Despite the sultry heat, he noticed she was trembling. 'I'm afraid I can't accept.'

His heart was beating so hard, he was sure it drowned his voice. 'But I love you. I want to—'

'No.' Her voice resolute. 'I have to feel free, completely free before I can accept.'

He looked at her with such tenderness that she felt a lump rising in her throat. As she replaced the ring on his finger, he took her in his arms. 'You're a wonderful woman, Maisie. You're fine and kind and honourable. I'll wait until you're ready, however long it takes.' He tilted her chin towards him and kissed her hard on the lips. She closed her eyes and for a moment everything – the fire, Betsy, Charles, Gaston – was obliterated from her mind. Like the butterfly, she felt light and carefree, fluttering gaily with the air-flows, upwards towards the sky.

The sound of wheels on gravel brought her back to earth with a bang. Through the trees, she could see Charles, levering himself with difficulty out of the back of a taxi. She froze in Scorpio's arms. 'I've got to go.'

'I'm coming with you.'

She shook her head. 'No, please don't. I don't want any trouble until the funeral's over.'

'You're probably right.' He bit his knuckles in sheer frustration. 'The mood I'm in right now, I'd probably end up decking the bastard.'

'Take my car. The keys are in the ignition.' She reached up and kissed his cheek. 'I'll ring you later at the hotel.'

'Maisie? Maisie!' Loud and peremptory, Charles's voice boomed out from the drawing room.

Scorpio gazed down at her, more loath than ever to let her go. 'Don't worry.' She squeezed his hand so hard that the scorpion ring gouged a deep red imprint on the soft white flesh of her palm. She looked at the tiny wound of love and gently rubbed it with her finger. 'I can cope with anything now.'

Charles was pouring himself a large drink as she walked in from the garden. His back turned, he did not notice her at first. He drained the Scotch in one, then swiftly poured himself another. She made to say something, then quickly changed her mind. For the first time in her life, she realized, she was seeing the reality. Charles slurped his drink, more slowly this time. Slung carelessly over an armchair, his light linen jacket slithered to the floor. She could see he was sweating profusely: under his arms and between his flabby shoulders the dark damp patches stained his striped cotton shirt. Stretched tight around his buttocks, his expensive Savile Row trousers looked as if they had been made for a much slimmer, neater man. The rolls of flab flapped over his waistband. They looked like buttered crumpets stacked haphazardly on a plate. Charles grabbed a handful of cashew nuts and stuffed them into his mouth. Maisie shook her head in pity and contempt. Dissolute and greedy, the creature standing before her was nothing but a stranger.

'I'm so glad you made it back.' Her tone was mordant.

He turned, the spidery veins of his cheeks purple with alcohol and heat. Loose and baggy, his heavy jowls reminded Maisie of a bloodhound. Suddenly, she felt an uncontrollable desire to laugh. The scales had fallen from her eyes. At last, she had broken free.

He shrugged and poured himself another drink. Then, with a wobbly hand, he held up the bottle. 'Want one?'

She shook her head. 'No thanks. There's too much to be organized.' She sat down on the sofa and watched as he meandered across to the fireplace.

'So, the old man's kicked it, then?'

She inhaled deeply, determined to stay calm. 'Would you like to see the body?'

His laugh was hard and mirthless. He took another slug of his Scotch. 'What on earth for?'

'To pay your last respects,' she replied icily.

'For God's sake,' he snorted, 'it was enough hassle having to see him when he was still alive. Forgive me if I pass on the corpse.'

Maisie's eyes came to rest on the solid lump of malachite which adorned the escritoire. It was all she could do to stop herself from throwing it at him. Instead, she gripped a cushion.

'We've been granted special permission to hold the requiem at St-Louis-des-Invalides,' she said.

Charles's fleshy lips curled into the most cynical of smiles. 'But of course! Gaston Gautier, fearless Resistance fighter, let's have the full charade for one of the nation's greatest heroes.'

She gripped the cushion harder. 'We were waiting for you to arrive before we set a date.'

'How kind to involve me in the family plans, I'm really so terribly touched.' His words were slurred.

'The day after tomorrow then,' she concluded crisply, 'if that's all right with you.'

'All right with me! *All right with me!* Since when did anyone in this family give a toss whether things were all right with me?'

He drained the remains of his drink and lurched across the room for another refill.

A rumble of thunder was audible in the distance. Outside, the storm clouds were gathering, grey and threatening, in the hazy afternoon heat. Maisie got up and began to close the windows. Despite the recent showers, the garden still looked parched and dusty. A single raindrop splattered on her hand. She looked at it, glistening cool and delicious against her hot, clammy skin. In the flower garden nearby, a delighted gardener hurried to put his tools away. She waved at him as he scurried past. 'The rain always comes in the end,' he shouted. 'It's just a matter of holding out.'

She walked back into the drawing room and resumed her position on the sofa. 'About the scripture readings. I thought you might like to do one.'

His eyes bloodshot, Charles shot her a look of deepest disdain. 'Can't you get it into that stupid head of yours? I don't give a fuck who reads or sings or dances on his grave. Where the hell was *he* when *I* needed *him*?' He staggered over to where she was sitting and shouted in her face, '*Nowhere!* That's where your big-deal national hero was. *Nowhere* to be found!'

The stench of alcohol made her want to retch. She turned her head away. He resumed his ranting around the room, banging into furniture as he went. Then, suddenly, he caught his foot in a rug and fell heavily against a bookcase. As the rows of books came tumbling out, one hit him on the temple. Furious, he picked up an onyx box from a nearby table and flung it against a mirror. It shattered instantly. For a moment, Charles stared at the grotesque, distorted creature who stared back at him from between the cracks. He slumped down into an armchair and buried his head in his hands.

She closed the door behind her and moved quietly across the hall. Walking up the staircase, she stopped for a moment to listen. It might have been the rain outside, but it sounded like someone crying.

*

Lugubrious in the storm, the drawing room of Gaston's apartment was suddenly lit by a flash of lightning. Busy on the telephone, a startled Laura said a swift goodbye and put down the receiver. 'Looks like Maisie's got everything fixed.' She resumed her previous position, supine on the floor.

Sharif looked up. 'So at last they tracked down Charles?'

She nodded. 'It seems like he just tipped up. No questions, no explanations – typical Charles. He didn't even ask how Papa died.' She stared into open space. 'God, I really hate that man.'

'Is he causing any problems?'

She shook her head lethargically. 'He's not interfering with the funeral arrangements, if that's what you mean. Maisie says she doesn't mind what he does just so long as he appears.' A sudden thought occurred to her. 'Would you like to come as well?'

'If you'd like me to.'

'You mustn't feel obliged.'

'I don't.'

'I'd have invited you before but . . .' she looked suddenly bashful, 'but this is a Roman Catholic service.'

'Yes?' He raised a quizzical eyebrow.

'And, well, you're a Muslim.'

'So I am!' His eyes were twinkling with mischief. 'Do you suppose the church might collapse on top of me?'

It was the first vague flicker of a smile Sharif had seen in days. After her father's death, a distraught Laura had cried like a child in his arms. Calm and strong, he had held her close and wiped away the tears. Now that the sobbing had subsided, he knew he must keep her occupied. Activity was always the best defence against the apathy of depression.

'May I see a picture of your father? I feel I almost know him.'

She walked across to the Louis XV desk in the corner of the room. After some rummaging she found an old family photo album and pulled it out. Flicking through the pages, she came to rest on a picture of a tall handsome soldier.

'That's him.' She settled down next to Sharif. 'That's Papa receiving the Croix de Guerre from General de Gaulle.' She turned over the page. 'Oh, and that's my mother, Caroline. This one was taken on her wedding day.'

'She looks just like you – very beautiful.'

But already Laura was far too engrossed to hear. It was as if her entire childhood was being relived before her very eyes. Happy images of herself and her father lay scattered throughout the album. In the workshop in Paris, on holiday in Cannes, on the slopes in Gstaad – a relationship of love and admiration shone through on every page. The most recent pictures had been taken in London and showed Gaston happy and relaxed. A tear rolled down Laura's cheek. 'I do so miss him.'

He slipped his arm around her waist. 'Of course you do,' he said, and kissed her hair, 'but I'm here to look after you now.'

Outside, the rain had stopped. High above the Parisian rooftops, a rainbow swept majestically across a powder blue sky. Despite the storm, the atmosphere remained heavy and humid but, for the moment at least, the thunder had disappeared.

The morning of the funeral was bright and clear. By half past ten the church of St Louis-des-Invalides was full. Crowded into the pews and side aisles, hundreds of people had come to pay their last respects to their dear friend Gaston Gautier. Looking pale in her black silk suit, Laura stared straight ahead at the simple oak coffin resting on the catafalque. Around it burned six large candles. As if in silent supplication, their wispy trails of smoke rose up towards the small red sacristy light shining bright above the altar.

Streaming in through the stained-glass windows, the sun was refracted into a dancing kaleidoscope of colours on the cold stone floor below. As the mourners arrived, ushers shepherded the men to the right and the women to the left of the church. Maisie glanced furtively across at Charles who sat, expressionless, alone in the front pew. Not once did he look at his father's coffin. Instead, his eyes were fixed unblinking on the tabernacle beyond.

Displayed on a red silk cushion, Gaston's medals shone in the surrounding candlelight: *Chevalier de la Légion d'Honneur,*

Croix de Guerre, Croix des Résistants – Laura swayed, hypnotized as she stared. Reverberating around the cupola, the massive organ swelled and at last the choir took up the strains: 'Out of the depths, I have called to you, O Lord'. The smell of incense assailed her senses. She felt as though she was drifting away.

The organ stopped and the congregation fell silent. From the back of the church, the sound of heavy footsteps could be heard marching slowly up the aisle. As the footsteps drew nearer, Laura turned to see an old man, his back straight as a ramrod, proudly bearing the French Resistance flag. He stopped in front of the catafalque and, for a moment, stared at the array of medals gleaming up at him from the cushion. His lip seemed to tremble. Then, with a strength and control which belied his age, he saluted the coffin with the flag. Up in the gallery, a solitary trumpet sounded the Last Post.

The mass passed in a blur. It was only half-way through the Bishop's sermon that Laura's attention wandered back to the service. 'But, above all,' continued the Bishop in clear, ringing tones, 'Gaston Gautier was a man of principle. Today we live in a world of cynical expediency. Values of tolerance, compassion and honesty are being cast aside by this get-rich-quick society. Throughout his life, Gaston Gautier was one of those who fought for a better world. But the price of that struggle was high. His battle for the Resistance was only won at huge personal cost to himself and his family.'

Laura glanced briefly across at Charles, but his face betrayed not a flicker of emotion.

The Bishop tapped the edge of the pulpit. 'A *better* world, brethren, that was the world Gaston Gautier and his comrades fought and died for. A world where men and women of all races, colours and creeds could live in peace and harmony. A world of courage and of honour. Courage and honour – those were the principles on which our dear friend based his personal, his public and his professional life. Today, brethren, we his friends mourn his loss. Our nation mourns a hero. But Gaston Gautier lives on in our hearts and our minds. So long as there are men and women of courage and honour, there is still hope that we may all achieve that better world he strove for.'

The Bishop paused to clear his throat. When he resumed, his voice was no more than a whisper. *'Au revoir, mon cher ami.'* He waited for some time to regain his composure. 'In the Name of the Father and of the Son . . .'

Laura had just about dried her eyes by the end of the mass. To the strains of the 'Pie Jesu', the members of the congregation filed past the coffin, each with his own silent memories. After some prompting, Charles joined Laura and Maisie who were already standing in the side aisle. For over half an hour they stood there, accepting the condolences of the crowd.

Laura was astounded. Apart from the host of family friends, there were hundreds of total strangers. 'He saved my life,' said one wizened man as he shook her hand. 'Mine and thirty others on that particular occasion.'

Daniel Baudon and Serge Birnbaum came up and embraced her warmly. 'It was a lovely service,' sighed Serge. He caught sight of Sharif, joining the end of the queue. 'And nothing if not ecumenical. Your father would have loved it.'

Laura forced a smile. 'I'm sure he would. Are you joining us later at the apartment?'

'But of course. There are people here I haven't seen in forty years.'

'And, Daniel, you'll be coming too?' She turned to find him glaring daggers at her half-brother.

'What? Sorry. I'm afraid I was miles away. Yes, my dear, of course I'll be there. You can bank on us old timers in a fight.'

She was about to ask him what he meant but her attention was already distracted by another comrade shaking her hand.

Gradually, the mourners found their way out of the church and into the large open courtyard. Some hung around to chat, others moved off towards the Père Lachaise cemetery where Gaston was to be buried. Without a word, Charles left the family group and hurried to join the throng. Maisie put a hand on Laura's arm. 'Would you like to stay here on your own for a minute? I can always tell the cortège to wait.'

She nodded gratefully. 'If you wouldn't mind. There are just a few things I'd like to say before we bury him.'

She walked to the altar and knelt down at the rails. The

smells of candle wax and incense still hung heavy in the air. She closed her eyes and tried to pray, but somehow the words failed to come. Startled by a sudden rustle of silk, she opened her eyes again. In the shadows of the side altar a woman sat saying her rosary. She was so heavily veiled that it was impossible to distinguish her face. Laura peered at her intently. There was something oddly familiar about her. Her fine, tapering fingers seemed to caress the beads as she prayed silently.

'Mummy,' gasped Laura in disbelief, 'is that you?'

Slowly, the woman raised her head. 'I was hoping no one would spot me here. I didn't want you to feel awkward.'

The joy of reunion mixed with tears of grief left both women speechless for some time.

'But you should have said you were coming,' chided Laura at last.

Caroline blew her nose. 'Don't be silly. I didn't want to cause a scene. Most of Gaston's friends hate the sight of me. What's more, I can't really say I blame them.'

'But Papa would have wanted you here today and that's all that matters to me.'

Caroline lifted her veil and began to wipe her eyes. Laura looked positively thunderstruck.

'Good Lord! Have you gone and had a face lift?'

'Nothing quite so radical.' Caroline's eyes sparkled brightly through the tears. 'I've given up the sauce, that's all. I decided you didn't need a lush for a mother.'

Outside, Maisie was nervously tapping her foot. It was a good ten minutes since she had left Laura to her thoughts and now the driver was getting fidgety. She made her way back into the church. 'Laura, I'm afraid you'll have to—' Her bag fell to the floor with a resounding clatter. 'Caroline! I don't believe it!' It was over twenty years since the two women had spoken to one another and Maisie's final words had been far from amicable.

Quickly Caroline stuffed her rosary beads into her pocket. 'I must be off.' She kissed her daughter's cheek. 'I'll be in touch very soon.'

Laura was clearly upset. 'But you must come to the cemetery.'

'I'm sorry.' Caroline turned to Maisie. 'I must be holding everything up. I don't want to ruin your plans.'

Like incense from a crucible, Maisie found her resentment evaporating.

'Thank God, you're back,' she said and gave Caroline a hug. 'Your daughter never needed you more.'

CHAPTER TWENTY-FIVE

Glass in hand, Charles welcomed the mourners as they trooped back from the cemetery. At Gaston's apartment, a magnificent buffet had been laid out and the finest wines of his cellar uncorked as he had wished. Quaking with apprehension, Caroline clung to Laura's arm as they ascended in the lift.

'Well, if it isn't the bolter herself,' sneered Charles as the two women walked into the entrance hall. 'And to what do we owe this unexpected pleasure?'

Caroline stared straight past him and into the drawing room beyond. 'Good afternoon, Charles.' She made to move on, but found him blocking her way.

'He hasn't left you anything, if that's what you're hoping.'

Following right behind, it was impossible for Maisie and Scorpio not to overhear. 'It's OK.' Maisie put a restraining hand on Scorpio. He glared at Charles but he seemed oblivious to everyone except Caroline.

'So help me, I'll end up killing him,' murmured Scorpio and continued on into the drawing room.

Charles was like a dog with a large, meaty bone. 'And how's the handsome husband?' he continued, relentless. 'My contacts in the racing world tell me he's cleared off with a stable girl.'

Laura gripped her mother's arm even tighter. 'Mummy, is it true?'

'For God's sake, Charles,' interrupted Maisie, 'why don't you just—'

'Your contacts are quite right.' Caroline's voice was calm and steady. She turned to face her daughter. 'I was going to tell you, but now it seems Charles has pre-empted me. Ralph has moved in with one of his grooms. I'm seeking a divorce.'

'I'm so sorry.' Laura looked genuinely downcast. 'Are you going—'

'And isn't she looking well on it?' interrupted Charles, unstoppable. 'So how much do you intend to take the second husband for?'

'Cut it out!' Despite her best intentions, Maisie found herself losing her temper. 'I'd have thought you of all people would have the decency not to talk about money!' She pushed him aside and shepherded the women into the drawing room where drinks were already being served.

'Just as hateful as ever!' Laura helped herself to a glass of champagne.

Caroline's hand was still shaking as she took a tumbler of mineral water from the waiter. 'You don't believe him, do you – about the fortune hunting?'

'Of course not.' She put a comforting arm around her mother. 'Since when has anyone taken any notice of anything he says? Goodness knows how I'm going to work with him now that Papa's no longer here.'

Maisie spluttered champagne down the front of her dress. 'How stupid of me!' She cast around, looking for something to mop up the stain. As if from nowhere, the ubiquitous Madame D appeared with a napkin and handed it to Maisie.

'It's good to see you again,' Caroline ventured tentatively.

It took some moments for Madame D's eyes to focus on the face. '*Mon Dieu*, Madame, is it really you?'

Caroline nodded nervously. She would not have been at all surprised if the housekeeper had ignored her altogether. 'Yes, Madame D, it's really me. I'm afraid it's been some time . . .'

'Monsieur would have been so happy!' Suddenly her eyes were brimming with tears. 'Welcome home, Madame. We've all missed you very much.' She shook Caroline's hand so earnestly that her water spilled on to the floor.

'I didn't want to intrude, but Laura insisted and so did Maisie and, well, I wanted to see a few things for myself.'

'Come,' said the housekeeper. 'There's something I want to show you, something I think you ought to see.' She led Caroline out of the drawing room.

'Where's she taking her?' asked Maisie, thoroughly intrigued. 'To Papa's bedroom, I'd say.'

'Any particular reason?'

'He always kept two photos by the side of his bed.'

'One of you, I suppose?'

Laura nodded. 'Yes, it was taken the day I was christened.'

'And the other?'

'The other's a portrait of my mother. It was the first thing he saw every morning.'

Laura noticed her old mentor Maurice as he wandered into the room. She moved across to greet him, leaving Daniel to talk to Maisie.

As soon as she was out of earshot, Daniel was down to business. 'Have you told her yet?'

Maisie shook her head. 'No, not yet.'

They could hear Charles's voice, loud and aggressive, as it resounded in the hall. Daniel's lip curled. 'He's so busy shooting his mouth off, I'm surprised he hasn't given the game away himself.'

'I've decided to leave it until tomorrow,' continued Maisie. 'Laura's had enough to cope with for one day.'

Daniel looked slightly dubious. 'I suppose so, but I'm running the Sandton story in this week's copy of the *Gadfly*. We've got to mount our opposition soon.'

Maisie lowered her voice even further. 'Thank God Caroline's back. I've just heard she and Ralph are splitting up.'

Daniel's rumpled face broke into an impudent, schoolboy grin. 'I could have told you that months ago.'

'Your spies must be very good.'

'They are, but they didn't need to be hot to winkle that out. Ralph's been knocking off his stable girls for years. It was only a matter of time before he found one he actually liked!'

'Poor Caroline. No wonder she hit the bottle.'

Emboldened by a few glasses of champagne, Daniel stared Maisie straight in the eye. 'And you, how did you manage?'

Maisie's gaze moved across the room to where Scorpio was standing. 'I really don't know,' she smiled wistfully, 'but I intend to make up for it now.'

Increasingly raucous, Charles's voice seemed to permeate the entire apartment.

'Do we have a plan of campaign?' asked Maisie.

Daniel frowned. 'It's difficult to know what to do until we discover the precise details of the deal. All the same, a seriously nasty smear campaign is always a good idea.' His grin grew wider. He looked like a naughty elf. 'And Sammy Sandton's such an easy target.'

'If you need money, just let me know.' Her voice was surprisingly cold. 'Everything I have is Laura's too.'

As a waiter passed, Daniel held out his glass and gratefully accepted a refill. He turned his attentions back to Maisie. 'I'm looking forward to the fight. It's nice to have right on your side and, besides, scandal is good for circulation.' He gestured towards Scorpio, deep in conversation with Serge. 'That rock star friend of yours . . .'

'There's absolutely no truth in the rumour.' She fluttered her eyelashes mischievously as she sipped her champagne.

'I wouldn't dream of suggesting otherwise.' Daniel tapped the side of his nose. 'At least, not until I hear it from a highly dubious source. Anyway, I know he's supposed to be a recluse nowadays but do you think he'd come on board?'

'You bet! He's as determined as I am to stop this deal. How do you think he could help?'

Daniel sipped his drink and thought. 'How about a song? I don't know – something to upset the Sandtons.'

Maisie giggled. 'I hear Daphne Sandton's the Edmund Hillary of social climbers. That shouldn't be too difficult.'

'Do you honestly think Scorpio might consider it?'

'I don't see why not. He's already promised Serge and Sharif that he'll help promote their film.'

'Excellent!' Daniel looked like the cat with the cream. 'Who knows? Perhaps we can merge the campaigns. "Stuff Sammy Sandton" and "Turn out for *Tor*" – there's copy in this, you know!'

Sharif joined Serge and Scorpio over by the fireplace.

'I'll leave you two for a moment.' Scorpio stared across at Maisie. 'There's someone who seems to be enjoying herself far too much without me.' He disappeared into the crowd.

'Besotted!' Serge whispered in kindly approval. 'Rather like someone else I know.'

For once, Sharif was in no mood to respond to his friend's good-natured ribbing. Dull and listless, his pale blue eyes seemed sunken above his cheekbones. 'I think I ought to be getting back to the hotel.'

'Something on your mind?' The old man's gibes turned swiftly to concern.

Sharif nodded wearily. 'It's my mother. I discovered last night that she's had a relapse.'

'I'm so sorry.' Serge patted his shoulder in sympathy. 'When will you be flying home?'

'As soon as possible.' He looked gloomily across the room to where Laura was standing. He thought she looked almost contented as she chattered away to her mother. 'It couldn't have happened at a worse time. I feel I'm abandoning Laura at the time she needs me most.' A waiter appeared, carrying a tray of canapés. He declined with a toss of the head. He had no appetite whatsoever.

Serge, on the contrary, chose a tiny smoked salmon sandwich which he swallowed in one swift gulp. 'I think you should take her with you.' He wiped his fingers punctiliously on a napkin.

'But my mother, my sister . . .' He threw up his arms in a gesture of hopeless frustration.

'Look, we still have crew up near Darra. She could stay with them. That way, there wouldn't be awkward questions.'

'But there's so much here that needs to be done.'

Serge filched another canapé from the waiter. 'When Charles's shenanigans come to light, I can assure you she'll be worse than useless. What she needs now is time to rest – *reculer pour mieux sauter*, as we say – and where better than the mountains?'

'But I'm not sure—'

'Do you want to help or not?' His tone was suddenly sharp and incisive. It was the voice he used on set.

Sharif felt mortified, like a star actor chastised for fluffing his lines. 'I'm sorry. I haven't really had time to think this through.'

Serge lit one of his monstrous cigars. 'It won't be for long, a few weeks at most, time to let her calm down and recover. Maisie and Daniel can hold the fort until then.' The smoke of his cigar wafted across to where they were standing.

'The wronged wife and the poison pen.' Even Sharif managed a smile. 'Poor Charles, I don't give him a chance!'

'You're not leaving already?' Maisie caught sight of Maurice as he tried to slip unobtrusively out of the room.

'Such a sad day,' he blustered, his eyes full of tears. 'I must go now before I make a fool of myself.'

'I understand,' said Maisie kindly. 'We'll all miss Gaston very much, but we'll do our darnedest to keep things the same.'

Maurice bit his lip. 'I'm sorry, Madame, but really I must be on my way.'

Daniel's antennae were finely tuned. He could sense that something was wrong. 'Is there anything you'd like to tell us?'

'Not today.' Maurice's voice was choked. 'It wouldn't be right to mention it today, not the day of Monsieur's funeral.'

In the entrance hall, a sudden crash brought the party to a temporary standstill.

'It's all right!' shouted Charles. 'I've always hated Chinese porcelain.'

'Philistine!' muttered Maurice under his breath.

'It's him, isn't it?' Maisie intuited the worst. 'What's he gone and done?'

Maurice fiddled with his cufflinks, a present from Gaston to mark his first twenty-five years with the company. 'He's sacked me. He's sacked us all, in fact, everyone in the workshop over fifty years of age.'

It was at that moment that Charles himself staggered into the drawing room. He lurched forward and, missing his footing, sent a lamp flying from the commode. It fell to the ground and shattered. Everyone turned to look.

'I think it's time I took you home.' Maisie's face was pale with anger.

'I'll take myself home, thank you very much, when I've had my little say.'

There were embarrassed rumblings around the room. Charles swigged at his glass, then reached out to rest it on a table. He miscalculated badly and it crashed to the floor. The slivers of crystal, like minuscule projectiles, attacked a gaggle of stiletto heels. Ignoring the accident, Charles coughed loudly in an attempt to clear his throat. 'I'd just like to say how happy I am to see my father's family and friends gathered here today.'

There were embarrassed titters amongst the guests. Maisie looked at Laura standing rigid next to her mother.

'As I always say, death brings out the best in people. Take my former stepmother, for example . . .'

All eyes in the room were suddenly trained on Caroline. She stared unblinking back at him.

'Such a good sort, don't you think? Not what you'd really call a sticker – just around long enough to screw up my father's life completely.'

Out of the corner of her eye, Laura could see Sharif moving quietly across the room. Like a tiger, he looked ready to pounce. 'I think you've said enough,' she murmured to Charles.

He swerved around, surprised by the sight of the stranger moving towards him. 'Who the hell . . .?'

'Let him be.' Laura's voice was calm. 'I'd like everyone here to know what kind of man my brother really is.'

Charles smiled cynically and took a deep bow. 'My dear sister, never the one to sully her precious hands with anything so nasty as a fight. And why should she indeed? Why should she bother hustling when she gets half of everything, just the same?'

He loosened his tie even further and ordered another Scotch. 'And while I'm at it, I suppose I'd better mention Maisie – my dear supportive wife.'

Scorpio bristled like a Rottweiler.

'She was always in league with them against me. Oh, yes, they thought they had it all worked out – I'd do the work and

Laura would reap the rewards.' He paused for a moment before bringing his tumbler down hard on the table. 'But the House of Gautier was supposed to be mine. These bastards have been trying to rob me.'

'For God's sake, shut up!' Daniel Baudon's face was crimson with rage. 'That's nonsense and you know it!'

Charles wiped his mouth with his sleeve. 'I'm sick of people telling me what's what around here. Now it's *my* turn to tell *you* a few things. Now Father's dead, the company's to be split fifty-fifty between Laura and me.'

A murmur of approval rose up from the guests.

'That's the good news, sister dear.' He sniggered loudly. 'The bad news is that Father didn't trust you not to behave like your sainted mother. In his wisdom, he decided that you'd have no voting rights until your thirtieth birthday.'

Maisie grabbed him by the arm. 'You've gone far enough. I think this can wait—'

'Why wait?' He shook her off. 'I've waited over fifty years for this. I've waited since the day my mother was hauled off by the Gestapo.'

The room was so quiet that Maisie could hear her own heartbeat, tapping a fast, syncopated rhythm. Smugly, Charles surveyed the scene. He was pleased to see his father's friends all looking so utterly shell-shocked.

'As things stand right now, I have complete control over all company decisions.' He waited a second before firing his final missile. 'And I've decided to sell the House of Gautier to Sandton and Sons of London.'

Sharif leapt to catch Laura as she collapsed semi-conscious to the ground. The din all around was deafening. Clearing a passage through the crowd, Caroline helped him to carry Laura into her bedroom. Gently, he laid her down on the bed and Caroline covered her with a blanket. As she stroked her daughter's hair, she seemed almost unaware of Sharif's presence.

'You really do care for her, don't you?' he said softly.

She nodded. 'I've got a lot of making up to do.'

'I can't believe it.' Laura groaned and opened her eyes. 'I knew he hated us, but I still can't believe he'd do that.'

Sharif knelt down beside the bed. 'I promise you, we'll stop him.'

Dazed, she closed her eyes again. 'I only wish I believed you could.'

In the drawing room, pandemonium had broken out. Shocked and angry, a group of Gaston's friends had surrounded Charles and were now haranguing him.

'I think you'd better leave,' said Serge, tugging him by the sleeve.

Charles turned on him, incensed. 'This is my father's house. I'll leave when—'

A thudding right hook caught him full under the jaw. For a second he weaved drunkenly around before slumping to the floor.

'I've been wanting to do that for ages.' Scorpio rubbed his knuckles. Somehow, Charles clambered up again. He jabbed around, trying unsuccessfully to punch his assailant. Unable to focus, he managed only to connect with a large commode. He shouted out in pain. As he held his knuckles to his mouth, he noticed a trickle of blood. 'I'll get you . . .'

Serge grabbed a burly waiter. 'Get him out of here,' he yelled above the fracas. 'My driver's outside – the one in the Merc. Tell him to take this idiot home before someone *really* hurts him.'

Drunk, and down to the dregs of his stamina, Charles knew he had no option but to leave. The waiter bundled him out of the drawing room and down to the car below. Serge stared up at Scorpio in open admiration. 'You pack one hell of a punch.'

'That was just a bit of gentle sparring.' He stared out of the window to where Charles was being bundled into the back of the car. 'Now the serious fighting starts.'

CHAPTER TWENTY-SIX

It was early evening before an exhausted Maisie returned home to the Bois de Boulogne. A watery sun hung low in the sky and a chill breeze seemed to herald the beginning of the summer's demise. Shivering, she pulled her cashmere stole around her shoulders as she hurried from her car. From the drive, she could see the lights burning in Charles's bedroom. She let herself into the house and ran swiftly up the stairs.

Slightly more sober after a few hours' sleep, Charles was busy packing. Suits, ties and shirts lay strewn all over the bed as he made his final selection.

'Leaving?' she asked as she entered the room. He did not bother to look up but continued to stuff his clothes haphazardly into a suitcase.

'Yes, and for good this time, thank God.'

Suddenly Maisie exploded. 'You snivelling bloody coward! You've had your say and now you think you can just crawl off, like some lizard under a stone!'

There was something demanding in her tone that forced him to turn round and face her. 'I thought I'd made myself perfectly clear. I've had enough of the lot of you.' He tried to resume his packing but she brought the lid down on his fingers.

'What the hell—' His voice was an amalgam of pain and astonishment.

'Just look at yourself!' she sneered. As he glanced at himself in the dressing-table mirror, he could see his jaw, red and swollen, where Scorpio had hit him.

'It's OK,' he said, with a feeble attempt at bravado. 'I'll pay you bastards back. Now, if you don't mind, I'm leaving for London tonight. I'll let you know where to send my effects.'

Suddenly Maisie burst out laughing. 'You still think you're giving the orders, don't you? Well, let me tell you something. You've had it now! Without your father's name and company, you're a pathetic, clapped-out nothing.'

The blood was pounding in Charles's eardrums. He felt his head would split. 'I don't need lessons in nepotism from you! Where the hell would you be without old John P. Appleford's millions?'

Her lips contracted into a thin, tight line. He knew he had drawn blood. Like a predatory animal, he continued on, pawing relentlessly at his prey. 'You must realize by now that I always despised you. I only married you for your money. Surely even someone as stupid as you must have finally understood that!'

Always! Always! The words went around and around in her head until she began to feel quite dizzy. So, then, her worst fears had all been founded. Their marriage had been a deception right from the start. Something inside her snapped.

'OK, Macho Man, let's lay it on the line. I know all about you. I know the *real* reason why we never had any children.'

Charles turned deathly pale. 'What the hell are you talking about?'

'You!' she shouted, on the attack once more. 'You, you selfish, arrogant bastard! *You* and *your* infertility!'

He spun round on his heels, his fists clenched threateningly. 'Shut up or I'll hit you. You don't know what you're saying. This is hysterical talk.'

'I've seen the letter!' Angrily, she picked up a vase. 'I've seen the results of the tests! For twenty years you made me feel guilty, twenty years when I might have had children of my own to love and care for. But no! Because of your stupid, selfish pride, you never dared admit that it was *you* who had the problem!'

With surprising force she hurled the vase at the top of Charles's head. He saw it coming and ducked in time but, for a split second, he had seen the murderous look in her eyes. Suddenly he felt frightened. 'Get out of my house!' Her voice was cool again. It was as if the boil had suddenly burst and all the poison had spewed out. 'You think you've got it all worked out but, mark my words, with every breath in my body and every cent I own, I'll fight your bloody deal.'

Back at Gaston's apartment, Caroline and Laura waited nervously for Maisie to call. No one had wanted her to confront Charles that evening, but she herself had insisted. She was determined to exorcize her own personal ghosts and, in the end, even a reluctant Scorpio was obliged to let her go.

As the evening shadows drew in, Laura sank further and further into depression. She had rallied sufficiently to bid farewell to the guests but the effort had cost her dear. Anxious to cheer her, Caroline had invited Scorpio and Sharif to stay on for dinner but no one seemed very hungry.

'Will you live here for a while?' ventured Scorpio over a delicious but barely touched summer pudding.

Caroline tried her best to sound perky. 'If Laura and Madame D will have me.'

The housekeeper smiled benignly as she cleared away the plates. 'We'd both love that, wouldn't we, Laura dear?'

The group looked at Laura, hoping for some response, but all she did was stare in silence at her father's empty armchair.

The once long nails of Scorpio's strumming hand had been chewed down to the quick. 'That bloke's a maniac!' he exploded suddenly. 'Do you think I should ring? Or maybe go straight over?'

Caroline shook her head. 'Maisie wants to deal with this one on her own. I think you have to let her.'

Obviously ill at ease, Sharif took Laura by the hand. 'I don't know how to tell you this, but I have to return to Peshawar. My mother's been taken ill again. I have to go and see her.'

She hardly seemed to be aware of what he was trying to tell her.

'I want you to come with me.'

He waited for a response but, from her vacant expression, he knew she was miles away.

The phone rang outside in the drawing room but Laura made no effort to move.

'Shall I get it?' asked Caroline.

'Please do!' Scorpio was like the original cat on a hot tin roof. 'If that bastard's touched a hair on her head . . .'

She went off to field the call. Two minutes later, she returned, a huge smile on her face. Scorpio's eyes searched hers.

'Maisie's fine,' she said in answer to his unspoken question. 'She says Charles has left for London and this time he's gone for good.'

'Anything else?'

Caroline paused, slightly puzzled. 'Yes, she says she'd like you to come right over and to bring the scorpion too.'

Sharif and Scorpio left together. Never sparkling that evening, conversation had now dried up completely and Caroline wanted time alone with Laura.

'I'll have a word with her,' she said, as she led the two men into the entrance hall.

Sharif looked very tired. 'She *must* come away with me to the mountains. There are things she'll remember up there.'

Caroline smiled gratefully up at him. 'Leave it with me. I'll convince her somehow.'

Eager to be off, Scorpio kissed her lightly. 'Don't forget, if you start feeling down this evening . . .'

'I won't,' she said, opening the heavy front door. 'You see, at last I know I'm home.'

CHAPTER TWENTY-SEVEN

It had taken the combined persuasive powers of her mother and sister-in-law, but eventually Laura accepted the need for a break. With a new-look efficiency which startled Maisie, Caroline made phone calls, organized reservations and even packed Laura's suitcases. For the first time in her life, the spoiled child bride was acting like a mature and responsible mother. Caring and protective, her every thought was focused on her daughter's health and well-being. The Peter Pan who was Caroline Jay had finally left Never Land.

After a tearful farewell at the airport, Laura and Sharif boarded the plane, both equally subdued. After take-off, Laura reclined fully in her comfortable seat and, snuggling down under a blanket, requested not to be disturbed.

Sharif tucked a pillow under her head. 'Shall I wake you up for lunch?'

She shook her head. 'No thanks. I think I'd rather just sleep.'

'You ought to eat more. You're starting to look like a stick insect.'

'Very *à la mode*.' The vague parody of a smile soon faded into a frown. Her head felt like a cement mixer as she rubbed her eyes. 'I don't know what it is, but I just can't think straight. Papa dying, the company about to be sold – it seems like everything around me is collapsing.'

He took her pale slim hand in his strong, rugged one. 'You're feeling too down to count your blessings, but the truth is you've got your family rallying around you. And, whatever happens, you know you've always got me.' He kissed her forehead tenderly. She smiled, more convincingly this time, and leaned across to rest her head on his shoulder. Her eyelids, leaden with fatigue, soon fell shut and within minutes she was asleep.

She slept fitfully, her repose troubled by distorted and disjointed images traipsing through her mind. First, a grotesque gargoyle appeared, shouting threats and imprecations. Next came a great bird of prey. Powerful and majestic, it swooped down to attack the gargoyle and sent it scurrying off. A child looked up to thank the bird, but already it had flown away. Over the intercom, the captain warned of turbulence and advised all passengers to fasten their seat-belts. Laura came to with a start and sleepily groped for her belt. To her surprise, she found it had already been secured. She turned and found a pair of light blue eyes still focused, unblinking, on her.

It was late afternoon in Peshawar as the plane came in to land. As they emerged from the cool, air-conditioned cabin on to the bubbling tarmac, Laura and Sharif felt the full force of the dull August heat like a blast from a metal smelter. A car was waiting for them at Arrivals and soon they were careering off towards the foothills and up towards Darra. Sharif spoke in Pukhtu to the driver who replied in short, clipped sentences. The film crew, it transpired, was now busy on the still photographs which were to be used for promotional purposes. Sharif listened carefully to every snippet of gossip the driver told him. By all accounts, there were still plenty of loose ends for him to tie up.

'I'm feeling very bad about this.' Laura watched as the lights of Peshawar faded gradually into the distance.

'About what?' Sharif seemed quite lost in his thoughts.

'About your coming up here with me this evening. Shouldn't you really be with your mother?'

As he stared up at the mountains, a towering range of cumulus clouds seemed to emphasize their dramatic mass. 'I'll go first thing tomorrow.'

His response served only to exacerbate her guilt. She realized that she had been so obsessed with her own problems, she had not even stopped to consider his. 'Is she still in hospital?'

'No,' he sighed, frustrated, 'she discharged herself as soon as they'd let her. Right now, she's at home with my sister.'

Laura's guilt turned to positive shame. 'I haven't been much of a friend, have I? You're up to your neck in my family and all its problems and I know almost nothing about yours.'

'There's not much to tell. My mother has cancer – the doctors discovered it soon after my father died. She's in terrible pain most of the time, but she never complains. She says it's the will of God, and gets on with her good works, helping the poor of Peshawar.'

'And your sister?'

'My mother thinks it's high time she was married.' His laugh was awkward and embarrassed. 'I need time to do some thinking before I see them. There are a few pressing issues we need to discuss.' Laura stared silently out of the window and wondered if she might be one of them.

The car moved slowly up into the foothills. The sky was hanging low, a bank of shimmering fire. Gliding out from behind the clouds, a bulging, gibbous moon illuminated Sharif's handsome profile. Laura longed to kiss him but here she felt she must hold back. Here they were in a different world. A long dark shadow crossed her face.

On their arrival at the camp, she was shown to Serge's trailer, which still reeked of his cigars. Never had she felt quite so physically and emotionally drained. Without even bothering to unpack her suitcases, she tumbled into the narrow camp bed and was soon immersed in a heavy, dreamless sleep. She was awoken next morning by Sharif carrying a mug of tea. 'I'm off to Peshawar.' He handed her the mug. Still dozy, she struggled to focus on his face. He looked tired and preoccupied, as if he had not slept a wink.

'Will you be gone long?' At once, she could have kicked herself. She had not intended to sound so clinging.

He looked at her bony shoulders. The white cotton T-shirt which served as her night dress did nothing to conceal the dramatic loss in weight. She seemed to have halved in stature in the space of a single week. He felt the desperate urge to take her in his arms, to nurse and to console her. He forced himself to resist the temptation. 'It depends on my mother,' he said.

She reached out to embrace him but he knew that would be

too much for him. Already he was on his feet and standing by the door. 'Go back to sleep,' he ordered, rather too sharply. 'I'll be back as soon as I can.'

For the next two days, she slept a dull, drugged sleep, never once emerging from the trailer. On Sharif's orders, the cook woke her with meals at regular intervals but she barely touched them before returning to her slumbers. There were so many problems to deal with and she had neither the will nor the strength to confront them. Sleep seemed the only sensible refuge. It dulled the pain of loss and betrayal. Sleep was a welcome friend.

On the third morning, she woke to find that Sharif had returned. Despite her relentless questioning, however, he seemed reluctant to discuss what had happened. His mother, he simply reported, was doing as well as could be expected. There seemed something in the way he said it which precluded further conversation.

It was a bright, silver-gilt morning and, after breakfast, Sharif suggested a ride up into the mountains. Laura willingly agreed. After two days cooped up in a stifling trailer, she was feeling the need of some physical exercise. They rode for about an hour, barely a word passing between them, as they trotted higher and higher. Overhead a skein of wild duck clattered and swirled. The riders stopped for a while and watched as the birds disappeared, receding black specks, into a lustrous azure-blue sky.

'If only *we* could fly away,' sighed Laura wistfully.

'If only,' agreed Sharif, rather less wistful, and urged his horse onwards again.

Dressed in a local *salwar kameez*, her head covered by a floppy turban, she could already feel the heat of the sun as it began its daily ascent. Ahead in the distance, the snow-capped mountains stood like faceless sentinels, defending the frontier from intruders. Already the horses were sweating as they picked their way between the stunted thorn bushes and scrub-covered ridges. Paddy birds flew up and circled noisily overhead. Her legs aching from the unaccustomed exercise, Laura dropped her reins on the horse's withers and stared up to study them. Sharif pulled in alongside her and together they listened to the sedge warblers as they twittered angrily to one another. Soon their attention was diverted by a flock of sarus cranes as they flapped their heavy wings and lumbered into flight.

'They remind me of myself,' Laura smiled, 'struggling to get out of bed.'

Sharif gestured towards them as they soared now quite effortlessly across the sky. 'Yes,' he added pointedly, 'but just look at them once they're off.'

It was fast developing into a stifling day. As they rode on, the outcroppings of trap rock seemed to disappear into a distant grey-blue haze. Here and there, stunted thorn bushes tried hard to relieve the barrenness of the landscape. As they climbed higher, Sharif seemed to brighten visibly. With every step further into the mountains, his face grew more relaxed.

'You take your strength from this place, don't you?' said Laura.

He nodded. 'It reminds me of who I am.'

'Are you saying you sometimes forget?'

'It happens.' He reined in his horse beside her. 'There are times when we all forget just who we are and that there are bigger things than us.'

The heat was almost unbearable. The sky had lost its earlier blue and hung low and leaden. Thick and grey, the slow-moving clouds were permeated by a relentless summer sun. Sharif could see that Laura was wilting.

'Shall we stop for lunch?' He pointed towards a cave about two hundred yards in front of them.

She shot him a grateful look. 'I hope you ordered a hamper to be brought up ahead.'

'Nothing quite so glamorous.' He tapped his saddle bag. 'Bread, chicken and water – it's not quite Fortnum and Mason's, I'm afraid.'

Sitting on a brightly coloured rug in the womb-like shade of the cave, Laura fell ravenously upon the chicken curry, mopping up every last drop of sauce with great wodges of unleavened bread.

'I'm glad you seem to be enjoying that.' He looked on amused as, greedily, she gulped her water.

285

'I certainly am. Any more *naan*?' She looked hopefully at his saddle bag.

Smiling, he pulled out a brown paper sack and produced another one. 'You realize that's your third.'

'Don't remind me!' She tore off a gobbet and dipped it in the remains of his sauce. 'I'll soon be as fat as Charles.'

It was as if the sun outside had suddenly stopped shining. A cold draught swept in to envelop them as they sat together in the cave. The very mention of Charles's name had cast a pall upon their picnic. Sharif moved swiftly to exploit the opening. 'You know you have to stop him.'

Her appetite gone, she dropped the *naan* she had been savouring with such relish only a few moments earlier. 'I don't have the energy for a fight.'

Sharif's nostrils flared ominously. 'Your father was a war hero. I refuse to accept that his daughter's a coward.'

Outside, the horses whinnied, switching their tails in a fruitless effort to drive away the flies. Unable to meet Sharif's eyes, she began to clear away the debris of their meal.

'I've been thinking about things,' she ventured tentatively. 'This takeover, well, it wouldn't be the end of the world.'

'*What?*' His voice boomed out so loudly that the horses almost bolted. 'I just can't believe I'm hearing this.'

Her hands trembled as she tried unsuccessfully to screw the cap back on to the water bottle. 'I mean, I'd end up a very wealthy woman. I could work as I pleased and go where I wanted.' She wafted a hand vaguely in the direction of the mountains. 'There's a lot to be said for that.'

'There's *nothing* to be said for running away!'

'What on earth do you mean?'

He grabbed her urgently by the arm. 'I mean you've got to fight, if not for yourself, then for your father – for the name of Gautier.'

'But it's hopeless!' Surprised by his sudden aggression, she could feel the tears welling up in her eyes. 'Charles has been planning this deal for ages. It's virtually a *fait accompli*.'

'No, it is not!' There was a cold, sharp timbre to his voice, the sound of steel on steel. The tears began to trickle down her face but, for once, he refused to console her. 'What about Maisie and Scorpio?' he continued, as relentless as the midday sun. 'They're back at home, organizing *your* fighting fund and you're already talking of quitting.'

'I'm glad I've seen this side of your nature,' she replied, still shocked by his outburst. 'I thought you were supposed to be a friend of mine, but you're just cruel and uncaring.'

A suggestion of pain flitted swiftly across his features but was soon dispatched to that emotional limbo where self-doubt ought to reside. 'Have you forgotten *everything* we ever talked about?' He was on the attack again. '*Me, me, me* – that's all I've heard from you so far. Your entire family heritage is now at stake. Surely that's got to be worth a struggle.'

'But I'm so tired,' she whispered, her slight frame heaving. 'I'm so unbelievably tired.'

Sharif felt quite dreadful. It cut him to the quick to speak so brutally to her, but time was of the essence. Laura could no longer afford the luxury of gradual recovery. From Peshawar, he had taken the opportunity of telephoning Maisie and the news was not encouraging. Charles was already on the warpath and any opposition needed Laura's whole-hearted support.

Desperately, he racked his brains, searching for a way to bring her to her senses. Right now, lectures on honour and revenge were the last thing the poor girl needed. A fly flew sluggishly past his nose. Irritated, he tried to swat it. Then suddenly the answer struck him. He leapt up, grasped her hand and led her out of the cave. Around the horses, the flies were buzzing in their droves, slow and sleepy in the sunshine. He caught one in his fist.

'Fetch me a glass of water,' he ordered. 'Make sure you fill it right up to the top. And bring the salt as well.'

Puzzled, she did as he requested, returning with a brimming glass and the shiny silver salt cellar. She gave them to Sharif.

'Now watch this carefully.' He tipped the fly into the crystal clear liquid then covered the glass with the palm of his hand so the insect could not escape. The creature struggled frantically to save itself from drowning but, at last, when the agonized twitching of its wispy black legs had ceased completely, Sharif fished it out. He showed the fly to Laura as it lay motionless in his hand. 'Dead, wouldn't you say?'

She nodded, mystified. 'Absolutely.'

He smiled. 'Right then. Now watch this.'

He placed the creature on a rock and covered it with salt. They stared for what seemed like ages but was, in fact, just over a minute. Then suddenly, the slightest of movements under the mound precipitated a miniature saltslide. Laura could not take her eyes off the strangely undulating pile. A few moments later, two silver black wings, then a pair of monstrous compound eyes cracked through the sun-caked salt. Next, with small but resolute kicks and jerks, the legs began to fight free. Soon the entire blue-black bloated body lay heaving on top of its sometime tomb. For a while, the exhausted insect lay there, just soaking in the sunshine. Then, it tried its wings, still encrusted with salt, and, with a strength quite staggering for its minuscule dimensions, gradually flapped them clean. Next, it arched its back and stretched its minute legs. Laura gasped. It seemed as if the creature had succeeded in coming back from the dead. She stared in wonderment at the Herculean strength of the tiny insect. Even in this insignificant creature it seemed that the instinct for self-preservation was ferocious. Suddenly, Laura felt herself urging it on, willing it to survive. For a while, the fly tottered round and round in circles, occasionally collapsing with exhaustion. Then, finally, with a swift running jump off the end of the rock, it hurled itself into the air, stretching its wings as it went.

'He's done it!' In her excitement, Laura found herself clapping. 'He's made it back from the dead!'

The fly buzzed round them for a while, as if in a lap of honour. Then, at last, it disappeared into the midday heat, a proud and deserving victor.

'How on earth did you do that?' Her eyes were wide with sheer amazement.

Delighted, Sharif smiled. 'It's a trick I learned from an old Bengal Lancer. The fly is drowned all right, but the combination of sun and salt draws the water from its body. Then the insect does the rest itself.' He paused for a second. 'Fortunately, this one was a fighter.'

Suddenly the penny dropped. She grinned at him. 'So I'm the fly, am I?'

He nodded. 'You could say that. And we'll be your salt and sunshine.' He patted the Lee Enfield rifle slung casually across his shoulder. 'You know, up here we have a saying, "He is not a Pathan who gives a pinch for a blow." Your brother has betrayed you, Laura. It's your duty to pay him back.'

She glanced at the rifle as it glinted threateningly in the sunshine. 'OK,' she said slowly. The lines of tension had disappeared from her face. She now seemed perfectly calm. 'Badal, if you insist, my friend, but we'll do it Western style.'

They returned to camp later that afternoon and, after brief refreshments, Sharif decided to go and check on the photographic crew and their progress. 'These characters seem to be taking an eternity.' He gazed at Laura and wondered how such a transformation could be possible. Their return ride together had been such fun, all smiles and laughter, so different from the silence of their mournful outward journey. 'I'm beginning to feel that they don't really want to finish this job.'

She stared up at the mountains. 'Who could blame them?'

He drained the dregs of his tea. 'I don't expect to be gone that long, but why don't you take a nap? It's been a long day in the saddle and this evening I'm taking you to Peshawar.'

Her eyes shone bright with anticipation. 'To see your mother?'

The question cast a dampener on his spirits but he recovered before she could notice. 'No.' He stood up and gently kissed the top of her head. 'Something very special. Now promise me you'll sleep.'

Although she was tired and aching, Laura's mind was too busy for sleep. As she opened the door of her trailer, she realized that she had still not unpacked. She heaved one of the suitcases on to the bed and unzipped it. 'Mummy!' It was difficult not to be impressed with the perfection of Caroline's handiwork. Neatly folded, each item of clothing had been meticulously interleaved with sheets of tissue paper. One by one, Laura removed the selection of shorts, jeans and T-shirts. There was not a crease to be found anywhere.

At the bottom of the suitcase, she discovered a large flattish parcel, carefully wrapped in Cellophane. She tore off the covering and was surprised to find the dossier she had first seen in her father's office. Written in Caroline's distinctive script, a note had been taped to the cover. She peeled it off and read it. 'Your father always intended this for you. Look at it! Lots of love, Mummy.'

She opened the worn brown file and, casually at first, began to flick through the contents. She was soon so immersed that all other thoughts were shifted to the back of her mind. Once again, it was as if the history of the House of Gautier was being unfolded before her very eyes. Dated 1878, a faded sepia photograph, taken by Niepce and Daguerre, depicted a Parisian society hostess wearing a fabulous Gautier parure. She turned the page and fell upon an invoice from 1912. Crinkled and yellowing, the bill gave details of the wreaths sent to the Gautier clients drowned with the *Titanic*. Press cuttings on the Gautier stand at the Universal Exhibition of 1867; sketches of commissions undertaken over the years – kings and courtesans, *grandes dames* and gigolos – it seemed anyone of any note or notoriety had passed through Gautier's doors.

Her hands began to tremble as she contemplated this extraordinary legacy. It seemed as if her father was talking to her through this collection of notes and pictures. Honour, excellence and tradition, everything in the dossier seemed to recall these, her father's favourite watchwords. Brusquely, she snapped the dossier shut.

'It's OK, Papa,' she said to the gentle ghost whose presence she could feel. 'I swore I'd never let you down and, believe me, I never will.'

It was Thursday evening and already the crowds were converging on the streets of Peshawar. After parking the jeep, Laura and Sharif joined the flow and allowed themselves to be swept along by the seething mass of locals. She tugged him by the sleeve.

'Are we going to a rally?'

'Hardly.' He grinned. 'In this country, rallies tend to end up with hundreds in the slammer.'

She stared, quite uninhibited, at the hotch-potch of humanity as it moved unerringly along. Judging by their clothes, the men and women here seemed to be drawn from every conceivable class and background. 'A concert, then?' she prodded. 'The last time I saw a crowd this big they were all screaming for Madonna.'

Wryly, he shook his head. 'Can you honestly see Madonna performing in a Muslim country?'

'There are times when I feel like strangling you!'

'That's the spirit.' He goaded her cheerfully. 'Only, save the homicide for Charles!'

Inlaid with mosaics of myriad reds and greens and golds, the domed roof of the shrine gleamed and glittered in the torchlight. Tiles and frescoes took up the colours, adding them to the floral tributes heaped around the tomb inside. By now, the crowd had fallen completely silent. Some, their eyes shut tight, were kneeling and chanting formal prayers. Others crowded around the tomb and raised their hands in silent supplication. It was then that the singing started, slow rhythmic singing, the singing of ancient and mystical songs. 'We call it *qavvali*,' whispered Sharif, but already Laura was swaying, eyes closed, to the rhythms of the music. The strange, haunting sounds washed over him. He closed his eyes and the words of *Fatiha*, the invocation at the beginning of the Koran, filtered gradually into his mind. The tinkling of bells, the smell of flowers and incense began to fill their senses. Evening turned to dusk and dusk to dark but no one seemed aware of time. The entire congregation was joined together in an act of spiritual communion.

At last, the music came to an end. Dispersing into the night, the crowds began to wend their way slowly, contentedly homewards. Laura's eyes flickered as she re-emerged into consciousness.

'Shall we go?' whispered Sharif.

She nodded, loath to let her voice disturb the tranquillity of the moment. Tonight she felt at ease with herself and at peace with the rest of the world. Happy and relaxed, they began to make their way out of the shrine. And neither noticed the pair of bright blue eyes which followed them through the throng.

After locating the Suzuki, they began the long and tortuous haul back to camp.

'It was beautiful,' said Laura at last.

'I'm glad you enjoyed it.' Sharif lit a cigarette and inhaled deeply.

'I know it's wrong of me,' she continued, 'but nowadays I only seem to pray when I want something badly.'

The smoke from his cigarette drifted outside and up to the stars. 'And what did you pray for tonight?' The jeep shuddered slightly as he moved down into first.

'You tell me first.' Her tone was slightly joshing.

'That's something between me and the *pirs*.' There was no humour in his voice.

'I'm sorry.' For a second, she thought she might have upset his feelings and resolved to delve no further. He was right, after all. What passed between the *pirs*, those 'saints' of mystical Sufism and their supplicants, deserved to be shrouded for ever in secrecy.

Sensing her discomfiture, he relented slightly. 'I prayed for the possible,' he replied, 'and for the impossible as well.'

It seemed too wonderful a night to become embroiled in riddles. Laura wound down her window and held her hand out in the air. The breeze felt deliciously cool against her skin. If only this magical evening could go on for ever. She wished her stay in the mountains would never end. 'Please, could you stop?'

Immediately, he slammed on the brakes. The Suzuki ground to a halt by the side of the road. 'You're not feeling ill, are you?'

'I never felt better in my life. It's just that I'd like to go for a walk.'

It was a madcap request and she knew it. Hidden in the gloom, wolves and brigands might be stalking the foothills, looking for unsuspecting prey. Tonight, however, there was no place for fear in Laura's pounding heart. A wisp of cloud trailed past the moon, unveiling its ghostly beauty. Laura's face, serene and resolute, was suddenly bathed in its silvery light. Sharif caught his breath, speechless at the sight of such ethereal beauty. She seemed like a wraith, to be caught and held for fear she might melt away.

His every instinct told him he ought to resist, but tonight he wanted to please her. He hopped out of the jeep and retrieved his rifle from the back. Stippled in the moonlight, the landscape, for once, was disturbingly unfamiliar. He put his arm round her and her body felt warm against his. They walked on, savouring their own foolhardy behaviour and inhaling the cool night air.

A sudden rustling made Laura jump. Immediately, Sharif had his rifle at the ready, his finger on the trigger. She watched as his eyes scanned the landscape, searching for the source of the noise.

'Stay here,' he whispered and crept stealthily towards the disturbance. Laura could feel her legs begin to give as she stumbled for cover behind a rock. Crouching down, she peeped out and saw the rifle glinting in the moonlight. Sharif now had it pointed directly at a bush. 'Come out!' he ordered. In the silence of the ink-black night, it seemed as if his voice would carry to the peaks of the snow-capped mountains. He waited but nothing happened. Laura felt her stomach begin to churn. Sharif was standing perfectly still, his rifle poised to shoot. 'I said, come out!'

Petrified, she bit her knuckles. Then, suddenly, in the thick evergreen hollow of the korinda bush, a twig cracked. It sounded like the report of a gun. By now, she was barely able to breathe.

'This is your last chance,' shouted Sharif. 'I'm telling you to come out.'

The whole bush began to shake as a small cheetal stag trotted out. It stared arrogantly at Sharif, shook its horns, then bounded off into the shadows. Laura felt the tension draining from her neck to her spine and thence towards her feet. She ran across to where Sharif was still standing and collapsed, laughing, into his arms. He held her so tightly she could feel his breath, moist and warm against her cheek. Then suddenly she felt his lips, soft yet probing against hers. He swept her up and carried her to a grassy verge where gently he laid her down. Then, together they made love beneath the wondrous, wheeling stars.

'I love you.' He ran his fingers through the tousled mass of her hair. Nestling happily in his arms, she looked up to contemplate the black infinity of sky.

'And I love you too,' she whispered. 'I can withstand anything now.'

*

The day after Laura's departure, Sharif returned home to a distinctly icy reception. 'It's good of you to find the time to visit.' His mother barely looked up from her needlework as he kissed her cheek.

'I'm sorry.' As usual, he was determined to make allowances for her health. 'But I've been so busy, tying up loose ends.'

'Not too busy to go to *qavvali!*'

'No.' The smile froze on his face. 'Everyone needs time to relax.'

'Your sister saw you.' Khatija let her embroidery fall to her lap. 'She says you were there with a woman.'

'I won't deny it.' Sharif's jaw set hard. 'Laura's a friend of mine.'

'Another friend?' Her voice was heavy with sarcasm. 'You keep an interesting selection of friends, nowadays. Like that Jew you've been working with.'

'Yes, Mother.' He could feel the anger rising in his voice. 'I'm proud to say that Serge Birnbaum *is* a friend of mine. I couldn't have made my film without him.'

She sniffed, and picked up her needlework. 'And what about this hippie you've been seen about with?'

'I won't have you denigrating Laura like that!' The vein in his temple had started to pulse. He struggled to keep his temper. 'She's wonderful. I love her.'

'Don't be so ridiculous!' Khatija's pinched face was etched with anger. She clenched her tiny fists. 'Do what you want with the woman. But keep your cheap Western morals and sordid affairs in Europe where they belong.'

Furious, Sharif got up to leave. 'You don't know what you're talking about. Laura is—'

'I have no wish to hear. This thing is a passing fancy. It's of no consequence to me.'

'But how can you—'

'Go now. I'm too tired to argue. You're becoming all things to all men, Sharif. Very soon, you'll be nothing at all.'

Something inside him suddenly snapped. 'Just because I won't fit into your nice, neat strait-jacketed world. You can't bear it, can you, Mother? You can't bear the fact that I refuse to be blinkered. Ever since I started work on my film—'

'Ah, yes,' she sneered. 'The film. The film about honour and family values. Tell me, have you read your own script?'

'But of course I have!'

She fixed him with a thousand-year-old stare. 'Then I suggest you read it again.'

CHAPTER TWENTY-EIGHT

ammy Sandton sat behind his recently purchased *bureau plat* and did his best to try to look smug. The acquisition of the House of Gautier was virtually, as his wife put it, *dans le sac* and he knew he ought to be a happy man. For some reason, however, Sammy most decidedly was not. Daphne was ecstatic, a condition which did their already active sex life no harm whatsoever, but, buried deep within his working-class psyche, something niggled. Although it was unspoken, Sammy sensed his sales director's heartfelt disapproval. If only Ray would come on side he knew he would feel better instantly. After twenty years at Sandtons, his old East-End friend was the only person Sammy really trusted. Ray's instincts were rarely wrong. Increasingly tight-lipped and taciturn, his persistent lack of enthusiasm was starting to worry his boss.

The assembled group of advisers, brokers and public relations experts was positively humming with excitement. Seated in a green leather armchair on her husband's right-hand side, Daphne Sandton smiled beatifically as she clutched her file of press clippings. The House of Gautier was *her* baby. It had been her dreams and aspirations which had propelled her husband into the deal and, since the death of Gaston Gautier, she had ensured that negotiations moved forward rapidly. 'Just a brief presentation,' she chirruped, turning watery doe-eyes on her husband. The office fell silent as Daphne produced a square gilt frame from her capacious leather handbag. She stood up and handed it to Sammy before kissing him noisily. He stared open-mouthed at the offering.

'I knew you'd like it,' she trilled, resuming her seat. She graced the company with a practised Olivia de Havilland simper. 'It's from *The Times*, a copy of Gaston Gautier's obituary. So wonderful, don't you think, him being a war hero and everything?' Oblivious to the frozen smiles on the faces all around her, she turned her attentions back to her husband. 'I thought you could hang it in the Gautier boardroom in New Bond Street, that is, when you take possession. I always think people like to know a bit about the history of a place.'

Sammy caught Ray's dead-fish eye and shuffled uncomfortably in his chair. The offending article was swiftly relegated to the top drawer of his desk. 'Thank you, darling. That was very thoughtful of you.' He cleared his throat. 'Thank you, ladies and gentlemen, for coming along this morning. I thought you'd all like a brief update on the state of play so far.'

Daphne shuffled her cuttings. 'So much publicity. I think you ought to congratulate Maddy, dear.'

Irritated at the interruption, Sammy nevertheless forced a smile. 'Yes, thank you, Maddy. You're doing a wonderful job.'

Maddy Wheatcroft, Sandton's financial PR consultant, nodded politely. Brought in at vast expense to cover the Gautier takeover, she was already sick to death of Daphne and her ludicrous personal publicity demands. There was plenty Maddy felt like saying but wisely decided to hold her peace. She might indeed be doing a wonderful job, she thought, if only this dreadful woman would leave her alone. In Daphne Sandton's myopic eyes, however, this whole multi-million-pound deal was nothing more than a massive ego trip.

Daphne leaned across and patted the young woman on the hand. 'You will try the editor of *Tatler* again, won't you, Maddy dear? The new mistress of Gautier – I'm sure I'd make good copy for them.'

A former Roedean lacrosse captain, Maddy felt an incredible urge to slap Daphne's stupid, over made-up face. Instead, she bit her lip. 'I'll certainly do my best, Mrs Sandton.'

Strategically placed as far away from Daphne as the office would allow, Ray yawned loudly and checked his watch. Sammy took the hint. 'If we could please get back to business,' he said, tapping the desk with his fountain pen. He turned to the dapper figure seated straight in front of him. Simon Lovell-Smith, Sandton's stockbroker, beamed back at him encouragingly. 'Perhaps, Simon, if you could tell us what's happening in the market.'

The broker's report was succinct and, in his own words, extremely promising. Despite the recession, Sandton's discount sales and aggressive marketing had kept their share price high. Thanks to some judicious unbundling before the property crash there was, he concluded jovially, more than enough money in the coffers to complete the Gautier deal. 'Any questions?' he asked at the end of the report. The room remained stonily silent. He cast around, anxious for a further excuse to display his expertise.

Ray sniffed. Ignoring the broker's expensively capped smile, he addressed himself straight to Sammy. 'And what about the rest of us here at Sandton's? With your posh new shops and your rich snotty clients, how are we supposed to fit in?'

Sammy could feel the colour rising in his cheeks. Trust Ray! With his no-nonsense approach, he had put his finger on the very niggle that was twisting around in his own guts. How, wondered Sammy, was *he* going to fit into the rarefied world that was Gautier? He opened his mouth, but somehow the placatory words he sought simply refused to come.

'You and I should have this out over a drink down the pub,' he heard himself saying instead.

Ray nodded slowly. The last time the old drinking mates had been down the pub together was the evening before Sammy met Daphne. 'You're on,' replied Ray, some slight vestige of a smile breaking over his lined and crumpled features. 'It's a while since I've hammered you at darts.'

Daphne rustled her cuttings loudly. Both Sammy and the situation seemed to be slipping out of her control. Men and their strange bonding rituals was something she would never understand and what Daphne did not understand alarmed her. She glared across at Ray, her eyes suddenly hard and cold. He met her gaze and stared back at her. He knew she had never had any time for him or any of Sammy's old mates. Well, the antipathy was mutual. Daphne gave up, pasted on a smile and turned to Sammy again. 'Darts, darling? So very working-men's-club, don't you think?'

Sammy made to answer, but already she was digging out another file from the bottom of her bag. 'Horses – now there's real class for you, the sort of thing we at Gautier ought to be involved with, in my opinion.' She opened the file and retrieved a sheaf of papers. 'The Gautier Platinum Stakes, that's the kind of image we want to project.' Daphne fluttered her eyelashes in her husband's direction. 'You know, Sammy, I've been on to this trainer, Gosden – lovely man, very Oxbridge – down in Newmarket. I asked him to keep an eye out. He was *so* polite, such breeding, you know, said he was busy but he'd let me know.'

Ray winced and stared fixedly out of the window.

'I've always loved horses,' continued Daphne, specifically for Maddy's benefit. A passion for horses always looked good in glossy magazines. 'In fact, my family has always been associated with bloodstock.'

It was all too much for Ray. 'Father an undertaker, grandfather a butcher,' he muttered under his breath. 'Now there's real bloodstock for you.'

Intuiting the probable drift of his mumblings, Sammy tried to change the subject. 'First things first,' he said, making a pitiful stab at levity. 'We haven't acquired Gautier yet.'

But already Daphne's mind was in overdrive: images of herself in a large, expensive hat at Royal Ascot; the cheering crowds; the thundering hoofs; the Winners' Enclosure; a presentation to the Queen. 'Yes, Your Majesty, I do so agree, Your Majesty. What a lovely brooch, Your Majesty. Do you know, I believe it's one of ours . . .'

'I'm off,' said Ray, standing up abruptly. 'I've got a meeting with my sales people at midday.' He looked pointedly at Daphne. 'Some poor buggers are going to have to pay for all this lah-di-dah!'

'See you at the Crown, then, this evening at seven?' Sammy's voice was almost pleading.

Daphne's face had turned thunderous. 'But, darling, we've been invited—'

'You've got it,' smiled Ray as he opened the door. 'And don't forget to bring your own arrows.'

A small grey cloud seemed to hang over Daphne's well-coiffed head. For the first time in their marriage, Sammy had actually ignored her wishes. She sat back in her armchair, pouting prettily. She would find some way of teaching him a lesson. Perhaps tonight she would tell him precisely where to stick that new vibrator.

The company accountant droned on interminably with proposed restructuring plans. 'And, of course, the Gautier workshops in Paris, Rome, New York and London will all have to be closed.' He handed out a balance sheet. 'The savings, as you can see, will be enormous. After the takeover, Sandton contacts in Taiwan and India will be dealing with all jewellery manufacture.'

Maddy Wheatcroft could feel the colour draining from her cheeks. The House of Gautier and all it represented was being undermined with every word. The figures on the balance sheet blurred into an amorphous blob. Maddy felt like a family ne'er-do-well, selling the ancestral silver. The day she accepted this account, she had hoped to promote concepts of quality and class. The travesty being suggested here was seriously off line.

'I'm sorry,' she stammered, 'I know it's not my position to say . . .' She faltered for a second.

Sammy smiled at her encouragingly. 'Please, all suggestions gratefully accepted.'

Maddy thought of the repayments on her new Knightsbridge flat and considered holding her tongue. She could not afford to lose this account. On the other hand, however, it was lunacy to sit by and allow Gautier's most precious asset, its exclusivity, to be offloaded overnight. Red-faced, she stumbled on. 'I was just thinking, even from a purely PR point of view, we ought to try and safeguard Gautier's special status.'

Daphne spotted her opening. 'Thank you, Maddy. That's precisely what I've been trying to get across. Now if Gautier were to sponsor the Platinum Stakes . . .'

It was with huge relief that Sammy saw the red light winking on one of his telephones. He picked up the receiver and heard the breathless tones of his new secretary, a Daphne-clone hand-picked by Daphne.

'I'm so sorry to interrupt your meeting, sir, but I've got your brother on the line. He says it's urgent.'

'My brother!' Sammy could not have sounded more surprised if Daphne had elected to enter a convent.

'Yes, sir. Kevin Sandton. He's ringing from Newcastle. I thought you wouldn't mind, but it's a reversed-charge call.'

Sammy sighed ruefully. Yes, that sounded like Kevin all right. A social worker up in Newcastle, Kevin despised everything his elder brother stood for. Money, power, materialism, none of these had ever meant anything to Kevin. The so-called 'brains' of the family, he had sailed through grammar school and on to university at Keele. Sammy, by contrast, had left school at sixteen and joined his father in the jewellery business. His old man had died young. A lifetime of outdoor, market stalls had had disastrous consequences on his chest. In addition, fifty smokes and six pints a day had done little to alleviate his bronchial condition. The day of his father's funeral, Sammy promised his mother that he would take care of Kevin's education. Two degrees, a Ph.D. and a plethora of sociology publications later, Kevin had at last found a remunerated job. Content with the delinquents, drug addicts and drop-outs of society, he now thought it only right that his rich brother, Sammy, should continue to support him in his philanthropic endeavours. Their mother, Muriel, thought Kevin was a saint. For Sammy, the description 'parasite' sprang more readily to mind.

'Put him through,' he ordered gruffly. There was a click as the line was connected. A social chameleon as well as worker, Kevin had soon adopted an almost perfect Geordie accent.

'Hi there, bro! How's the bauble business doing?'

Sammy clenched his teeth. 'Well enough to continue paying for your flat and your car.'

The sarcasm was lost on Kevin. Everywhere around him, people accepted being bailed out as a normal way of life. Taking Sammy's money was as natural as whingeing about the government. 'There's a bit of a problem, Sam.'

Sammy felt his heart sink. The last time Kevin had 'a problem', the 'problem' was already six months pregnant. Sammy would still be paying the poor girl maintenance well into the next millennium. 'What is it *this* time?'

'The old queen . . .'

'Mum?'

'Yeah. Seems like she's fallen down the stairs.'

Sammy's face turned ashen. Beads of perspiration appeared on his forehead. He took out his handkerchief and wiped them away. 'Is it serious? Has she broken anything?'

The image of his mother, small and frail yet independent and stubborn, flashed sharply into Sammy's mind. He could almost see a laid-back Kevin shrugging casually at the other end of the line.

'Dunno. Don't think so. It was the neighbour who rang me to say she was worried about her. Looks like Mum's refusing to go to hospital.'

Sammy looked at the row of consultants and advisers staring across at him. There was not a single one of these gannets on less than two hundred pounds an hour. Sammy put his handkerchief back in his pocket.

'I'll go and see her right away.'

Kevin sounded hugely relieved. 'Would you, bro? What a star. I mean, you know, I'd go myself, but, like, the train fare down from Newcastle . . .'

'I'd pay your bloody train fare!'

Kevin tittered, embarrassed. 'Well, there's also this course I'm on at the moment, "Geriatric Care in the Community", I wouldn't like to miss out on it. We've had some very useful lectures.'

Something inside Sammy snapped. 'Good old Kevin! Time for every stray dog and every lost cause, but never a minute for your mother.'

'But look, bro, I don't think—'

But Sammy had slammed down the phone.

*

Parked outside the tiny terraced house just off the East End's notorious Brick Lane, the gleaming blue Bentley caused quite a stir. Alarmed by the group of adolescent hooligans who sprang, as if from nowhere, to study the vehicle and its 'removables', Sammy's chauffeur suggested moving on. 'Perhaps, sir, you'd like to ring me on the mobile when you're finished. It might be safer if I circled.'

Sammy was not amused. 'For God's sake, man, this is the place where I grew up. Do you think I can't deal with a couple of kids?'

He hopped out of the car and, after surveying the ogling group, pointed to the biggest and meanest-looking amongst them. 'Here, you, what's your name?'

Dressed in a reversed baseball cap, a Tochini tracksuit and Reeboks, the teenager stared impudently back at him. 'They call me Mack. Who's asking?'

Sammy suppressed a smile. He had been just the same himself when he was that age, insolent and arrogant. He liked that in a kid.

'I'm Sammy Sandton.'

A low hum of approval buzzed around the group. Everyone knew about Sammy Sandton, the local boy done good. All over the East End truants without a GCSE to their names all shared aspirations to 'do a Sammy'. Mack's sullen, pustule-ridden face was suddenly wreathed in smiles. 'Glad to meet you, Sam.' He extended a silver-ringed hand. Across his knuckles, the tattoo of a boa constrictor stood in livid contrast to the grey-white pallor of his skin. Sammy squeezed the boa solemnly. Wide-eyed, the smaller children cheered.

'I'm here to see my mother,' said Sammy, taking his wallet from his inside breast pocket. He pulled out a twenty-pound note. 'While I'm with her, I wouldn't want anything unfortunate to happen to my car.'

He handed the note to Mack, who shook his close-shaven head vigorously. 'No need for that. I'll take care your car. You and me is mates.'

Sammy rang the bell of the miserable two-up-two-down

house he used to call his home. It seemed like an eternity before he heard the sound of footsteps, shuffling slowly towards the door. 'Who is it?' The voice was shrill yet somehow frail. He began to fear the worst.

'It's me, Mum, Sammy. I heard you'd taken a fall.'

A heavy bolt was drawn back with a resounding clunk and the door shuddered open, shedding flakes of blistered green paint in the process. 'I've never known such fuss and nonsense,' muttered Muriel Sandton as she allowed her elder son to peck her on the cheek. Sammy followed her hobbling figure as it disappeared down the dark narrow corridor and into the tiny sitting room. It was wearing the pink and white checked nylon overall he had rarely seen it without. Muriel slumped down in a battered brown velveteen armchair and heaved her right leg on to an old hand-embroidered footstool.

Sammy looked on, concerned. 'What on earth happened? You ought to be in a nursing home.'

She sniffed disparagingly. 'I slipped on the stairs, that's all, it's just a bit of a cut. No need for everyone to get worked up.'

The slit in her overall revealed a large white bandage extending from the ankle to the knee cap. He gawped at it, horrified. 'Have you been to see a doctor?'

Muriel shrugged. 'The district nurse came round and sorted me out. She wanted me to go to casualty, but I told her I wasn't having any of it.'

'But, Mum, she's right, you know.'

Muriel shook her head. 'I said to her, I said, "Look, love, I spent the war in the East End with the WVS. Some of the injuries I dealt with during the raids, why, them youngsters they call doctors nowadays just wouldn't know where to start."'

'But, Mum,' protested Sammy feebly, 'you're not getting any younger. Won't you let me hire a nurse?' Muriel's eyes flashed dangerously. Sammy knew he was on shaky footing. 'Just until your leg's fixed. She could do your messages – help you around the house.'

'I'm not having no other woman living under my roof. Besides, the neighbours do my messages for me. We ain't West Hampstead here, you know.'

Normally, Sammy would have given up and changed the subject, but today he was determined to bring things to a head. On this occasion, his mother's injuries had not been serious, but next time it might be a broken leg, a broken hip or worse. True, she was a stubborn and wilful character but that was why he loved her. During the war, her kindness and bravery had been legendary throughout a badly bombed East End. Sammy had always been proud of his mother. He knew she was one in a million.

'You know, Mum, it'd be much easier on your pins if you were in a bungalow. I was looking at a property the other day, so nice, pretty little garden – I'd have someone come and do it for you—' Muriel stamped her one good foot. 'Look, if I've told you once, I've told you a hundred times. I ain't leaving this place till they carry me out in a box. I'm happy here. I've got all my friends and memories around me. If I left here, why, it would be like deserting your dad. Now, I know you mean well, but we'll have no more about this moving lark.'

Defeated, Sammy bent down to pick up Blacky, the old tom cat who had fathered even more illegitimate offspring than Kevin. 'She's a hard case, isn't she, Blacky?' He stroked the cat's smelly and rather mangy coat. 'I reckon she's the only person I know who isn't trying to take me to the cleaners.' He immediately bit his tongue. Nothing was ever lost on his mother.

'How's Daphne?' she asked pointedly. 'The district nurse showed me some pictures of her in a magazine when she came.'

Blacky miaowed loudly as Sammy put him down on the floor again. Immediately he began to claw the almost threadbare nylon hearth rug.

'She's very well,' replied Sammy, colouring. His mother had never cared for Daphne. As Kevin had been pleased to report, she called her a cheap little gold-digger. Muriel had even gone so far as to boycott their wedding, claiming an appointment with her chiropodist. The snub had not been lost on Daphne who now refused to have Muriel in her house. Sammy sighed. It was just another tension in his already stressful life.

Struggling now for things to say, he scanned the room. The mantelpiece and sideboard were crammed full of photographs. A few were of his father, looking tall and handsome in his RAF uniform. The rest were all of Kevin. Our Kev, thought Sammy wryly, the apple of his mother's eye. The living room was nothing but a shrine to Kevin and his various achievements: studio portraits of Kevin in a gown and mortar board; snaps of Kevin receiving scrolls, diplomas and degrees; photos of Kevin pontificating at study groups and conferences. Sammy felt a sudden wave of sibling jealousy. It had always been the same, ever since they were nippers. Sammy had always been his father's lad and Kevin had been his mum's.

'So, son, you're keeping busy?' Muriel stroked the cat, now happily ensconced on her knee.

Sammy nodded. 'Yes, very busy. In fact, it's still a bit of a secret, but we're taking over Gautier.'

'That's nice, dear. Cup of tea?'

'The *House of Gautier*,' he repeated, deflated. 'You know, the king of jewellers and the jeweller of kings, the most famous jewellers in the world.'

Muriel stared up at one of Kevin's many images and continued to stroke the cat. 'Yes, dear, very nice. And Kevin's doing so very well in Newcastle. Such a good boy. You know, he phones me every week.'

I should know, thought Sammy bitterly. I'm paying all his bloody bills.

'He wanted to come down and see me, but he's ever so busy up there. Such good work he's doing. If only the country had more like him!'

Sammy stood up abruptly. 'I'll make the tea.' He strode into the kitchen and shoved the kettle under the tap. It was always the same, he thought. Nothing *he* ever did – ever *had* done, for that matter – really counted with his mother. If he arrived with news that he had been appointed prime minister she would respond with some tale of Kevin's latest triumph. Kevin! Sammy smacked the plug into the socket and angrily flicked the switch. Kevin and his horde of every-which-way-challenged dropouts! Where the hell was the success in that?

He opened the pantry door and looked around for the tea caddy. At last he spotted a box of Typhoo tea bags and an old biscuit barrel, its chromium handle corroded green, on the bottom greaseproof-papered shelf. Leaning across for them, he stumbled against a pile of wicker baskets hidden against the wall. Looking down, Sammy found about a dozen Harrods' hampers and a crate of vintage champagne. On further inspection it transpired that none of them had ever been opened. A look of pain crossed Sammy's face. These were the gifts he had been sending his mother over the past decade or so. Suddenly he felt small, as if he were eight years old again. It was Christmas and he had spent the best part of a month making a special greetings card for his mother. With enormous pride he had left it under the tree, together with her present, a box of Coty's L'Aimant talc. On Boxing Day, the young Sammy had found his card on the windowsill in the sitting-room. Kevin's card had been given pride of place in the middle of the mantelpiece.

Sammy replaced the tea and biscuits on the shelf and briefly blew his nose. All his life, he had striven to gain approval from his mother, but somehow it still eluded him. He scalded the tea-pot the way she had shown him forty years ago and added four tea-bags – he knew she liked it strong. Next, he opened the biscuit barrel and found the usual mound of soft, stale Nice biscuits. He laid several on a plate and thought of the phalanx of advisers he had just left haggling in his office. Thank God they couldn't see him!

'Nothing like a nice cup of tea,' said Muriel, pouring her slops into a saucer. The cat hopped down from her knee and started lapping up his treat.

Sammy chewed his lip. 'Are you sure there's nothing else I can get you?'

'Nothing, thanks. The district nurse brought me all the papers.' She gestured towards a pile by the side of the settee. 'The rate I read, it'll take me months to get through that lot.'

He stood up and moved the stack closer to his mother's armchair. The latest issue of the *Gadfly* slipped out and fell to the floor. 'I see your district nurse is into trendy stuff.' He laughed and stooped to pick it up, stopping to glance at the page where the magazine lay open. The smile froze on his face. Wearing a crown and draped in the tricolour, a cartoon depicting the late

Gaston Gautier seemed to be glaring straight at him. Sammy stared back at it. Slithering out from behind Gaston's foot, a fat slug-like creature bearing Charles's overblown face was wriggling along on its belly. 'A worthy successor?' ran the caption beneath and a two-page article followed.

'Do you mind if I take this?' Sammy's voice was ominously quiet.

Muriel nodded. 'Please do. I never seem to know what they're on about in that magazine. Too many nods and winks for my liking. I like my scandal straight.'

He smiled wanly, rolled up the magazine and pushed it in his pocket. 'Right then, Mum. I'd better be off. Remember, if there's anything you need . . .'

'I've told you,' she interrupted tetchily, 'I'm perfectly all right.'

'You're sure you're in no pain?'

Muriel shrugged. 'Nothing I can't cope with. Anyway, whoever said things were supposed to be easy? Like your dad used to say, life is six to four against!'

His mother's lack of expectation made Sammy feel guiltier than ever. People like Daphne and Kevin were easy to accommodate: they wore their price tags clearly appended. But Muriel anticipated little and demanded even less – an old cat, some happy memories, the warmth and friendship of her neighbours. And yet, mused Sammy enviously, she seemed totally content.

He returned to the narrow corridor where he had dumped his briefcase. Kneeling down, he opened it and retrieved his mobile telephone. He returned to the sitting room and handed it to his mother. 'Look, Mum, this'll save you having to move if you need to call anyone.' He saw her eyes glaze over as he explained the various dials and buttons. 'Don't worry about the bill. They'll send it to me.' He paused, but could not deny himself the dig. 'Our Kevin's got one the same.'

The gentle sarcasm was lost on Muriel. Her face brightened as she punched in her darling Kevin's number. For a full five minutes, it was constantly engaged. 'Never mind.' Lovingly Muriel stroked the mobile. Any device which could conjure up Kevin so easily was a precious gift indeed. 'I'll try again later.'

Sammy kissed his mother affectionately. 'I'll call round again tomorrow. But if you're feeling worried in the night—'

Muriel sat upright in her chair. 'Look, son, if fire-bombing and doodlebugs couldn't frighten me, what can possibly worry me now?'

As he emerged into the street, Sammy felt strangely comforted. His mother's guts and independence still filled him with righteous filial pride. An image of his wife, forever wheedling and manipulating, flitted swiftly across his mind. Critical and unflattering, he swatted it like a fly. Daphne, at least, made him feel good about himself. She applauded his achievements. The little boy with the unopened card paid generously for that.

The sight which greeted him outside almost stopped him in his tracks. Armed with what looked like someone's old thermal vest, Mack was busily buffing the hub-caps of Sammy's glistening Bentley. His group of admirers hung around, thrilled with their leader's handiwork.

'You've done a brilliant job!' Sammy opened the back door and threw his briefcase onto the seat.

Mack shrugged his shoulders and tried hard to look cool. 'I didn't have nothing better to do.'

Once again, Sammy took his wallet out of his pocket. This time he offered the boy a fifty-pound note. The kids around fell silent. Half a ton was a lot of dough.

Mack pulled himself up to his full height and looked Sammy straight in the eye. 'I don't want nothing. Like I said, Sam, you and me is mates.'

Sammy made as if to argue but, regally, Mack held up his hand. 'I might ask you for something one of these days. But, in the meantime, if your mum needs owt, tell her to give Mack the Lad a shout.'

Sammy eased back into the luxuriant upholstery of his car and told his chauffeur to head for the Crown. His appointment with Ray was two hours away but he was desperate for a pint. He unrolled the *Gadfly* and was soon immersed in a coruscating article on 'The Life and Times of the House of Gautier'. The traffic near St Paul's was moving at a snail's pace. All around, horns were blowing and frustrated lorry drivers were shouting genial abuse at one another. Unaware of the hullabaloo, Sammy read on eagerly. For the first time, the real Gaston Gautier was emerging before his very eyes. Honourable, brave and clearly much loved, he appeared far more sympathetic than his miserable louse of a son.

The car phone rang as the car swerved to avoid an idle jaywalker. Slightly shaken by the near miss, Sammy fumbled to pick up the receiver. To his annoyance, he found it was Charles. On the mahogany dashboard, the digital clock flashed five o'clock. By the sound of Charles's voice, however, he had already had plenty to drink. 'Just one more thing,' he slurred after five minutes of inconsequential blather.

Sammy drummed his fingers on the top of his briefcase. 'Yes?'

'It's a little matter of goodwill.'

'Goodwill?' snapped Sammy. 'What the hell are you talking about?'

'The goodwill attached to Gautier. I don't think that element has been properly reflected in your offer.'

The aggravations of the day started to collide in Sammy's head. He could feel a migraine coming on. 'Look, sunshine, as far as I'm concerned, we've already shaken on the deal.'

'Come on, now.' Charles had reverted to wheedling mode, an approach that sickened Sammy. 'We're only a few hundred thousand adrift. In a deal this size, that isn't going to kill you.'

Sammy could feel the blood pounding around his head, exacerbating his migraine. 'You know what? I can't stand blokes who agree deals then start bitching over every detail. It's like punching below the belt.'

Splayed out on his bed in his suite at the Connaught, Charles heard warning bells ringing. He jumped up, phone in hand, and started pacing round the bedroom. So far, this deal had been plain sailing. Through Daphne he had been able to manipulate Sammy into accepting his every demand. But now, for some reason, the worm was turning. He decided to change tack.

'I think there's been a misunderstanding. I've had one hell of a day. A few weasels from the press have been on my tail—'

'Yes.' Sammy's tone was icy. 'I've just been reading all about you in the *Gadfly*. It seems that shaking on a deal then reopening negotiations has always been one of your strong points.'

'I'll sue those bastards for every penny they've got! It's nothing but a pack of lies. That bloody wife of mine—'

'Well, let's have a little look, shall we?' Sammy was beginning to enjoy himself. 'The sources mentioned here – what do we have? a property developer in Hong Kong, a Gautier franchisee in Rome, a diamond cutter in Antwerp – quite a few of them, Charlie old son. Now, remind me, what was it you were saying about goodwill? You know, I'm beginning to wonder if a decent East-End boy like me should be dealing with the likes of you.'

Back in his hotel room, Charles collapsed, a crumpled figure, on to his pillow. 'Is our meeting still on for tomorrow?'

'If I've arranged to meet you tomorrow, Charlie, then meet you I certainly shall.' He paused, before continuing with deliberation. 'Unlike *some* people, Sammy Sandton is a man of his word. Ask anyone in the City.'

After six pints of Murphy's and eight games of darts, Sammy's migraine was quite forgotten. He and Ray had shared a wonderfully convivial evening down at the Crown, beating the resident darts team and swapping yarns with all the locals. Arm in arm, they strolled out of the pub just a little after closing time.

'I haven't enjoyed myself so much since—' Sammy broke off. It seemed disloyal to say what he really wanted to say.

Six pints over par himself, Ray had no such inhibitions. 'Since you started going to those high-falutin' wankers' dos that wife of yours drags you off to.'

Sammy nodded dolefully. 'You're right. I can't remember the last time I had a skinful with the lads.'

Ray patted him on the shoulder. 'That's the problem. There are some of us who really watch out for you, Sam, and we reckon you're losing the plot.'

It looked, for a moment, as if Sammy might turn nasty. Then, all of a sudden, a broad smile began to spread across his face. 'Do you remember when I was still boxing, how they all used to underestimate old Sammy – everyone that is, except you and Dad. I'll be OK, Ray, you know I will. I've always been a survivor.'

The driver was waiting patiently as the two friends lurched merrily back towards the car. He opened the door and allowed them to tumble, still singing, into the back seat. Twenty minutes later, a far happier Ray was decanted into the family home at Peckham.

It was way past midnight when the Bentley purred its way along the Sandtons' tree-lined drive. Upstairs in the mansion's master bedroom, Daphne heard the car approaching and put the final touches to her négligé. The black, diaphanous creation had been her hair-stylist's suggestion. After her behaviour that afternoon, she knew that Sammy was bound to be sore. Her refusal to accompany him to his mother's house had been met with stony silence. Invoking an entirely fictitious commitment, she had spent the afternoon shopping in Knightsbridge. Diplomatically, she kicked a large box into her wardrobe and slammed the door shut. Even if it was for the Red Cross ball, two thousand pounds for an outfit was expensive even by her own standards. She would make it up to him. Poor darling! The Gautier deal was causing him more headaches than he had ever anticipated. By now, he would be in need of some serious relaxation. She added a generous dab of Opium to her cleavage and inhaled its cloying scent. If anyone knew about relaxing Sammy, there was no doubt it was her.

The moment she heard the singing on the stairs, she knew there was something wrong.

'"My old man said follow the van, And don't dilly-dally on the way . . ."'

'Sammy?' Already her plans seemed to be going awry. 'Is that you?'

'Who the hell else might it be? "Off went the van with me old man in it, I followed on with me old cock linnet . . ."'

Angrily, she pulled on her dressing gown and marched from the bedroom on to the landing. On the stairs, an ataxic figure was weaving its way uncertainly upwards.

'Are you drunk?' she shouted.

He stopped for a second, leaning for support against the banister. To her horror, she noticed that his tie was missing. Slung across his shoulder, his jacket was horribly crumpled and along one sleeve was an ominous brown patch, the detritus of Ray's misjudged sixth pint. He smiled blearily. 'You could say that. In fact, you could say old Sammy here was absolutely legless.' He seemed to find that extremely funny and swayed perilously to and fro. For one terrible moment, she even thought that he might tumble over the banister and on to the Carrara marble floor below. She raced down the stairs to help him and together they stumbled back into the bedroom. It was then that he caught his foot in the hem of her black diaphanous nightdress and went flying across the bed.

Still desperate to make amends, Daphne peeled the clothes off the semi-conscious body. Then gently she began to tease its nipples with her tongue. The body groaned and rolled over and within minutes, it was snoring. The stench of beer was appalling. Daphne opened the window and, as the cool evening breeze blew in through the casement, she realized she was crying. Tonight was a devastating personal failure. For the first time in their marriage, Sammy had failed to get it up.

CHAPTER TWENTY-NINE

Maisie felt for her scorpion ring, a reassuring presence on her hand. 'I never realized the English countryside could be quite so beautiful.'

The long, winding lane was deserted and a lazy bee hummed hypnotically about their ears. As they rounded the bend, an overgrown honeysuckle cascaded on to their path. Scorpio paused to pick a sprig and handed it to her. She breathed in its heady perfume. 'If only Charles could be made to see sense.'

'Out of order!' He tutted loudly. 'You promised we could spend one whole hour together without mentioning either Gautier or Charles.' Clancy jumped up from behind a blackberry bush and barked his whole-hearted approval. 'Come out of there this instant!' Scorpio laughed. 'You'll end up tearing yourself to pieces.'

Thrilled to have his master home again, the dog was skipping around like a two-month-old puppy. He leapt over the bush and, paws covered in mud, began playfully to grapple with Scorpio, whose white cotton T-shirt was soon absolutely filthy.

'Cut it out!' He did his best to sound annoyed, but neither Clancy nor Maisie was convinced. Scorpio stooped down and picked up a large, boomerang-shaped stick which he hurled far, far off into a field. Tail wagging, Clancy raced off in ecstatic pursuit. Scorpio shook his head and placed his arm around Maisie's shoulders. 'You'd never believe the difference in that animal. He was so cowed and battered when I found him.'

She snuggled up closer to him. 'I guess that must make two of us.'

314

He kissed her soft, bouncy hair. 'OK, you win. I'll lift the ban on Charles, but only because I'm curious to know why you stuck with him so long.'

A large green frog hopped suddenly across their path. It stopped for a minute to study them with its large, protruding eyes. Then it croaked a salutation before hopping off back to the pond. Maisie stared thoughtfully after it. 'I remember reading that if you put a frog into boiling water, it'll hop straight out again. But if you put it into cold water and gradually raise the temperature, it'll stay right there till it boils.'

Scorpio shuddered. 'You come across some interesting literature.'

'It was in some scientific journal. It didn't occur to me at the time, but now I realize that human relationships work in precisely the same way. If I'd known what Charles was like at the beginning, I'd never have gotten involved. But life went on and without even being aware of it, I began accepting more and more. All the time my self-respect was quietly being whittled away. Then one day, I suddenly opened my eyes and realized I'd almost been destroyed.'

A manic Clancy returned and laid the stick at Maisie's feet. She smiled and hurled it high into the sky. The dog bounded off, his eye on the projectile, determined to retrieve it wherever it might land. 'Par-boiled only.' Scorpio pulled her closer to him and kissed her tenderly. 'But thank God I hauled you out in time.'

Flo was in the garden as they sauntered up the drive. She started waving as she saw them. Instinctively Maisie quickened her step. 'It might be news about Laura. She should've landed by now.'

'You've got to stop worrying about everyone,' remonstrated Scorpio, gently. 'She'll be all right, I promise you. Bruce is there to meet her.'

It was no use. Already Maisie was sprinting up the garden. Scorpio chased after her, amazed at the speed with which she moved.

The usually placid Flo was distinctly agitated. 'I'm sorry, Mrs Gautier—'

'Maisie, please, you really must call me Maisie. I don't intend to be Mrs Gautier that much longer.'

'I'm sorry, Maisie, but your husband, Mr Gautier . . .' Her voice faltered. 'I'm sorry, I'm just not used to being spoken to like that.'

Scorpio's face was livid. 'What the hell has he been saying now?'

'Well, it did seem as if he'd been drinking, but the things he said about Maisie and Laura. I really wouldn't care to repeat them.'

His eyes glinted dangerously. 'I told you we'd never make him see sense.'

Maisie sighed, frustrated. 'Flo, I'm sorry you've had to put up with this. Did he say where he's staying?'

'At the Connaught. He said he'd seen the latest copy of the *Gadfly* and that he was going to sue the lot of you for libel.'

'Just let him try.' Maisie's voice was cold and hard. 'Scorpio, I'm going to call him back.'

'Why bother?'

'Please, just one more time. I must try and reason with him before this turns *really* nasty.'

Since his meeting with Sammy Sandton early that morning, nothing had gone right for Charles. Immured in his hotel suite, waiting for Yolande to fly in from the Seychelles, he poured himself another Scotch and stared disconsolately out of the window. He had played his hand very badly. After calling his bluff over the 'goodwill bonus', Sammy had gone on to subject him to a series of humiliating climb-downs. For once, Daphne had been absent from the meeting and Sammy on his own presented a different and far more daunting negotiator.

His spirits rose as the phone rang. He lurched for the receiver. 'Yolande?'

'I'm afraid not.' Maisie's tone was crisp. 'I'm afraid it's only me, your wife.'

'You bloody bitch! What the hell do you think you're playing at? If you think a few articles in that tacky magazine—'

'I'm not calling you to swap insults – the divorce lawyers are already being paid quite handsomely for that.'

Her composure made him want to scream. She sounded like a nursery school mistress dealing with a particularly awkward child. 'I'll have you for adultery,' he shouted.

'For goodness sake, *do* grow up!'

'It didn't take you long, did it? You've already moved in with your boyfriend.'

She decided not to take the bait. 'Look, Charles, I'm phoning with a perfectly straightforward business proposition. If you accept, it could save the whole family an awful lot of grief.'

'Family? Don't talk to me about family. What a pile of bloody vultures. I hear Caroline is still at my father's, picking over the bones. Wait till I get back to Paris, I'll soon have her kicked out—'

'If you know what's good for you, you'll try no such thing.' Maisie's voice was ominously quiet. He felt almost frightened of her. 'Now then,' she continued pleasantly. 'You realize we're not going to stand by and let this Sandton deal just happen.'

'If you try—'

'Oh, do shut up and listen. You can't threaten me any more. It's obvious you want out of Gautier, but why not walk away gracefully? Give me some time to raise the money and I'll buy your stake from you. Then the House of Gautier would still remain within the family.'

He let out a loud, hollow laugh. 'You really haven't understood a thing, have you? I keep telling you. I don't have a family.'

'Don't be so ridiculous! Whatever you say, you still have Laura—'

'Don't talk to me about *her*!' He sounded beside himself. 'I'd rather see Sammy Sandton in charge than that bastard sister of mine!'

Trembling with rage, Maisie spoke softly into the receiver. 'OK, if that's the way you want to play it, then I'm warning you. That piece in the *Gadfly* was just a shot across the bows. From now on, we're talking war!'

Tight-lipped, she returned to the drawing room to find Clancy leaping around, bashing his tail against the french windows. She

317

looked out to see Scorpio's Range Rover progressing slowly up the drive.

'Laura!' She opened the window and raced across the lawn. By the time she reached the car, the genially Neanderthal Bruce was already hauling suitcases out of the back. A tanned and smiling Laura got out and embraced her friend.

'You're looking just great!' exclaimed Maisie, staggered at the transformation.

Laura smiled. 'I've been doing a lot of thinking. Perhaps, I should have tried it sooner.' She noticed Scorpio, hanging back discreetly, and bounded off to hug him.

'So,' he smiled, stepping back to admire her, 'it looks like you've been taking a few lessons in survival from our friend the Pathan.'

'I suppose I have.' Her eyes twinkled in the sunlight. 'At least, he taught me there are *some* things you can't take lying down.'

'Not even one bloody photographer,' moaned Bruce as he deposited the luggage in the hall. 'You'd have thought one of the tabloids would've wanted a snap of her or something. Not a dicky-bird – and there's me, all ready for a scrap.'

Scorpio slapped him jovially on the shoulder. 'Don't you worry. The way things are panning out, you'll soon be back in business.'

Delighted at the prospect, Bruce dashed off to pump some iron.

Over tea, Maisie and Scorpio briefed Laura on the current state of play. 'So you see,' explained Maisie disconsolately, 'Charles just won't give me the time to launch a counter-bid. If he'd only let me have a few months or so, I could get the Appleford trustees on side.'

Laura shot her friend a grateful look. 'You're too good to me, Maisie.'

'Who else am I going to be good to?'

'There's always me,' Scorpio chipped in.

Maisie ruffled his hair. 'Yes. I'll have to see about you later.'

They were still poring over cuttings from the financial press when Flo appeared with the message that Caroline was on the line from Paris. Sprawled out on the floor between a slaveringly affectionate Clancy and a copy of Gautier's year-end accounts, Laura jumped up and bounded into the study. Soon mother and daughter were chatting animatedly. From developments in Paris, it was clear that battle had already commenced.

'Poor Charles,' mused Caroline, 'he's such a pathetic creature. He's always been so full of spite and hate. I suppose we ought to feel sorry for him.'

Laura's sentiments were far less generous. 'Come off it, Mummy. He's hell bent on destroying Gautier. That's why he's got to be stopped.'

Caroline grimaced. 'I hear he's drinking heavily.'

'So what? He always did.'

'I mean, worse than ever. Mind you, I'm not surprised. You should read what they've been writing about him over here.' There was a rustle of newspapers at the other end of the line. 'Let's see. *Le Monde* – "Charles Gautier: ingrate and traitor". *La Libé* – "Charles Gautier: unfit to run an English vineyard" – gosh, that's heavy. *Le Canard Enchaîné* – look, there are so many of these things, I think I'd better fax them across to you.'

Laura chuckled. 'Looks like good old Daniel's been stirring it.'

'And in the very highest of places. There are going to be questions in the National Assembly. We've already had one minister on television, banging on about France's cultural heritage being hived off to British philistines.'

'I love it,' said Laura gleefully. 'It's bound to get picked up here. I only hope that Sammy knows what a philistine is!'

Laura was still laughing at her own little joke when she returned to the drawing room. 'Seems like the battalions are ranging.' She poured herself some more tea from the silver pot on the table.

Scorpio put down his cup and waltzed across the room to where his ultra-sophisticated sound system was concealed. Theatrically, he produced a compact disc from an unlabelled plastic box and slotted it into the CD player. As he settled back in an armchair, Maisie and Laura stared at one another, puzzled. 'It's just my contribution to hostilities.' He grinned and closed his eyes to listen.

A fortnight later, Daphne Sandton was taking breakfast in her recently refurbished garden room. It consisted of a glass of hot water with a slice of lemon followed by a sliver of papaya, and hardly warranted the two hours she would regularly devote to it. Breakfast, she always claimed, was her 'personal thinking time'. Until recently she would spend it wondering how to get a mention in the Nigel Dempster column. That morning, as usual, Sammy had left at some ungodly hour for a breakfast meeting in the City. Idly, she sifted through her correspondence and was depressed to find only one 'stiffy'. She ran her pearl pink fingernail across the expensively embossed invitation. What a disappointment! She would have to have a word with the committee chairperson, Pilar del Establecimiento. After all, she *had* promised faithfully to deliver the Princess of Wales to the ball! She flicked the invitation to one side. The function had now been downgraded to an appearance from Himself.

Irritated, she glanced at the heap of magazines and newspapers Sammy insisted on having delivered every day. She found herself increasingly frightened of reading them. Nasty stories about Charles, unflattering remarks about herself – since the news of the projected takeover had broken, the vitriol had been relentless. Even the quality broadsheets were at it now. Daphne would never have believed it possible, but she was actually beginning to wish that the media would ignore her.

After scanning the Court Circular, she pushed aside *The Times*. Their recent financial columns had been so scathing about Sammy that he now refused to read them. Her hand wavered for an instant, then came to rest on the *Sun*. The cover story seemed harmless enough – a senior politician picked up at a sado-masochist brothel. Voraciously, she read on.

Her heart sank as she turned the page. Featured prominently inside, a large cartoon depicted a goofy-looking serpent slithering its way into Gautier's New Bond Street premises. Her eye was drawn inexorably to the caption: 'Sammy Snake – On The Make'. Mortified, she snapped the paper shut and swiftly turned on the radio. However low she was feeling, the wild and wacky Dicky Butcher programme always managed to brighten her day. 'Now then, now then, what have we got here?' Dicky's cheerful Cockney voice sang out across the airwaves. 'Well, well, if it isn't a new recording from my old mate, Scorpio. Scorpio, sunshine, if you're listening, I've got to tell you, we all thought you'd gone and snuffed it. Which reminds me, since you're obviously back in the land of the living, remember that fiver you owe me? You know, that bet we had on the Arsenal? Hurts me to take a mug's money, it does, but now I'm waiting for the cheque.'

Daphne was feeling so much better she even managed an entire spoonful of papaya. The stress of the deal had been taking its toll. Already she had lost a stone and now her cantilevered cleavage was shrinking most dreadfully.

Dicky was still going strong – a seamless continuum of trivia and chat. 'A new release – well, Scorpio, son, that *is* a turn-up for the books. What have we here? I dunno – this producer of mine keeps giving me these notes. Look, love, why don't you just leave a bloke alone to do a bit of broadcasting and whip off and get me a coffee? Now let me take a dekko. Well, folks, you heard it here first. "Reclusive rock star, Scorpio, is coming out of retirement to help promote *Tor*, a film in which he sings the title song. La la la. Two-month tour of the UK and the States . . . La la la . . . you know, the usual hype and drivel these PR people send you . . . Anyway, in the meantime, he's come up with his first release in five years. He says it's to help with what he calls "another worthwhile cause".'

The Filipino maid sidled into the garden room to clear away the breakfast dishes. 'Later, for goodness sake.' Daphne dismissed her with an impatient wave of the hand. 'Can't you see? I'm listening.' The woman drifted out again. Nowadays, it was impossible to know what Madam really wanted.

Daphne's foot was tapping. The introduction to Scorpio's new single was fantastic. Loud and lively with an irresistible rhythm, the song was bound to rocket straight into the bestseller charts. Gradually, she could feel her whole body responding to the music. The old maestro had lost none of his appeal. Raw and sexy, his voice attacked at the most visceral of levels. Her mind wafted off. Memories of parties when Scorpio was in his heyday. Her first flirtation with boys and booze. That bonk in the back of the Escort . . .

All of a sudden, Daphne's foot stopped tapping. Her hand, it seemed, was frozen to the breakfast table. Loud and clear, Scorpio was hammering out the song's refrain:

'But can you truly say you're happy,
When your girl's done up all crappy?
Does she really feel a queen
When Sandton's ring's turned her finger green?'

Furious, she stood up and hurled the offending radio out of the window into the pond outside. One large white carp popped his head up as if in mild surprise, as it sank bubbling to the bottom.

'Not Scorpio!' she wailed. 'I can take it from anyone but him.'

She picked up the phone and began to dial her husband. Still at breakfast, Sammy was infuriatingly incommunicado. She raced into the study and looked up Maddy Wheatcroft's home number in the contact book. She punched in the digits so hard that the acrylic nail tip of her forefinger snapped off and went flying into an ashtray. 'Damn and blast!'

'I'm sorry.' Sitting in her kitchen, slowly drinking her early morning coffee, Maddy had picked up the phone at once. 'Is this an obscene phone call?'

'No, it is not!' Daphne was livid. To cap it all, she would now have to spend the entire afternoon at the nail clinic, organizing a new prosthesis. 'It's me, Daphne Sandton, and I want to know what the hell you think you're doing for a living.'

Maddy rubbed her forehead. It sounded as if Daphne had been sniffing too much of her own malodorous perfume. All this on top of her own ghastly hangover! She was too tired to think of something placatory, but Daphne was off again.

'Have you been listening to *The Dicky Butcher show*?'

Maddy rubbed her spinning head and took a deep breath

before answering. 'Well, yes, actually, I listen to it every morning. Brilliant, isn't he?'

'So you heard it, then? You *must* have heard it. Scorpio's new single.'

'Sure.' Maddy poured herself another cup of coffee and vowed never, ever again to drink champagne and vodka chasers with City FOREX dealers. 'It's kind of catchy, isn't it? In fact, I can't get the lyrics out of my head. "But can you truly say you're happy/When your girl's done up all crappy . . ."' In amongst Maddy's half-fried neurones, the penny suddenly dropped. 'Oh, my God!'

'Oh, my God! Is that all you can say – oh, my God? I want you to get this record banned immediately.'

Maddy was sobering up swiftly. 'Now, calm down, Mrs Sandton. I'm afraid it's not going to be as easy as you imagine. I'll have to—'

'I don't care what you have to do, but whatever it is, do it quickly! Everyone knows who he's talking about. I'll be the laughing stock of the Red Cross ball!'

It was all too much for Daphne. Suddenly she burst into tears. For over a minute, she just sat there, sobbing down the phone. Maddy felt almost, but only almost, sorry for the woman. 'Is Mr Sandton around?' she asked.

'No, and I can't get hold of him.'

'Listen, why don't you take a nice long bath? I'll be over as soon as I can.'

Daphne sniffed. 'Would you? I'm beginning to feel that everyone everywhere is having a go at me. Surely, it can't go on much longer?'

'I'll be right over,' repeated Maddy, side-stepping the question. Swiftly, she replaced the receiver. She grabbed her handbag and keys and daubed on some lipstick in the hall mirror. She knew she must speak to Sammy as soon as possible. At the previous night's party, she had met an old flat-mate who now acted as Scorpio's personal publicist. And according to Miranda Bentley, the fun had just begun.

CHAPTER THIRTY

For the first time in the entire promotion campaign, Miranda was feeling nervous. Working in tandem with Serge Birnbaum's gigantic publicity machine, Scorpio had pushed himself almost to a standstill. Hype, claimed Serge, had always been his middle name, but for this film, a low-budget production featuring no 'big name' stars, Scorpio had been drafted in to provide the essential focal point. After a relentless schedule of interviews and concerts, there were few people in Europe or the United States who had not now heard of *Tor*. Advance box-office receipts were already impressive and a confident Serge was predicting 'serious success'.

This week, however, was fast developing into a nightmare. Scorpio's forthcoming appearance on *The Ricky Rich Show*, Britain's highest rating chat show, filled Miranda with justified trepidation. A waspish left-wing barrister, Ricky Rich had carved himself a reputation as a formidable interviewer. Funny and iconoclastic, his Saturday evening slot was considered compulsory viewing by the vast majority of the British public. All over the country, harmless housewives and their hen-pecked husbands seemed to revel in the weekly spectacle of celebrities being thrown to a well-briefed media lion. After the adulation of the previous few months, Miranda wondered how an exhausted Scorpio was going to manage the inevitable onslaught.

Sitting in her Bloomsbury office, the nerve centre of Scorpio's promotional activity, she lit up a cigarette. *The Ricky Rich Show* was now a mere twenty-four hours away. A disaster there and she knew Scorpio might well go scuttling back into his shell. To her increasing consternation, however, Scorpio himself seemed unconcerned.

'I can always call it off,' she ventured hopefully. 'We could say you had laryngitis.'

Scorpio looked hurt. 'Over my dead body!'

'That's what bothers me,' quipped Maisie. 'They tell me this guy Ricky Rich eats guys like you for breakfast.'

Scorpio shrugged. 'I keep telling you, don't worry. If he decides to have a go, I'll set Bruce on him after the show.'

Bruce's well-worn face creased into a gap-toothed grin. For him, the last few months had been like a new lease on life. Ten paparazzi, three obnoxious journalists and one particularly insistent fan – he felt good when he thought of the casualties he had been responsible for during the US coast-to-coast tour. 'Just leave him to me,' he chortled. 'I've never decked a chat-show host.'

Miranda raised her eyes to heaven. Already she could see the headlines and the ensuing case for criminal assault. Scorpio did his best to calm her down. 'Look, Miranda, I can handle it. Sex, drugs, alcohol – there's nothing he can throw at me that I haven't openly admitted.'

'But the Sandton deal,' she objected. 'He's bound to give you a hard time on that. He's sure to drag up . . .' Her voice petered out.

'Me?' suggested Maisie helpfully.

'I'm afraid so.' She looked pleadingly at Scorpio. 'Believe me, this is no holds barred TV.'

Scorpio leaned across the table and gently touched Maisie's hand. 'Are you sure *you* can handle this?'

She nodded decisively. 'I know Charles is peddling all sorts of rumours, but the truth is, I never did anything wrong. What have I got to be afraid of?'

He looked up, deadly serious. 'Miranda,' he said, 'you've got twenty-four hours. I want every last bit of shit there is on Mr Ricky Rich.'

By Saturday evening, Miranda was in a state of terminal panic. Her research on Rich had revealed some extremely juicy tit-bits which she had dutifully handed over to Scorpio. As he studied them in the car on the way to the studio, his features never altered.

'Very interesting.' He snapped the file shut.

Miranda's once well-manicured nails had been chewed to jagged stumps. 'We don't want a slanging match, or worse still, a libel suit.'

Maisie sat next to Scorpio, totally immersed in her own thoughts. In her own far quieter way, she, too, had been busy over the previous few months. After much haggling with the Appleford trustees, she now had the money to buy out Charles's stake. All the same, she knew that he would never sell to her as long as Sammy Sandton remained an option. The negative publicity surrounding the takeover had depressed the Sandton share price. The deal, however, was still progressing. It seemed that Sammy was a man of his word and was proving a stubborn opponent. Maisie was even beginning to feel a grudging respect for him. To some extent, she even identified with him. As she of all people would know, it was easy to be taken in by Charles.

The hordes of fans had been waiting for hours in the miserable autumn drizzle. As the car pulled up outside the studio, they surged forward screaming, 'Scorpio! Scorpio!' Bruce and the security guards swung into action, shepherding Scorpio, Maisie and Miranda safely into the building where they were met by a fresh-faced researcher, who led the ladies off to the so-called 'hospitality suite'. A more senior member of the production team diverted Scorpio down to 'Make-up'.

There was a huge flurry of excitement as the rock star entered the room. Ensconced in their seats and in the process of being 'done' were the other sacrificial lambs for Ricky Rich's show. The reformed-alcoholic footballer leapt up to shake Scorpio's hand, to which Scorpio responded amiably by asking for his autograph. Buried underneath a headful of Carmen rollers, the ex-nun turned bestselling, bodice-ripper novelist flushed pink with pleasure when he addressed her. 'Of course you may have a copy,' she replied, signing *Passion in the Presbytery* with a flourish. She handed it, trembling, to Scorpio. 'I never told this to anyone before,' she confided, 'but I left the convent because of you.'

After some discussion and even more bitching, it had been decided that Justin, the senior makeup artist, should take charge of Scorpio. He sat him down in the dentist-style chair and covered him with a white nylon cape. Forefinger pressed to perfectly pursed lips, Justin studied his latest challenge. 'We're looking a little peaky, aren't we? Too many late nights, I'll be bound.' He patted Scorpio's cheek with the tips of his fingers. 'Broken veins, oh dearie me! Fetch me the green powder, would you, Daryl?'

By the time Scorpio emerged into Hospitality some fifty minutes later, he was looking like a man half his age.

'There are eats over there on the table.' The fresh-faced researcher pointed across to a distinctly unappetizing finger-buffet.

Scorpio glanced at the heaps of carbonized chipolatas and dubious quiche and felt it safer to decline. 'Just a glass of mineral water, please.' He took a seat between Miranda and Maisie, who had both opted for a glass of plaque-stripping plonk.

In an effort to calm her nerves, Miranda was now trying to decipher the Gothic script on the bottle's illuminated label. '"The joint product of at least five European community countries."' She sniffed. 'Typical, isn't it? Not one of those cowardly bastards is prepared to take the rap alone.'

Less jittery than Miranda, who clearly felt that her own reputation was on the line, Maisie did her best to make conversation. 'The researcher tells me that Ricky never turns up here before the show. It seems he doesn't want to be disabused of any preconceived ideas.'

'Don't worry.' Scorpio smiled at her encouragingly. 'Tonight I'll bury that bastard.'

Back home at Le Bijou, the Sandtons were settling in for an evening's television. Daphne did not agree with TV dinners – in her view, they were common – but for once she was prepared to make an exception. The prospect of her fallen idol, Scorpio, being torn to shreds on *The Ricky Rich Show* was just too irresistible to miss. With napkins strategically spread to obviate spillage on the sofa, she and Sammy sat down to saviour a delicious Chinese meal.

'Saturday night in front of the telly,' sighed Sammy happily. He shovelled another helping of sweet and sour pork on top of his special fried rice. 'You know, we really ought to do this more often.'

Daphne's over-plucked eyebrows shot up. She made a mental note to book theatre tickets for the next six Saturdays at least. Content with his remote control and a pint of lager, Sammy flicked the ON button just in time for the opening credits.

Ashen-faced, the reformed-alcoholic footballer returned to the hospitality suite and demanded an extremely large Scotch. Now on air, the nun-turned-novelist was being subjected to a dreadful grilling herself about her own intimate sexual behaviour. Maisie winced as Ricky pushed shamelessly on. Judging from the howls of mirth from the auditorium, the audience were lapping it up.

'Time to go.' The researcher looked at Scorpio almost apologetically. She led him backstage just in time to witness the nun-turned-novelist bursting into tears.

'Here he is,' said Daphne excitedly and made Sammy turn up the volume. The audience applauded loudly as Scorpio took his seat opposite the Grand Inquisitor of British Television. With a swift sideways sneer, Scorpio sized up the opposition. It was the first time he had seen Ricky Rich in the flesh and he did not take to what he saw. Of indeterminate middle age, Ricky's face was somehow shrivelled, like an apple that had been picked and stored too soon. His eyes were small and rather too close together, yet sparkling with intelligence and malice. He smiled unctuously at his guest. Scorpio crossed his legs and sat back casually in his armchair. After what he had witnessed that evening, stitching up this bastard would be a pleasure.

Back in Hospitality, the man dispensing drinks had become extremely chatty. 'It's Ricky's usual technique,' he confided. Miranda held her glass still until it was full right to the top. 'A few soft lobs to begin with then, wallop! They just don't know what's hit them!'

On set, Ricky smiled amiably at the camera. 'So, this film *Tor* you've been promoting, tell us what it's all about.'

Scorpio scanned the audience and made eye contact with an elderly lady seated in the second row. He decided to talk to her. 'Well, there's this community of tribes called the Pathans who live in the North-west Frontier Province . . .'

'Provence!' Daphne sipped her Lapsang Souchong, unimpressed. 'Some people have no imagination! You'd have thought that man Peter Mayle had already done the place to death.'

Sammy turned up the sound even louder in an effort to ignore her running commentary.

The atmosphere in the studio was electric. As Scorpio talked, Ricky rolled his eyes to camera. It was always good for a few cheap laughs. 'Very interesting,' he scoffed when Scorpio had finished. 'I must say, you're getting very right-on in your old age. It hardly seems a minute ago that you were at Hong Kong airport, being busted for possession of cannabis.'

The audience fell silent. After the velvet glove treatment, this was the first real sign of Ricky's iron fist.

Scorpio's smile was dazzling. 'Yes, time does fly, doesn't it? I bet you can hardly remember being picked up that evening in the gents' lav at Piccadilly. What was the rap, remind me, loitering with intent?'

Underneath his pan-stick, Ricky turned beacon red. His eyes narrowed even further. 'Those allegations were never proved.'

'Well, they wouldn't be, would they, sunshine? Not with your old man a judge. Quite a big mason, wasn't he?' Scorpio pulled up his trouser leg and wiggled his bare calf at the camera. The audience hooted with laughter.

In Hospitality, the formerly reformed-alcoholic footballer was now three Scotches up. He poured himself another. 'Good lad, Scorpio! You show the little prick!' The rest of the room was deathly quiet.

'Oh God.' By now, the researcher was looking decidedly less fresh-faced. 'Ricky's going to kill him.'

Unused to counter-attacks, Ricky was flustered for a moment

but soon regained his composure. He began quizzing Scorpio on his campaign to halt the Gautier takeover. 'And you're on record as saying you'd like to publicly humiliate Sammy Sandton.'

Hamming it now, and enjoying every minute, Scorpio put his hand to his heart. 'Not guilty, squire.'

Incensed, Ricky checked his clipboard. If she had got it wrong, he would sack the bloody researcher, single parent or not. 'Are we to take this as a climb-down? Are you telling us here tonight that you never said you were out to publicly humiliate Sammy Sandton?'

Scorpio stared deep into the camera. 'I've got no personal grouse against Sammy Sandton. In fact, he seems like a regular sort of bloke. I just want the House of Gautier to stay with the family who's owned it for the last hundred and fifty years.' A stir of approval went up in the audience. 'To publicly humiliate Sammy Sandton!' Scorpio shook his head in mock outrage. 'How dare you accuse me, Ricky, of splitting an infinitive?'

At home, Sammy was guffawing loudly into his lager. 'What a lad! I don't know what the hell he's talking about, but he's got that clever-dick on the run. Do you know, I never could stand Ricky Rich.'

Ricky could feel the interview slipping further and further out of his control. Anger began to cloud his judgement and he decided to go for the jugular. 'But, of course, Scorpio, your fight for Gautier is not entirely disinterested. Let's face it, everyone knows you're knocking off Charles Gautier's wife.'

A fearful hush descended on the studio. For a split second, Ricky thought his guest might punch him and decided it was a risk worth taking. A punch-up on air would do his ratings no harm whatsoever. He watched as Scorpio turned slowly to the camera, then back towards him again. His eyes were blazing, but his voice was calm. 'Maisie Gautier is the woman I love. When she's free, I intend to marry her.'

Ecstatic cheers erupted from the auditorium. Out of the

corner of his eye, Scorpio saw the floor manager drawing a finger across his throat and recognized the signal for time running out. Ricky turned to the camera, ready to wind up, but Scorpio continued. 'But what about that sixteen-year-old in Bermondsey?'

The colour drained from Ricky's cheeks.

'You know, the kid you knocked up five months ago. Why don't *you* try making an honest woman out of *her*? That is, if the present Mrs Rich doesn't mind.'

The music started, the final credits rolled and all hell broke loose in the studio. His face contorted with rage, Ricky Rich could barely bring himself to speak. In ten short minutes, the image he had so assiduously cultivated over the years had evaporated into thin air. 'You fucking bastard! I'll sue you for all you're worth.'

Scorpio produced a buff envelope from his inside pocket. 'Photocopies of sworn affidavits. If I were in your shoes, I'd find myself a decent lawyer.'

Back home in West Hampstead, Sammy found himself cheering. Disturbed by this reaction, Daphne nibbled on a cracker. 'I think Scorpio's behaviour was appalling!'

'I don't know. You can't help liking the bloke.'

The phone rang and he leaned over to answer it. A dab hand now with the mobile, his mother was ringing him from the pub. 'We've all been down here watching that Scorpio on *The Ricky Rich Show.*' An atmosphere of general hilarity formed the backcloth to her conversation.

'Yes.' Sammy pulled the ring off another can of lager. 'He really kippered that clever dick all ends up. I'd say old Ricky has had his chips.'

Down the line, he could hear Muriel ordering another port and lemon. 'And a packet of pork scratchings,' she added before turning her attentions back to Sammy. 'Look, son, I've never interfered with your business, but I couldn't help hearing what Scorpio was saying about them Gautier people.'

Sammy took a swig of lager straight from the can. 'I was listening too.'

Muriel sounded tipsy. 'And all I want to say is, you can't trust a bloke who's shafted his dad. That just ain't on, it ain't.'

'It's OK, Mum.' Sammy settled back on the sofa and put his arm around Daphne's bony shoulders. 'Our share price has never been so low and now I've got an anorexic for a wife. This deal is costing me too much grief. I'm calling the whole thing off.'

CHAPTER THIRTY-ONE

'What the hell do you mean, the deal's off?' Charles banged his fist down so hard on the desk that the bank of telephones jumped.

Sammy focused his steely blue eyes on the dissolute figure opposite. Flushed and wheezing, this Gautier bloke was such a pathetic sight. Suddenly Sammy realized that he had never really liked him at all. 'Off, as in fuck, I'd have thought that was fairly simple.' His eyes wandered past Charles's head and towards the office door beyond.

The unspoken message was not lost. The veins in Charles's neck began to throb. 'So you think you can just call it a day like that, do you? You think you can string me along, waste my time . . .'

'Now just hang on a minute, sunshine.' Sammy's voice was hard and threatening, like broken beer bottles on concrete. 'If it hadn't been for you and all your farting around, this deal would have been tied up months ago but first we had the value of your stock, then all that "goodwill" bollocks. Every bloody thing we ever agreed, you came straight back and welshed!'

A sudden thought struck Charles. Perhaps, this was Sammy's eleventh-hour bid to improve his own position. He smiled his most charming, placatory smile. Fair enough! He, Charles, had struck a hard enough bargain. There was still plenty of room for manoeuvre. 'You're a tough opponent, Sammy. Come on, we're good friends, what is it you want?'

'Look, mate,' snorted Sammy, 'first you and me was never mates. And second, I don't want this deal at any price. It's cost me too much already.' He turned ostentatiously to the pile of papers on his desk. 'And now, if you wouldn't mind, I'm a very busy man.'

Red blotches had appeared on Charles's face. Shaking with anger, he leaned across Sammy's desk. 'You bastard!'

Unmoved, Sammy stared at the contorted features now spewing out their venom. 'Go on. It makes a change to hear you being sincere for once in your bloody life.'

Charles could feel the blood racing to his head. He could hear himself shouting out loud, 'You! You and your tacky little wife—'

Sammy's face froze. 'I'm warning you, Gautier, leave Daphne out of this.'

'The woman's a laughing stock. Stupid, pretentious, jumped-up nobody! As if the likes of you could ever have anything in common with the House of Gautier—'

The punch sent him sprawling backwards across the room. For a moment, he lost consciousness as he hit the skirting board. Coming to, he was dimly aware of Sammy's powerful frame, towering above him. '*You're* the bloody nobody! You might have been the son of somebody and the husband of somebody but you'll always be a nobody. Now get out of here before I give you the hiding you deserve.'

Charles touched his jaw gingerly before clambering to his feet. There was a time in his life when he might have considered retaliation, but those days were now long gone. Still reeling, he grabbed his briefcase and tumbled unsteadily towards the door. 'You'll be hearing from my solicitors!' His hand grappled unsuccessfully for the handle.

Sammy laughed the deep, uninhibited roar he had not heard himself use in months. 'Try it!' He opened the door for Charles and pushed him into the corridor. 'And I'll have you kebabed on toast.'

Passing the boss's office, Ray noticed a crumpled figure fumbling its way towards the lift. To his surprise, he recognized Charles Gautier, his lip cut and the area around his mouth already swelling. 'Everything all right?' asked Ray, chirpily.

Charles stared at him with unconcealed loathing as he pressed the 'Down' button gingerly. 'This whole place stinks.'

The lift doors opened and he lurched inside, fell against the carpet-covered wall and waited impatiently for the doors to close.

'Not now you're out of it, it don't,' said Ray and strode happily off to his sales meeting.

Sitting in the *Gadfly*'s office in the heart of Soho, Daniel Baudon was only vaguely surprised to have Sammy Sandton on the line.

'So you promise you'll lay off?' Sammy rubbed his knuckles contentedly. That punch had been a hell of a belter.

Daniel scribbled on a notepad with his biro. 'If the deal's off, we've nothing more to say. Believe me, Sammy, this was never meant to be a personal campaign against you.'

'Why don't you pull the other one? Anyway, no hard feelings. You done what you thought was right. I'd have done the same myself, I reckon, for any old mate of mine.'

'It's big of you to take it that way.' Daniel felt a sudden surge of sympathy for him. 'Look, we've got a whole pile of cartoons of you down here. Let me send them to you as a peace-offering. You can hang them on the wall or burn them. It's entirely up to you.'

'Daphne would love them,' said Sammy enthusiastically then, suddenly more subdued, 'That's why I don't want any more aggro, you understand. My missus has been taking it bad.'

'You have my word on it, but our campaign against Charles will continue. We assume he's still intent on selling his shares?' Daniel paused for a moment, weighing up the odds. 'I don't suppose you'd help us with useful info, would you?'

The image of Charles's face, distorted with contempt, was still livid in Sammy's memory. 'If you're not doing anything for lunch,' he replied, 'I'll meet you at The Ivy.'

The level of the whisky had fallen to the half-way mark in the bottle. Slumped in his father's favourite armchair, Charles poured himself another large shot and settled back, half dozing. The events of the day had left him shell-shocked. His eyelids flickered and his head felt heavier and heavier as gradually it lolled towards his shoulder. A knock on the boardroom door brought him to with a start. Sally, his late father's secretary, popped her head tentatively into the room. 'I'm sorry to bother you, sir, I know you asked not to be disturbed, but your sister is here to see you.'

Charles glanced at his watch. Five o'clock. He had been drinking since his return from Sandton's office at twelve o'clock that morning. His tongue was thick with whisky and his mouth tasted bitter and dry. He could smell his own breath, rank and fetid, whenever he exhaled. 'What the hell does she want?'

Sally pursed her lips. She had read in the papers of Charles's plans for the company and knew where her sympathies lay. 'She says she has a business proposal to put to you. I think you ought to see her.' Sally was surprised at her own temerity but, as Gautier London's most long-serving employee, she felt that it was high time that certain things were said.

Wearily, he rubbed his eyes. What had he to lose? He was up to his neck in trouble. 'Give me fifteen minutes,' he agreed, struggled to his feet and staggered off towards the washroom.

It was a good twenty minutes later when, slightly less dishevelled, he returned to the boardroom. Seated at the head of the table, Laura looked up from the notes already laid out before her. 'Ah, there you are.'

Instinctively Charles felt for the knot in his tie. Her tone made him feel like the office junior, hauled up in front of the boss. He stared at her in surprise. It was difficult to believe that this was the same hapless Laura he had last seen at the funeral.

'Sit down,' she ordered. 'This won't take long.'

Like a startled rabbit, hypnotized by oncoming headlights, he found himself obeying. She fixed him with a long, cool gaze. Unable to meet it, he turned away and reached for the whisky bottle.

'We hear the Sandton deal is off.'

His hand quivered. He missed the tumbler and spilled a good

measure of single malt on the table. 'How on earth do you know?'

She uncapped her fountain pen and underlined something in her notes. 'We know *everything* about you. The details of the deal Sammy Sandton was offering, the extent of your gambling debts, the cost of the new helicopter and the house in Hydra . . .'

His hand began to shake even more alarmingly. He put his tumbler down. 'Who the hell . . .?'

She raised her eyebrows slightly. Daniel's briefing notes were nothing if not exhaustive. Over a long and bibulous lunch, Sammy had come up trumps. 'It doesn't really matter how we found out. The point is that we *know*.'

'We? *We?*' As he hammered the table, the tumbler shook and more whisky spilled over the rim. The tiny rivulets of liquid rolled over the edge of the table and on to his crumpled trousers. 'Who the fuck is *we*? I suppose Maisie's had a detective following my every move?'

'Paranoid as ever!' Laura's voice was cold. 'Really, Charles, you flatter yourself. Maisie's far too happy to worry about you and your . . .' she glanced at the almost empty whisky bottle, 'personal habits.'

As a pathetic gesture of independence, he took another slug. 'Just tell me what you want and get out!'

'Nothing would give me greater pleasure.' She reverted to her notes. 'You're up to your neck in debt, Charles, and your creditors – ' she smiled up sweetly, 'those gambling types are not very pleasant, I'm told – your creditors are after your hide.'

'I'll manage.' He did his best to look unconcerned.

'I'm sure you will. Concrete *sabots* off the pier at Piraeus – I can see the obituary now.'

'Your concern is most touching.'

She tapped her fountain pen lightly on the table. 'I'd love to spend the day just chatting with you, but *my* life, at least, is too busy. I'm here to make you an offer.' She waited for a moment, wondering if the same old mindless vindictiveness would rear its ugly head. On balance, she guessed it would not. The sight now in front of her did much to encourage optimism. In a matter of months Charles seemed to have aged a decade. Physically bruised and mentally battered, she reckoned he must be ready to negotiate now.

'Let me guess.' His voice sounded suddenly weary. 'I suppose you want to buy me out.'

She nodded. 'We'll give you precisely the same terms as Sandton promised.'

He looked up, clearly surprised. 'I'll never understand you people. If the boot had been on the other foot I'd have screwed you into the ground.'

'I know,' her tone was bereft of emotion, 'but I don't want any more damage done to the company or staff morale.' She opened her briefcase, pulled out some papers and handed them to him. 'You'll find all the details in here.'

He scanned the documentation with an expert if somewhat bleary eye. He knew he would have to look at it more closely in the morning but, at first sight, it did appear to be the same deal he had constructed with Sandton. 'I'll get my lawyers on to it.'

'There's no point trying to prevaricate, Charles.' She stood up, ready to leave. 'You have until tomorrow lunchtime to come to a decision. Think about it. Those debts of yours are pressing.'

As she reached the door, she heard him calling after her. 'Do you swear it's the same deal I had with Sandton?'

'Exactly the same.' She paused on the threshold, hoping for a final response.

'In that case,' he said, 'I agree.'

The champagne corks were already popping as Laura arrived at Scorpio's house. She bounded into the drawing room and was delighted to find Sharif who, together with Serge, had just flown in from New York.

'Congratulations!' He held her tight and kissed her. Happy, relieved and exhilarated, she felt positively light-headed.

'It's what your father would have wanted,' added Serge and gave her a great big bear hug.

Still tipsy from his three-hour lunch with Sammy, Daniel Baudon had decided to keep on drinking. 'To the House of

Gautier,' he said and raised his glass. The swiftly assembled War Council followed suit.

'You old rascal!' Scorpio slapped Daniel affectionately on the back. 'Admit it. You're going to miss baiting Sammy.'

Daniel snorted loudly as the champagne fizzed up his nose. 'Listen who's talking! If you ask Sammy, he'll tell you it was that song of yours which really did him in.' He took a deep breath and began to sing in a monotone B flat. 'Can you truly say you're happy/When your girl's done up all crappy . . .'

Over in the corner of the room Maisie sat quietly fondling Clancy's ears. Disturbed at her silence, Laura wandered across to sit by her. 'Come on, brighten up! This is supposed to be a celebration.' A sudden frown crossed her face. 'Are you having second thoughts? I know it's an awful lot of money.'

'It's not the money that worries me.' She patted Laura's hand. 'Whatever is mine is yours. It's just—'

An agitated Flo interrupted their conversation. 'I'm sorry, Laura, it's your brother on the phone. I told him you were busy, but he insists on talking to you.'

A look of dread clouded Maisie's eyes. 'That's just what I was anticipating. You'd better go talk to him.'

Alone in the study, Laura picked up the receiver. Charles was in no mood to waste time on polite precursors. He moved straight to the point. 'There's one detail we didn't quite cover earlier.'

'I'm listening.' She sat down in the large leather swivel chair and placed her champagne on the desk. A stream of bubbles raced merrily to the surface.

'The Star of Heaven,' he said.

She watched as the tiny, busy bubbles evaporated into the air. 'What about it?'

'Have a little guess.' His laugh was raucous and without humour. 'You thought you had me over a barrel. But I'll have the last laugh, after all.'

Laura's stomach began to churn. 'You're not seriously suggesting that you should have the Star of Heaven?'

'Oh, but I am.' His tone was harsh and cold. 'Let's just call it a little memento of our dear departed father.'

'You bastard!'

'Now, now. Temper will get you nowhere.' His wheedling made her all the more angry.

'But you know as well as I do that Papa wanted it to go to the V and A.'

'Do I? Do I? Actually, I have no such recollection. Tell me, was it written down anywhere?'

'You *know* it wasn't! Papa died before he got around to it. But you *do* know—'

'Now you listen here,' he interrupted. 'As you said yourself only this afternoon, staff morale is low. Insecurity is such a terrible affliction. Soon, even Father's most faithful retainers will be leaving in droves.'

'You mean, those you haven't already sacked!'

'Let's call it streamlining, shall we?'

'How dare you talk to me about streamlining? Maurice has been with—'

'Let's not get bogged down in trivial details.' His voice turned suddenly harsh. 'Where was I? Ah, yes, the Star of Heaven. As someone said to me, why, only this afternoon, you have until tomorrow lunchtime to decide.'

And with that, the phone went dead.

By the time she reappeared in the drawing room, celebrations had been put on hold.

'What does he want?' asked Maisie, fearing the worst.

Laura slumped down heavily on the sofa. 'Only the Star of Heaven.'

Maisie shook her head. 'I knew he was bound to pull a fast one.'

Sharif moved to sit beside Laura. 'You can't give in to him.'

'No, you can't,' Scorpio added. 'Call him back immediately and tell him to go and stuff it.'

Daniel nodded his agreement. 'Just wait until the *Gadfly*'s finished with him. He'll wish he had never been born.'

'We *have* to give it to him!' An adoring Clancy yelped his surprise at the sharpness of Maisie's tone.

'Come off it,' said Scorpio, equally stunned. 'We can't let that bastard blackmail us.'

'He's just trying it on!' Serge drew deeply on his large cigar.

'I suggest we just ignore him. We'll have him crumbling in a couple of months or so.'

Sharif's blue eyes were clouded with anger. He clasped Laura by the hand. 'You can't give in. You must fight back. It's the only language he understands.'

'I agree with Maisie.' A strange look stole across Laura's face. 'The name of Gautier has suffered enough. He can have the bloody diamond!'

'No!' chorused the four men.

'This is not the time for compromise,' pleaded Sharif urgently. 'It's the time to seek revenge!'

Laura turned her head and stared deep into his eyes. 'Perhaps that's what I'm doing.'

CHAPTER THIRTY-TWO

Charles glanced out of the helicopter window and on to the Aegean below. Above, the sky was cloudless, its brilliance reflected in the glorious azure water. Every so often, a soft breeze would catch the surface of the sea, whipping it into battalions of curling, foaming waves. Yolande watched as they rose, confident and proud, before disappearing back into the deep. To her they looked like snow white stallions, charging into some mystical abyss.

The helicopter flew on, past innumerable reefs and islets, towards the bare, rocky island of Hydra. Relaxed, she settled back to enjoy the view, the brightness and the light. Charles, she noticed, was still distinctly ill at ease, his fingers gripping the controls.

'They call them "God's castaway stones",' she shouted, pointing down to the string of barren, hilly isles. Determined to make him loosen up, she patted his hand encouragingly.

'I know.' He jerked his hand away.

Peeved, she put on her Ray-Bans and resumed staring at the sea.

At last the helicopter was circling the island. Long and mountainous, Hydra looked rugged and inhospitable from the air. As he banked, she gasped in open admiration. An almost perfect semi-circle, the harbour was as beautiful as it was unexpected. Around it, the town of Hydra rose like an amphitheatre into the hills. It stood out like a jolly tie against a pin-stripe suit, a startling riot of colour.

'Look, down there,' gasped Yolande, all excited, 'can you see that lovely white church? It looks like a wedding cake. And the tiles on that roof – did the builder replace yours? – I think the red looks wonderful.'

Charles said nothing as, expertly, he manoeuvred the helicopter along the hills and towards his recently renovated home. The clearing in the terraced garden was not enormous, but he put down without difficulty.

'It's just fantastic!' shouted Yolande as they waited for the rotor blades to come to a complete standstill. 'So much better than the boat!' She jumped out, clearly delighted. On her first (and she had threatened last) trip to the island, the hydrofoil from Piraeus had taken three hours and nearly everyone on it had been sick.

They carried their suitcases into the hall and dumped them on the black and white marble floor. 'Want a drink?' asked Charles as he wandered into the drawing room.

Yolande gazed appreciatively at the restored wood ceiling, carved in intricate geometric patterns. 'Things seem to be coming on,' she said, before following on after him.

The room smelt stuffy and unused. She opened the french windows and walked out on to the balcony. The view over the sea was magnificent. 'Charles,' she gasped, 'come quickly!' She watched, entranced, as the sun drooped its flaming pennants into a pool of liquid light.

The bottles in the cabinet rattled as Charles located the Scotch. 'Around here, there's a sunset every evening,' he said. 'I'm off to take a shower.'

Annoyed, she poured herself a dry martini and began to drift around the house which was about to become her home. It had taken almost two years, but the run-down building had at last been transformed into a haven of peace and beauty. The fragrance of the olive and lemon groves outside wafted in through the open windows. As she inhaled the heady smells, she felt immediately more relaxed. Returning to the drawing room, she sat back in an old embroidered armchair to survey the results of her own handiwork. Purchased on the mainland, and transported to the island at huge expense, a selection of Italian paintings now graced the walls. Pieces of fine Italian porcelain

343

and Venetian glass were also artfully arranged around the room. Over the fireplace hung a beautiful Brussels tapestry, depicting the Adoration of the Magi. Heavy mahogany furniture, richly upholstered, conferred further warmth and depth. Yolande gazed contentedly out of the window. A line of fishing caiques left the quay and disappeared gradually over the horizon.

'The fucking water's off!' A towel around his midriff, Charles stormed angrily into the drawing room.

Irritated by the interruption, she stared pointedly at the grey-white flab which hung in rolls over the top of the towel. 'It'll be on again later.' She sniffed and sipped her martini.

'Stupid bloody place! Why can't they drag themselves into the twentieth century?'

She bit her lip. 'I thought that was why you bought this place – to avoid the hassle of civilization.'

'I bought it to avoid all the people who annoy me.'

'Which seems to include just about everyone.'

Even Charles was unable to ignore such obvious sarcasm. He thought of the night ahead and swiftly decided to relent. 'I'm sorry, *chérie*. It'll take me a while to wind down.'

'Then I think you'd better start right now.' There was no shred of sympathy left in her voice.

He switched to self-pitying mode. 'That family of mine. You've no idea what shits they've been. I'm totally exhausted.'

'Nonsense!' She was becoming increasingly tired of these performances. 'They gave you everything you asked for – even that bloody great rock!'

Miffed at her disapproval, Charles got up and poured himself another whisky. He noticed her glass was also empty, but decided to ignore it.

The gesture was not lost on Yolande. 'Of all the petty tricks!' She strode across to the drinks cabinet and fixed herself another drink. 'We don't seem to be getting off to a very good start, do we?' She returned to her armchair and sat down, determined to have it out. 'Look, Charles, you've now got everything you ever wanted. What more will it take to make you happy?'

He stared across the sea to where the sun had contracted into a fierce red globule. Suddenly, the globule dived into the calm, inky water and plunged the world in darkness. Without a word, Charles drained his glass and went off to change for dinner.

Set in the town square and a constant hive of social activity, Xeri Elia Douskos was Yolande's favourite Hydriot restaurant. The trip from the house was a bone-shaking mile by scooter – cars were banned on the island. Yolande was smiling as they arrived, exhilarated by the ride.

'What a mess!' she said, surveying the unruly tangle of her hair. The young waiter looked at her in frank admiration as he led them to their table. 'On the contrary, you look wonderful!'

Half-drunk already, Charles was getting grumpier by the minute. 'Bring us a bottle of retsina and be quick about it.'

The waiter said nothing. With a flourish, he opened Yolande's napkin and placed in on her lap. Then, he waltzed off into the kitchen and returned with a plate of dimpled, juicy olives. 'For you, Madame. I know how much you like them.'

'How many times do I have to ask?' Already the pitch of Charles's voice had escalated to aggressive. 'I'm waiting for my retsina.'

Under the table, Yolande delivered a swift kick to his shins. 'I'm sorry,' she said, fixing the young man with a dazzling smile. 'My friend has been working too hard.'

'Of course.' The waiter shot Charles a look of purest contempt. 'Now, if Madame would like retsina, I shall bring some right away.'

The evening went from bad to worse. Not even the lobster, freshly landed and totally delicious, could improve Charles's hateful mood. 'Wonderful!' cooed Yolande as the waiter cleared away the detritus.

Charles's dinner lay barely touched. The young man raised an eyebrow. 'Anything wrong, sir?'

'Just take it away!' Charles sneezed loudly into his napkin. 'And bring us another bottle.'

Yolande began to drum her fingers impatiently on the table. 'I think you've had enough!'

'Who asked you?'

As he cleared away, the young man's hand touched hers. She looked up and met his dark brown eyes, full of sympathy and yearning. She pictured herself in those muscular arms, beneath that slim, tanned body. Then, disturbed by her own imaginings, she stood up and went to the ladies'. The waiter followed her longingly with his eyes.

The look was not lost on Charles. 'You couldn't afford her,' he said dismissively, and took out his bulging wallet.

Yolande was still seething when they arrived home after a perilous ride up the hill. Without a word, she headed straight for a spare bedroom and fell, angry and exhausted, into bed. She awoke a few hours later to find a reeking Charles fumbling awkwardly for her breasts.

'I love you, Maisie,' he mumbled, semi-conscious. 'Believe me, I'll never upset you again.'

She was out of bed in an instant and marching towards another room. Angrily, she slammed the door before feeling suddenly quite sick. It was as if someone had just punched her hard and low in the pit of the stomach. She raced into the bathroom and vomited violently into the lavatory. It was no use, she told herself, heaving into the bowl. Charles would never change. Now she knew for certain she had been wasting her time all along. She crawled back across the floor and tumbled into bed. Cocooning herself in the crisp white sheets, she cried herself to sleep.

Charles groaned as, gradually, he came to the next morning. His throat parched and sore, he fumbled for the tumbler of water he normally kept beside the bed. His hand thrashed around, encountering nothing but air. Confused, he struggled to open his eyes but the lashes seemed matted together. Crinkling up his thumping forehead, he fought to prise them apart. At last, the right eye flickered open followed slowly by the left. For a moment, his head stopped spinning long enough to ascertain just where he was. Slowly, he realized that he was not in his bedroom. He heaved himself up and plodded off down the corridor.

'Yolande! Yolande!'

The door of the master bedroom creaked open, but there was no sign of her inside. He pulled on a towelling tracksuit and ambled slowly down the stairs. She must be making breakfast, he concluded, and made his way towards the kitchen.

The kitchen was as clean and pristine as the occasional housekeeper had left it. He opened the fridge and searched through the provisions she purchased whenever he returned. He found some orange juice and slurped it greedily from the carton. The acid hit his stomach like a bullet. He promised to put himself on a diet soon and wandered off into the drawing room carrying the juice.

'Yolande!'

To his surprise, that, too, was empty. Anxious now, he raced back up the stairs again. Calling her name, he lurched from bedroom to bedroom, but neither Yolande nor any of her effects was anywhere to be found. He lumbered back into the drawing room and collapsed, breathless, into an armchair. The events of the previous evening were a total blur, but it looked as though he must have upset her. He wiped the beads of sweat from his forehead with the sleeve of his tracksuit. So, he concluded, she must be playing her little games again. He stood up and flung the french windows open wide. A string of pearls or a pair of earrings and he knew everything would be all right. He smiled a slow, self-satisfied smile. It had always worked before.

He was startled by a sudden noise on the balcony. 'Yolande?'

He stepped out into the sunlight to be greeted by an emaciated black cat. 'Shoo!' he shouted, angrily flinging the empty juice carton at its head.

He returned inside and waited, hoping to hear the sound of footsteps returning up the road. None came. The house seemed enveloped in silence. He strained his ears but all he could hear was the rustling of leaves in the olive groves and the lapping of the waves beyond.

'Sod her!' he shouted to the echoing walls. 'Sod the bloody lot of them!'

CHAPTER THIRTY-THREE

T he entry points to Leicester Square were all completely blocked. Flushed with excitement, Laura clung to Sharif's hand in the back of the gleaming black Bentley. Ahead, a squad of policemen on motorcycles tried desperately to clear a passage through the cheering crowds. A young woman spotted Sharif through the smoked-glass window of the car and started hammering on the door. A mass of fans converged on the Bentley and began to rock it from side to side.

'Sharif! Sharif!'

He smiled at them and waved. Not even in his wildest dreams had he anticipated this. Thanks to Scorpio and Serge, the film had generated massive publicity and his own round of promotional interviews had met with equal success. He gazed out at the sea of faces and wondered how he would cope. Right now, every newspaper, every colour supplement, every magazine seemed to be carrying his face. His natural chivalry and devastating looks had taken Fleet Street by storm. Even the most hardened newspaper harridans had been bowled over by the newcomer's charm. All over the country, pin-ups of Tom Cruise and Richard Gere were being relegated to the dustbin. Now a generation of besotted adolescents demanded posters of Sharif.

The sound of screaming sirens grew closer. Blue lights flashing, another phalanx of police outriders moved in to encircle the car. Slowly, the Bentley pushed forward towards the Odeon. Women screamed, a teenager in ethnic clothing fainted and a policeman in a helmet called for help on his walkie-talkie.

Laura stole a glance at Sharif. 'Now you know what it's like to be a star.'

He looked curiously despondent. 'It's about the last thing I wanted.' He sighed.

She squeezed his hand even tighter. 'Well, it looks like you'll have to get used to it.'

The crowd broke through the police cordon and again encircled the car. Instinctively, he put a protective arm around her. 'I've tried to be a spokesman for my people. I only hope the message gets through.'

It was a good fifteen minutes later before the car pulled up outside the Odeon, Serge's choice for the royal première. The cinema was ringed with an impressive platoon of police and security guards. Its red neon lights stood out starkly against the evening gloom: *Tor*. For a moment Sharif paused to look up. Laura tried to read his expression but tonight his face told her nothing at all.

'Happy?' She slipped her arm through his.

'I'm not sure.'

Puzzled, she wanted to quiz him further but already the opportunity was lost. All around, lights flashed and camera bulbs popped as they were ushered into the building. Pushing and shouting, the paparazzi were having a field day. The line-up for the royal première of *Tor* read like a *Who's Who* of entertainment. Already pop stars and movie idols had been photographed in their dozens. 'Over here, Sharif! Come on, mate, give us a smile!'

Laura shuddered as the pack surged relentlessly forward. She clung more tightly to his arm. The pack yelped its whole-hearted approval. 'Come on, Sharif, give her a kiss. Is there any truth in the rumour—'

Even inside the foyer they could still hear the racket thundering outside. Looking decidedly dapper in evening dress, Scorpio came across to greet them. Relieved to see a familiar face, Laura embraced him warmly. 'What a scrum!'

He smiled nonchalantly. 'It feels just like the good old days!'

Maisie appeared, dazzling in a simple black Valentino gown, and kissed her. 'You look just wonderful, honey!'

Laura glanced down at the ravishing, off-the-shoulder creation she had chosen for the evening. 'Thanks. Although for all the interest shown by certain parties I may as well be wearing a bin-liner!'

'For goodness sake!' exploded Sharif suddenly. 'There are more important things—'

'Children, children!' Serge Birnbaum had attended too many premières not to expect a few first-night nerves. He put one arm around Laura and the other around Sharif. 'Come now. My two favourite people in the whole wide world. Tonight, of all nights, I will not tolerate tantrums.'

'Mr Birnbaum, sir.' A well-built young man in evening attire sidled up with a walkie-talkie. 'The Princess is due to arrive in five minutes' time.'

Serge produced a large white handkerchief and swiftly mopped his forehead. In his long and successful career, he had met kings, queens and presidents from all over the world. None had managed so far to faze him in the slightest. Tonight, however, was different. He fiddled nervously with his bow-tie. 'I'd better go. Such an honour, you know, the Princess of Wales herself.'

Scorpio could not contain himself. 'And you such a great Republican!'

Held up by the crowds of star-spotters, photographers and film crews, the Princess had arrived at the Odeon a full fifteen minutes late. Nevertheless, she still spoke to everyone in the line-up before Serge whisked her off to her seat. The audience fell silent as he took his place beside her. A tense smile frozen on his face, he settled back to watch his latest production.

For two hours, the guests sat spellbound by the story. After a while, Serge could feel himself loosening up and actually enjoying the evening. Even to his relentlessly critical eye, the shots of the scenery were breathtaking. He made a mental note to pay a bonus to his chronically overworked crew. The story raced on until, at last, the hero blew up the cocaine laboratory. The special effects were so phenomenal that members of the audience stood up and cheered. Serge smiled mischievously. The première was in aid of drug rehabilitation. Many of those cheering so vociferously had kept the cocaine trade in business for years.

The final scene brought gasps as the hero and his lover were forced to part. Then the credits rolled to the haunting sound of Scorpio's smash-hit theme song.

In the dark, Serge noticed the Princess fumbling in her evening bag. She brought out a handkerchief and swiftly dabbed her eyes.

The entire audience was on its feet, some weeping, others cheering, everyone applauding. The noise was overwhelming. Scorpio swung a tearful Maisie around, and kissed her hard on the lips. 'They love it!' he cried ecstatic. 'They absolutely love it.'

Happy yet sad, relieved yet excited, Laura could not contend with the morass of emotions swirling around inside her head. Already, Sharif was besieged by people intent on shaking his hand. Soon he could feel himself being borne away by the host of enthusiastic well-wishers. He struggled to find Laura, temporarily separated from him in the fray. He reached out blindly, found her hand and pulled her back towards him.

'It was brilliant,' she shouted between tears and laughter. 'What's more, they got the message.'

As if from nowhere, a broad-shouldered security man appeared and shepherded them into a private room. Scorpio and Maisie were already there, looking slightly tousled. Wryly, Maisie surveyed the rip at the bottom of her gown. In the stampede to congratulate Scorpio, someone had stepped on it and torn it. 'Are all these people coming to the party?' she asked.

Scorpio straightened his jacket. 'You bet. And a few hundred more besides.'

'Looks like Serge has pulled in all his markers.' Deftly Laura pushed a maverick hairpin back into her chignon. She glanced at Sharif who, to her consternation, was still looking very uptight. 'Everything all right?'

'I'd like to leave early this evening,' he replied, and went off to talk to Maisie.

By the time she met the Princess, Laura was feeling too euphoric to worry about Sharif's odd behaviour. Resplendent in a silk Caroline Charles creation, Diana had kind words and compliments for everyone. Even Sharif seemed to brighten as she asked him about his people and their country. Smiling nervously, Serge guided the Princess through the throng of celebrities and back towards her car.

He returned to the room in raptures. 'She thinks it's wonderful!' he exclaimed. Uninhibited now, the assembled company sent up a raucous cheer. He beamed broadly at everyone and waited for silence. 'What's more, ladies and gentlemen, I happen to *know* it is.'

Over a thousand people had been invited to the post-show party. Spilling out on to three floors of the Savoy, the celebrations were already in full swing by the time Laura and Sharif arrived.

'For he's a jolly good fellow!' shouted one notoriously savage reviewer. Fellow revellers joined in, toasting the new movie idol with Serge's free-flowing champagne. 'And so say all of us! And so say all of us!'

Sharif smiled uncomfortably and selected an orange juice from the waiter. Still dazzled by the cameras outside the hotel, Laura blinked and looked round. Captains of industry mingled happily with super-models. Pasty-faced politicians hustled to rub shoulders with polo-playing pop stars. And, urged on by their respective managers, three buxom starlets converged on Serge.

In one flower-festooned corner, Scorpio came face to face with Sammy Sandton. Maisie froze as the two men sized one another up. Then suddenly, Sammy began to laugh, a loud, warm, engaging laugh. He extended his hand. 'Congratulations, Scorpio! You gone and got yourself a belter.'

'No hard feelings, then?' Scorpio looked surprised.

'No, mate. It's like you say, you got to be "true to who you are".' He winked comically. 'And I'm an East-End barrow boy. That's how I made my fortune.'

Over by a silk-sheathed colonnade, Daphne had attached herself to a rising young actor and was now hanging on his every word. 'But, Peter, I said, you can't seriously expect me to play Coriolanus with that same old Oedipus complex. Been done to death, I said, just *so* old hat. Couldn't I play him as a glue sniffer or a dyslexic, perhaps, something to make the man *relevant*?'

Daniel Baudon's evening suit smelt of mothballs. It had been years since he had been invited to such a grand occasion. He moved in and out of the crowd, eavesdropping shamelessly.

'Lock them up, I say.' The new hard-right Tory minister had attracted quite an audience. Daniel stopped to listen. 'All these dropouts and drug addicts, none of them any use whatsoever in a capitalist economy. Regulated work camps – now there's an idea. That would keep crime off the streets.'

'And ladies of the night?' enquired Daniel loudly. 'Perhaps the minister has some interesting views on cleaning up the streets around Shepherd Market?'

The Young Turk quailed as he recognized the editor of the *Gadfly*. He glanced at his horsy wife, clad in Aquascutum pastels, and deftly changed the subject.

Wandering on, Daniel spotted Serge, surrounded by large expanses of female flesh. He pointed to an alcove. With practised charm, Serge extricated himself and moved briskly to join his friend. Hidden in the alcove, he lit up a cigar. 'God I'm tired of being hustled.'

'The price of success, *n'est-ce pas*?' Daniel accepted a cigar. 'I thought this was supposed to be a low-budget production.'

Serge nodded. 'And so it was – *very*!'

'But this party alone must have cost you a packet.'

Serge shrugged, very Gallic. 'We can afford it. With the distribution contracts I've negotiated, we're bound to net a fortune.'

Daniel puffed slowly on his cigar. 'I'm not sure Sharif is interested in fortunes.'

'Maybe not.' Serge stared vaguely into the distance. 'But right now he's hot. He can exploit that to promote whatever he wants – his views, his values, his culture, it's entirely up to him.' He drained his glass. 'But I've delivered my part of the bargain and tonight I intend to enjoy it.'

*

The dinner of beluga, duck and soufflé looked delicious, but neither Laura nor Sharif had any appetite.

'There's something wrong, isn't there?' Half-heartedly, she pushed the pudding around her plate.

He shaved off a desultory spoonful of soufflé, then left it lying untouched. 'I wish we were back home together. I'm tired of noise and crowds.'

Badly off-key, a table of tipsy revellers began to sing snatches of Scorpio's song.

'I *do* know what you mean.' She folded her napkin and replaced it on the table. 'It's been a difficult time for both of us. Couldn't we just slip away for a holiday? I've got these friends in Martinique.'

He began to toy with his glass.

'Please,' she insisted, 'we could go at the end of the month. I'd be off tomorrow if I could, but I've got to go to Paris. Charles sacked so many of our staff and I've got to try and coax them back.'

He felt his heart getting heavier and heavier as she rambled on enthusiastically. 'Martinique is so lovely at this time of year. They've got this darling little house just on the beach.'

'Laura . . .'

'We wouldn't have to see anyone if we didn't want to. I could cook. Lots of fish. The fish out there is just wonderful.'

'Laura . . .'

'And the fruit . . .' Her voice wavered. 'You don't want to come, do you? For goodness sake, Sharif, please tell me what it is!'

Wearily, he rubbed his eyes. 'It's my mother.'

She felt she could have burst into tears at such a simple explanation. 'You should have told me sooner.'

'What? And ruin the entire evening for you?'

'It's been ruined anyway. You've been so distant with me these last few days, I thought you'd found another . . .' She could not bring herself to say the word 'lover'.

Sharif could have kicked himself for his own insensitivity. 'Don't be silly!' He reached out and tenderly stroked her cheek. 'You're the only woman I'll ever love. You have my word on it!'

The tone of his voice, the feel of his skin, the warmth of his body next to hers – Laura wanted to be anywhere with him, anywhere but here. 'I'm coming with you.'

'But your trip to Paris?'

'I'll cancel it. The company can wait.'

She looked so beautiful, so resolute and wilful, he almost found himself agreeing. He looked down and shook his head. 'No.'

'But I'm so fed up and weary. I want some time alone with you.'

Sharif's jaw set hard. 'No, Laura. You must go to Paris and repair the damage. Why else did we fight for Gautier?'

She knew he was right and deep down she agreed. That did not make the pain more bearable. 'Your mother,' she asked, trying to be less self-centred, 'is it very serious this time?'

He fiddled nervously with his cufflinks. 'I've spoken to the doctors. They don't think she'll pull through.'

She felt an overwhelming surge of tenderness and guilt. 'I'm so sorry. You don't need all this hassle from me.' She picked up her evening bag. 'Come on. It's time we went home.'

He caught her hand as she rose from the table. 'Tonight, at least, we're allowed to be selfish.' She smiled as, arm in arm, her head on his shoulder, they slipped quietly out of the room.

By midnight, the party was positively humming. As the clock struck twelve, a group of session musicians appeared on the stage and launched into a medley of vintage Scorpio. The guests were thrilled. Some sang along, word perfect, to the music. Others, more energetic, started rock 'n' rollin' around the dance floor. At first, it started as a single voice, but soon the whole room was chanting, 'Scorpio, Scorpio', insisting that he perform. High on pure adrenalin, he jumped on stage and grabbed the lead guitarist's instrument. Immediately, the group raised their game. Strutting around like a teenager, he began to belt out a string of old hits. The crowd cheered more loudly still.

Maisie was feeling ecstatic. Light-headed from a combination of excitement and champagne, she suddenly found herself being twirled around the dance floor. Surprisingly light on his feet, Serge rolled her away and then back towards him again.

'My God,' she laughed, breathlessly, 'is there anything you can't do?'

'Sure.'

'What?'

'Keep this up much longer!' He twirled her round once more.

As if on cue, Miranda returned with a pile of first editions. She waved at Serge. 'Quick!' He dragged Maisie off the dance floor and fell upon the reviews. With an expert eye, he scanned the papers, first the broadsheets then the tabloids. Too nervous to read, Maisie waited for the verdict. It was not long in coming. With a whoop of joy, Serge threw the papers high up into the air.

'It's official!' he shouted and flung his arms around her. 'We've got a smash hit on our hands.'

CHAPTER THIRTY-FOUR

On Hydra, the foreign newspapers arrived approximately four days late. One afternoon, after an extended siesta, Charles sauntered down to the harbour and waited for the boat to come in. The afternoon sun was still hot and, after seeking shade under the awning of a nearby bar, he shouted for a bottle of ouzo. If the owner thought the order excessive, he did not bat an eyelid. Wealthy, bored expatriates were a regular feature of his establishment. If they wanted to drink themselves into oblivion, that was very good for business. He plonked the bottle down on the table and went back to join his card game.

Charles stared out over the infinity of blue and tried to formulate a plan. Yolande, it appeared, had gone for good. Since her departure, he had called her Paris number over a dozen times a day and had only ever managed to communicate with her answering machine. In desperation, he had even called Air France, but the personnel woman was decidedly sniffy. Mademoiselle, she informed him, had recently resigned and that was all she was prepared to divulge.

Quite obviously in love, a young couple sat down in the corner of the bar. Holding hands across the table, they stared deep into one another's eyes, quite oblivious to the rest of the world. Charles began to feel uncomfortable. Their presence was like a reproach to him, a comment on his loneliness. He pulled a notepad out of his pocket and began to scribble furiously. The island was full of artists and writers. He hoped he might pass for one.

The small boat bearing the papers appeared on the horizon

as he poured himself another drink. No one on this island was interested in time. He knew it would be at least another hour before the knotty-armed fisherman delivered the bundles to the shop. He glanced down at his notes. 'Change will', he had written in large black capital letters. A sudden sharp spasm wrung the breath out of his chest. As he doubled up in pain, he could still see the lovers in the corner, embracing tenderly. With difficulty, he straightened up and tried to breathe as normal. His whole torso ached. He downed a gulp of ouzo and waited as the fiery liquid filtered down, but afforded little relief.

He picked up the pen he had dropped on the table. 'Beneficiary?' he wrote and stared back out over the sea. The waves lapped hypnotically against the white-painted walls of the harbour. A mangy-looking mongrel happened by, foraging hopefully for food. After a few insults, the bar owner relented and threw him a meaty bone.

Charles underscored the word 'beneficiary' and added an extra question mark. The more he thought about it, the more the solution eluded him. Who on earth could he leave his money to? Even if she had hung around, he would never have left it all to Yolande. And now she had walked out on him, he was damned if he would leave her a *sou*.

'Deserving causes?' he wrote, and sneered into his drink. He had spent his entire life working for the one and only deserving cause he believed in. Charity, indeed! In his view, charity began and ended at home. Liberal do-gooders like his father – such people made him sick!

The idea struck him like a bullet. He wondered why he had not thought of it before. This would be the ultimate insult to the memory of Gaston Gautier. A cruel, mirthless smile crossed Charles's face. He picked up his pen and wrote the words 'Jean Le Pen' next to the word 'Beneficiary'. Then, settling back happily in his chair, he contemplated the perfect act of revenge.

Over in the west, the sun was slipping into the sea as he meandered down to the harbour. Like small blurs of light, the bobbing fishing boats looked as if they belonged to a broad Impressionist canvas. Charles lurched into the newsagent's and picked up every French and English publication he could find.

The owner, a man in his eighties, smiled and tried to make conversation in his archaic, rusty English. Charles ignored him and, having paid his bill, set off back towards his house.

He kicked off his shoes in the hall and padded into the kitchen where a leg of roast lamb had been left to cool on the table. Worried about her employer's erratic eating habits, the housekeeper had hoped to tempt him with it. Charles hacked off a chunk, then shuffled into the drawing room for his early evening Scotch. Collapsing into his chair, he reached for his stack of papers and idly opened one.

'That bloody bitch!' He brought his tumbler down hard on the table. From the pages of the *Mail*, photographs of an ecstatic Maisie smiled blissfully up at him. Sick with envy, he scanned the column. A picture of Laura, arm in arm with some dark-haired swarthy type, soon attracted his attention.

'Trollops, the pair of them!' He tried to throw the paper across the room, but the pages separated in the mild cross breeze before fluttering back to earth.

Next he grabbed the *Guardian*. At least, he felt, there was no chance of idle society gossip there. 'TOR' ran a front-page headline. 'East meets West in a collision of ideologies'. Despite his hostility, he could not stop himself from reading on. 'Brilliant' was the conclusion of the review inside, 'a modern masterpiece'. He tossed the paper aside and turned to the next. There was no respite to be found. Everywhere, it seemed, images of Maisie and Laura popped up to laugh at him. Dancing, smiling, partying, *living*, their joyous faces made him want to scream. Jealousy gnawed the pit of his stomach as he staggered out onto the balcony. 'So they think they've got it made,' he shouted, accosting the sky. 'Well, I'm not beaten yet.'

After two days of frantic phone calls, Charles felt he had the matter well and truly sewn up. With the reluctant assistance of his father's old friend, Harry Blumstein, the transport and insurance formalities had all been successfully completed. He sipped his morning coffee and pondered the upset his latest move would make. The Star of Heaven would be arriving in Athens later that afternoon. He would then transport it home to Hydra. Once there, the fabulous diamond would disappear from sight. He would keep it under lock and key, far away from prying eyes. Charles spread a layer of apricot jam on his doorstep of home-made bread. That would knock the smile off Maisie's stupid face! And off Laura's, too.

The white and gold of the helicopter glistened in the watery, early-morning sunshine. Charles threw his briefcase on to the passenger's seat and heaved himself into the pilot's position. For a split second he thought of the engineers in Athens, forever banging on about switches and screws and pre-flight checks. Justifying their own existence, he sniffed, and immediately switched on the engine. The jets took a grip on the rotors which quickly accelerated to their operating speed. He put on his headphones and tried to contact the control tower. At first, there was no reply. 'Lazy bastards,' he muttered under his breath and impatiently flicked the switch. 'Athens, can you hear me?'

At last, a heavily accented voice replied and asked for an initial reading. Charles quoted his co-ordinates and final destination. The voice in the control tower gave him the all clear and soon the helicopter was whirring its way up into the sky. The warm sun filtered through the perspex and on to the side of Charles's face. Blinking in the light, he stared down at the tiny toy town of Hydra as it disappeared from sight. From the air, even the bright white church looked small and insubstantial, like a freshly cooked meringue shell. He glanced at his watch. Ten twenty precisely. The flight to Athens would take just over thirty minutes. Smiling smugly to himself, he sat back to savour the view.

The craggy islands below seemed like war-hardened veterans, standing guard on their glorious sapphire sea. Defending what was rightfully yours – the idea appealed to Charles. He could feel the heat of the sun streaming into the helicopter. Gradually, his eyelids began to droop and a wonderful sense of peace and well-being began to permeate his body. His arms, his hands, his fingers all started to grow heavy. As, slowly, his head lolled to one side, the joy-stick moved out of his slackening grip. In an instant, the helicopter was out of control and spiralling towards the sea.

He came to with a start and grabbed the controls. Frantically, he struggled to arrest the descent but the engine refused to respond. Like a moth attracted to a flame, it continued on its mission of self-destruction, determined to be at one for ever with the flickering blue beyond.

'May Day!' screamed Charles to the control tower. All the warnings – pre-flight checks, safety procedures – everything he had ever been told flashed past him in a second.

'May Day! May Day!' By now, he had even unclasped his safety harness and was wondering whether to jump.

The heavily accented voice was calm as it requested his position. By now, however, he was far too distracted to make a rational response. 'May Day! May Day!'

Then, suddenly, the screaming stopped altogether.

It was a chilly, autumnal morning in Sussex. Around Scorpio's house, the naked trees looked forlorn and skeletal, like a lost tribe of Giacometti statues. Maisie walked on through the sodden leaves, oblivious to the dark, threatening sky above. Cavorting around her heels, Clancy was insisting on a game.

'Oh, all right, then!' Relenting she took a ball out of her mackintosh pocket and threw it into the air. The dog was after it in a trice, snapping it up as effortlessly as a frog might an unwary fly. Within seconds the ball was resting beside her green wellington boots.

'No wonder your master's so fit!' She picked it up and once more sent it scudding through the air.

She returned to the house, pink-faced and exhilarated. As she removed her boots in the hall, a mud-spattered Clancy danced playfully all over the parquet. 'For goodness sake, calm down,' she ordered, 'and wipe those paws on the mat.' Clancy looked so down in the mouth she just had to kiss him better. Delighted, he responded by licking her all over the face.

She wandered into the kitchen and switched on the kettle for tea. Noisily, Clancy lapped his water from a special earthenware bowl. In the oven, the succulent beef casserole she had prepared bubbled merrily away. For a moment she felt like pinching herself. A kitchen, a dog and a casserole – the very cliché of domesticity! And yet, in all her rich and privileged life, she had never felt so happy. She picked up *The Times* and, settling down at the kitchen table, started on the crossword.

After a few initial successes, she became stuck on twenty-six across. 'Many a poisonous type's converse on board – six letters.' 'Poisonous type, poisonous type?' The words Gautier and Charles sprang to mind. The sound of the phone interrupted her thoughts. Smiling, she picked up the receiver. It was bound to be Scorpio on his way home to lunch. He would help her finish the crossword.

The resonance on the line seemed to herald an international call. A slight pause ensued before the operator spoke. 'Mrs Gautier?'

She hesitated. Already Mrs Gautier sounded so alien to her, like a person from a previous existence. 'Yes, this is Mrs Gautier speaking.'

The operator's voice was clipped and efficient. 'Please hold.'

After a series of clicks, she was put through to a foreign-sounding man who spoke correct but laboured English. He announced himself as Nicolas Georgiadou of the Athens coroners' office. 'It is my duty to inform you of some very unpleasant news.' His tone was the perfect administrator's amalgam of disinterest and politeness. 'I'm afraid your husband, Charles Gautier, was killed two hours ago in a helicopter accident. As next of kin to the deceased, we would like you to come and identify the body.'

'Oh, my God!'

'It's a mere formality, of course,' continued the man. 'The cause of death was drowning. But I must warn you that you may find the body a little . . .' he coughed, for the first time slightly ill at ease, '. . . a little disfigured. The rescue services had to cut it from the wreckage.'

She nodded and calmly noted down names and addresses. 'I'll fly to Athens this evening,' she confirmed. 'That means I can be with you at nine tomorrow morning.'

She stared out of the window and tried to conjure up some slight twinge of regret. None came. After twenty-three years of marriage, Charles's death evoked nothing in her but the most enormous sense of relief. Ever since their separation, his existence had felt like a disease in remission, threatening to erupt at any time and wreck her current happiness. She heard a car coming up the drive and ran outside to greet Scorpio.

As he leapt out to hug her, the box of orchids he was carrying fell with a clatter to the ground. 'You'd think I'd been away for months!' As he bent down to pick up the flowers, Clancy bounded up and jumped ecstatically from one to the other. Scorpio laughed and patted his head. 'I hope you've been keeping an eye on this lady of mine. I can't have anyone spiriting her off.' He turned and caught the look on Maisie's face. 'My God, whatever's the matter?'

She stared at him, unsure of how to break the news. 'Charles has been killed in an accident.' The words seemed very brutal.

'I see.' He could feel his heart pounding as he ground the pebbles beneath his feet. 'And how do you feel?' He dared not look at her. Perhaps, deep down, she still had some residue of affection for the man who had been her husband. The thought shot through him like a physical pain.

'I know it's terrible,' she said, at last, 'but I'm glad he's dead.'

He pulled her close to him and kissed her. 'I'm afraid I'm worse than you. My first thought when you told me was that we can get married right away.'

The phone was ringing as they reached the front door. Maisie dashed into the drawing room and was surprised to hear Harry Blumstein on the other end of the line. 'I'm in Athens,' he explained, almost apologetically. 'I believe you've already been notified . . .'

'Yes, about half an hour ago.'

'May I offer my condolences.' A member of the old school, Harry felt obliged at least to *say* the right thing.

'Come on, Harry. You're not sorry and neither am I. Let's skip the formalities.'

'That's fine by me.' He sounded relieved. Insincerity had no place in his makeup and, besides, he was far happier to talk business.

'The real reason I'm calling is to tell you that the Star of Heaven is here with me.'

'But why on earth?'

Maisie's expression grew harder and harder as the reasons were explained.

'I'm leaving for Paris this evening,' concluded Harry. 'What do you want me to do with the stone?'

Maisie thought quickly. 'Deliver it to Laura at Gautier. I'm not sure what the situation is but in the meantime it may as well stay there.'

She rang off and was on the point of calling Laura when the phone rang once again. This time it was Leon, one of the Gautier trustees, on the line from Geneva. 'News travels fast,' said Maisie, after thanking him for his expressions of sympathy and concern. There seemed no point washing the dirty linen of her marriage in front of a relative stranger. Leon paused deliberately. She could almost hear the whirrings of his mind as it decided how much to divulge.

'I learned of the tragedy from Charles's housekeeper. You see, I was phoning him to confirm our meeting the day after tomorrow.' Maisie stayed resolutely silent. He sounded desperate to get something off his chest. She would let him get there in his own time.

'We were to meet in Athens,' he continued awkwardly. 'Charles was going to sign the final papers, transferring his Gautier stock.'

Suddenly Maisie's legs felt weak. 'Oh, my God,' she murmured, 'so the deal still hasn't been done.'

'I'm afraid not. These things always take much longer than people anticipate. And there's something else as well.' Leon's voice sounded hollow and distant. She forced herself to concentrate on what he was saying. 'I'm not sure that I should be telling you this, but I was due to fly to Athens with the family lawyer.' His voice dropped to a whisper. 'I believe your husband was about to change his will.'

'I don't understand what you're driving at.' Maisie's head was spinning. 'Charles had every right to change his will. It's no secret we were getting divorced.'

A paradigm of discretion, the Swiss banker was finding it difficult to break the habits of a lifetime. 'You understand that I'm making this call in a *strictly unofficial* capacity.'

She recognized the hallmark of the Swiss financial mafia. 'Of course, this is a purely *personal* call, or, if you'd prefer, there's been no call at all.'

Leon laughed politely. As with bridge, it was always wise to check that your partner was playing the same conventions. 'Under normal circumstances, of course, I would not be doing this, but Gaston Gautier was a personal friend of mine. I feel I owe him something.'

The tension in her stomach was like a stiletto jabbing away inside. She wished that Leon would get just get on with it but the flood gates of confession had opened and he was in full flow. 'You must understand that I never agreed with Charles's behaviour. Legally, however, his position was watertight . . .'

There followed five more minutes of self-exculpation before finally he came to the point. 'So you see, Madame, in the absence of a new will, you now stand to inherit everything.'

Maisie's jaw dropped. 'I'm sorry?'

'I believe the only will Charles ever made was the one he signed on your wedding day.'

A smile began to play around the corners of her mouth. 'That was Daddy's idea. In those days, Daddy only had to say, "Sign here, son," and Charles had his fountain pen out.'

'Well, that's the will that stands. Your husband died before he could change it. Thank goodness, for once, that the Gautiers were always so bad with their paperwork.'

Maisie's eyes were shining. 'Let me get this straight. Are you telling me that Charles's Gautier stock is mine?'

'Everything – the stock, the house, the Star of Heaven – everything.'

She let out a low, unladylike whistle. Slumped across her feet, a neglected Clancy pricked up his ears and began to wag his tail. 'Thank you.' She planted a great big kiss on top of the dog's head. 'I can't tell you how much this means to me, to all of us, in fact.'

Scorpio was overjoyed when he heard the news. 'So you've

acquired Charles's stock without spending a dime of Appleford money.' He sat down on the sofa and put his arms around her. To his consternation, he could feel she was trembling. 'Are you sure you're OK?'

She buried her face in his shoulder. 'It's just the shock, that's all. For a while, I thought Gautier might be up for grabs again. I couldn't have broken that to Laura.'

He could feel her warm tears, seeping through his shirt and on to his skin. 'You really do love her, don't you?'

'As if she were my own.' She raised her head from his shoulder and nuzzled her cheek against his. 'I'm going to give her Charles's shares, then the company's completely hers.'

'Quite right!' With his hand he cupped her chin and gently kissed her lips. 'It's the way it ought to be.'

'So, you don't mind, then, that I'm bowing out?' She stared mischievously up at him.

'On the contrary, I'm delighted. I want my wife to devote herself one hundred per cent to *me*.'

Playfully she ruffled his hair. 'That doesn't sound very politically correct.'

'Why ever not?' He scooped her up into his arms. 'When I promise to spend the rest of my life just looking after her?'

CHAPTER THIRTY-FIVE

Laura put down the receiver and stared blankly into space. The conversation with Maisie had left her feeling stunned. Desperately she struggled to think, but her head was just a maelstrom of fierce, conflicting emotions. Shock, guilt, relief, joy – all were swirling and whirling around in her mind. Sorrow was the only feeling which did not seem to pass her way.

'*Badal*,' she murmured softly.

Madame Goffinet looked up from her dictation pad. A lady of the old school, she had no time for new-fangled technology such as dictaphones and the like. She peered at Laura through her gilded half-moon spectacles. 'I'm sorry, dear,' she queried. 'I'm afraid I didn't quite catch what you said.'

Laura smiled back at her. There were some employers, she was well aware, who might object to being called 'dear'. Madame Goffinet, however, had known her since the day she was born. She was allowed to take such liberties.

'*Badal*,' she repeated slowly. 'To the Pathans, it means revenge.'

The driving rain in rue de la Paix tapped hard against the window. '*Badal, badal.*' To Laura, the word seemed everywhere. She tried to resume her dictation but her concentration had evaporated completely. 'I'm sorry,' she said, after a few false starts. 'I'm afraid I'm not really with it this morning.'

Madame Goffinet was far too discreet to voice her curiosity. She closed her dictation pad and stood up to leave the office. 'Never mind, dear, we can do it later when you feel like it. Is there anything else for now?'

Laura hesitated for a second. An announcement was perhaps a little premature but she resolved to take the bull by the horns. 'Would you please ask the staff to meet me in here at one? Something quite unexpected has just come up and I think they ought to know. And now if you'd excuse me . . .' She leapt up and hurried off to the ladies' room, only arriving in the nick of time. She slammed the lavatory door behind her and was violently sick.

A bemused Madame Goffinet walked down to the workshop where she was met by a host of happy faces. It was just like the *bon vieux temps*, she mused, when Gautier *père* was still alive. She hailed Maurice, recently re-engaged after his summary dismissal. He looked up from the lapis lazuli flower he was carving and nodded contentedly. Everyone in the company was in agreement. In the few weeks since Charles's departure, Laura had managed to work miracles. Fearing for their jobs, many long-term employees had become morose and bitter under her brother's cynical regime. Standards in the workshop had plummeted and no one, not even the boss, appeared to give a damn. Within weeks of Gaston's death, the very spirit of Gautier was in serious jeopardy. Laura's arrival at the head of the company had been like grace to a tortured soul.

An announcement to the entire workshop was not Madame Goffinet's natural style. In her thirty years with the company, she had only ever been heard to raise her voice on one occasion and that was the day when Maurice was sacked. Gracefully, she drifted from workbench to workbench. With a greeting here and a kind word there she delivered the news of Laura's convocation. A hum of excited anticipation began to trail her around the room. Nowadays news was always good news. They counted the minutes until one o'clock.

Near the window at the far end of the room, Gautier's latest recruit sat huddled intently over her work. Spellbound, Madame Goffinet watched as, slowly, she levered the tiny baguette diamonds into the proboscis of the butterfly brooch. 'It's so beautiful!' she murmured.

Delighted, Caroline Jay looked up. 'I'm so glad you like it. It's all Laura's idea, really, a revival of the J line. Do you remember at the beginning, all the fun we had with that?'

Madame Goffinet smiled benignly. She did indeed remember. Those first few years of marriage had been the happiest of Monsieur Gautier's life. In her view, of course, the young Madame Gautier had behaved quite appallingly but at last she was making amends. 'I do indeed. And with your work still as brilliant as ever, the new range is bound to succeed.'

Caroline secured another stone in its minuscule platinum mount. 'The phoenix from the ashes, *n'est-ce pas*, Madame Goffinet?'

The secretary was on the defensive at once. 'It was just a tiny bad patch, that's all. No one ever believed that the company was *really* in trouble.'

Caroline glanced down at her right hand. Now that she had given up alcohol the tremor had disappeared completely. 'Who was talking about the company?' she asked, and flashed her a perfect smile.

Madame Goffinet glanced at the clock in the workshop and knew she ought to push on. After informing Caroline of the meeting, however, she found herself still hovering. 'I'm not sure it's my place to mention it,' she ventured awkwardly, 'but I think there's something wrong with Laura.'

Caroline put down her tools and turned to face her. 'Do you know, I was beginning to think it was my imagination.'

Relieved to have her suspicions corroborated, Madame Goffinet decided to go further. 'I can't quite put my finger on it, but ever since she got back from London she's been acting rather strangely.'

Caroline nodded, concerned. 'I know she's been under a lot of pressure. Things have changed so quickly and she's been working terribly hard. All the same, I think you're right. It's time she and I had a heart to heart.'

The news of Charles's death was received with total silence. Laura looked from face to face, but none of the Gautier employees showed the slightest flicker of regret. It was dreadful, she thought dispassionately, that a man should leave this world so unwanted and unloved. As if to mark a hiatus, she quietly cleared her throat. 'I am now assuming complete control of the House of Gautier.'

The group erupted into a loud, spontaneous cheer.

She blushed. 'I only hope I'm worthy of that confidence.'

The room fell so quiet, she could have heard a pin drop. Everywhere, eyes were trained on her, searching for direction and leadership. She stared resolutely back at them. When she spoke her voice was low, but calm and completely even. 'Since my father's death, this company has been rudderless. That's the reason I wanted to talk to you today, to put your minds at rest. It is my intention to run this company precisely as my father ran it . . .' She was aware of Maurice, beaming encouragingly across at her. 'And his father and grandfather before him. For one hundred and fifty years the name of the House of Gautier has been synonymous with innovation and excellence. With your help, ladies and gentlemen, I vow to continue that tradition.'

The staff were still chattering as they filtered out of the office. Caroline hung back, watching as Maurice embraced her daughter. 'You know we'd all swing for you,' he said and kissed her on both cheeks.

Laura looked up at her mentor and gripped him by the hand. 'And I for you,' she said quite fiercely. 'You realize we're all in this together?'

'We most certainly do!' Caroline walked across the room and put her arm around Laura's shoulders. 'So how about shouting your mother some lunch? I'm absolutely starving.'

At the bistro, Laura seemed oddly restrained as she pushed her favourite risotto round and round on the plate. Caroline talked on, determined to get to the root of the problem. 'Oh, I almost forgot.' She helped herself to her daughter's untouched salad. 'Your friend Jenny rang this morning, just after you'd left.'

Laura brightened slightly. 'How is she?'

'She didn't really say. She just told me to tell you that the police have located your parrot.'

'They've found Backbencher?' Laura managed a smile. 'That's wonderful. I'll have him flown here immediately – business class, of course!'

A po-faced waiter replenished their glasses with mineral water. Caroline waited until he had disappeared before mimicking his expression. 'No wine! *Nom d'un chien!* What is this country coming to?'

Laura was grinning.

'That's much better.' Caroline reached over to pat her hand. 'Now let's have it. What's on your mind?'

Laura began to play with her bread roll. 'I'm afraid I'm going to have to move . . .'

A sudden wave of guilt engulfed Caroline. She had been so gloriously, selfishly happy in Gaston's flat that she had ignored her daughter's needs.

'You should have said sooner,' she stammered. 'Of course you're not moving. *I'll* move. I'll find—'

'No!' Laura's tone was adamant.

'But I—'

'No, Mummy,' she insisted. 'You must stay in Papa's flat. It's what he would have wanted. But, if you like, you can help me look for somewhere else – something bright and spacious for me and the—' She hesitated for a split second, then swiftly retrieved herself. 'For me and Backbencher to live.'

There followed an awkward pause as the waiter served the coffee. 'And the bill, please,' added Laura. He grunted, noncommittal, and shimmied on his way.

She took a half-hearted sip of coffee and wrinkled up her nose. 'I don't know if I told you, but I'm off to Delhi in two days' time.'

'A buying spree, I hope.'

'Yes, there are some stones I'd like to take a look at.' The coffee slopped over the rim of her cup as she replaced it on the saucer. 'Charles sold everything he could lay his hands on. Our stocks are totally depleted.'

'Are you flying up to Peshawar afterwards?'

'Yes.' Laura started to fidget. 'Do you think that's a mistake?'

Her mother's eyes were warm. 'Only you know the answer to that.'

'I mean, I wouldn't want Sharif to think I was running after him or anything. It's just . . .' She rolled a sugar lump along the tablecloth. 'It's just there's something I need to tell him.'

It was then that the penny dropped. 'Oh, my God!' exclaimed Caroline. 'I should have known. The apartment, the coffee, the food, the mood swings – it's all been staring me in the face. I remember I was exactly the same when I was having you.' She moved across to the other side of the table and hugged her daughter tightly.

Laura responded to the gesture by bursting into tears. 'I only found out for certain yesterday,' she sobbed. 'I was going to tell you as soon as I could, but I wanted to tell him first.'

'Of course you did.' Caroline stroked her daughter's soft, silky hair and thought how much of her life she had missed. She resolved not to make the same mistakes with her new grandchild. That baby would have *all* her attention.

'So, do you still think I should go and see him?' Suddenly the chief executive was sounding very much in need of a mother.

'Yes,' replied the mother deliberately, 'and in my view, the sooner the better.'

It was some days before Charles Gautier's obituary appeared in the papers. Over a leisurely breakfast with his wife, Sammy Sandton looked up from *The Times*.

'Looks like old Charlie boy has come a proper cropper.'

'Yes, I saw that.' Daphne buttered herself a second piece of wholemeal toast. Nowadays, she was eating much better. 'I didn't know whether to mention it or not. You said you never wanted to hear that man's name again.'

'Well, he's dead now and that's that. I can't say I'm particularly sorry.'

'I am.'

Sammy looked up, offended. 'About Gautier?'

'No.' Daphne kept buttering. 'About all the hassle I caused you. I never did say sorry properly.'

Sammy reached across the table and put his hand over hers.

'We all make mistakes, you know, darling. You don't have to apologize to me.'

'Oh, but I do.' The tears were glistening in Daphne's eyes. 'Not only for Gautier – although that was bad – but for all the other grief.'

'I don't know what you're talking about, sweetheart. You're the best wife a man could have.'

'No.' She shook her head, determined to make amends. 'I've been mean and selfish and daft. I went round to see your mum the other day—'

'*You* went to see my mum?' Sammy shivered involuntarily. 'What did the old queen say?'

'We had a good old natter, her and me, and decided to let bygones be bygones.'

A huge grin spread across Sammy's face. 'You don't know what that means to me.'

'I've invited her over to stay the weekend. I hope that's all right with you?'

'I'm chuffed to death, really I am. That's one hell of a weight off my mind.' He stood up and went over to kiss her.

'There's something else as well,' she said, when at last she surfaced for breath.

'Yes?' He braced himself for the inevitable. 'You want me to top up your account?'

She shook her head, quite hurt. 'I hope you won't be mad at me, but I've told Maria her son can live here.'

CHAPTER THIRTY-SIX

A bitter, wintry wind swept down from the foothills, rattling the bedroom windows. Fitfully, Sharif tossed and turned, but it was a hopeless battle for repose. Another sleepless night. Weary and frustrated, he switched on the bedside lamp and watched as a comforting yellow glow suffused the bedroom of his childhood. He sat up and, with tired, bloodshot eyes, scanned the memorabilia of his youth. Little had changed in the twenty years since he had been first dispatched to England. From Peshawar to Winchester and thence to Oxford, the room bore eloquent testimony to the hybrid nature of his upbringing. Next to his prayer mat stood a red-scarred cricket bat, two cultural icons side by side.

The wind outside howled its relentless threnody. He rolled out of bed and shivered. Although it was large and elegant, his mother's house was always freezing in the winter. Open fires and storage heaters were no match for the icy gusts which rolled down from the Himalayas. He moved swiftly across the red-tiled floor and opened his wardrobe door. Inside his clothes were neatly arrayed. An evening suit hung next to his *salwar kameez*, a loose green *kurta* next to his Levi's. On the rack below, Nike sports shoes and Gucci loafers were slotted in between his well-worn local *chappals*. Without thinking, Sharif reached for his tribal clothes and dressed hurriedly.

The horses whinnied a friendly greeting as he opened the stable door. Deftly he saddled his favourite mount and within minutes they were off, up into the hills, the raw mountain air attacking their sinuses like a whiff of nitric acid. He breathed deeply and urged his horse into a gallop. He loved the sheer aggression of this remorseless, attacking wind. It cleared his head and it focused his mind. He wished it could lighten his heart.

The dawn was breaking, silver-white against grey, as they reached their destination. In a single, liquid movement he dismounted and tied his horse to a korinda bush nearby. Exhilarated now and eager for more, it pawed the ground. Sharif stopped to stroke its wide, intelligent head before walking off towards the cave.

He did not know how long he sat there, huddled in his heavy woollen shawl. Shielded from the force of the wind, far away from disease and dilemma at home, the cave seemed a haven of peace. A neutral creation of nature alone, it spoke neither of East nor West. Gradually, the salve of serenity began to soothe his ailing spirit. He sighed and pulled the shawl around his shoulders more tightly still. The previous week had been traumatic and he needed time to think. Since returning home, he had experienced nothing but misery and confusion. Motionless on her death-bed, his mother lay drifting in and out of consciousness. So far, he had not even managed to engage her in a coherent conversation. And yet, from the look in her drugged and hooded eyes, she seemed desperate to speak.

The events of the previous months flashed past, a colourful collage of images. Laura with her twisted ankle, up there all alone in the mountains. Laura and the reborn fly, outside this very cave. In her flat, at her work, by his side, images of Laura crowded his head, confusing him once again. As he stared, her face was in the filigree of frost which laced the stones around. As he listened, her name was in the wind as it swept across the Frontier. Even here, the echoes of her voice seemed still to whisper around the cave. He picked up a stone and sent it skidding across the floor. For the first time in his life, he felt that his certainties had deserted him. The prospect of Laura's impending arrival filled him with both delight and despondency. He was desperate, perhaps too desperate, to see her. Never before had he felt so dependent on another human being. He needed her as he needed the mountains. She was part of the warp and weft of his being. She was in his very soul.

But Peshawar, he knew, was not Paris or London. To have her here and not with him would be intolerable. Right now, he had his grief to cope with and that was as much as he could bear. Grateful to the wind for its mind-numbing ferocity, he untied his horse and jumped nimbly on to its back. It snorted as the raw cold tickled its flaring nostrils. Quite suddenly, Sharif felt famished.

Galloping joyously across the final ridge, he suddenly reined in his mount. Wheeling high above his mother's house, a flock of jet-black crows cawed urgently to one another. He could feel his fingers turn to ice. On the Frontier it was said that crows only gathered when catastrophe was in the air.

When he arrived home, his sister was waiting anxiously in the hall. A raven-haired, olive-skinned beauty, Tahira had only just turned nineteen. Sharif felt a surge of fraternal concern as he noticed the large black bags under her eyes. So far, it had been she, not he, who had borne the brunt of their mother's illness. He vowed to take care of things now.

'Mother's been calling for you,' she said, hugely relieved to see him. 'She's been awake this past half-hour and refuses to take her medication. She says she wants to stay awake to say what's on her mind.'

Propped up on a pile of snowy white pillows, Khatija looked more frail than ever. He bit his lip as he entered the room, battling to hold back the tears. He kissed her lightly on the forehead, determined that she should not see him cry.

'Sharif?' Her eyes flickered open. He sat down on the bed and took her hand in his. It felt almost weightless, like a leaf that might be blown away by the merest summer breeze.

'It's all right, I'm here now. I'm here for as long as you need me.'

She closed her eyes again, as if the strain of vision were too great. 'I don't have very long, and there are things we must discuss. Your sister – she's very headstrong . . .'

He squeezed her tiny hand. 'There's no need to worry about Tahira. She'll be well looked after. I promise to take care of that.'

She fell silent for a moment, as if gathering her resources.

376

'And you, Sharif,' she began, 'I hope that you, too, find contentment.'

His heart began to pound. The dreaded miasma that had assailed him since his arrival had now been given form. 'But I *am* happy.' He caught his mother staring up at him. Her eyes, like his, were a piercing pale blue. Disconcerted, he stared out to the mountains.

'This woman of whom you once spoke to me. Is she still in your thoughts and your heart?'

'Yes.' He turned to face her again. 'I love Laura and I always will. Some day, I intend to marry her.'

With a strength that belied her ravaged frame, Khatija hauled herself up on to her elbows. For a moment, she was once again the redoubtable matriarch Sharif still remembered. Even during his father's lifetime, she had ruled the domestic scene with a rod and will of iron. Like a seven-year-old about to receive chastisement, he stared down at the floor.

'*Some* day?' Her voice was laced with sarcasm. '*Some* day when she finds a free day within her busy schedule?'

He could feel his neck muscles tensing. He did not want this conversation. 'Mother, you're upsetting yourself. You really must rest—'

'I cannot rest!' Her fingernails dug into the flesh of his palm, leaving small white crescent-shaped marks. 'She is not one of us, my son. She does not understand our ways.'

'But we love one another. We'll manage to work things out. She's—'

His mother interrupted him with an impatient flick of the wrist. 'You speak of love. You mean romantic Western love, the kind which disappears like morning mist in the heat of the summer's sun.'

'It won't be like that for us.'

She stared at him, unblinking. 'It is like that for *everyone*. And when the passion disappears, what then, Sharif, what then?'

'But that's just it. We're not just lovers, we're friends and companions. I know we belong together.'

Khatija's breathing had assumed an ominous rattle. Her face

contorted in a spasm of searing pain. Sharif made to call for the
nurse but immediately she stopped him. The proximity of death
seemed to redouble her resolve. 'This must be done,' she
snapped imperiously and then, relenting, reached out once more
to take his hand. 'Be realistic. This Laura of yours is a wealthy
Western woman. She runs a major company. All her life, she's
been free to come and go and do as she pleases. Do you think
such a woman would be happy here, hidebound by the restric-
tions of a Muslim wife?'

He slumped forward. At last his mother had verbalized it, the
very question he himself had never dared contemplate. After
initial heavy shelling, the atom bomb now exploded. 'I have
chosen a suitable wife for you.'

He looked up, wild-eyed. 'You've done *what*?'

Buoyed up by her own unshakeable beliefs, Khatija continued, 'I thought about it long and hard. It's been decided that
it will be Mumtaz.'

'Mumtaz?' Sharif's head was reeling. 'But I've only ever met
her once. She's just a child—'

'She's a good, modest Pathan girl. She'll make a fine wife and
mother.'

'But I don't love her. I love Laura.'

'Our families have known each other for five generations,'
she continued, ignoring his protests. 'Her father hunted wild
boar with yours.'

He jumped up and, like a caged wild cat, started pacing
around the room. Among his people, he was well aware,
arranged marriages were a time-honoured tradition. In Peshawar,
on the Frontier, throughout the whole of Pakistan, everyone was
obliged to comply.

'Not me! Not me!' In despair, he banged his fist against the
wall. 'I don't love her. You can't force me. I'd rather leave the
country.'

'Oh, yes!' His mother was trembling with anger. 'Leave the
country and do what? Abandon everything that makes you who
you are? You've already been away too long, Sharif. You've
forgotten the way of the Pathans!'

It was as if his feet had been pinioned to the ground,

depriving him of motion. Suddenly the energy seemed to drain from his body. He sank limply into a chair. '*Tor*,' he murmured. The word seemed to stick in the back of his throat. He shook his thumping, aching head, all too conscious of the irony. *Tor*, the title of his recent hit film. *Tor*, the reality of his dilemma. His mother's voice was weak, but her message was ominously clear. 'The dowry has already been settled,' she said. 'The marriage is agreed.'

Sharif felt totally crushed. His mother, his people, his code, his traditions – everything was conspiring against him. To call off the wedding would be a terrible affront, an insult that would have to be avenged. An implacable family feud was bound to result. Who could tell where it would end? 'You have me cornered,' he whispered, his features sunken with despair.

'I did this for you and your happiness.' She closed her eyes. 'In time, you'll see I was right.'

He found his sister waiting anxiously outside the bedroom. She looked up to gauge the extent of the damage but, apart from his eyes, unnaturally dull, his face gave nothing away. 'She's sleeping,' he informed her, very matter-of-fact.

'Did she . . .?'

'Yes, she did.' He picked up his shawl from where he had dropped it. 'I'll speak to you later when I get back. Right now, I need some air.'

The crows had dispersed as the rain appeared, sweeping in torrents across the foothills. Sharif galloped on, his whole being numb, grateful to the elements. The rain joined the tears as they streamed down his face, but the wind kept his secret safe.

CHAPTER THIRTY-SEVEN

I t was probably her imagination, but Laura felt sure she could feel the baby moving around inside her. A boy or a girl? It did not matter, she decided, just as long as it had Sharif's eyes. She settled back contentedly in her first-class seat and pulled the PIA blanket up around her chin. His eyes, his smile, his sculpted features and finely chiselled nose – every detail of his image was there, imprinted on her mind.

'A drink, Mademoiselle Gautier?'

The flight to Peshawar was under-booked and first class almost empty. The cabin crew had virtually nothing to do and she found their attentions overwhelming.

'No thanks.' How she longed to be left alone with her thoughts! 'I'll call if I need anything.'

Mademoiselle Gautier – already she had become quite used to the name. The decision to change had been prompted by Caroline. A Gautier to run Gautier, she had argued and the logic was irresistible. Laura Gautier. The very name conferred *gravitas*. In Delhi, her welcome could not have been warmer. Hardbitten doyens of the diamond business had treated her with the greatest of deference. For generations, such men had dealt with the House of Gautier. The very name demanded respect. It had been a successful trip but, for all their deference, her Indian counter-parts had proved tough negotiators. She smiled at the recollection. Never had she imagined that she, too, possessed their genius for brinkmanship and haggling. Despite raised eyebrows and hands uplifted, she knew they had been impressed.

'You are indeed your father's daughter,' one had remarked,

ruefully shaking his head as he agreed her terms. 'I applaud you, Mademoiselle Gautier. You strike a hard bargain indeed.'

Mademoiselle Gautier, Mademoiselle Gautier – the name swirled round and round and her head felt heavier and heavier. At last, it drooped sideways on to her shoulder, and soon she was fast asleep.

'Do you, Laura Gautier, take this man, Sharif Khan, as your lawful wedded husband?' The organ music swelled so loud that it blotted out her response. Bewildered, she looked to the priest for guidance, but he had disappeared. She tried instead to focus on Sharif, but her view seemed oddly blinkered. Her flimsy white veil had disappeared and now she wore a heavy black *chaddar*. It clung to her nostrils, her mouth, her face – she felt as though she was suffocating. She tried to pull it off, but the fabric seemed to grow until it enveloped her completely. In terror, she shouted out to Sharif, but he just stood there looking at her, impotent to help.

She awoke with a start and tore off the offending blanket. Sweating profusely, she called for a glass of water, which she downed in one gulp. She noticed her hands were trembling and tried to steady them by gripping the arm rest. Even so, her heart was thumping hard, like a manic blacksmith beating his anvil. She retrieved her briefcase from under the seat and settled down to do some paperwork. Nowadays, she found that she even enjoyed that. She flicked the gilded catches and opened the maroon leather case. At once, her eyes were drawn to the velvet-covered object nestling snugly in the corner. She took it out and unwrapped it. The pencil beam of her seat light caught the tiger's ruby-studded eyes. They glared at her ferociously as if challenging her to a fight. She ran her finger down the length of its perfectly executed body. It was a superb piece of work and she was proud of it. As she rewrapped the golden creature in its cloth, she decided she would give it to Sharif over dinner that evening. Set with the stones they had once purchased together, it had always been meant for him.

He was waiting for her at the airport, but the moment she saw his face she knew something was wrong. Sunken-eyed and haggard, he looked as if he had not slept in weeks. He greeted her at the airport with a punctilious politeness which made her blood run cold. Peshawar was not Paris and she had not been expecting ostentatious demonstrations of affection. All the same, there was something disturbing about his coolness and restraint. It seemed based on something more profound than the dictates of local custom.

'How's your mother?' she ventured, searching for explanations.

'Fading.' His monosyllabic manner did not encourage further small talk. In silence, she followed him out of Arrivals, feeling completely unnerved.

The Suzuki was waiting outside the airport building. The porter hauled her luggage into the back of the car and Sharif paid him off. He opened the off-side door and she jumped into the passenger seat. His fingers, she noticed, were stiff with tension as he turned the key in the ignition. For the first time in their relationship, there seemed to be a barrier between them. Suddenly she felt very lost, a child deserted by her faithful guide in a strange and alien land. 'I think you'd better take me straight to the hotel,' she said. 'We can talk things over tomorrow.'

The engine started with a roar. He crunched the gears into first and set off without indicating. 'We're going to the mountains,' he replied. 'We've got to get out of this place.'

The freezing fog hung in icy, impervious tendrils along the snaking road. Somewhere behind the thick grey cloud, the winter's sun was struggling to emerge. Despite the efficiency of the fan heater, Laura's teeth were chattering. She pulled up the collar of her cashmere coat and held on tightly to the dashboard. Sharif was driving far too fast, manoeuvring in and out of the morning traffic like a man pursued by demons. She gritted her teeth. Further platitudes – his mother, her trip – seemed pointless. The silence hung like a pall between them, defying communication. She noticed his knuckles, white against the steering wheel, and longed to reach out and touch him. One look at him, however, and the thought evaporated from her mind. Unnaturally straight, his body radiated stress. He seemed to have constructed defensive ramparts. But to shield himself from what or, more important, whom?

The crowded city roads gave way to the sprawling suburbs and, at last, they were climbing up into foothills. As the traces of civilization grew increasingly sparse, so Sharif began to relax. The sun pushed its way through the clouds, shedding a little watery light on the snow-shrouded Himalayas. Immersed in their thoughts, they drove on in silence until a certain peace prevailed. A fierce cross-wind shook the jeep but neither cared, cocooned together inside. Laura stared out of the window and up to the mountains beyond. They looked so mournful in the grey-silver light, yet at the same time defiantly majestic. It was like travelling in a capsule, she thought, sealed off from the pressures of time and space, just living for the moment.

Sharif swerved off the road and brought the car to a shuddering halt. Turning, he tried to face her, but for once his courage failed him. The words erupted of their own volition, a volcano beyond his control.

'I'm going to be married.'

A terrible pain spread through Laura's chest, twisting her ribs and stealing her breath. It was as if her heart had just imploded.

'I hardly know her,' he continued desperately. 'It's been arranged for us.' He paused for a second, overcome by emotion, willing his voice not to falter. If he stopped to look at her now, he knew he would be totally lost. Lost in the feel of her hair and her skin. Lost in the warmth of her touch. 'I don't love her, Laura. It's you I love. But I have to go through with it.'

He waited but, to his surprise, there were no hysterics. She sat absolutely still.

'I understand.' Her voice was perfectly level. 'It's what you have to do.'

Her very calmness did for him. Tears, anger and recriminations he could have dealt with, but not her comprehension.

'I can't bear it!' As he banged his fist on the dashboard he skinned his knuckles. A drop of blood fell on her coat. 'I can't bear the thought of losing you.'

She reached out and put a restraining hand on his forearm. He clasped it so hard, she thought her fingers might break. As she winced, he dropped it at once.

'As if I haven't caused enough pain already!' He buried his head in his hands. 'I'll never forgive myself!'

The sun broke through the cloud cover, a welcome shaft of light. She leaned over to stroke his tangled hair, then suddenly stopped herself. 'I've been thinking about us, Sharif. I don't think it would have worked.'

He lifted his head to look at her. 'We could have *made* it work.' His eyes were blazing – but not with conviction, with the anger of sheer despair.

'I don't believe I could.' There! She had said it. She had taken responsibility, let him off the hook. The pain in her chest was almost unbearable. This was the bravest thing she would ever do.

'Oh, Laura. Tell me you'll always love me, too!' From the look of anguish on his face, she knew she must keep her secret. She would tell him, of course, in the fullness of time, some day when there was a continent between them to buffer this appalling sense of loss.

'You know I will. You'll always be part of me.'

They drove back slowly to the Pearl Continental. A neutral blend of East and West, the hotel seemed a suitable no man's land to bid a final farewell. For some minutes, they sat outside in the jeep, searching for things to say. But words did not come easily to breaking hearts. In desperation, Laura opened her briefcase. 'Here.' Brusquely, she handed the tiger to Sharif. 'I want you to have this.'

'But I can't—'

'Please!' Her voice was strong and resolute. It brooked no contradiction. 'It was you who taught me to fight like a tiger for the things I care about.' The afternoon sunlight engulfed the creature. It shone like a ball of fire. 'Think of me whenever you look at it!' She jumped quickly out of the jeep. 'And never forget, I'll always love you.'

He felt an overwhelming urge to stop her as she ran up the steps. But what would he say? And what could they do? For that moment, it did not seem to matter. He jumped out of the jeep and raced after her. 'Laura!'

But already the plate glass doors had swished together. The Frontier was now closed.

He clambered back into the Suzuki and roared off down the road. Unthinking, he drove on and on, until at last he was on his way home. Home! The journey had been long and often confusing but now he was almost there. Home to his family, his people, his duty. Home to the few remaining certainties in an ever-changing world. He rummaged in the glove compartment and pulled out a cassette. He glanced briefly at the label – the complete soundtrack of *Tor*. He slotted it into the player and Scorpio's deep, clear voice began to filter through the speakers.

> 'And even though it causes pain
> You know you'd do the same again,
> Be true, my love, be brave and true
> Although it means me losing you.'

He swung the car off the highway and on to the slip road home. On the seat beside him sat the indomitable tiger, a memento of the woman he loved.

CHAPTER THIRTY-EIGHT

As she waited for her daughter at Roissy, Caroline resolved not to probe. A busy airport was not the place for an interrogation and, besides, Laura would tell her in due course. One point, however, was already quite clear. If the previous day's phone call was anything to go by, things in Peshawar had not worked out as planned.

To her surprise, Laura appeared looking stunning in a cashmere cape. As they embraced, Caroline could feel her resolve evaporating by the second.

'Was he angry – about the baby, I mean?'

Laura manoeuvred her maverick baggage trolley towards the elevator. 'I didn't tell him.'

'You didn't tell him?' Caroline looked flabbergasted. 'But surely that was the whole point of going. I'm sure if only he knew . . .'

From the distant look on Laura's face, it was obvious she was not listening. 'If you wouldn't mind, Mummy, I'd like to go straight to rue de la Paix.'

'To Gautier? At this time of night?' Caroline's curiosity suddenly turned to concern. 'Can't it wait until tomorrow?'

The elevator doors opened and the two women got out.

'No. I have to go there now.'

On Laura's instructions, the Star of Heaven was on display in Gautier's window. She had decided it would stay there until it could be transferred to the V and A. Together, mother and daughter stared in awe at the fabulous diamond. A symbol of permanence, born at the beginning of time, it would continue for all eternity. Laura closed her eyes, but the image still remained. Like a spirit, the diamond's inner fire permeated everything around. Sharif's face returned to her thoughts and, despite her pain, she smiled. He had taught her so much about herself, he was now inseparable from her. Honour, family, belief, tradition: like the diamond, these would be her touchstones in a fickle, changing world.

This time she knew for sure that it was not her imagination. With the slightest of tremors, the baby inside her made its presence felt. Suddenly, Laura was overcome by an enormous sense of optimism. She placed a protective hand across the tiny, growing presence. An artist and a warrior, part Gautier part Khan, this was a creature of East and West, a child for the new millennium.